DE

BY

TERESA HILL

AND

VEGAS TWO-STEP

BY

LIZ TALLEY

MILLS & BOON

Dear Reader,

Writers will tell you story ideas are all around us, and they truly are.

This idea came from a newspaper story about two elderly residents of a retirement home falling in love, much to the outrage of their respective families. Love in the eighties took on a whole new twist.

I took that idea and played with it, twisted it this way and that, turned it just so. It's what writers do to make a story our own.

Who were these people who fell in love? What were they like? What reasons would their respective families have to be upset about that? How complicated could I make this? How much fun could we all have along the way?

The result is the kind of life in our eighties and even nineties that I hope all of us have: busy, fun, active, surrounded by friends and lots of love, along with glorious adventures. (And maybe a little scheming and meddling in our loved ones' lives.)

Happy reading,

Teresa Hill

RUNAWAY VEGAS BRIDE

BY
TERESA HILL

First published in Great Britain 2011
by Mills & Boon, an imprint of Harlequin (UK) Limited,
Eton House, 18-24 Paradise Road, Richmond, Surrey TW9 1SR

ISBN: 978 0 263 88878 2

23-0411

Harlequin (UK) policy is to use papers that are natural, renewable and recyclable products and made from wood grown in sustainable forests. The logging and manufacturing processes conform to the legal environmental regulations of the country of origin.

Printed and bound in Spain
by Blackprint CPI, Barcelona

Teresa Hill lives within sight of the mountains in upstate South Carolina with one husband, very understanding and supportive; one daughter, who's taken up drumming (earplugs really don't work that well. Neither do sound-muffling drum pads. Don't believe anyone who says they do.); and one son, who's studying the completely incomprehensible subject of chemical engineering (Flow rates, Mom. It's all about flow rates.)

In search of company while she writes away her days in her office, she has so far accumulated two beautiful, spoiled dogs and three cats (a black panther/champion hunter, a giant powder puff and a tiny tiger-stripe), all of whom take turns being stretched out, belly up on the floor beside her, begging for attention as she sits at her computer.

To my son, John, on the occasion of his 21st birthday
and first trip to Vegas.

May your math skills and all those poker probabilities
you memorized serve you well.

And please stay far, far away from the
Love Me Tender Wedding Chapel.

Chapter One

"Darling, I'm in love!"

Jane Carlton choked on her hot tea, then covered the phone with her hand and mouthed to her assistant, "Did you say this is my grandmother?"

Lainie nodded, looking concerned. "What is it? She sounded okay. Is she okay?"

Jane threw up her hands as if to say she had no idea, then tucked the phone into her shoulder once again and said, "Gram?"

"Yes, dear. Did you hear me?"

"I…maybe," Jane admitted. "Say it again?"

"I'm in love!"

The words came out sounding like lyrics in a musical—theatrical, whimsical, larger-than-life.

There was just one problem.

The women in Jane's family didn't do love. They didn't do forevers.

Oh, they had men in their lives. But they made no mistakes about it involving anything as substantial and long-lasting as love.

Jane had learned that the hard way.

"Gram, I thought—"

"I know. I know! That's why it's so amazing! Me, in love, finally, at seventy-six! Who'd have believed it?"

"Wait," Jane said, shaking her head. "Gram, you're eighty-one—"

"He moved into one of the cottages a week ago! The most amazing man I've ever met in my life, Jane, and… Oh, here he comes! Leo! Over here! Over here!"

Jane's grandma sounded like a teenager.

This was so bizarre.

Was it some kind of sudden-onset dementia that had her believing she was only seventy-six? Worst yet, could that have taken her back in her own mind to her teenage years in the four days since Jane's last visit?

Because that's what she sounded like, a ridiculous kid in love.

"Say you'll come and have dinner with us so you can meet him," Gram said. "Tonight? All right? It's lasagna night. Goodbye, my darling girl."

Thursdays.

Lasagna night.

One of Jane's big dates of the week.

Thursdays was lasagna with Gram, her great-aunt Gladdy and a few of their friends from their active retirement village—they stressed the word *active* in all things—called Remington Park. Sunday afternoons were spent taking Gram and Gladdy shopping, maybe to a movic or brunch.

There it was, the sad truth about Jane's big dates.

Oh, she could have found a man to go out with. Men were everywhere. But a man she truly wanted to spend time with? A man who could be depended on to show her a good time that topped a hot bath, a glass of wine and a good book?

There certainly weren't a lot of those around, Jane had found in her twenty-eight years.

She put down the phone—forgotten by Gram, who'd gone in search of Leo, the supposed love of her life—and sighed, trying not to think Gram had more of a social life than she did.

"Is she all right?" Lainie asked, hovering as she tended to do.

"Well, she's either forgotten her own age or she's pretending to be five years younger to impress a man. Please tell me we won't give a flip about impressing a man when we're eighty-one. I mean, at that age, who really wants one? They're bound to be more trouble than they're worth in their eighties. I mean, I think men in their thirties are more trouble than they're worth."

Lainie frowned. "Jane, you think all men are more trouble than they're worth."

Jane considered, decided she couldn't argue that point. "And?"

Lainie looked sad, as if she might just feel a bit sorry for Jane. "I'm just saying… Don't you ever get lonely?"

Absently drumming the keys on the powered-off calculator on her desk, Jane considered. "Not really. I have my work, my family. I guess I'm a little lonely now that Bella's gone—"

"Bella was a dog, Jane."

"I know. I've never met a man who was nicer to me than my dog was."

Then there was no even trying to hide it. Lainie definitely felt sorry for her, which made Jane wonder if it was really that sad, to have a beloved and recently deceased dog who was nicer to her than any man she'd ever met. But really, Jane felt lucky to have no illusions. To be honest with herself and in the way she'd put together a life of her choosing. And it was a good life. A good, satisfying life most of the time.

Sure, every now and then she got lonely, but didn't everyone?

"Men are so unpredictable," she complained.

"Life is unpredictable," Lainie insisted.

"No, life with men is unpredictable." Jane smiled, quite satisfied with that catchphrase.

She quickly scribbled it down on a list she kept handy for just these occasions. She'd come up with another great catchphrase for her work with the poor, unhappy women who hadn't yet come to the wisdom she had, wisdom she happily shared with others in her Fabulous Female Financial Boot Camp seminars. Where she preached financial independence with the same fervor of a good old-fashioned preacher trying to save lost souls. The women in her seminars were lost, too, in a wilderness of financial ignorance, irresponsibility and the completely mistaken idea that they were helpless to assist themselves, to take control of their own financial destiny.

Men were what messed up everything.

Most women would be so much better off without them.

Jane didn't come right out and say that, exactly, to the

poor, lost female souls who came to her. She didn't want to freak them out too badly right away, and Jane knew she could really freak people out if she wasn't careful, being so passionate and insistent in getting her ideals across. She just told women that unless and until they were in charge of their own lives, they would never have any true independence or stability, and that who, if anyone, should be in charge of their lives except themselves?

Empowerment and enlightenment, Jane promised in the advertisements for her seminars. *Changing women's lives for the better.*

Jane was completely in charge of her own life, and it was wonderfully predictable, dependable and sane.

And she liked it that way.

Wyatt Addison Gray IV got *the look* the minute he walked in the door at the main offices of Remington Park.

The administrator, a most aptly named Ms. Steele, was waiting for him, all starched and pressed and so buttoned-up it looked like her blouse might be strangling her, even as she stood there.

Wyatt asked himself, How bad could it possibly be? The man had only been here for a week. How much havoc could an eighty-six-year-old man possibly cause in seven days?

And come to think of it, why couldn't his uncle be immobile like so many men his age? Maybe just stuck in a wheelchair that conveniently didn't move, the wheels sabotaged for his own good? Was that too much to ask? Drugged into a mild haze that left him feeling no pain and causing no trouble? What would it take to arrange that? It wasn't really illegal, was it? Drugging and restraining a troublesome eighty-six-year-old?

Wyatt tried to fortify himself for what was to come, put on his best I-can-fix-this smile and extended a hand. "Ms. Steele. What can I do for you?"

"You promised there wouldn't be any trouble," she said, attacking from the first word as she stood in the doorway to her office.

"Yes," he said, pretending he believed every word he was about to say.

No trouble.

No problem.

Nothing to fix.

She gave a curt nod that said, *Inside my office. Now.*

Wyatt smiled reassuringly and then tried to appear calm and confident—none of which he felt—as he complied with her unspoken command.

Ms. Steele seated herself behind a desk organized with rigid precision, pen here, clock here, phone here, files neatly housed in a small holder on her desk, paper in a short stack that looked like someone had taken a ruler to the edges.

Ooh, Wyatt thought, feeling like he was a teenager and had been summoned to the headmaster's office at boarding school. *Again.*

He sat back, determined to at least seem relaxed, and smiled. "What can I do for you?"

She huffed like she was already disgusted with him and his uncle, and Wyatt hadn't even begun to make his explanations yet.

"You think those of us in the eldercare community don't know each other?" she began. "Don't talk? Don't get together to share our problems and ideas on how to address them?"

Oh, hell.

He hoped not. Though he probably should have thought

of that and negotiated a confidentiality clause with the other retirement homes his uncle had been in.

"Well, we do talk to each other," Ms. Steele said. "And I did some checking. I don't know how I let you talk me into taking him without talking to some people first—"

Wyatt knew exactly how he'd done it. It was, simply, what he did—talk people into things they didn't want to do. He was a divorce lawyer, and what he'd found, mostly, was that by the time they got to him, people really didn't want to divorce their spouse. They wanted to torture their spouse, mercilessly and without end, and the way to do that was to keep fighting about the divorce.

So he usually let them fight it out for a while, chalking up billable hours like crazy, until most of the fury had burned out, that gleam in their eyes about revenge giving way to exhaustion and growing financial distress, and then he talked them into what they really needed to do. Agree to the divorce.

It sounded cold and maybe a little as if he was taking advantage, but truly, he wasn't. People needed that time to let their emotions rage, he'd discovered. It wasn't pretty, but it was all about processing those bad, messy feelings that came from the breakup of most relationships. And without that processing time, people simply couldn't move on.

He gave them that time, at an outrageous sum per hour, as most attorneys did, and then when he felt they were ready, he got them to agree to the actual divorce.

Wyatt liked to think he provided a much-needed service to the miserably married public, that he gave his clients a nice balance of hand-holding, emotional venting opportunities and, in the end, closure. For that, he was incredibly well paid and had learned how to talk almost anyone into anything. A skill that he never imagined he'd need in such abundance in looking after his beloved but troublesome elderly uncle in the man's waning years.

Problem was, certain things about uncle Leo showed no signs of waning. Most distressingly, his interest in women.

When they'd come to Remington Park, Wyatt had been at his most charming, most reassuring, pushing to seal the deal without ever seeming like he was pushing, seeming like a man with no troubles at all, when he convinced Ms. Steele to take uncle Leo.

"Kicked out of three retirement homes already!" Ms. Steele commented.

It wasn't a question. She knew it was true. *Damn.* "Look, he just went a little…you know—"

"No, I don't," Ms. Steele said. "The man's eighty-six, not sixteen!"

"He and my aunt Millicent were together for eleven years," Wyatt explained.

Ms. Steele didn't seem impressed at all with the number.

Wyatt frowned. "No one in my family's ever stayed married that long. This was the marathon of marriages for the Gray family men—a record likely to stand for the ages if history is any guide—and uncle Leo was faithful to her the entire time. He swears it. But then, when she was gone… I mean, he was devastated. Truly, he was. But he also felt like…"

"He was running out of time?" she suggested.

Wyatt nodded. "I suppose."

"Had to get everything while he still could?"

That sounded more selfish than he'd ever considered Leo to be, but still, Wyatt conceded, "It's possible."

"A little like a kid in a candy store, given the fact that there are so many more women than men at his age? Or even in the age group ten or twenty years younger than he is? So many lonely women with no one to talk to? No one to flatter them? Flirt with them? Hold them? Convince them to let him take care of certain physical needs they might have forgotten, that he can bring back to life, like magic?"

"Okay, yes. He likes women," Wyatt admitted. "Always has. And they like him."

"Don't expect me to see this as some sort of public service he's offering. Servicing—if you will—lonely women," she said, looking every bit as dour and imposing as the last administrator who'd kicked uncle Leo out of her facility. "Because I certainly don't see it that way."

"And how do you see it?" Wyatt asked, thinking if he knew where she was coming from, surely he could fix this.

"Like he has caused women who've lived together happily, some of them for years in the same cottage, to now be at each other's throats! Like they were in high school, fighting over a boy! I won't have it. I can't—"

"Look, he's a flirt—"

She frowned down her upturned nose, holding a file folder in front of her. "He's doing more than flirting."

Damn, Wyatt thought. Leo's still got it. At eighty-six! A part of him couldn't help but feel a sense of admiration and reassurance about his own twilight years.

Eighty-six and still going.

On the other hand, he could really go for Leo moderately drugged and confined to a deliberately sabotaged wheelchair in an all-male home right now.

Did they have those? All-male homes? Wyatt would have to look into it, if he couldn't salvage this situation.

"Look, these women… He swears he doesn't make them any promises. No commitments. I told him he had to make that clear up front, so no one would get hurt." He'd thought about actually drafting a release, spelling it out in writing. No expectations of any permanent arrangement. And getting them all to sign before Leo got too close. "I mean, surely women still aren't looking for a long-term commitment in their eighties? Please tell me they're not?"

Ms. Steele looked aghast.

"He can't help it if women like him," Wyatt said.

"The women here got along just fine with each other until he came," Ms. Steele reiterated. "So I don't think the women are the problem. He is. And if he causes any more of an uproar here, he's gone. I mean it. And you'll have to take him out of state to find him a new home. I won't have him doing the same thing to anyone I know in this business."

Okay, so…it wasn't that bad yet? They still had a chance. What a relief!

"He'll be great," Wyatt vowed. "Quiet, kind—without being too kind. Friendly without being too friendly. A model resident. I promise."

Bigger lies had seldom fallen from Wyatt's lips, he feared.

He wrapped up his meeting with Ms. Steele and went to find his uncle.

Remington Park was actually a series of small cottages, each housing eight to ten residents who had their own bedrooms and shared a common kitchen, living room and dining room. Those cottages were set around larger, more traditional assisted living apartments and a nursing home facility for people who needed a higher level of care. Once they could no longer live in the cottages comfortably, they could move next door to assisted living or the nursing home, without leaving all the friends they'd made within the community.

The whole complex also had extensive walking trails, gardens, a few small shops, a pool, a rehab center and cafeteria, and boasted of the fitness and activity level of its residents.

Wyatt thought it seemed homey, those little cottages—kind of like old-fashioned boarding houses. Plus there were the more traditional care options. He hadn't thought, as he clearly should have, that with the place being this big, there were bound to be tons of women.

As he walked down the path that led to Leo's cottage, he saw them. Some of them frail-looking and hunched over, some of them glossy, white-haired, beauties-in-their-day women, bare arms pumping with each step, wearing walking shorts, their toned, tanned legs moving at a pace that might even leave Wyatt breathless as they went about their exercise.

As Leo liked to say, eighty was the new sixty.

Wyatt just shook his head and thought he had to get to the gym more. He could take out some of his frustrations over Leo there, and he wanted to be in good shape, still able to chase women if he wanted to when he was in his eighties.

He got to Leo's cottage, then to Leo's room, but seeing it was empty, went to the kitchen and asked the young woman in the cheery yellow polo shirt the staff wore where his uncle was. But she wasn't sure.

"He doesn't spend much time in his room," she said, looking like she was trying to be diplomatic and maybe was a little scared.

Wyatt wondered if she was the one who had squealed on Leo to the dragon-lady administrator. Poor girl. She didn't look like she was much past twenty and certainly no match for Leo at his most charming or most manipulative.

"Do you have any idea where he spends most of his time, if not in his room?" Wyatt tried.

"Well, he has a new lady friend," she admitted. "I mean…at least one new one that I know of. It's hard to keep up, you know?"

"I know," Wyatt admitted.

"There's a bench on a little hill in the formal gardens overlooking the outdoor pool. You know where the outdoor pool is?"

Wyatt nodded, remembering from the tour.

"I've heard him say how much he likes that spot." She leaned in closer, whispering. "The view…of the ladies at the pool, sunbathing… You know what I mean?"

"Oh, yes."

Bathing beauties had always done it for the Gray men.

"You might try there," she offered.

Wyatt thanked her.

He found the gardens, followed the sound of low laughter and a faint blend of '40s big-band music to the little hill overlooking the outdoor pool.

There was the bench, but no Leo.

Then Wyatt heard giggling.

Leo had always had a knack for making the women laugh.

Around a bush, a cypress tree and a decorative rock wall, there was a more secluded bench and Leo with his arms around a lovely white-haired woman, her head laid back against his arm as she gazed up at him adoringly. He bent down to kiss her, his hands starting to wander.

"Leo," she said, still giggly, pushing one wandering hand away. "We just met!"

Wyatt rolled his eyes and swore under his breath.

Leo copping a feel at eighty-six, just like a damn teenage boy with more hormones than functioning brain cells.

Was there some sort of anti-Viagra? Something they could slip into Leo's nightly bourbon and Coke? Maybe that would do the trick.

Wyatt strode forward, calling out to his uncle as he did. The lady jumped up and away from Leo, blushing like an innocent young miss.

Leo got to his feet, too, smiling for all he was worth. "Wyatt, my boy. What are you doing here?"

"Oh, I think you know," Wyatt said.

Chapter Two

Leo introduced his lady-friend, Kathleen, who shook Wyatt's hand and said, "Leo's told me all about you. He just adores you."

Wyatt smiled as best he could, put an arm around Leo's shoulder that left no doubt Leo was to stay right there. "Leo's a real character, isn't he?"

"I hope you'll be joining us for dinner," Kathleen added. "It's lasagna night, and we could all get to know each other better."

"Mmm," Wyatt said, making no promises.

Although maybe he could prevent a fight from breaking out over dinner, if he stayed. Leo had a bad habit of inviting more than one woman to share the same meal with him. It wasn't a forgetfulness-that-comes-with-age thing, either. He'd been double-booking himself for decades.

"Well," Kathleen said, looking from Wyatt to Leo and then

back to Wyatt again. "I suppose you two could use some time to catch up. Leo, I'll see you at six o'clock at my cottage. Don't you forget this time or I'll have to come find you."

She gave him a kiss on the cheek and then walked away.

Leo watched her go, trim, toned legs in neat, short socks and sneakers. He'd always been a leg man.

Wyatt just shook his head. "For a woman you just met, she sounds a tad possessive. She's ready to hunt you down if you don't show up on time for dinner."

"Damn, that's a pretty woman. You should see her in a bathing suit," Leo confided, shaking his head appreciatively. "Seventy-six, and she's still got it."

"She's lovely," Wyatt agreed.

"Kind of reminds me of your father's third wife. What was her name? Elaine?"

"No, Elaine was number four. I can't remember number three's name at the moment. She was the one who only lasted a few months. I was at boarding school practically the whole time."

"Oh, yeah. The redhead. I'd forgotten about her," Leo said, then had the grace to look a bit sorry. "So, the Dragon Lady summoned you, boy?"

Wyatt nodded. "And it only took a week. That's a record, Leo."

"Yeah, that woman really needs a good man to loosen her up, make her smile once in a while, you know?"

Wyatt rolled his eyes. "Don't tell me you're going to fix everything by taking the Dragon Lady out for a spin, so to speak?"

"No, no, no. Not me! I'm just saying, a good roll in the sack would do wonders for her."

Wyatt sat down on the bench and buried his face in his

hands. The men in his family tended to think good sex fixed everything, when it was usually the beginning of all their problems. How could they not know this by now? Especially at Leo's age?

"I'm not here to talk about the Dragon Lady's sex life or lack of a sex life."

"Yeah, yeah. I know," Leo grumbled. "Bunch of damn uptight prudes! They expect a man's life to be over at my age. Well, I'm tellin' you, boy. Leonardo Gray's life is far from over! And I intend to enjoy every last minute of it."

"Well, if you want to enjoy it here—" Wyatt began.

"I do. I like it here. Beautiful women all over the place. Women who really know how to take care of themselves, too. Did you get a good look at my Kathleen? Great legs."

"Yes, she has gorgeous legs," Wyatt agreed. "And if you want to be here to admire them, you've got to tone down the charm, Leo. The flirting with everyone you see. You know how women get their hopes up when you're around. They tend to always think you're offering them more than you are. Things more permanent than you want."

Leo made a disgusted sound. "Permanent? What the hell is permanent when you're eighty-one—"

"You're eighty-six, Leo."

"I know that! Don't you think I know that! But I can't be saying it all the time. Otherwise, I might forget and say it in front of the women. They get a little squirrelly at the idea of a man not that far from ninety. Not that I'm scared of it. Hell, it's just a number. If I'm still around, I'll still have it when I'm ninety. You wait and see!"

Wyatt just groaned at the idea of Leo the Ladies Man, still havin' it at ninety.

* * *

Jane arrived promptly at five minutes to six.

She prided herself at being on time, always, which she accomplished by consistently being five minutes early for any appointment. Being on time was a mark of respect for others and a sign of good organizational skills, she thought, both virtues Jane strived to portray to the world at large.

She walked into the cottage Gram and Aunt Gladdy shared with four other women, all friends from childhood who'd grown up together in Maryland and even if they'd moved away at times, came back home in their later years.

Gram could have lived independently, but she and Gladdy had shared a house off and on for sixty years. In fact, the first apartment they'd ever lived in on their own had been in the same boarding house. They were both attending secretarial school in hopes of snagging their rich bosses as husbands, something they both had managed to do, although neither one's marriage had lasted long. They happily moved in together again and again, as various entanglements with men began and inevitably went bad over the years.

When Gladdy broke her hip a year ago and was facing a couple of months in rehab, maybe more, Gram missed Gladdy so much, she moved into Remington Park with her. Once there, they found so many old friends in residence, they didn't want to leave. Gram said it was like being back in the boarding house and twenty-one all over again. It was the homeyness of that little eight-person cottage that did it, that and all the activities.

Gram said she hadn't realized how much fun it was to have people around all the time and to have so many things to do, right there where they lived. She and Gladdy had always been social creatures, and as long as they were happy, Jane was happy.

She'd never expected anything like Gram falling in love.

Jane said hello to Gram's friend Ms. Bea, who was knitting in her favorite chair in the corner of the living room, and Alice, who was heading for the door in a terry cloth swimsuit cover-up, blowing kisses at Jane as she went.

The cottages' favorite aide, Amy, was in the dining room setting the table. Amy was twenty-one and had a five-year-old of her own, Max, who all the ladies of the cottage adored and secretly looked after on days when Max didn't have kindergarten or Amy's babysitter was a no-show.

"Hi, Amy. Dinner smells delicious," Jane said, putting a bakery box on the counter. "I brought cupcakes for everyone, including you and Max."

Amy beamed at her, grateful for every little thing anyone did for her and her son. "Jane, you spoil us."

"And you spoil everyone here, so we're far from even. But I have to try," Jane said, more grateful than she could ever express to know that Gram and Gladdy were so well taken care of and happy here. "So, given any thought to my offer to help get your application together for the culinary arts institute?"

Amy made a face. "I told you, this is the best job I've ever had. These ladies are sweet and happy almost all the time, and they take care of me and Max as much as I take care of them. I worked a lot harder than this at home when I was twelve taking care of my younger brothers and sisters for free. This is a piece of cake."

"But you're such a wonderful cook—"

"And I cook here, and people love my food," she reasoned.

"But, I know the pay for aides in a retirement community is not good." Abysmal, actually. How could any woman live on that, and the workers here were primarily female, as the lowest-paid workers most usually were, Jane knew.

"Yes," Amy admitted. "But all I have is my GED. You don't make a lot of money with a GED."

"Which is why going back to school is so important," Jane said.

"And costs a ton of money. Where would I get the money?"

"There are programs to loan money to people who are furthering their education. I'll bring the paperwork here. We can fill it out together."

"And then what? Classes at night? Working all day? When am I going to see Max? I'm all he has. And I can't afford to pay someone to take care of him all the time." Amy looked tired suddenly, taking care of too many people for too long with no one to help her.

"Do it now, and you'll be grateful for the rest of your life and Max's. No more living paycheck to paycheck. Think about it. Job security, health insurance. You can do it. I know you can," Jane promised, trying not to break into her basic speech on education and financial well-being with all the bells and whistles, the cheerleading, the chants, the whole bit.

She tended to do that, even when she wasn't on the podium conducting a seminar, and it made some people uncomfortable.

"I'll think about it," Amy said. "But I just don't see how I can make it work."

"I do. I've helped thousands of women just like you get back to school and get good jobs—"

"Jane?" Gram said, as she and Gladdy came around the

corner and into the kitchen. "Don't nag, dear. Amy loves it here, and we can't imagine this place without her."

"Sorry, Amy." Jane took a breath and hoped she truly did look sorry.

Gram thought Jane was too militant in her ways, crusading for women's financial freedom and security.

Of course, Gram and Gladdy's idea of financial security was a man, a well-to-do man. Jane had finally convinced them to at least ask for gold and diamonds as gifts from their various admirers. Gold and diamonds held their value quite well and could always be sold, if need be. Stock certificates and bonds in divorce settlements worked well, too. They'd been involved with enough men, by this age, to have accumulated smartly diverse and extensive investment portfolios, something of which Jane, who'd handled their finances for years, was very proud.

"Don't worry." Amy laid her hand on top of Jane's. "It's fine. And it's nice to have someone who cares."

"I do," Jane promised. "If you ever decide to leave here, or they catch you bringing Max to work one day, promise to call me."

"Jane!" Gram said again.

"You know the administrator would fire Amy if she ever caught Max here during Amy's working hours," Jane argued in her own defense.

"We love Max and Amy, and we are very good at hiding Max when necessary," Aunt Gladdy said. "Plus, we have our eyes out for a nice young man for Amy. We're going to find her someone fabulous!"

Jane groaned, then looked pleadingly at Amy. "A man is not the answer."

"They are to some things," Amy countered. "I've been alone a long time, if you know what I mean."

"Okay, men have their uses," Jane admitted. "Limited at best, but they are not the answer."

"Well, I don't know about that," a lively older man claimed, smiling as he took his place by Gram's side and leaned over to give her a little kiss on the cheek. "I'd have to say it depends on exactly what the question is."

Though he looked younger, Jane would bet money he was at least eighty, maybe older, just because she knew men seemed to think they were entitled to a younger woman, the younger the better.

Her father had already married and divorced two women younger than Jane. Why was that, exactly, that they thought they were entitled to younger and younger women? Didn't they know how ridiculous they looked? Running around with wives younger than their daughters?

Jane had never been able to figure that one out.

And she feared she disliked Leo Gray on sight.

Gram gave him a dazzling smile, which faded fast after Leo greeted her and then turned to give Gladdy the same treatment, little kiss on the cheek and all. Gladdy glowed for a moment, then caught Gram's look and eased maybe an inch farther away from Leo.

So… Gladdy liked him, too?

Not good, Jane thought. Really not good.

She tried to comfort herself by remembering that in all their years together, Gram and Gladdy had never fought over a man. Surely they wouldn't start now.

Gram put her hand on Leo's arm and said, "Leo Gray, meet my favorite granddaughter, Jane Clayton. Jane, darling, this is Leo."

Jane held out her hand, only to find Leo clasping it in both of his and slowly bringing it to his lips for the barest hint of a kiss. "Well, she is just as adorable as you said, Kathleen. I can see now what you must have looked like as a girl, you gorgeous thing."

Adorable?

Girl?

He made it sound like Jane was six. She fumed but said nothing, not wanting to embarrass Gram.

This was going to be a very long dinner.

"Men have their uses. Limited at best…"

Wyatt caught that much as he followed Leo through the cottage door, then hung back, not wanting to walk into the middle of that particular conversation. Leo, of course, had no reservations about getting into anything with any number of women, kissing his new lady-love, Kathleen, and her friend, which Wyatt could see didn't go over so well with Kathleen.

Jeez, right in front of her like that? What was Leo thinking?

And the granddaughter, Jane, the *adorable girl,* had just met Leo and already she was fuming on her grandmother's behalf.

Wyatt decided navigating this room was going to take all the diplomatic skills he possessed, that he'd rather step in between feuding spouses on the way to divorce court than this particular group.

Bracing himself, he walked to Leo's side.

"My nephew Wyatt dropped by for a few minutes. To take care of some business for me," Leo said. "He met Kathleen in the garden by the pool earlier. Gladdy, my dear, Jane, meet Wyatt. Wyatt, these two lovely ladies are Kathleen's cousin Gladdy and her granddaughter, Jane."

Wyatt smiled and nodded to Gladdy, a shorter, more gently rounded version of Kathleen with the same pretty white hair. He would have done the same to Jane, but she stood ramrod straight and extended a hand, giving him a firm, businesslike handshake, which he returned in the same manner, fighting the urge to snap to attention and salute at the way she held herself.

He hoped he passed her little test, being properly businesslike and not trying the bowing-over-the-back-of-the-hand kiss Leo favored in greeting all women, whether they were five or one hundred and five.

Wyatt anticipated Jane might have slapped him if he'd tried it. He'd seen her reaction to Leo's patented move, after all.

She was obviously going for the classic power-suit look some women favored, and she might have pulled it off. She had the matching skirt and jacket in power-red, a no-frills white blouse, hair raked back from her face in a severe knot and carried her leather briefcase by her side.

It was just that Jane was pint-size, maybe five foot two, Wyatt guessed.

She looked like a dress-up doll in that outfit. Like a little girl who'd been sneaking into her mother's closet.

It was cute, really, if a man liked that sort of thing, though he was certain that was not the look she was going for.

His mouth twitched, amusement warring with the need not to offend her or to show any undo interest. After all, she already thought Leo was an awful flirt. Wyatt didn't want her to think all the Gray men were like that.

"Well, it was lovely to meet you all," Wyatt said. "I

won't keep you from your dinner. Leo, just don't forget what we talked about, okay?"

"Wyatt, you're not staying for dinner?" Kathleen asked.

"Oh, honey, it's my fault," Leo said. "I didn't know he was coming by today, and I didn't call in time to make a reservation for him."

Wyatt hadn't been here for dinner yet. He usually took Leo out to a restaurant nearby. But he knew guests were welcome, for a slight meal fee and with a few hours' notice, to make sure there was enough for everyone in the cottage who wanted to eat that evening.

"Sorry, ladies. Another time," he responded, thinking how happy he was to escape this little group.

"Oh, you're welcome to stay," Amy piped up from the kitchen. "We have a resident who has a sore throat and just told me that she wasn't coming to dinner tonight. So there's plenty."

Wyatt tried to keep the pained expression from his face, knowing it might be smart to stay and see firsthand what the problem was, maybe even talk to Leo's new lady himself and set her straight about Leo's abysmal record with women, much as he dreaded the idea.

"Well, in that case, I'd be happy to join you," he said.

Leo held out a chair for Kathleen, and Wyatt did the same for Gladdy, then hesitated over doing so for Jane, feeling she would see it as an insult to her abilities to pull out her own chair, rather than plain, old-fashioned manners.

He played it safe and stood back, indicating that she should take her choice of seats, the one next to Gladdy or Kathleen. Leo, of course, seated himself between the two women at the small, round table. Jane picked the seat next to Gladdy, leaving Wyatt the one next to Kathleen.

Everything was fine for a while. The food was actually outstanding. He joined the others in heaping praise on the very young-looking girl who had made and served the meal.

Amy, a bit flustered by the attention, fumbled the fork on his empty plate as she removed it, and Wyatt and Jane both hurried to bend over and pick it up.

And that's when Wyatt—and unfortunately Jane—saw it.

They already knew Leo was leaning comfortably toward Kathleen, his arm stretched across the back of her chair, his hand cupping her far shoulder. But now that they'd bent over to pick up the fork, they could see he was also holding hands under the table with Gladdy! He pulled his hand away when they bent over, but not quickly enough.

Jane gave an outraged huff, her mouth falling open, eyes shooting sparks at Wyatt under the table. Wyatt, hoping he looked properly shocked to Jane, picked up the fork and slowly straightened.

He handed the lost fork to Amy, then got another zinging look from Jane. Gladdy, he noted, had the grace to blush and carefully bring both her hands to the top of the table, clasping them together almost in a prayer-like motion.

Begging them not to tell?

Leo, the idiot, looked relaxed as could be, and Kathleen perhaps a bit confused, but smiling all the same in that lovely way of hers.

Wyatt wiped his mouth with his cloth napkin and as unobtrusively as possible, leaned toward Jane and whispered, "Meet me at that bar across the street after this? We need to talk."

Her seething look said, *Yes, we certainly do.*

Chapter Three

"What in the world is wrong with that man?" Jane demanded, upon entering the bar, not even bothering to sit down.

Wyatt had selected a table in the far corner, wanting privacy and anticipating that this conversation might get loud at some point. Not thinking she'd walk in and stand there, all puffed up and mad, trying to glare down at him. A ridiculous attempt, given how tiny the woman was.

Even sitting down, he could very nearly look her in the eye.

And she was really adorable when she was spitting fire like that. Not that Wyatt would dare tell her. She already had a terrible opinion of the men in his family.

"Is he demented in some way that isn't quite obvious to a person untrained in geriatric medicine?" Jane asked, hands on her hips, still filled with anger.

"Unfortunately not," Wyatt told her.

"Unfortunately?" She enunciated each syllable like he might be demented himself and didn't quite understand the big word.

"Yes. If he was actually impaired in some way, he'd have some excuse for his behavior," Wyatt admitted. "Jane, I'm very sorry, but there's simply no excuse. It's just the way he is. Always has been. He's like a kid in a candy store where women are concerned."

He had her agreeing with him for a minute, maybe even sympathizing, and then she started seething again.

"Kid in a candy store? Like women are all laid out in a row, his for the taking, waiting for him to pick which one he wants?"

"Unfortunately, yes. He's just that…" Wyatt would have said confident, but stopped himself. He thought she might have hit him, if he had. "Look, I know it's…offensive, especially to someone like you—"

"Someone like me?" She practically spit the words at him.

"A modern woman," he said, trying desperately to save himself now. "An enlightened woman. A strong, successful, extremely capable woman."

Who doesn't think she needs a man for anything at all. He got it. He understood her perfectly, he believed. Oh, yes, he did, because his last words placated her a bit.

"Look, the man was born in a different era. He was raised to see women and relationships differently than we do today," Wyatt tried, not about to explain that his father, twenty years Leo's junior, thought of women the same way and that he'd been raised much in the woman-as-candy-in-a-store philosophy, too.

"That's really no excuse for his behavior," Jane said, not quite as militant-sounding as before.

"I know. Believe me, I do, and I'm sorry." Wyatt dared to pull out the seat next to him and offer it to her. "Jane, please, sit down. Let's talk about this. Let me get you a drink. God knows, I need one after dealing with Uncle Leo."

She looked a bit miffed, like she'd been winding up for a really great fight or a rant on women's rights, and he was depriving her of that opportunity by agreeing with her and apologizing. It was one of Wyatt's greatest weapons—being able to soothe outraged females. He was a master at work right now, even if he did say so himself, much like Leo in that gigantic candy store of women.

Jane sat, still looking as if she didn't trust him a bit, but not foaming at the mouth or anything. With Jane, he decided, that was progress.

He motioned for the waitress who'd been hovering a few feet away, figuring out if they were really going to start a fight at the bar and how she might handle it. She came to the table, looking a bit nervous but calming down as Jane stayed silent.

At his quiet question about her drink preference, Jane looked a bit sheepishly at the waitress and murmured, "White wine spritzer, please."

Wyatt tried to contain a grimace at the idea of wanting to dilute good wine with anything, at the idea of such a sissy, girly drink. Jane didn't seem girly at all. Maybe she didn't approve of really drinking. She was prim and buttoned-up after all.

"You're going to make fun of my drink?" she asked, apparently not going to let him get away with anything.

"I wouldn't dream of it," Wyatt insisted. Then asked for a bourbon, straight up.

Jeez, the woman was prickly.

The waitress nodded, promised to bring their drinks right away, and then escaped, looking quite happy to get far, far away from them.

Wyatt sat back in his chair, trying to look relaxed and in perfect control of the spitfire that was Jane. "So, as I said before, my uncle's attitude toward women is inexcusable. Outdated, sexist, arrogant, immature. I realize that. I freely admit it and apologize sincerely for it."

Jane gave him an odd look, hopefully discarding the next three insults she had planned to hurl at him over Leo's behavior.

Good. They were getting somewhere.

"If there was anything I could do to change the way he behaves, believe me, I would have done it years ago. It's caused him and me enormous amounts of trouble and grief. But I fear, at eighty-six—"

"Eighty-six? He told Gram he was only eighty-one."

"Well, he's not," Wyatt went on. "Honestly, a woman can't believe a word that man says, and unfortunately, I simply cannot change him. I've tried. So, at this point, all I can do is be completely up front about…how he is…and hope that saves women like your grandmother and great-aunt from being hurt by him."

"That's it? That's your solution?"

Wyatt shrugged, trying to look both reasonable and helpless at the same time. "I don't know what else to do. He's a grown man. I have virtually no control over him. Any more than you can control your grandmother—"

"My grandmother's not the one running around with two different people at the same time."

Wyatt could only pray it was merely two women for Leo at the moment.

"I was just hoping," he explained quietly, "that your grandmother might be more…reasonable…to deal with than my uncle. That once we explain to her…the way he is…"

"You want to tell her that he's a complete cad and a liar?" Jane asked.

"Better than her finding out on her own. And, actually, I thought you might tell her. That the news might be easier coming from you. But if you think it should come from me, of course, I'll do it."

Jane's mouth fell open, literally.

The waitress returned with their drinks. Jane didn't touch hers. Wyatt downed his in one long gulp.

"Another, please?" he asked the waitress before she left.

Jane leaned toward him, whispering urgently, "My grandmother thinks she's in love with him!"

Wyatt sighed, feeling a headache coming on. "He's only been there a week."

"I know. It's ridiculous, I admit, but she does! What in the world does he do to these women?"

Wyatt could only shake his head in wonder. He refrained from saying that surely any woman who could believe she was in love in a week's time was, perhaps, just asking to get hurt.

He wouldn't dare say that to Jane.

She sat back in her chair, looking sad and worried. "You have to understand, my grandmother has never been in love before. She's had men, of course. She's a beautiful woman.

Been married a number of times, and been genuinely happy for a time with a man, but she's never claimed to be in love. She doesn't even believe in love, as far as I know."

"So what the devil happened between the two of them?"

"I have no idea."

Jane sat back in her chair, taking a sip of her wine spritzer. What could this man possibly find offensive about a white wine spritzer?

But on the topic of Leo, she had to concede to herself at least, that for a man, Wyatt Gray was being exceedingly reasonable, much as she hated admitting it.

He had acknowledged his uncle's bad behavior and didn't really try to make excuses, merely admitting he was incapable of controlling the man. Jane had tried for decades to change Gram and Gladdy's attitudes toward life in general and men in particular without much success. Except for getting control of their finances. So she had to empathize with Wyatt's own troubles where his uncle was concerned.

"What about Gladdy?" Wyatt asked finally. "She doesn't think she's in love with Leo, does she?"

"I have no idea. I couldn't believe they were holding hands under the table. It's like something twelve-year-olds would do."

Jane felt awful remembering that soft, warm glow on Gladdy's face. She'd looked delighted with their intimate dinner at first, and Jane had simply thought Gladdy was happy for Gram, silly as that would be, because Gladdy didn't believe in love any more than Gram did.

"They've never fought over a man before," Jane confided. "And they grew up together, moved into their first apartment together and have lived together off and on ever since. The thought of a man coming between them is unthinkable."

And yet, Jane had seen with her very own eyes the way Gladdy looked at Leo and Leo looked at her. And Gram! That little weasel of an eighty-six-year-old man!

"I suppose we could start by talking to Gladdy," Wyatt offered. "Appeal to her sense of friendship and devotion to your grandmother, and at the same time, tell her the sad, hard truth about Leo. That might, at least, keep him from coming between the two women."

Jane nodded sadly. "It would be a start."

"Just tell me what you want, Jane. I'll do whatever you think would be best. If you want me to talk to Gladdy, I will. I'll be unmerciful in explaining Leo's lifelong habits with women."

"Short of hog-tying your uncle to his bed and locking him in his room—"

"Believe me, I've wished I could."

Which actually had Jane smiling a bit.

Wyatt Gray was a reasonable man, and Jane had found that so few men were. She regretted how things had started out between them.

"I'm sorry if I behaved badly toward you at first," she said, because a polite, well-bred, empowered woman always acknowledged her own unfair treatment of others and apologized. "Gram and Gladdy… Well, I just adore them both, and looking out for them hasn't always been easy, but believe me, they need someone to look out for them and I try my best."

Wyatt gave her a reassuring smile and let one of his hands settle softly over hers on the table between them. "I'm sure you do your absolute best for everyone you care about."

Which was just so nice of him.

People sometimes thought Jane could be overzealous and maybe even a bit aggressive in her attempts to take care of others, when she truly never wanted to do anything but help. Women could just be so mixed up about some things, have such wrong ideas, and she felt it was her calling to straighten them out, to educate them, to help extricate them from the troubles they found themselves in. It wasn't a job to Jane. It was her calling, her mission in life.

"That's incredibly kind and generous of you," she admitted. "Especially when I yelled at you at first."

"It's completely forgotten," he promised, smiling once again.

She could see a bit of Leo in him when he smiled like that. The dangerous charm, that wicked twinkle in his eye. Not that he was flirting with her or anything like that. He'd been perfectly respectful during their exchange. Some men thought flirting was as natural and expected as breathing in any exchange between the sexes, even the most businesslike. Something of which Jane naturally disapproved.

But Wyatt hadn't been like that at all.

Still, the dangerous charm was there lurking below the surface in the man, even if he didn't turn it on every time with all women. But when he did…

Jane shivered just a bit, thinking he really was too good-looking for any woman's good and likely too used to getting his way with women, just as Leo was. She couldn't let herself forget that.

Not that Jane ever really forgot herself with a man.

"Well," she said, feeling a little warm and uneasy suddenly. "I suppose the best thing would be to talk to Gladdy first. I'll try it myself and see how it goes."

"And if that isn't enough, I'll talk to her. Just give me a call," Wyatt offered, pulling out a business card and scribbling down a phone number on it. "My office and personal numbers. Feel free to call anytime, Jane."

She pulled out a card of her own, wrote her private number on it and handed it over to him. Picking up his card, she saw Wyatt Addison Gray IV, attorney at law, with what she knew was a pricey downtown address.

"What kind of law?" she asked.

"Divorce." His mouth twitched, trying to hold back what she suspected would be a mind-numbingly gorgeous grin. "I have to admit, it seemed to come naturally to me. I saw so many of them in my family as I was growing up."

Jane nodded. "Me too. What was the longest marriage in your family?"

"Leo's last one. Eleven years."

"Wow. Impressive," Jane declared. "We never managed to do better than six."

Wyatt shrugged, as if to say, *What are you going to do?*

"I think we're going to work together well to handle this little problem," Jane told him, quite pleased with herself and Mr. Wyatt Addison Gray, Esquire.

"I do, too, Jane."

Jane felt like a dynamo the next morning, charging through her routine with even more enthusiasm and effectiveness than usual. Powering through her morning kickboxing class, getting to the office early, proofing the copy for her latest ad campaign for her Fabulous Female Financial Boot Camp, even sketching out ideas for a series of advanced classes for women who'd mastered the principles laid out in the first seminar.

She felt like she could do anything.

Her assistant, Lainie, showed up at the usual time, looking puzzled at the way Jane rattled off a list of things she already needed Lainie to take care of.

"You didn't have one of those energy drinks again, did you?" Lainie asked. "I told you, Jane, your system really can't handle those. You're already on overdrive. You don't need the boost."

"Of course not." Jane looked puzzled. "After all, a well-rested, well-nourished woman doesn't need artificial stimulants."

She reached for her notepad, always close at hand, and started scribbling.

"Sorry," she said, quite pleased with herself. "I need to write that down. I'm thinking about working on a book of my philosophies. Financial advice for women is such a nice niche market these days, and it would be a wonderful cross-promotion for my seminars. Don't you think?"

"Sure," Lainie said, still frowning.

"What?"

"It's just that…you seem…happy."

"I am almost always happy," Jane insisted.

Lainie looked skeptical. "I think you might have been whistling when I walked in."

Jane thought back. Had she been? And what if she was?

"How did things go with your grandmother yesterday? Did you meet this man she claims to love?"

"Oh, yes," Jane said. "A complete cad, but Wyatt and I will take care of the situation."

"Wyatt?"

"The man's nephew. Wyatt Addison Gray IV. I have to say, I disliked him on sight as we sat down to dinner, but then we went across the street to this bar and had drinks afterward, and he was completely open and honest and reasonable. Altogether, a remarkable man."

Lainie gaped at her. "You met a man you think is reasonable?"

Jane nodded.

"And honest?"

"I told you, a remarkable man," Jane repeated even more emphatically than before.

"And you had dinner and drinks? Like…a date?"

"I date," Jane insisted.

"Not in this calendar year," Lainie reminded her.

"I'm just very selective about the men I find worthy of my consideration and time."

Lainie's bottom lip curled over her teeth, and she looked like she might bite herself to keep from replying to that, but finally gave up the battle and said, "And when you do, you don't show up in the office whistling the next morning. If I didn't know you better, I'd say you and Wyatt Gray didn't end things with dinner and drinks last night."

"Of course we did. I would never take a man home with me that I'd just met, and going home with him would be just as risky and irresponsible." And Jane never took irresponsible risks. "Besides, this wasn't a date. It was dinner at the retirement park with Gram, Gladdy and Wyatt's uncle, the cad. Assessing the situation we're facing with them."

"And the drinks afterward?" Lainie prompted.

"A place to talk without them present, where Wyatt and I found out that we're in complete agreement that the relationship between his uncle and Gram has to be stopped. We plotted our strategy to make that happen."

"Of course," Lainie said. "I just got so excited when you said you met a man you think is reasonable."

"Well, I'm sure there are a few of them in the world," Jane admitted.

Granted, that might be considered a rather large concession on her part to the quality of men alive on the planet at this moment. But she did consider herself a reasonable woman, and a reasonable woman would have to concede that Wyatt Gray had not been what she'd first thought.

"I'll even admit we had a very interesting and enlightening conversation," Jane said, thinking she was being exceedingly reasonable and fair-minded now.

"Okay, tell the truth. He's gorgeous, isn't he?" Lainie asked with a knowing gleam in her eyes.

"That had absolutely nothing to do with…anything," Jane insisted, thinking, oddly, that she felt a little…tingly inside and just a tad overly warm all of a sudden.

How odd.

Lainie laughed.

"It didn't," Jane corrected. "You know I always say the worst thing in the world a woman can do, besides depend on a man financially, is to judge one by his looks. I would never, ever do that. In fact, the best-looking men are almost always the most spoiled and immature."

It was true. She knew it. Long experience with the women in her family had proven it.

"We must be talking Greek God in a designer suit here," Lainie claimed.

"He was beautifully dressed," Jane admitted, again only trying to be fair.

And still, feeling that unusual, unsettling tingly warmth inside her.

"You know, I may be coming down with something," she told Lainie. "Does it feel warm in here to you? Could you check to see if anyone messed with the thermostat?"

Chapter Four

Jane waited until Gram was at her regular tennis lesson two days later, because normally Gram and Gladdy were practically inseparable, and then went to do her duty, to save poor Gladdy from Wyatt's ill-behaved uncle.

Jane pasted on a fake smile, walked into Gladdy's room, and—

"Oh, my God!"

It looked like Gladdy and Leo were…necking on the love seat! Gladdy had her head on Leo's shoulder, and his was bent over hers. When Jane burst in, Gladdy gave a start and her head popped up, banging into Leo's forehead.

Jane stood there, astonished and really, really mad on both Gladdy's and Gram's behalf.

"Oh, Jane, dear, will you ever learn to knock?" Gladdy asked, practically giggling.

Giggling?

Jane worked herself up into a good, steaming rage and pointed her finger at Leo, who didn't look guilty in the least over what he'd done. "You," she said, advancing on him. "Get your hands off my aunt! Right now! Now!"

She'd beat him off with her briefcase if she had to. Jane lifted it up and back, preparing to take a swing.

Leo Gray stood up, all too slowly for Jane's current mood, smoothed out his shirt, brushed back the bit of hair on the sides of his head and looked for all the world like he was the insulted party here.

"Girly," he said. "You've got to learn to have a little fun."

Jane's mouth fell open.

Girly?

He'd called her *Girly!*

"I'll have you know that I am a twenty-eight-year-old adult woman! I am no girl," she yelled after him, as he left Gladdy's room. "I should have you arrested for this!"

"Arrested?" Gladdy said, taking her arm and pulling the briefcase out of her hand. "Jane, what are you doing?"

"I came to warn you about that awful man! Did he force himself on you? Tell me, because if he did, I'll—"

"Leo Gray's never had to force himself on a woman in his life," Gladdy insisted. "I mean, have you looked at the man? I know you're not seventy-five years old like me—"

"Gladdy, you're eighty," Jane reminded her.

"Shhhh. He doesn't know that. A woman should never admit to her real age and never look her real age. There's no reason to in these days. Speaking of which, Jane, darling, is it too much to ask for you to use that nice age-resistant face cream Kathleen and I bought you for Christmas? You have beautiful skin, dear, but you want to keep it that way. You'll care about these things one day. At least, I pray that you will."

"That I'll worry about wrinkles one day? That's what you pray for?"

"No, that you'll learn how to enjoy a man and want to look your best for him."

Jane sank down into the love seat Leo had just vacated, suddenly so tired and frustrated, she could have cried or screamed. That awful man!

"Are you sure you're all right?" she asked Gladdy.

"Of course, I'm all right. I'm better than I've been in years, in fact. Nothing like a fabulous man to make a woman feel young again. I think I'm going to get my hair done and have a facial. What do you say, Jane? A facial? My treat?"

Jane felt like she might turn into a stark raving lunatic at any moment. "A facial? Gladdy?"

"Good skin care is nothing to scoff at, Jane."

"What about Gram? You love Gram. You always have, and she thinks she's in love with that man, that awful man—"

"He's far from awful, and Kathleen has never been in love in her life," Gladdy insisted. "You know that. You know what the women in our family are like."

"Yes, but she told me that she loves him. I've never heard her sound this way, and if she knew what the two of you were doing behind her back… Not even behind her back," Jane remembered. "The other night, at dinner?"

"We were holding hands. It's hardly a crime, hardly anything at all. What a prude you can be sometimes, Jane. I just hate that for you. I want you to be happy in every way, including having a man in your life."

"Prude?" Jane was so hurt, she could hardly speak.

Frustrated, infuriating tears filled her eyes. *Prude?* "I am not!"

"You're objecting to hand-holding, my darling. If that isn't prudish, I don't know what is. I was holding hands with boys in first grade."

Jane gasped, hurt. *Prude?* She opened her mouth to object again, and then realized if she didn't get out of there right that minute, she was going to cry. And Jane Carlton never cried, especially in front of anyone!

"I…I…I have to go. I can't talk to you about this right now," she said, then got up and fled.

She was outside, hurrying down the walkway toward her car, not really watching as carefully as she should have been, when she literally ran right into Leo Gray.

"You," she said, "Necking with my aunt? Behind my grandmother's back! My grandmother who thinks she's in love with you? You rat!"

He didn't crumple or anything from the impact of their collision. The man was solid for his age. But then he grabbed her by the arms. She hated grabby men.

"Get your hands off me this instant!" she yelled.

"Calm down, girly," he said, having the nerve to seem amused. "I'm just trying to make sure you don't fall down."

"I don't need any help to keep from falling down. Let go of me this instant!"

She jerked herself away with everything she had, but he was stronger than he looked, and he didn't let go. A haze of red came over Jane's vision. She was so mad now, she couldn't even see, couldn't remember ever being this mad in her life.

It was all his fault!

Every bit of it!

Her grandmother would be brokenhearted. He'd been necking with Gladdy, Gladdy who'd called Jane a prude! And this awful man had the nerve to tell her she needed to relax?

Before she truly thought of what she was about to do, Jane pulled back the hand with her briefcase and got ready to whack him with it. She got the backswing in and was bringing her hand forward when, only then, her mind cleared just a bit so she could actually see what she was doing.

She was about to hit an old man.

A nearly ninety-year-old man!

"Oh, my God!" she cried, changing her mind right at the end of her backswing, as she started swinging her arm forward.

Could she stop it now? Was it too late?

And then she gasped as she was lifted off her feet—literally—and hauled around in the other direction.

Wyatt saw Jane and Leo having what looked like angry words, but he wasn't really worried at first.

Then Leo put his hands on Jane, holding on to her.

Not the smartest thing to do, Wyatt was sure.

Then he saw Jane wind up to take a swing at Leo with her briefcase.

"Good God! Jane!" he yelled, barely getting to her in time.

He was in the wrong place to get between her and Leo. He was behind Jane. So he just put an arm around her waist, hauled her back against him and swung her around the other way.

Leo ducked and her briefcase went flying, landing harmlessly in the petunias in the flower bed to the right.

She screamed in pure outrage, like she was being mugged in a dark alley, kicking her feet in the air, her arms coming back to grab him. She hit him in the eye, then grabbed and thankfully got nothing but his hair. Afterward she took that handful of hair and yanked hard.

"Jane," he hollered at first, because she wouldn't have heard him over the racket she was making otherwise. "It's Wyatt. Shhhh. I'm not going to hurt you. I would never hurt you."

He got another arm around her, this one across her hips, her body completely plastered against his as he spoke softly into her right ear. "Shhh. It's all right."

She stopped kicking out with her feet, stopped squirming and went still. Maybe that was even worse, because then her hips were pressed against his abdomen—sweet, curvy Jane hips. She was breathing hard, and as he lowered her to her feet, her whole body rubbed along his.

Damn, Jane.

She really would be outraged if she knew the direction of his thoughts at the moment.

He put her down and she turned around, right there in front of him, looking shocked, still more than a little mad, and all rumpled and…sexy.

Very, very sexy.

Her hair had come tumbling down from that well-disciplined knot she'd had it in yesterday. It tumbled about her shoulders and her face. Her cheeks were flushed, eyes glistening with unshed tears.

A look of horror came over her face as she glanced from him to Leo to the crowd of retirees Wyatt now realized had come to watch this scene.

"Oh, my God!" she said, like she'd just woken up from a nightmare.

He took her carefully by the arms, to steady her and nothing more, not because he just needed to have his hands on her. "It's okay," he promised quietly, then turned and addressed the crowd. "Everybody's fine here. Just a slight misunderstanding. Let's all move along now. Nothing to see."

Jane's mouth fell open, and for a moment, it looked like she was going to hide her face against Wyatt's chest to keep from having to see anyone. Not that he had any objections.

He had the feeling Jane Carlton very seldom, if ever, let herself really lose it like that, and while he wasn't a man to condone violence, he had to admit, if any man could push a woman over the edge, it would be one of the Gray men. Leo probably deserved to be whacked with much more than the briefcase.

His mouth twitched. He was aching to grin, but tried to maintain his stern facade as Leo came cautiously closer. Wyatt eased Jane's face against him in a loose embrace, while she hid for a moment.

Over the top of her head, he mouthed to Leo, "What the hell did you do now?"

Leo shook his head, pretending an innocence Wyatt was sure was completely fake.

"Get out of here," he mouthed.

Before he turned Jane loose on the man.

Wyatt waited until Leo was far enough away. He felt fairly certain Jane wouldn't chase after him, if she saw him, and then reluctantly stepped away from her.

She was shaking and felt so tiny in his arms. "You okay now?" he asked.

When she finally lifted her head, she looked a bit dazed and still horrified. "I can't believe I did that."

Again, Wyatt had to fight not to grin, because she looked like she was confessing to mass murder.

"Leo's fine," he said. "Not a scratch on him."

"I almost hit another person!" she cried. "An old man!"

"Now that would offend him terribly. Calling him an old man and thinking he was too frail to take you on in a fight."

"I don't fight!" Jane cried. "I can't… I would never… I've always been devoted to nonviolent ways of settling disagreements. I abhor violence in any form."

"An admirable principle," Wyatt assured her.

"But I could have really hurt him. I mean, I take kickboxing and self-defense classes."

Wyatt couldn't help it. He chuckled at that.

Jane, kickboxing? It was laughable, given her size. If her little suits weren't so severely cut, he'd swear she had to shop in the girl's department.

"I could have hurt him," she insisted. "I've had abused women go through my seminars. And every now and then, a man gets mad at the things I've taught a woman and shows up at the office. I thought it was important to learn to protect myself, that every woman should."

"Of course," Wyatt agreed. Mad men came looking for her? Pint-size Jane? He didn't like the sound of that at all.

"But I never believed I could resort to anything like that myself. Wyatt, this is horrible. This is completely unacceptable. One minute, I was fine, and the next, I just saw red, literally, and I was taking a swing at him."

"Jane, I've nearly decked him a time or two myself, and I assure you that I too abhor violence. I've had abused women in my office, as well, trying to work up the courage to divorce their abusers."

"I'm so sorry," she said, still aghast at her own behavior, standing on the walkway at the retirement park, looking around like she'd just found herself on another planet.

"It's all right. I promise. And I'm sorry I grabbed you like that. I was just trying to keep you from hitting him."

"And I'm so glad you did."

"What did he do to make you so mad?"

"I went to talk to Gladdy about him, and I caught them necking in her room! And he was so awful! He called me names and said I just needed to learn to have some fun. Fun! He's going to hurt my grandmother and Gladdy's feelings terribly, and he thinks it's fun!"

Jane realized she'd said it like *fun* was a dirty word, which she didn't believe, and she wasn't really a prude, was she?

"But I wasn't really going to hit him, Wyatt, I swear! I changed my mind. Midway through that swing, I realized what I was doing and changed my mind. I just wasn't sure if I could stop in time. My briefcase was already headed for him, and I just… I don't… This is sooo awful!"

"Jane, it's fine. Everyone's fine."

"And then you grabbed me, and I didn't know it was you, and I—"

"I know. I didn't mean to manhandle you. I just had to act fast, and…well, I'm sorry."

And then she looked horrified again, raised her hand to the side of his face and said, "I hit you!"

His right eye throbbed a bit. "It's nothing," he insisted.

"No. It's turning red and a little puffy." She touched it, with her fingertips, featherlight, trying to find the extent of the blow. "Oh, my God, Wyatt! I could have put your eye out!"

"I seriously doubt that."

"No, I've been trained to do that." She seemed absolutely convinced that she could. "A man attacks you, you go for the eyes. It's one of the most vulnerable spots on the body. Eyes, nose with the heel of your hand, groin—"

"Okay, thankfully, I came out of this unscathed."

"No, we have to get something on that eye. Ohhh," she fretted. "I feel awful about this. You have to let me help you."

"Well, if you insist," he said, turning himself over to her tender care.

Gladdy, Leo and Kathleen watched from the cover of the rhododendrons fifteen feet away.

"Ladies, I'm afraid I overplayed the scene," Leo said.

"Nonsense. Jane overreacted," Gram stated. "Gladdy and I should have warned you about that. Poor Jane does tend to overreact."

"She's got some fire in her, all right. I like that in a woman," Leo admitted. "Couldn't believe she actually took a swing at me. Didn't think she had it in her."

"It was the 'girly' remark," Gladdy said. "And I may have overplayed things a bit myself with her."

"Of course not. It worked perfectly," Kathleen insisted. "Look at them. Jane feels terrible about what she did and Wyatt's comforting her. It's so sweet. They've known each other for less than three days and there they are. I'd say our plan to get them together is a rousing success."

"Well, in that case, ladies," Leo said, "would you care to join me for a celebratory drink? I have champagne chilling in the minifridge in my room. We can decide on our next move and commemorate the success of this one."

* * *

Wyatt took Jane back to his apartment, which was a mere four blocks away—a sleek, shiny, modern, expensive loft in a high-rise on the edge of town.

Jane taking charge was something to behold. She pushed him down to sit in the middle of the big, cushy sofa the minute they had walked in the door, and told him not to move. He complied.

She got ice from the kitchen, lectured him mildly about the need to take care of himself properly once she found out he didn't even have an ice pack, explained that one should always be prepared for life's emergencies, then said they'd make do with a ziplock bag wrapped in a hand towel.

She came to stand behind him, took his head in her hands and eased it back against the sofa cushions. Then she placed the makeshift ice pack on his right eye.

"Keep that there while I search your bathroom. You must have some ointment and bandages somewhere."

He sprawled on the couch, leaning back as instructed and holding the ice to his eye. He never imagined a woman giving orders to him would be so sexy. Normally, he was a take-charge kind of guy. Not that he ordered women around, either. Just that…well, he couldn't help but wonder now exactly how Jane would be in bed.

Would all those spitfire tendencies come out? That take-charge attitude, demanding what she wanted from him?

Wyatt had a hard time imagining Jane knowing what she truly wanted in bed, much less demanding it. She was cute, but didn't seem to have much use for men, and any woman who'd been truly satisfied in bed would have at least one use for a man, he reasoned. He suspected she was very good at pushing men away, at keeping them at arm's length, and not that good at really letting herself go in any situation.

Not that he thought he'd see her in his bed anytime soon. There had to be a dozen women he knew who'd be so much less trouble than Jane, although, he thought, once there, Jane would be interesting and definitely a challenge.

And Wyatt would admit to being a man who liked a challenge.

She came back a moment later and he felt the couch cushions give with her weight, as she knelt on the seat beside him, bracing her side on the back of the couch as she leaned over him.

Removing the ice pack, she frowned down at him, her face maybe an inch from his as she inspected his eye.

"It's all red and puffy now," she complained, sighing heavily, her warm breath brushing across his cheek, his ear.

He shivered just a bit, wondering what she'd do if he pushed her backward to lay on the couch, stretched out on top of her and started giving a few orders of his own. Would she give him a smile and wind her arms around him? More likely, she'd try to hit him again or really put his eye out this time.

The woman thought she was a champion kickboxer, after all.

Wyatt grinned, laughing a bit, unable to help himself.

"What? There's nothing funny about this. I feel terrible, Wyatt."

"Well, I don't," he said. "It's really nothing, Jane. I can hardly feel it anymore. I assure you, I'm fine." As long as she didn't figure out where his thoughts were going at the moment.

She put the ice pack aside and came up with some kind of ointment, which she then very carefully spread with her fingertips along his eyelid, his brow and the side of his face. And as she got closer and concentrated harder on getting it in exactly the right place and not his eye, her body leaned into the side of his, one breast pressed against his shoulder.

He felt like someone had installed a giant neon Trouble sign in his apartment when he wasn't looking, and that it had just flickered on and was blinking in a fire-engine red color.

Trouble, trouble, trouble!

He had real problems to deal with. Leo and his penchant for getting kicked out of retirement complexes had Wyatt worried that there would be no place in all of Maryland that would take his uncle, once Ms. Steele put the word out about him. And the easiest way to fix that problem was for Wyatt and Jane to work together.

If he made her mad, came on to her, offended her, hurt her, he doubted they'd be working together to solve the Leo problem any longer. So Ms. Jane Carlton was definitely off-limits. It would be more trouble in the long run than any short-term fling with her would be worth.

So what if she smelled really good? And had the sweetest, gentlest touch in a little spitfire of a body? Which he suspected no man had ever properly awakened before. Surely he was capable of exercising some kind of discipline where a woman was concerned.

He shifted his weight, thinking to ease away from her, and instead, set her off balance and her whole body fell against his. No question now. Those were her breasts pressed against him, her neck and her sweet, sassy Jane mouth right at the corner of his own.

She gasped in surprise, her eyes suddenly all big and round and so close to his, not blinking. Neither of them breathed for an instant.

He could have her flat on her back in a moment. Or take her by her thighs and pull her across his lap facing him, palm those pretty hips he'd had pressed against him earlier and pull her tight against him. He knew it, and if he knew anything about women, she was thinking the same thing.

Discipline, Wyatt. It's not just a word.

"Jane," he whispered, hardly able to believe he was actually doing this, taking her arms in his hands and steadying her, then easing her away from him, to sit on her knees on the cushion beside him. "I'm sorry. I didn't mean to throw you off balance like that."

She just looked at him, sexy and baffled and maybe embarrassed, which was the last thing he wanted.

"And I'm just not sure what you want here," he confessed. "But I know what I want, and I really don't want to offend you."

She seemed a little dazed, innocent. *Damn.*

"What I want?"

"Yes," he said.

"I…I was just trying to fix your eye."

"Okay." He smiled what he hoped was an I-understand-perfectly smile and not an I-wanted-to-jump-your-bones one. "That's what I thought you were doing. My mistake."

"Mistake?"

She looked a little sad then, a little embarrassed. He could feel her withdrawing from him, even though she hadn't actually moved an inch.

"I'm just… I'm a guy, okay? Some women would say, I'm not a very nice guy. That I…well, when a woman gets this close and is…touching me…I get ideas. Ideas that, I'm afraid, were not the same ideas you were having, and… well, you're a beautiful woman, Jane."

She scrambled to get off the couch, to get away from him, hot color blooming in her cheeks as she got all flustered. "You thought…I was coming on to you?"

He nodded, thinking honesty probably wasn't the best policy here, that he'd offended her, when, he swore to God, he'd been trying to do the exact opposite. To keep from offending her.

Women. They could just be so hard to read, and sometimes it seemed there was no way to win. No way at all.

Come on to her and offend her? Don't come on to her and still offend her?

What was a guy to do?

"I am so sorry," she said.

"Jane, it's no big deal—

She blushed even more furiously. "I would never—"

"Never?" Now that hurt. "Never?"

"I'm not… I mean to say, I don't—"

"Don't what?" Now he had to know. Never with anyone? No way. Not in this day and age. Or no way, no how, with him? That seemed like overstating it a bit. "What do you mean, never?"

"I don't…throw myself at men."

Okay, that he believed, though in his thoroughly male opinion it was a shame.

The world should be full of women who threw themselves at men. Of course, it was, he'd found, but not many of those women were like Jane.

"I'm sorry. For everything. And I just… I have to go," she said.

"You really don't," he claimed.

"I do." She turned and fled.

Wyatt swore softly and succinctly, his body humming with desire, still feeling her pressed against him, her soft hands on his face.

He was an idiot. A complete idiot where women like her were concerned.

Chapter Five

Jane Carlton did not come on to men.

At least, she didn't think she did.

She didn't mean to.

Her face burned when she remembered being on the couch with Wyatt the day before. He'd thought she was making a pass at him? And he'd been trying to say…he'd welcome that?

Surely not.

"You're frowning again," Lainie said, standing in the doorway with a batch of message slips with Jane's calls on them. "What in the world happened to you yesterday?"

Jane, if puzzling over anyone's behavior except Wyatt's, would have normally turned to Gram and Gladdy for advice on men. Between the two of them, she doubted there was any situation Jane might find herself in that they hadn't already been in themselves. But she couldn't talk to them about Wyatt. Not when she was trying to keep his uncle away from both of them.

She figured Lainie was her best shot for help here.

"Can I ask you something about men?" Jane blurted out before she lost her nerve.

Lainie giggled.

"Why is that so funny?" Jane asked, finding Lainie's reaction slightly offensive, maybe more than slightly.

"It's not funny. I'm just so happy, Jane!" she said, like Jane had announced she was eloping or something.

"It's just a question."

"Okay. Go ahead. Please." Lainie sounded so eager. "Anything I can do to help."

"You think I need help with men?"

"Oh, definitely."

No hesitation there. Jane pictured herself as a virtual wrecking yard of relationships, like there might be a sign that said, *Abandon all hope, ye who enter here.*

"It's about…coming on to men," she said, wishing she'd never started this whole thing.

"Oh!" Lainie clapped her hands together like a kid who'd just received a terrific present. "This is sooooo good! Jane, I'm so proud of you. You actually want to make the first move with a man!"

"No, I didn't say that. I'm just…trying to find out if I already did."

"Well, that's even better! Tell me! Tell me everything," she begged.

Jane thought about how she might explain, then decided it would probably be better to just show Lainie. There was a love seat in Jane's office, after all.

"Shut the door," she instructed, then got up and walked

over to the love seat. "I just…sit down and let me show you."

"Okay." Lainie sat.

Jane knelt on the love seat, conscious now of how hard it was to keep her balance. "Lean your head back."

Lainie did, and Jane eased closer.

"Now, you've hurt your eye, and I'm…I'm trying to fix it. That's it. Just trying to fix it. Like this, except you're a lot taller than me, so I had to reach up higher. If I did that, would you think I was coming on to you?"

She reached up to a point past Lainie's eye and then looked down and realized her breasts were practically in Lainie's face when she made that move.

"Oh, no!" Jane cried.

Lainie lifted her head before Jane could move away, and then…sure enough, breasts in her face.

While Lainie giggled, Jane went to brace herself against Lainie's body to get out of the way, but before she could do that, she heard a voice.

A man's voice, Wyatt's, clearing his throat and then saying, "Ladies, I'm so sorry. There was no one at the desk out front, and I…seem to have caught you at a bad time."

Jane froze, her mouth dropping open.

This could not be happening.

Lainie looked over Jane's shoulder. She could see Lainie taking the whole thing in. Mulling it over. Wyatt, how gorgeous he was. His eye, no doubt at least a bit bruised. Jane's worry about coming on to a man. Jane shoving her breasts practically in his face while she tried to fix his eye and needing to reenact the whole scene to figure that out.

She was a complete idiot.

She looked to Lainie, mouthing, *Don't leave me. Please don't leave me alone with him. Please!*

"Sorry." Lainie laughed and got up from the couch. "I'm sure I have…something to do at my desk."

Jane hung her head down and stayed there, sat back on her heels on the love seat, thinking if she never had to turn around and look at him, she might live through this day with just a shred of her dignity intact.

She heard Lainie introduce herself and Wyatt's gloriously deep, beautiful voice saying, "Wyatt Gray. So nice to meet you."

And then Lainie disappeared, closing the door behind her.

Jane stayed where she was and said, "If I paid you…like a million dollars, would you turn around and go away? So that we never had to talk about this?"

He laughed. Beautifully. The sound like a current zinging through her body.

And then he walked over and sat down beside her. She still perched there on her knees, not wanting to shove any part of herself into his face, either accidentally or on purpose.

He looked like a man who couldn't be more pleased with himself or his life at this moment. Wearing a gorgeously expensive suit that wrapped faithfully around his altogether impressive body, he sat there, slightly blackened eye and all, looking completely at ease and holding a huge bouquet of exotic-looking flowers in his hand.

"Jane, I'm seldom wrong about these things, but with you… Well, I suppose it's a possibility. I just haven't had a lot of dealings with women like you. You don't…like women, do you?"

"What? Of course, I like women. Women are great, women are—"

"Sexually," he clarified.

"Oh. You mean…me and Lainie? Me and…women? That way?"

He nodded.

"No! I… No! Not that there's anything wrong with that. But, I like men." She got all flustered then, and kept talking, which she tended to do when flustered. Fill the silence and try to move on. "Granted, not a lot of men. But I do…like…men. I mean, I have to admit I like them more in theory than reality, but… Well… Oh, my God!"

She buried her head in her hands and gave up.

Too much information, Jane.

Way too much information.

"Well, I'm happy to hear that," Wyatt responded. "That you like men. And that you find at least a few of us…acceptable and interesting."

The flowers, looking lush, exotic and expensive, came into her field of view, even with her head hanging low so she didn't have to look at him.

"These are for you," he continued, still sounding amused. "A small token of apology, nothing else. No reason for you to worry."

"But *I* hit *you,*" she said, taking the flowers and feeling completely inadequate at the moment as a girl. This whole girl-stuff thing had just never come naturally to her. Or maybe she just hadn't tried hard enough or cared enough. But she'd always felt a little awkward in this area.

Even more than usual with Wyatt.

"I know, but I embarrassed you yesterday in my apartment, and it certainly wasn't my intention."

"No. It was me. I was… I'm so sorry—"

"Jane," he interrupted. "Take the flowers and say thank you. Then forget about the whole thing. It's as easy as that."

Easy for him, maybe.

"Jane?" He touched his fingers gently to her chin and urged her to raise her head and look him in the eye.

His poor, bruised eye. It was a faded black shade. She'd really hit a man.

"I'm telling everyone a hulking two-hundred-fifty-pound man did this to me, and that I got it defending a lady's honor. My female clients are impressed and the men are intimidated."

She was sure the women were impressed.

"Take the flowers and say 'thank you,'" he reminded her.

She took them and mumbled, "Thank you."

He sat there looking as relaxed and gorgeous as could be, despite the black eye. "Now, what are we going to do about Leo and your sweet grandmother and great aunt?"

Two days later, Jane was in the middle of a youth-regenerating apricot-mint facial and pedicure—thinking it would give her some alone time with Gladdy to explain what a rat Leo really was—when she got the call.

Ms. Steele, the Remington Park administrator, insisted on seeing her immediately.

That had never happened before.

Jane promised to be there within the hour because Gladdy insisted that no meeting was worth cutting short a facial and pedicure.

As she sat in the waiting area outside Ms. Steele's office, Jane had a sinking feeling she knew what this was about. That Ms. Steele had heard about Jane attempting to slug Leo Gray on the grounds of Remington Park.

How humiliating!

She remembered it seemed like tons of eyes were staring at her when that freakish red haze cleared—when she stopped trying to kick Wyatt in the shins and pull out his hair, thinking she was under attack and all her self-defense training she'd never had to use before was kicking in. So it wasn't that surprising Ms. Steele would have heard about it. From what Jane had seen in the time Gram and Gladdy had been here, Ms. Steele kept a very close eye on the goings-on at Remington Park. As a business owner, Jane could only applaud that kind of devotion and attention to detail.

But at the moment, she was horribly embarrassed.

She sat there getting more and more nervous, wondering how in the world she might explain herself, when Wyatt, blackened eye and all, strolled in.

Her face fell. "You've been summoned, too?"

He nodded, taking the seat beside her, looking much more at ease here than she did.

"I feel like I've been called into the principal's office," Jane fretted.

He laughed. "I'm going out on a limb here, but I bet you were a very good girl growing up, Jane. I bet you've never been called to the principal's office before."

"Only for good things. Like accepting awards and organizing school fund-raisers," she admitted, sighing heavily. "How in the world am I going to explain getting into a fight on the grounds of my grandmother and aunt's retirement park?"

"Denial is always a good start," he began.

"Denial? You're sitting here with a black eye."

"And if denial is out of the question, I recommend, as a next step, downplaying the importance and scope of the situation."

"You sound like a defense attorney now. Either that or someone who's used to being in trouble."

He shook his head. "Never been a defense attorney, but I did play one in moot court competition in law school. Won my cases every time."

Jane wasn't surprised about the wins and noted he hadn't denied being in trouble himself. She shook her head and said, "I got Gladdy alone today at a salon. It was like talking to a Barbie doll. She ignored everything I said about your uncle and kept suggesting new skin care routines for me."

"Wait…salon?" He leaned in close, his nose practically touching the rim of her ear, sniffing her hair, then the side of her face. "Is that why you smell so good? Good enough to eat?"

She closed her eyes, feeling all tingly and warm at the same time.

Because a man was sniffing her youth-regenerating apricot-mint facial?

She felt him breathing in that smell, the heat from his body so close, radiating toward hers. The tip of his nose gently brushed her cheek. Was it an accident?

"What is it? Peaches?"

"Apricots," she admitted, not daring to move an inch.

She didn't think she'd ever had actual sexual intercourse that felt this good. Her breasts ached and she thought she wanted to shove them into his face right now. She could spread apricot-mint facial cream over her whole body and then practice her coming-on-to-him skills and see how he liked it.

Jane was even regretting wearing her customary white, no-frills, all-buttoned-up blouse, because honestly, how much good could a woman do trying to stick her breasts in a man's face when she was buttoned up practically to her chin? She was even considering undoing a few buttons, as unobtrusively as possible, when she heard a door open.

There was dead silence for a moment.

A throat was cleared quite pointedly.

When Jane glanced up, Ms. Steele, looking particularly steelish at the moment, was gaping at them both.

Face flaming, Jane turned to Wyatt. Sitting up straight in his chair now, he threw up his hands in a helpless manner and mouthed, "Sorry," before standing, extending a hand to Jane, then leading her into Ms. Steele's office.

They sat side by side in front of Ms. Steele's desk. Jane looked determinedly down at the floor so she couldn't see Wyatt, but she felt him, absolutely certain he was doing that easy yet elegant sprawl of his, perfectly comfortable in that chair, ready to brazen this out with the body language that said, *Problem? There is no problem here.*

The man had nerve, and it seemed he was impossible to embarrass.

What in the world must Ms. Steele think of them?

"I am so sorry for that…that…" What to call it? Jane couldn't think of a thing and sat there mute, feeling stupid all over again.

Wyatt shot her a hard look that said something like… *Denial and downplaying, remember? You're not helping, Jane.*

Jane dared to look up at Ms. Steele, who appeared to

be having a hard time believing what she'd just seen in her waiting room.

"I…" the woman began. "I wasn't aware that the two of you knew each other."

"Oh, we don't," Jane claimed, then realized how ridiculous that sounded, given the fact that they were just in the waiting room, Wyatt practically nuzzling her cheek. Would what he did really be considered nuzzling? Or had he just been smelling her fruity facial? "My grandmother, my aunt and Wyatt's uncle introduced us. They know each other. That's all."

"Oh, I'm aware that they know each other," she said, emphasis on the word *know.*

Jane felt like sinking down in her chair and trying to hide.

Wyatt, still brazening it out, asked, "Is there something we can do for you, Ms. Steele?"

The woman's lips got all funny and stiff, as if she sternly disapproved of Wyatt, maybe of both of them. Jane couldn't be sure.

"You could tell me," Ms. Steele said, "why I have very odd and difficult-to-believe, yet remarkably consistent reports, that you, Jane, attacked this man's uncle on the walkway outside the blue cottage shortly before noon yesterday."

Before she could say anything, Wyatt chuckled and said, "Oh, no. Nothing like that. She…uh…tripped. Jane wasn't looking where she was going. You know Jane, always on the move, always rushing about to get everything she has to get done…done. And she wasn't watching where she was going, and she tripped."

Now that was so brazen Jane couldn't help but admire his skill a bit. She supposed all lawyers lied. There were probably courses at law school on how to do it effectively. Wyatt Gray, no doubt, had excelled in those.

"I do know Jane," Ms. Steele said. "But I thought you two didn't know each other."

"Oh, just…you know…we were introduced one time by our relatives," Wyatt claimed. "And in fact, we all shared a very nice dinner at the blue cottage the other night. I have to say, the young woman working there, Amy I believe it was, makes outstanding lasagna. Doesn't she, Jane?"

Jane nodded. She'd be happy to talk about Amy and lasagna.

"So, Jane tripped, but she didn't get anywhere near my uncle, because I caught her," Wyatt said, not technically a lie. He had caught her. He pointed to his black eye and said, "That's how I got this."

Then he smiled that I-can-charm-any-woman-alive smile Jane had come to know so well. Except, sadly, Ms. Steele looked completely immune to it.

How could that be? Jane puzzled. She would have guessed no woman was truly immune to Wyatt at his gorgeous, most-charming self.

Ms. Steele cocked her head to the right and frowned at Wyatt. "So your story is… Jane tripped and you caught her?"

Wyatt nodded.

"You're nearly a foot taller than she is. How did you get hit in the eye?"

"I don't really know," Wyatt said. "It all happened so fast."

Ms. Steele rolled her eyes and gave a little huff, then turned to Jane. "I called you in here because I can't just ignore reports of fighting on the grounds of Remington Park. But I was sure it was Leo Gray who was responsible for this whole mess. I would never believe Jane attacked an old man for no reason."

"Oh, but..." *I did.*

Jane barely managed to stop herself as Wyatt clamped a hand down on hers. She took a breath, trying to think up some brazen lies of her own she might tell, but honestly, when was hitting an old man ever justified?

"It wasn't his fault. He didn't do anything to me. And I've never hit an old man in my life. I've never hit anyone...."

Except Wyatt.

He gave her a nod that said, *Well done, Jane.*

"I have no trouble believing the last part," Ms. Steele agreed, yet still seemed troubled.

"I am so sorry about this whole mix-up." Jane tried sounding her most earnest. "I strive to never cause trouble for anyone, and I'm sure Wyatt does, too. I've apologized profusely for giving him a black eye—"

"And I, of course, have forgiven her completely," he jumped in. "Knowing that it was most definitely unintentional on her part. So there's really no problem here."

With that, he got to his feet and urged Jane to do the same, as if his pronouncement that there was no problem was all that was needed to clear up this whole thing.

Jane smiled hopefully in Ms. Steele's direction, then did as Wyatt wanted and walked out the door ahead of him.

As he followed her, she could hear Ms. Steele call out to him, "We're not done with this, Mr. Gray."

Chapter Six

Wyatt thought they both deserved a drink after that little scene in Ms. Steele's office, and Jane, looking like she was still figuring out how her no-doubt neat, orderly life had come to this, let him steer her quite easily to the dark, quiet bar across the street. He set a drink in front of her before she ever uttered the first word of protest, and then she just sat there, looking bewildered, embarrassed and a little sad.

He really didn't want to make Jane sad.

"Why was Ms. Steele so sure this was all your uncle's fault?" she finally asked.

Wyatt frowned, wondering if he could bring himself to do the old denial-and-downplay routine with her.

No, he couldn't.

"Leo tends to…shake things up wherever he goes," he began, then had to admit that was definitely downplaying. "Actually, Jane, he chases after women like a man who's been celibate for years—which I'm sure he'd tell you feels like a reasonable equivalent of being married and faithful to one woman for the previous eleven years. And now that aunt Millicent is gone, he seems to feel the need to make up for lost time. He doesn't just go after one woman at a time. This thing with your grandmother and your aunt—I'm afraid it's not unusual at all for him. This is the norm."

She shook her head, disbelieving. "He's eighty-six!"

"I know. I keep hoping he'll get too tired for all of this, but so far…he hasn't even slowed down. He's been kicked out of three retirement homes, bringing complete chaos to the places. Women who've lived together happily for years suddenly turn on each other, when he favors one over the other, no matter how brief his attention span."

"He can't live by himself?" she suggested.

"He probably could, but he won't. You know how favorable the ratio of men to women is in these places. He thinks a retirement park is a paradise for men. And nothing I've said to him has been able to change him in any way. If he gets kicked out of Remington Park, I don't know what I'll do with him," Wyatt admitted. "And I'm truly sorry for any problems he might cause between your aunt and your grandmother."

"I love them so much," Jane said. "They make me crazy, but I just adore them."

"Yeah, I feel the same way about Leo. He was more of a father to me than my real father was. I mean, my father's not a bad guy or anything like that. He's just…well, he was more interested in his own life than mine. But Leo always took the time to look out for me, guide me, explain things to me. He was there if I needed help. I'd do anything for him."

"There should be some kind of pill to make men faithful," Jane said.

"If there was, Leo wouldn't take it."

"Well, I still feel like I have to apologize to him," she repeated. "I did take a swing at him, after all."

"I'm not sure he deserves an apology—"

"No, I have to. What I did was wrong, and I always apologize when I'm wrong."

"Okay." Wyatt nodded. "If you insist."

"I do. Will you come with me? Sometime tomorrow?"

"Of course."

They went to Leo's cottage, but he wasn't there.

Jane was a little afraid where they might find him and what he might be doing, but she was determined not to lose her good manners around him, at least not anymore. She felt oddly like her life could be on the verge of spinning off into complete chaos at any moment. How could that possibly have happened?

She couldn't blame it entirely on the Gray men. Her own behavior had been erratic, at best, and Jane preached that men could not make women crazy. Women allowed themselves to be crazy over men, but men could not force that kind of irrational behavior upon anyone. No one could. A woman was responsible for her own behavior at all times. She had to own her own decisions, her actions, her words, and Jane's had been abominable.

She and Wyatt walked into Gram and Gladdy's cottage.

Amy was in the kitchen, stirring something on the stove and baking something that smelled luscious. Leo Gray stood beside her. They both turned as the front door opened and Jane thought Amy looked particularly uncomfortable at the moment.

Jane frowned, whispering to Wyatt urgently. "He wouldn't hit on someone Amy's age. Would he?"

"I don't think so," Wyatt said. "But she doesn't look happy to have him here. Or maybe it's us. Maybe she thinks she's going to witness another scuffle."

Oh, Lord! He was probably right. Amy, sweet, kind, quiet little Amy, whom Jane wanted to help become a chef, had surely heard about Jane freaking out and attacking Leo Gray. Amy was looking at Jane like Jane had grown three heads.

"I will never live this down," she muttered.

"Come on," Wyatt said, putting a supportive hand at the small of her back and steering her to the kitchen. "Chin up. Smile. Be confident, gracious, polite. All the things I know you are, Jane. Put this behind you and move on."

"No. They all know." It wasn't her imagination. There were three little old ladies in the common area of the cottage, all staring at Jane like they'd never seen her before. "I'm infamous at Remington Park as the crazy woman who attacks old men with her briefcase!"

"Nonsense. One little slip does not a crazy woman make," Wyatt insisted.

They got to Leo and Amy's side, Amy now looking like she really wanted to run away, Leo looking calm and happy as could be, not at all like a man who created chaos everywhere he went.

"Hello, Amy," Wyatt said, turning on the charm. "I was just bragging to Ms. Steele yesterday about what an outstanding cook you are."

Amy blushed and stammered. "Uh…thank you. I'm making raspberry lemon bars."

"My favorite," Leo said, beaming.

Wyatt ignored that and did his best to charm and reassure Amy. "I'm sure they're lovely. I'm still thinking about the lasagna you made last week."

"I'll save you some to take home, if you're still here when they're done."

"Thank you, Amy. Now, could you excuse us a moment? Jane and I need to talk to my uncle."

"Of course," she said, looking uneasy again.

Wyatt gave a curt nod to Leo, to follow them into the empty dining area. He pulled out a chair for Jane, touching her reassuringly on her shoulder, then seated himself.

"She's not armed, is she?" Leo asked, still standing.

Jane felt like a worm, like one of the lowest creatures on earth and wished she could just crawl away right now.

"Uncle Leo?" Wyatt said none too softly.

Out of the corner of her eye, Jane saw Amy startle, heard the pan clatter on the stove like she'd lost control of it for a moment.

She was expecting the worst.

"Just sayin', you feeling better, girly?" Leo inquired.

"Now you're just trying to be annoying," Wyatt complained. "Let the lady explain why she's here."

"Mr. Gray," Jane began. "I am so very sorry about everything I did the other day, and I've come to humbly beg for your forgiveness. My behavior was completely unacceptable, and I am both shocked and humiliated that I resorted to violence as a way of settling our disagreement."

Leo grimaced, then shook his head. "Kathleen and Gladdy said you were kind of prissy."

Jane winced. Had they told him that she was a prude, too?

Because if he brought that up in front of Wyatt, she would happily just sink into the floor and try to disappear into the crevasses in the stone tile.

Wyatt shot his uncle a hard look. He might have even stepped on Leo's toe or something, because Leo gave a little yelp and eased away from both of them.

"Tell her you accept her apology," Wyatt insisted.

Leo turned to his nephew, chuckling as he asked. "She give you that shiner, boy?"

"Leo!"

"Okay, fine. I accept," he said, not looking either sincere or happy about being forced into saying it.

Wyatt didn't take his gaze off of his uncle. "Jane, would you excuse us, please? I'd like a moment alone with Leo."

"Of course," Jane conceded, eager to escape as fast as she could.

"What the hell is the matter with you?" Wyatt practically roared the moment Jane disappeared from sight.

"She is a prissy little thing. I still can't believe she hit me."

"She didn't hit you," Wyatt reminded him.

"But she meant to. The only thing that stopped her was you. And then she hit you."

Wyatt sighed, feeling a headache coming on, as it often did when he had to deal with Leo. "Did your doctor change your medication or something? Because you seem… particularly outrageous lately, even for you."

"I'm just enjoying myself here," Leo claimed, slapping his hands to his chest. "Life was meant to be enjoyed, boy."

"God help me," Wyatt muttered. "Are you trying to get kicked out of this place?"

"No, I love it here. This is the best old folks' home I've ever been in. Best-looking women, the friendliest, the fittest. I think this place is God's gift to Leo Gray."

"I doubt God sees it that way, and I know for a fact that Ms. Steele doesn't. She sees it as you potentially ruining this place, and she's this close to kicking you out." Wyatt held his thumb and his first finger an inch apart. "One more thing, and I swear, you're gone."

Leo made a disgusted, dismissive sound. "We done? 'Cause I'm supposed to meet someone in thirty minutes, and I need to spruce up a bit. A man can't just let himself go."

"Please tell me it's not one of Jane's relatives." Wyatt said, then wondered, would it be better or worse if it wasn't Kathleen or Gladdy?

"You gonna start policing my social calendar, boy?" Leo challenged.

Wyatt sighed. "There aren't enough hours in the day for me to control you."

Leo looked particularly pleased with himself. "Didn't think so."

"But I'm telling you, you're going to get kicked out of here, and Ms. Steele's going to blackball you with every retirement home administrator she knows, and she claims that will cover the entire state of Maryland. Think about it, Leo."

Jane found Gram and Gladdy in Gram's room whispering urgently to each other. They clammed up the minute they saw Jane.

That was odd.

"What are you two up to?" she asked.

Gram got a sad, disapproving look on her face. "Talking about you, my girl."

"We can't believe the things we're hearing, Jane. You attacked that sweet Leo Gray?"

"He is not sweet! He's trouble! How can you both not see that?"

"He is sweet as can be and just delightful to be around," Gram insisted. "Do you have any idea how boring most men in their eighties are? Sad and grumpy and complaining about one thing after another. Their backs, their head, their eyes. It's really disheartening what you have to choose from in men at our age, Jane."

"You could just give up on men altogether," Jane suggested.

Gram and Gladdy groaned, then looked at each other like it was too horrible an idea to even think about.

"Surely you've both had enough men by now," she tried.

"I hope to have a man in my life for as long as I'm breathing," Gram said.

Gladdy nodded her head, obviously agreeing. "You've just never learned how to truly enjoy a man, Jane. If you had, you'd understand."

"Enjoy a man?" She winced, remembering being called a prude and Gram and Gladdy feeling sorry for her, just because she didn't turn her life upside down for every man who showed the slightest interest in her. "I've had enjoyable men in my life before."

"Name one," Gladdy challenged her.

"I...uhhh..." She had to think, then came up with, "Andy Scovol. He was great fun. We did all sorts of things together, and I still miss him since he moved away."

"He was your best friend in fifth grade. That was eighteen years ago, and he wasn't a man. He was a boy. I bet you never even kissed him," Gram complained.

"Of course I didn't kiss him. He was my friend. It's okay to be friends with men, isn't it? Surely it's not all about sex."

Gladdy sighed. "Jane, we worry about you."

"And I worry about the two of you, too."

"Well, don't. We're fine."

"Fine," Gram agreed.

"But you won't be if you both keep running around with that man, Leo."

Gram gave a dismissive huff. "We told you. He's so much fun to have around."

"Well, you should know he's been having fun with both of you." There, she'd just blurted it out.

"Of course he has," Gram said. "We've had dinner together every day this week. We played doubles today in tennis, and we're going dancing downtown Saturday night."

"That's not all he's been doing." It had to be said, Jane knew. "I'm sorry, but it's not. His nephew says he's incapable of being faithful to any woman or of making any kind of long-term commitment."

Gladdy laughed. "Honey, we're both in our…seventies. How can a long-term commitment even apply at our age?"

Jane let the lying about their ages go. It wasn't the issue.

"He's been romancing you both. Gram, you think you're in love with him, and he was here, in this room…doing things with Gladdy yesterday."

Gladdy looked outraged.

"I'm sorry," Jane told her. "But he was."

"Doing…things?" Gram asked.

"Oh, pooh. I had something in my eye, and he was helping me get it out. I've already told Kathleen about it, and she understands perfectly. Don't you, Kathleen?"

"Of course I do." She patted Gladdy's hand with lifelong affection. "Gladdy and I would never let a man come between us."

"But...but you said you were in love with him." Jane tried.

"I'm quite sure I am. It's so exciting! Love at my age." She smiled like she didn't have a care in the world.

"See? I told you," Jane said to Gladdy. "Love. She thinks she's in love with that...cad!"

Gladdy rolled her eyes and said, "So what? Half the women at Remington Park are in love with Leo Gray. Jane, he's a wonderful man. I wish you could see that, and if I ever hear about you assaulting him again... Well, let's just say Kathleen and I are both greatly disappointed in you, Jane. Would you care to explain yourself?"

Jane frowned, her brow furrowing. *Everyone was in love with Leo?* That was it? That was their explanation?

Could she have completely misread the situation and thought Gram cared more about him than she actually did? Was no one's heart or lifelong friendship at risk here?

Jane sighed. It was hard work, taking proper care of two women in their eighties, especially two active, stubborn women who didn't want to be taken care of. "I just... I worry about the two of you."

"Well, we worry about you, too, Jane, darling," Gram said gently. "But we try not to overreact and let you live your own life, even if you're doing so in a way we disagree with at times."

"I'm...I'm sorry," Jane apologized, feeling ridiculous and so relieved.

Everything was okay. Nothing really bad was happening. She could relax, back off, never have to deal with Leo Gray again and maybe never see Wyatt again.

That was a good thing, wasn't it?

She felt vaguely disappointed and just…out of sorts. Which was silly, because this had to be a good thing.

Gladdy got up, came over to Jane, smiled down at her and gave her a little kiss on her forehead, like she used to do when Jane was little. "You're so sweet to fuss over us like this, but we're fine. Honestly. And I hate to rush off, but I made plans to meet a friend for bridge. Bye, darling. Bye, Kathleen."

"Bye," Jane whispered.

Gladdy left, and Jane for once relaxed that rigid posture of hers and fell back against her chair. "I'm so glad we got that cleared up."

But then she looked at Gram, and it appeared as if nothing at all had been cleared up, Gram's expression suggested that she had to tell Jane something and she was dreading it.

"What?" Jane asked.

Gram gave a shrug and a smile, then a sigh. "I just… Don't get upset, all right? You get upset over everything, Jane."

"Upset? Why would I get upset? You two said you're not fighting, that you haven't gone nuts over Leo Gray and that everything is fine. There's nothing upsetting about that. That's all good news. I'm happy. See? Happy Jane."

"The thing is, that isn't…entirely true," Gram confessed. "We haven't told Gladdy yet, although honestly, I don't believe it's going to be such a problem. I mean, I know she really likes Leo, but she hasn't said anything about being in love with him, and you know Gladdy. She doesn't do love."

"Neither do you," Jane said.

"Still…there's nothing official yet, but Leo and I've been talking, and… I'm fairly certain he's going to ask me to marry him! Jane, I'm just so happy, darling. Isn't it fabulous!"

Chapter Seven

"You can't do that," Jane said, after a long moment of stunned silence.

"Of course, we can. We can do anything we want."

"But…why would you want to?" Jane tried.

"Because that's what people in love do!" Gram gave her a huge, glowing smile.

Jane winced. Her head hurt. Her ears hurt. She could not listen to this anymore. She had no calm reasoning abilities left in her where Leo Gray was concerned.

"People in love do a lot of things," Jane said. *A lot of really stupid things.* "And you've only known him for two weeks, Gram."

"I know, but when it's right, Jane, you just know. This is right, and honestly, he's eighty-one—"

"No, honestly, he's eighty-six. He's lying about being eighty-one."

Gram laughed. "Well, I'm lying about being seventy-six, so I'd say we're even on that score."

"He was in Gladdy's room, necking with her just yesterday! That's what made me so mad! That's why I stormed off after him! Because he acted like it was nothing, to be messing around with you and her, like he could hurt you both and laugh about it."

"She said she had something in her eye, and I believe her, of course," Gram said sternly. "Now she may like him and enjoy spending time with him but she's not in love with him, and we'll all just sit down, talk this out and everything will be fine. You'll see."

"I don't think so, and I don't trust that man. You shouldn't, either."

"Things will be fine. Leo's going to tell her everything. Just wait and see."

Gladdy, just as Jane feared, was with Leo Gray!

When she finished with Gram, Jane went to the card room, where Gladdy wasn't, and then kept asking if anyone had seen her or Leo. She eventually tracked them down to a secluded bench near the tennis courts. Someone said it was a particularly favorite spot of Leo's to take his lady-friends.

Jane contemplated strangling him with her bare hands when she saw him and Gladdy sitting there, laughing hilariously, Gladdy's hand on his knee, Leo toying with a bit of Gladdy's long, pretty white hair.

Was the man on some new combination of Viagra and steroids?

This was ridiculous.

Jane crouched down behind a bush and tried to figure

out what to do next. It was like both Gram and Gladdy had completely lost all sense. Granted, they'd never been the most sensible women, but they hadn't been crazy, either.

Marry Leo Gray?

Gram would be safer jumping off a cliff.

He was like those wackos who founded cults and could get people to do anything he wanted, no matter how illogical or inherently dangerous.

Drink the Kook-Aid for Leo Gray.

And here was Jane, the only sensible one in the group. Well, maybe Wyatt was, too.

She had to see Wyatt again—and firmly ignored a little happy feeling that came along with that thought. There was simply no choice. He at least would help her.

She was getting ready to creep away from her hiding place behind the bush when Leo got up, kissed Gladdy on the cheek and headed Jane's way.

She gave a little yelp, fell to her knees and tried to crawl into the midst of the bushes. It was all the cover she could find that quickly, but it just wasn't big enough for hiding purposes. She was sure her butt was sticking out, and the stupid bush scratched her cheek, her arms, maybe even her ear and was likely ruining her pretty-yet-sensible, low-heeled pumps she'd just bought on sale.

Jane waited there, cuts stinging, knees sinking into the dirt, wondering how her life had been reduced to this—hiding in bushes—until she heard a man's voice.

"I'm telling you, there's something wrong with that little girl."

Leo, of course.

Groaning, even swearing under her breath in the bushes,

Jane couldn't bring herself to crawl out of there. It was too much. She had no dignity left, and Jane Carlton placed a great deal of value on her own sense of dignity. Every woman should, she believed. And hers was simply gone, all because of that man!

"You can come out now. He's gone," Gladdy said, sounding sad and worried herself.

Jane backed out on her hands and knees, then sat back on her heels, simply unable to look Gladdy in the eye.

"Honestly, Jane. Is there something going on that you're not telling us? Because you just aren't acting like yourself lately," Gladdy said.

"Of course I'm not acting like myself. I'm trying to save you and Gram from that man!"

"And we keep telling you, we don't need saving."

"Oh, yes, you do. Did he tell you what's really going on? What he did? What he and Gram are talking about?"

"Oh, please! What is going on? We're all going dancing together. We have dinner together. We just told you this. You remember, don't you, darling?"

"Of course I remember! There's nothing wrong with my memory! It's just…he's… I knew he wouldn't tell you. I just knew it."

"Tell me what?"

"About what's really going on here!" Jane was just all done in. She had dirt all over her knees and her new shoes, scratches on her face. She'd been caught hiding in a bunch of bushes, spying on her aunt, and two days ago, she'd nearly attacked an old man.

"Jane, everything's going to be fine. I'm sure of it. Kathleen and I are as happy as we've ever been. Life is very, very good."

"You're both crazy about the same man. This cannot end well!"

"Well, Leo will just have to pick one of us. Or… maybe not."

"Maybe not? What do you mean, maybe not?"

Gladdy hesitated, looking uneasy for once in the whole Leo Gray situation. "Jane, are you really sure you want me to answer that question? Because you have to think, before you ask some things, whether you really want to know the answers."

Jane shook her head. "What? What could I possibly not want to know?"

"Well…it wouldn't exactly be the first time Kathleen and I have…shared."

Jane got a funny feeling in the pit of her stomach. "Shared?"

Gladdy nodded.

"Shared…a man?"

"Yes," Gladdy whispered, a tiny smile on her pretty face.

When he got back to his office that afternoon, Wyatt got Leo's doctor on the phone. Wyatt was mostly getting the runaround about patient confidentiality and privacy laws, a thoroughly frustrating exchange.

"Look, he's just acting…funny," Wyatt finally said.

"Funny-sad or funny-odd?"

"He's definitely not sad, just…more stubborn about things," Wyatt explained. "And a little reckless."

"Ignoring what seem like perfectly reasonable requests?"

"Yes."

"And good advice from people trying to take care of him?"

"Exactly. What is that?"

"The most common complaint I hear from people trying to take care of older relatives," the doctor replied. "And unfortunately not a disease, as far as the medical profession has been able to identify."

Wyatt wanted to beat his head against his desk. "He's driving me crazy!"

"Me too, most of the time," the doctor admitted. "I can't get him to listen to a thing I say."

"Me either. What do we do?"

"Unfortunately, he's an adult, he's competent to make his own decisions—according to the law, at least—and he gets to go on making his own decisions until you can convince a court to find him incompetent."

Wyatt groaned.

"Look, you're always welcome to come with him to his appointments with me, if he'll let you, and then if you have concerns, I can try to play medical referee. If you're trying to look out for his health and safety, I'll back you up all the way. But I can't force him into anything."

"I feel like I'm the grown-up and he's the teenager," Wyatt complained. "Or maybe even a toddler."

"In my experience, most family members caring for older relatives feel that way eventually," the doctor sympathized. "Come to his next appointment. We'll talk."

Wyatt said he would, was just hanging up the phone with the doctor when his secretary buzzed, sounding agitated. "There's a woman here to see you."

"Lucy, I'm a fortunate man. There's almost always a woman here to see me," he spoke into the intercom.

"This one's different," Lucy claimed.

Wyatt shook his head. "Different, how?"

"She says she just crawled out of some bushes and she has to talk to you right now. It's about Leo."

Wyatt grinned broadly. Jane coming to him? This was a good day.

He opened the door, and then gaped at her.

She looked like a woman who'd been in a fight with a bush. There was a small twig of some kind sticking out of her hair, which was half falling down, half still in a droopy bun on her head. She had small scratches on her face and hands, leaves stuck to her skirt and bits of dirt clinging to her knees.

"Jane!" He went to her side, looking her over more carefully to make sure she wasn't really hurt. "What happened?"

"I hid in a bush," she said, as he took her hand and led her carefully into his office to a seat on his sofa. "Because I was spying on Leo and Gladdy, and then Leo left, and I didn't have time to really get out of the way. It was the bush or nothing. Not that it worked. They saw me anyway. And…I ended up like this."

"Lucy, would you get…anything you can find to help clean her up, please?" he called out the open office door, then turned to Jane, pulling stray leaves off her skirt, because that looked like the easiest place to start.

She looked so sad.

Wyatt carefully pulled the little twig out of her hair.

"Oops," she said. "I thought I got it all."

"It's fine now," Wyatt insisted, smoothing her hair back into place as best he could, which wasn't really all that well, but she didn't need to know that. He looked at her knees, dirt ground in, and asked, "You two didn't get into another fight, did you?"

"No," she responded meekly. "I refused to come out of hiding until he left."

Wyatt got an image of the scene in his mind, then said, "Good thinking, Jane."

Lucy returned with a damp cloth, and Wyatt gently cleansed the scratches on her face, which were red and angry looking but not deep.

"You poor thing," Lucy said, looking at Jane like she came from Mars or something.

She certainly wasn't Wyatt's usual type. He'd admit that. But it wasn't like she came from Mars, either. She was just…a little reserved, serious, all buttoned-up, although today's white blouse was coming untucked from her dark blue skirt in a couple of places.

"Lucy, will you run to the market on the corner and get some antibiotic ointment for these cuts?" Wyatt asked.

"No, it's okay," Jane said. "I can do that at home."

Wyatt shook his head. "You took care of me when I hurt my eye. I'm going to take care of you now."

That got Lucy's attention as she was walking out the office door. She'd been sure his black eye had something to do with a woman, and he'd refused to explain anything about it. Which made Lucy all the more curious. He gave her a curt nod to get out of there, then started cleaning up Jane's knees.

"So, do you think we're going to survive taking care of these three?" Wyatt asked, thinking he might at least get a smile out of Jane with that.

She looked even sadder. Her bottom lip started quivering. She sniffled once, then again. Tears filled her pretty blue-green eyes.

"No, no, no, don't do that," Wyatt begged.

He couldn't stand the idea of Jane crying. Not tough little Jane, who could handle anything. Her expression just crumbled. The harder she fought to control it, the more difficult it become.

Wyatt dabbed at the corner of her eyes with a tissue. "It's okay. Everything's fine. See? No need to cry."

Finally, she just blurted out, "Do you think I'm a prude?"

"No! My uncle called you a prude? I'll kill him—"

She shook her head, tears falling in earnest. "No, my aunt Gladdy did the other day, right before I ran into Leo and almost hit him. And I thought about it, but I didn't really think it was true. But today…today, I wasn't sure anymore."

Oh, God.

What had Leo done? What had Jane seen from those bushes to have her thinking she was a prude?

Ooh. Ick. This was like teenagers walking in on their parents having sex.

Jane was sobbing now, and Wyatt was thinking he probably wouldn't be too out of line if he just kissed her until she stopped. It wasn't as if he'd had many opportunities to grab Jane and kiss her, when he didn't think she'd maybe slap him for trying. But she was genuinely distressed now and kissing was a great distraction, he reasoned. Maybe taking advantage of the situation, just a little, but he felt certain he could stop her crying, and that was what was important. Wasn't it?

Poor thing had been attacked by a bush, called a prude and seen God-only-knows-what that had left her in this condition. Serious comforting was in order, Wyatt calculated.

He took a seat beside her and then just lifted her onto his lap.

Her eyes flew wide open, and she looked at him as if she wasn't quite sure what was up and that she might need to protest. He'd been right to be wary. Kissing her right now was not a good idea.

"It's okay, Jane," he said softly, then urged her to let herself lean on him, put her head on his shoulder.

She sat ramrod straight on his lap, stubborn to the core and resisting with all she had. She might just tell him she didn't need comforting, and if she tried that, it would be all he could do not to laugh. It would be such a ridiculous assertion, but he could imagine Jane trying to make it.

"Just for a minute," he suggested. "I won't tell. If anybody ever asks, you're the toughest woman I know. I'll swear to it."

She sniffled again and finally, ever-so-slowly, settled herself against him, her head falling to his shoulder, her sobs leaving her whole body shaking.

Wyatt closed his eyes and let his face find its way to her hair, inhaling the scent that was Jane, taking in the warmth of her body, the softness of her, the satisfaction of finally having her in his arms.

He was going to get her on her back on this couch and kiss her before this was over. He promised himself. As soon as she stopped crying.

So he stroked her hair, her back, promised her that everything was going to be okay. That he would handle anyone who said mean things to her and make it clear that they were never to treat her badly again.

Her head popped up off his shoulder and she sat up straight on his lap again. "I can't believe they called me that name!"

"I know," he agreed. "I'm sorry."

"That's one of those awful labels people use against

women, to try to rob them of their power by taking a dig at their femininity. It's patently unfair. Especially when it comes from another woman. Especially a woman who's supposed to love me!"

A woman? Well, at least it wasn't Leo. But still…

"Your grandmother?"

"No, Gladdy."

"She loves you, Jane. You know she does. She's just…old, and it's like old people think that their age comes with the right to be as outrageous, as demanding and as stubborn as they please."

"Yes! I take care of her and Gram. I try really hard to take good care of them, and be a good girl. I mean…a woman. A good, responsible, hard-working, intelligent woman."

"You are. You're all those things."

"And what do they do? They insult me and try to demean me with that word!"

"They should be ashamed of themselves. Do you want me to try to make them ashamed? Because I will," he promised. He could shame sweet, little old ladies for Jane.

"I don't think you could. I don't think anyone could. I don't think they have any shame. They never have!"

He hated asking. Really, he did, but he figured he had to know, because he was still afraid Leo had something to do with this. "So…Jane…what happened, exactly? To make you so upset today."

She looked too embarrassed to tell him.

This was going to be bad. Really bad.

"It was about…picking and choosing," she said finally. "Or…actually…not picking and choosing. Leo not having to pick between them, because…well, first, Gram said he had chosen her and that he was going to tell Gladdy everything.

But he didn't, and when I tried to tell Gladdy instead, she said maybe he would choose, but maybe he wouldn't have to."

Wyatt shook his head. "Because Gladdy doesn't want him anymore?"

"No, because Gram and Gladdy might…share."

Wyatt figured he must not have heard her right. Or understood.

"Share…?" And then he got it. No, surely he hadn't gotten it. "Share…Leo?"

Jane nodded, looking truly horrified.

Yeah, this was bad.

"You mean…" Wyatt had really disturbing pictures of sharing in his mind. "Take turns with him? One gets him one night and another…the other? Like on a schedule or something?"

"I don't know," Jane cried, looking pitiful and sad again.

"Like they'd really put up with him going from one bed to the other?"

Jane pressed her hands over her ears. "I don't know! I really don't want to know!"

"God, neither do I," Wyatt agreed. "That man's eighty-six! Something like this could kill him."

"I would think so!" Jane whimpered.

"Your aunt really said something about her and your Gram…sharing Leo?" Wyatt couldn't quite take it in.

Jane nodded. "She said it wouldn't be the first time!"

"With…they've already…shared Leo?" Oh, please, don't let it be that, Wyatt thought. He couldn't take it. It was too much.

"No. It was another man. Years ago. During the war. I'm not even sure which war. I was too horrified to ask. But apparently, there was a war on, men were scarce and they were lonely. This man showed up and they liked him, but they didn't love him or anything like that, and he stayed around for a while, and they…shared. It worked, Gladdy said. Got them all through a difficult time, and… I don't know. That's what she said."

"Damn, the women in your family are just full of surprises," Wyatt said.

Jane nodded, then started whimpering again. "Sharing? I mean, is this what modern women are putting up with these days, and calling it a sex life?"

"Not the ones I know," Wyatt assured her.

"Either that or… I mean, don't tell me that he's not going back and forth, because they're all… You don't think they're all in that bed together, do you?" she cried, tears falling once again. "Surely that's not what they meant!"

Wyatt shook his head. "No way. Not at eighty-six—"

"Even with drugs?"

"I don't think any drug is that good," he tried to reassure her.

"Because I would never do that, Wyatt. No way. If that means I'm a prude, so be it. I'll be a prude. But I just can't do that."

"I promise, you don't have to do that." He would never ask her to share, or to take part in any kind of sharing, except the one-man, one-woman kind of sharing. Jane would be plenty enough woman for him, he decided.

"I just…" She sniffed, looking thoroughly defeated. "I'm not the most…adventurous woman. I know that. I'm cautious. I'm careful. I admit that, but I'm not some kind of sexual dinosaur, either! At least, I didn't think so. Until now."

"Oh, Jane. I'm so sorry," he said, tucking her head to

his chest once again. Poor thing. She was just overwhelmed by the hijinks of three sexually adventurous, eighty-something-year-olds.

Who wouldn't be?

Wyatt let her cry a bit longer, rubbing her back, stroking her hair, trying to be a gentleman, promising that this would be okay somehow.

He really hated to see her this upset, especially about that ugly word—*prude.* He was fairly certain she wasn't a prude. And even if she did have some…prudish tendencies, he was sure he could fix those, that they couldn't withstand the kind of effort Wyatt Gray was willing to put forth on her behalf.

An effort he was eager to extend for Jane.

He just wasn't sure if she'd be happy about that or call him names in return, and he was seldom so uncertain with any woman. But this was Jane, and Jane was different. He tried patience, more soothing, more gentlemanly behavior, and then, when he wasn't sure he could stand it any longer, she finally stopped crying.

And then, finally, he kissed her.

Chapter Eight

One minute, Jane was devastated, thinking she was a prude and just unable to get the image of all that sharing out of her mind, and the next, she was lying flat on her back on the couch with Wyatt stretched on top of her, kissing her.

Not grabbing her, mauling her, rushing her. Just kissing her. Lazily, luxuriously, longingly. Jane wasn't sure she'd ever been kissed like that before.

He tasted like cinnamon and coffee. Sweet. A wicked little zing that rattled around her whole body from head to toe. His lips were the softest things she'd ever felt and he smelled glorious, and the weight of his big, hard body on top of hers, the heat, the power…

Jane did not feel like a prude at all.

She did exactly what she wanted to in that moment—something she had seldom wanted to do in her life with a man. She opened herself to him completely, throwing herself into the moment, kissing him back, feeling her heart pound and her body go limp. He had a hand in her hair, tearing it down from what was left of her hairdo after her tangle with the bush. He freed her hair and then stroked through it, holding the side of her face in one hand, nuzzling his nose against her ear. Then his mouth found the sensitive hollow of her throat, her neck.

She arched against him, heard him groan, thought about how she could just happily dissolve into a puddle in his arms, and let him do whatever he wanted to with her. Just like that.

His mouth came back to hers, and she felt his thrusting tongue. Jane thought about taking him into her body in another way. Heat pooled between her legs. A pulse throbbed. He wanted her, too. His body told her so as he rocked gently against her.

It was as if every sexual thought Jane had ever had came roaring to life, right here in this room, on Wyatt's couch.

"I am not a prude," she said proudly.

He lifted his head a fraction of an inch, grinned down at her. "No, you most certainly are not."

He started kissing her again.

It felt glorious, sweet and wicked at the same time, overwhelming.

And then Jane remembered—they were in Wyatt's office, in the middle of the afternoon. His secretary was coming back to give Jane first aid for her skirmish with the bush at Remington Park.

The bush, Leo, Gladdy, Gram, sharing…

Jane pushed Wyatt away. "I can't do this."

"Why not?" he asked, holding himself up on his elbows, but still stretched out on top of her.

"Your secretary's coming back with first aid supplies, remember?"

"No. Not until you reminded me."

"And besides, I don't have sex with men on the sofas in their offices," she said, then feared she was sounding prudish again.

Did women often have sex with men in their offices? Was that a requirement of non-prudishness, too?

"Am I supposed to?" she asked.

"Supposed to what?" Wyatt questioned, carefully climbing off her and sitting on the edge of the sofa.

"Have sex with men on their sofas?"

"Not unless you want to," he told her, running his hands through his hair, hair she thought she might have mussed up herself a moment ago.

Jane sighed. It was all so bewildering. What was normal and what was not? What was expected? In her admittedly not abundant experience, men wanted a lot these days. They expected a lot. Quickly. Very quickly.

"I'm sorry," she said.

He frowned. "Why? You're right. Lucy is coming back. I told her to. And I know you're not the kind of woman who'd be comfortable having sex in my office on a sofa during business hours."

She got worried. "But does that—"

"That doesn't make you anything except who you are, Jane, and there's nothing wrong with who you are. Any man who tries to tell you there is is an ass and probably just out to get whatever he can get as fast as he can."

"But you… I know you… I suspect you…wouldn't really have a problem with…something like this."

He shrugged. "Maybe every now and then, for something quick and different. But the thing I like best…is someplace totally quiet and private, no time constraints at all, no interruptions. And nothing to do with sharing."

"Really?" she asked in wonder.

He nodded.

"Oh." She was thinking about pulling him back down on top of her on the couch. He knew it, too. She could tell by that flare of heat in his eyes as he watched her watching him.

She sighed, took his tie in her hand and gave it a tug. Grinning like the no-doubt wicked man he was, he happily lowered his mouth to hers once again. If she was going to be wicked herself, she might as well start right now with the time they had until his secretary did get back.

"You're just trying to mess with me now," he said stopping with his lips a breath away from hers.

"Yes," she admitted.

"You know Lucy's coming back, and you know I know, so you think you're perfectly safe here with me. That I'm not going to really do anything."

"Yes," she agreed.

"That is so bad of you, Jane," he said, still not kissing her. "And you're supposed to be such a good girl."

She'd been watching his eyes, his mouth, waiting for it to descend that last inch and kiss her again, and she hadn't been paying attention to anything else. It wasn't until she felt cool air on her chest that she realized he'd unbuttoned her blouse.

He took the tip of his nose and skimmed it along the line of her bra as it rose and fell over her breasts, nudging it aside here and there. Then he started playing with her skin with his tongue, his warm breath heating her nipples as he got closer and closer to them.

She gasped, ran a hand into his hair and grabbed on, trying to pull him away, but in the end, not having the will.

He nibbled on her collarbone, on the side of her neck. She just melted when he did that to her neck and was starting to rethink the whole sex-in-the-office thing.

Who would ever really know? Jane could be quiet. At least, she always had been, before Wyatt. She didn't think Wyatt would be particularly quiet, though, and honestly, she wasn't sure she could be.

She was whimpering already.

"Can you be quiet?" she asked him. "Really quiet?"

He jerked back, just enough to stare down at her, as if he couldn't believe she had just said that. "No, but I can throw you over my shoulder and haul you out of here. I live right down the street. We can be in my bed in ten minutes flat."

She got a little scared then.

He laughed. "Didn't think so."

Oh, she'd ruined it! "I'm sorry."

"I'm not. I don't think you're quite ready for this, Jane. And I can wait."

"Really?"

"Well, I don't want to, but I'm capable of it. I'm actually looking forward to talking you into it."

"Talking?" she asked, not feeling so bad after all.

He grinned. "Whatever it takes."

He nearly had her blouse off by the time Lucy got back, because Jane did feel safe, she was truly enjoying herself and they couldn't seem to keep their hands off each other and honestly, why should they?

Lucy just waltzed right in, saying, "I got antibiotic cream and… Oh, sorry. I—"

Jane gave a little yelp, face flaming. She really had forgotten, there at the end, exactly where they were.

"It's okay, Lucy," Wyatt said, sitting up and keeping his broad back to her.

Jane couldn't see her, and she figured that meant Lucy couldn't see Jane as she buttoned up her blouse, wondering just how many times Lucy had walked in on a scene like this between her boss and some woman.

No, she wasn't going to think like that. She would just think about Wyatt and that wonderful mouth of his, those talented hands, the way he smelled, the wicked things he made her want to do.

"I'll just leave this stuff right here and leave you two alone," Lucy said, then whispered to Wyatt. "You know, your door has a lock on it."

"Sorry, Luce."

But he didn't look sorry. He looked like a man who was very happy with himself. Of course, why wouldn't he be?

"I bet you get every woman you want," Jane said, not upset, not mad, just…marveling that she could ever actually think about getting involved with a man like him. Even if it was nothing but sex. Great sex.

Surely a woman was allowed to have one highly satisfying, purely sexual relationship in her life. She'd decided Wyatt would be hers.

"You really want to talk about me and other women, Jane?"

"No, actually, I don't."

He nodded. "Good. I'd rather talk about you and me. Have dinner with me tomorrow night. I've been dying to see you in something other than one of those little power suits."

"You don't like my suits?"

"I do. I think they're adorable, which I know isn't the image you're going for. But I can't help it. You're just so cute."

"You're sounding less desirable to me with every word that comes out of your mouth," she warned.

"Because I like the way you dress?"

"Because I am not cute. Kittens are cute. Puppies are cute. Little girls are cute—"

"So I guess you wouldn't consider dressing up as a Catholic schoolgirl for me? Or maybe in a cheerleader outfit?"

Her mouth fell open, and she was just about to get really mad when he burst out laughing at her.

"You rat!"

"I like grown women, Jane. I have no doubt that you are one. And now that I think about it, wear one of your little suits. I always see you that way in my head, anyway. I think they're really sexy."

"Well, in that case, I wouldn't dream of dressing in any way other than to please you, the man."

"Hey, it was a compliment."

She'd gotten her blouse buttoned up and tucked back into her skirt. "I have to go. I have to get some work done, especially if I'm not working late tomorrow night, because I'm having dinner with you."

He handed her the bag of first-aid supplies Lucy had brought back from the store and said, "You're really not going to let me play doctor?"

"I don't think that would be wise," she said, heading for the door, not quite able to believe what she'd already done today with him or what he might expect after the obligatory dinner date tomorrow night.

He watched her go, stopping her just as she reached for

the door handle, his body wrapping itself around hers, trapping her between him and the door.

"Maybe one of those suits without any underwear? What do you say, Jane?"

"That you're crazy."

He dropped a little kiss on her cheek and then backed up and let her go.

Lainie stared at Jane when she walked into the office an uncharacteristic hour and fifteen minutes later than expected.

"What?" Jane asked. "Was I humming?"

Or grinning like a woman who'd nearly had sex with Wyatt in his office, or one who was contemplating all the sinful behavior she might partake with him the very next evening?

"Did you get mugged?" Lainie asked.

"Oh!" Jane touched the scratches on her face and grinned. "I forgot. I hid in a bush."

Lainie looked skeptical. "Why?"

"Because there was no other place to hide," Jane explained.

"Does this have something to do with that man? The amazingly reasonable one?"

"Oh, I don't think he's all that reasonable, really. He's actually…"

Outrageous. Wicked. Gorgeous. Jane sighed happily, then remembered where she was. "I can't talk about him now. I'm so far behind, and I need to get out of here early tomorrow. I have a date."

"A date? With him?"

Jane nodded.

"Has he…done something to you?" Lainie prodded, looking worried.

"Done something?"

"Drugged you, maybe? You're really not acting like yourself, Jane. You haven't been since you met him. And there are all sorts of things men can put into drinks these days to get women to do anything they want. This is serious."

"Wyatt Gray's never had to drug a woman in his life. They probably line up for the chance to give him what he wants."

"And that doesn't…infuriate you?"

Jane thought about it. At one point, it would have. She knew that. But it seemed she'd discounted the whole bit about what the women might want in this situation. Women could be taken advantage of, certainly, and they often were. Jane knew from experience with the women who came to her seminars. But she didn't think Wyatt took advantage of women. She thought he just enjoyed them, and they enjoyed him.

She wanted to enjoy him and very much wanted him to enjoy her.

"I think I may have been a little harsh in my judgments about men," she admitted.

Lainie started dropping things, everything she was carrying, actually. A coffee mug, some papers, little pink message slips for Jane. Flustered, she hurried to pick them up, then looked at Jane as if she'd grown three heads in the last five seconds.

"What has that man done to you?" she asked.

"I know most men are jerks. Believe me, I do. It's just that, not all of them are. There must be some decent men out there. Some who can be trusted in…certain…limited…situations."

"You want to go to bed with him," Lainie guessed.

Jane felt heat coming into her cheeks. "I'm allowed to have a sex life—"

"I know. You just never have before. Not in all the time I've known you, I bet."

Jane clamped her mouth shut, thinking back to exactly when she'd hired Lainie. Had it been that long? She wasn't going to answer that.

"Just be careful, okay? I don't want to see you get hurt," Lainie said.

"I won't. I know exactly what I'm getting into. I certainly know that nothing lasting will ever come out of this, and that I'm not his usual type, which has made him more interested than he'd normally be. But I know that in the end, we'll just go our separate ways, and that'll be it."

"And you're fine with that?"

She sighed. "I wouldn't say fine with that, but I'm an adult, and like you said, I get lonely at times. Wyatt's here, and I'm here, and he's…he's…he's the sexiest man I've ever met in my life, Lainie. I'm thinking about going to dinner with him in one of my power suits with no underwear. Does that sound…normal?"

"Not for you," Lainie yelped.

"No, I mean for a woman not like me. A woman who likes men. Really likes them. And really likes sex. For that kind of woman. Would that kind of woman do that?"

Lainie sighed. "Jane, are you sure he didn't drug you? Maybe I should come along on this date, just to make sure he doesn't…that he isn't…you know? A bad guy. Or we could run a background check on him. You have that friend on the police force. Just in case. How about that? A background check and a credit check. You can't be too careful."

"Yes, you can. I've been careful too long. And I'm done with it," Jane declared.

She was going to dinner without her underwear, after all.

Chapter Nine

The next afternoon Jane skipped out on much of the work she'd hoped to accomplish. Her heart just wasn't in it. She went home and took a bath instead. A nice, long, sexy soak, because she wanted to smell good all over.

The no-panties thing had been just a crazy idea at first, but Lainie had been so sure Jane had become demented or perhaps incapacitated by drugs someone had slipped her, that Jane had been insulted a bit. Granted, it wasn't like her to ever do that, but surely it wasn't completely out of the realm of possibility.

It was like the odds of her winning the lottery, maybe. Not probable, but not impossible.

She decided she was going to do it.

It's not as if it would kill her, and no one would ever have to know. It wasn't as if she'd promised to hop in bed with Wyatt tonight, even though she suspected he was fairly certain she would. And at this moment, she wanted to. But if later she got too nervous, too scared, or changed her mind, she didn't have to, and if she did, her pantyless state could very well go undetected.

It could be her wicked little secret.

Jane was not as stuffy or prudish as anyone thought. She liked that idea. That it was more like a dare she'd given herself, something she wanted to prove to herself.

Opening up her closet door, she frowned at row after row of power suits, all virtually identical except for their color. Was she really that boring? That predictable? It was just so easy this way. Buy good-quality suits that didn't go out of style, pick a color, pair it with a white blouse and she was ready to go, day after day.

Jane sighed. Wyatt had asked her to wear one.

She picked the brightest color she had—a hot, candy-pink—then got to all those white blouses. It was definitely not a buttoned-up, white-blouse kind of night, either.

In her underwear drawer, she picked up lace camisole after lace camisole. Jane wasn't a busty woman, and she wasn't going to endure a stuffed or even water-filled bra to try to make her look bustier every day, just to please some man who only wanted to look at her chest. But she did like camisoles with a little support that doubled as soft, comfortable bras. They were pretty, and some were even soft and pretty at the same time. Truth be told, she felt a bit sexy in those little camisoles. She just always wore her buttoned-up blouses over them.

Tonight…maybe she'd skip the blouse and wear one of her prettiest camisoles instead.

She found one in white satin, the neckline made of lace trim and cut straight across, so it didn't look like a bra or underwear necessarily. She slipped it on, thinking it certainly felt a little wicked against her skin.

Pulling on the slightly cropped jacket to her suit and buttoning the two buttons, she thought it looked sexy. She was showing some skin, but nothing outrageous, as long as she didn't take off her jacket.

She gave herself a pep talk that she could indeed do this, slipped off the jacket and then put on a robe, so she could take the time to do her hair and put on a little makeup, saving the panties or no-panties decision until the last possible minute.

Her hands actually shook as she put on mascara.

Why did women do this to themselves? Get so worked up over a man? She found lotion, to match the scent she'd used in her bath, smoothed it over her skin around and even beneath the camisole. Which had her thinking of Wyatt's hands under there, touching her everywhere.

Jane frowned, watching the clock move ever closer to the appointed time of their date. It wasn't as if the man was going to push his way into her apartment and strip her naked the moment he arrived.

At least, she didn't think so.

Maybe she could call Lainie and ask if…that might be something she should be prepared for, although how a woman prepared for someone like Wyatt to do something like that to her…

She set the bottle of lotion down, dropping the cap as she tried to put it back on. Maybe she should have a drink, and not a white wine spritzer.

He was just a man, she kept telling herself. Reasonable in some things perhaps, more good-looking than most, kind to his elderly uncle, but beyond that, just a man. She was probably all worked up over nothing.

Her doorbell rang.

Jane yelped, practically jumping out of her skin.

He was a full nine minutes early!

She dropped the robe, grabbed her skirt and put it on, along with the jacket and buttoned up. She'd never put on her panties, and she was feeling incredibly, sinfully bare, but looking in the mirror…

No one would ever have to know, she told herself as he rang the doorbell again and she went to answer it.

Wyatt stopped in the doorway and stared, a slow smile coming across his face.

"Pink is a great color on you, Jane."

She stood absolutely still, feeling cool silk and lace against her breasts and, down there, nothing but a slight breeze coming up her short, straight-cut skirt.

He reached out, letting his fingertips skim along the lace neckline of the camisole, his eyes dark and smoky looking. "If this is underwear, I've changed my mind. I approve."

"It's not underwear," she claimed. Not really. "It's a camisole top."

"Pretty," he said appreciatively.

He looked good enough to eat, she thought, in his sleek, dark, perfectly fitted suit. But he didn't needed to hear it. And given the look in his eyes, she really didn't trust him not to push her down on the couch and start taking her clothes off, right here and now.

"I'm starving," she said, taking him by the arm and steering him toward the front door. "We should go."

"Whatever you want, Jane. I intend to be a perfect gentleman tonight."

"I don't believe that for a second," she told him.

But she got him out the door, into his car and on the way to the restaurant. Jane leaned back in the soft leather seats of his sleek, roomy Mercedes, and tried to relax as he drove just a tad fast for her tastes, but seemingly in perfect control.

It was just dinner, she told herself.

His cell phone rang. He took it out of his pocket, glanced at the number, then clicked it off. "Sorry. Meant to do that before I picked you up."

"It's all right. Mine's not turned off, either, now that I think about it."

She fished it out of her purse, where it had been buried under everything and saw that she had three missed calls, including two from Ms. Steele while she'd been in the tub.

"Uh, oh. Was yours from Ms. Steele?"

Wyatt nodded. "But we're not going to think about her tonight. Tonight is for us."

"I know, but…she called me twice, which doesn't really bother me, but Amy, the sweet aide who's such a great cook, she called, too, and she never calls me."

"Jane, if you want to call her, go ahead."

"If I don't call, I'll spend all night wondering what's wrong." She hid the redial button and waited until Amy came on the line. "Amy, it's Jane. Is everything all right?"

"Jane, I'm so glad it's you. Do you…know where Kathleen is?"

"She's not at the cottage?"

"As far as we can tell, she's not anywhere at Remington Park. She missed her regular tennis lesson and we started looking for her. Then we figued out that Mr. Gray's missing, too. They didn't say anything to you about…taking off for a few days, did they?"

"No. What about Gladdy? She must know."

"We're looking for her right now, but I thought you might know what's going on or that, if you didn't, you'd want to know. We can't find Kathleen."

"We'll be right there," she told Amy. "Uh… I'm with Mr. Gray's nephew, so you don't have to call him. I'll fill him in. See you in a few minutes."

Wyatt groaned as she got off the phone. "Don't tell me."

"They can't find Leo or my grandmother. They're canvassing the whole place to find Gladdy right now, hoping she knows where they are."

Jane groaned unhappily. She'd so been looking forward to an evening with Wyatt, even if the prospect did scare her a bit.

"Can we throw uncle Leo into a dungeon in chains when we find him?"

"I wouldn't tell on you if you did." Jane sighed. "So, where does he like to take his women?"

"All sorts of places, but he doesn't drive anymore. It was a battle, but we finally got rid of his car. Does Kathleen still drive?"

Jane nodded. "Not often, but she does. She and Gladdy keep a car at Remington Park that they share. Gram and Leo could be anywhere by now."

They got to her grandmother and Gladdy's cottage to find it in an uproar of worried older women, a few security guards and Ms. Steele in full-battle mode, questioning a withering Amy, who looked as if she just wanted to hide.

At the sight of Wyatt, Ms. Steele made a face that actually scared Jane a bit. Amy came running over to her, whispering, “She wants to fire me, Jane, and I didn’t do anything wrong. I swear.”

Jane eased around to put her body between Amy and Ms. Steele. She’d protect Amy. So would Wyatt.

The administrator puffed up her chest and glared in their direction. “So, the two of you have no idea where Mr. Gray and Ms. Carlton might be?”

“No,” Wyatt said.

“Neither said anything to you about going away for a few days?” she grilled them.

“Nothing,” Wyatt insisted.

“What about Gladdy?” Jane tried. “Gram would never take off without telling Gladdy where she was going.”

“We still have people looking for her,” Amy said.

“Did you look in Gram’s room? Are any of her things missing?” Jane continued.

“I looked, but I really wasn’t sure if she’d taken some things or not. But her big suitcase is there,” Amy offered.

“There’s a smaller matching one, something made to fit under a seat on an airplane. What about that?”

“I didn’t see it.”

Jane headed for Gram’s room, Wyatt and Amy following her. At first glance, it looked as if everything was in place. Jane opened the top two drawers. They hadn’t been cleaned out, but Amy was right. It was impossible to tell if Gram had packed for, say…a few days.

She opened the closet, saw the big suitcase, pulled it out and unzipped it.

Empty.

“She keeps the smaller bag inside the big one, to save space,” Jane said.

She did a quick sweep of the room looking for the

smaller bag anyway. Wyatt helped, shaking his head when he came up empty.

"So, she's gone," Jane said.

They searched the grounds and Gladdy's room for another twenty minutes before Ms. Bea, one of the residents of the cottage, woke up from her nap and came out of her room to hear that Kathleen was missing.

"Oh, my goodness. I had no idea you were all looking for her," Ms. Bea said. "She gave me a note to give you, Jane, as she was rushing out the door this afternoon."

The lady pulled out a familiar envelope in light yellow—Gram's signature stationery—and handed it to Jane.

Tearing it open, Jane read:

My Darling Jane,
Please don't be upset. I know you think this is wrong, but I'm absolutely certain it's right, and at our age, Leo and I simply don't have time to waste. I hate that you won't be there for the ceremony, but we'll be back in a few days and have our own little family celebration then.
All my love,
Gram

Wyatt, reading over her shoulder, swore softly and shook his head.

"Eloped?" Jane yelled, then turned to glare at Wyatt. "They've eloped?"

"No. Leo wouldn't do that. He absolutely promised me that he would never get married again without letting me take care of the prenup," he claimed. "I've cleaned up too many messes of his before, after the fact, but never again. He swore to me."

"Gram, too," Jane admitted. "I made her promise the same thing. She actually has an investment portfolio thanks to me. I worked hard to make sure she'll always be taken care of financially, and she promised she wouldn't put it at risk."

Wyatt smiled at her admiringly, then took her face in his hands and gave her a quick, deep, satisfying kiss. "There you go. That's my girl. Woman, I mean. What a woman!"

He let her go, as if he might have forgotten where they were, or that he'd been surprised by the impulse to grab her and kiss her that way.

Jane looked around, seeing Gram and Gladdy's friends in the cottage beaming at them. Amy, too. Ms. Steele, on the other hand, looked at Jane as if Jane had surely lost her mind, no doubt thinking all the Gray men were troublemakers.

"So," Wyatt said, sounding very lawyerly once again. "We can hope they remember their promises to both of us and don't go through with this. Or that we can find them in time to stop them."

"How can we find them?" Jane asked. "We have no idea where they went."

"If they've run off to get married, they're headed for Vegas."

"How do you know?" Jane asked.

"Leo always gets married in Vegas," he stated, as if it was some kind of unwritten law.

"Sentimental, is he?" Jane guessed.

"Not so much about marriage, but about the city and this one little chapel on the strip, yes. What is that place called? It's an Elvis song."

"Doesn't every hurry-up wedding chapel in Vegas have something to do with an Elvis song?"

"'Love Me Tender.' That's it," Wyatt confirmed. "The Love Me Tender Wedding Chapel."

"Oh, this is so exciting!" Ms. Bea said. "So romantic."

No, Jane thought, *really, it's not.*

It was foolish, crazy and completely irresponsible. Gram barely knew the man, and Gladdy… What about Gladdy?

"We have to find Gladdy," she remembered.

They searched Gladdy's room again, and finally, there in her jewelry box was a little note addressed to Jane.

Jane, Darling,

I know you'll fret. Honestly, Jane, you fret too much. But Leo, Kathleen and I are going away for a few days by ourselves. Don't worry. Everything will be fine. Leo and I are going to explain it all to Kathleen, and I'm sure when we do, she'll understand. Leo and I can't help how we feel about each other, Jane. He's the most wonderful man. To think, when I come back, I'll be a married woman again!

All my love,

Gladdy

Jane let the note fall from her hand, simply unable to hold on to it any longer.

Beside her, Wyatt just said, "No, no way! He's not crazy. Irritating and infuriating, but not crazy."

"He's eloping with two women?" Jane fumed. "How does any sane man elope with two women? What does he think he's going to do? Make up his mind when they get there, and both women will put up with that? Give him whichever one he wants?"

"I don't know," Wyatt admitted. "It doesn't make any sense."

"Or maybe he's just going to marry them both!" Jane theorized, horrified. "Maybe he thinks he can get away with bigamy, too."

Wyatt actually looked hopeful at that.

"What could possibly be good about a man committing bigamy?" she countered.

"It would invalidate both marriages," Wyatt said, shrugging apologetically. "We wouldn't have to worry about the prenup thing."

"Oh, well, I suppose that's one good thing." And then she got mad all over again. "Wyatt, he's going to break their hearts! He thinks he can have both of them, and he's bound to break their hearts. We have to stop him!"

"I know, Jane. I'm so sorry. I've already called my travel agent. I got us two seats on the last plane out tonight to Vegas, but we have to get to the airport right now."

They made it.

Barely.

No luggage or anything, but they made the plane, settling into two seats in the very last row of first class only moments before the plane backed out of the gate.

Jane hadn't done anything so impulsive as flying off to Vegas at the drop of a hat in years, and she hated to admit it—given the fact that Gram and Gladdy were going to get their hearts broken—but she was a little excited about the whole crazy trip.

And to be making it with Wyatt. He really was a very nice man, even if his uncle was a troublesome, potentially crazy womanizer. She actually wished she had hit the old man with her briefcase now. But none of that was Wyatt's fault. She'd been looking forward to their date tonight, but she supposed a lunatic, last-minute trip to Vegas together was even better.

Date, she remembered. Something about the date, she was forgetting.

What? And then she got it.

Oops.

"What's wrong?" Wyatt asked.

"I just remembered. I'm not wearing any panties."

Chapter Ten

Wyatt was certain he could not have possibly heard her right.

Jane with no panties?

"What?" he repeated.

She leaned over to him this time, whispering urgently. "I'm not wearing any panties."

He looked down at her hot-pink suit, the color that had him thinking of tropical islands, the blazing sun, gleaming tanned skin and Jane. She came alive completely in that color.

And if that weren't bad enough, from the moment he'd opened the door to her apartment and seen her there, he'd been trying to figure out exactly what kind of top she was wearing.

Because it looked like underwear.

The cropped jacket of her hot-pink suit, buttoned with

two buttons at the bottom and open in a wide, deep V-neck to show off… Well, it really looked like underwear.

A lady's camisole was underwear, wasn't it?

Silky and lacy and one of those tricky fabrics that was part white flowers and part…sheer. A really unfair trick that had him thinking what he was seeing was, for all intents and purposes, bare skin. But he couldn't be sure. Maybe he was, maybe he wasn't.

It was just enough to drive him crazy.

Especially seeing it on Jane.

Buttoned-up-to-here Jane.

And now she claimed that under that pencil-slim, hot-pink skirt that stopped a couple of lovely inches above her lovely knees, she wasn't wearing any panties?

He stared at her waist, her hips, as if he could see through the fabric and find the answer. She'd turned in her seat, angling her body toward his, and the skirt was riding up even higher on the outside of her right thigh, but not nearly high enough for him to see how far up was pure skin and how far he might find the proof that she was lying.

Surely she was lying. This was Jane, after all.

"This isn't funny, Jane," he said, feeling hot and dizzy all of a sudden, seeing nothing but her, her legs and that gloriously sexy hot-pink skirt.

"I'm not trying to be funny. I was ready for our date. I was really excited about our date, and right before I left your office yesterday, you said to wear one of my suits without any—"

"Good God, I never thought you'd actually do it!" he yelled.

Passengers in the rows in front of them turned to stare. The first-class flight attendant, who'd been openly flirting with Wyatt as they got on the plane, despite the fact that he was traveling with Jane, now shot him a worried look, as if he might be trouble on this flight.

Jane leaned into him. "I wanted to surprise you."

"Well, you certainly did," he said, none too quietly.

"I thought you'd like it," she said, pouting a bit.

"Like it?" He laughed, sounding as if he was being strangled, all the blood leaving his head and heading south, leaving him decidedly uncomfortable. He shifted in his seat. No help there.

Did she have any idea what she was doing to him?

"I was trying to be…you know…non-prudish," she explained.

"Well, you succeeded."

"I thought you'd be happy—" she repeated.

"Jane, I'd love it, if only I could do something about it," he told her. "But it's a four-hour flight! You're telling me I have four hours to sit here next to you, knowing you're completely bare under that tiny hot-pink skirt and not do anything about it?"

"Oh," she said. "Well, I didn't mean to end up this way on the plane. It was just, with all the commotion over Gram and Gladdy being missing and finding out they'd both eloped with your uncle, I wasn't really thinking about my underwear or lack of it. Until right now."

Wyatt buried his face in his hand, then opened his eyes and stared at her legs again. Couldn't help it.

Jane had really nice legs, toned and lightly tanned.

He looked around at exactly where they were on the plane. It was small. In each row, there were two first-class seats on either side of a single aisle. No one was in the seats directly across from them, and the wall of the first-class cabin was behind them. There were two people in the row in front of them, on the opposite side of the aisle, and Wyatt had taken the aisle seat. If he angled his body the right way…

"What are you doing?" Jane asked suspiciously.

"Just taking stock of the situation we're in, of the options…."

"Options?" She looked aghast. "I want you to know right now that I am not doing anything with you in the lavatory of this airplane. So you can forget that—"

"I didn't ask you to. I wouldn't. I have trouble believing it's even possible myself. I can hardly get my whole body into one of those things, as small as they are these days, although I know people who swear it can be done. Still, it's just not my thing, to do it in an ultra-cramped airplane bathroom. Of course, I've never been on a plane for four hours with a woman with no panties on before."

"You sound so mad at me—"

"Jane, I think I'm going to lose my mind before we ever get off this plane. I'm starting to sweat, and we haven't even taken off yet. Because all I can think about is you…sitting there…and how much I want my hand under your skirt."

She pressed her thighs together as if he'd have a fight on his hands if he tried that.

"I know. Believe me, I know."

"Surely you're capable of showing some kind of restraint. You're a grown man, Wyatt—"

"Do you have any idea how many times I've undressed you in my head?"

She fell silent, looking a bit scared of him, as if he might turn into a raving, sexual beast at any moment and devour her.

"Yeah," he said. Maybe she was beginning to understand the problem now. "I've done it slowly. I've done it in seconds flat. I've taken suits of every color off you, unbuttoned crisp, prim, white blouses with excruciating attention to detail to every bit of skin I uncover. I've ripped buttons away with my teeth, Jane!"

She eased away from him, as far as the side of the airplane would allow, and just stared up at him with wary eyes. "Men don't do those kinds of things to me."

"This man is going to."

"Not here!" she whispered urgently.

"Four hours," he replied. "It's a four-hour flight. I really don't think you understand the urgency of my situation."

"How spoiled are you? You can't wait four hours for a woman?"

Wyatt saw that she still just didn't get it. Did that mean she hadn't even thought of him undressing her seventeen different ways, including with his teeth? Was she completely oblivious to him and this crazy attraction he felt for her?

Maybe all the Gray men had gone crazy at the same time.

Wyatt had an idea.

Jane watched him warily as an odd sense of calm came over him and he stopped arguing with her. His sudden silence, his seeming acceptance of the situation, made her all the more uneasy. But he just sat there, like a man perfectly at ease, big and gorgeous and sexy, taking up way more room than he should have in the seat beside her. He sat there as the plane took off and climbed into the air, wordlessly downing two bourbons during the beverage service, sat there as the captain dimmed the lights and people quieted down and settled in to get some sleep.

Which made Jane feel a little uneasy.

It was darker than she thought it should be, more private here in the last row of the first-class cabin, the curtains behind them drawn shut, the flight attendants settled in, too, up front, no one in the seats immediately to their left.

She clicked on her overhead light.

Wyatt laughed softly, reached across her and clicked it off.

Jane put her hands up to ward him off, but he didn't do anything else, just sat back in his seat, waiting.

For what?

Nervously, she scanned the cabin again, finding it even quieter now, soft voices heard here and there, but muffled, more like the impression of sound than sound itself, the hiss of the plane's ventilation system leaving a kind of white noise around them that enveloped them in a kind of privacy.

So, it was dark and quiet.

That was bad, Jane feared. Very bad.

The truth was, she had put this suit on thinking about him looking at her in it, looking at her as if he was going to devour her whole, which is exactly how he'd looked at her when he found out the secret to this outfit. She'd had vague thoughts about him undressing her very slowly, very carefully, almost politely, although she had known even then that the polite part was definitely more her fantasy than anything he'd ever come up with. And she'd been right about that. He had fantasized about ripping off buttons with his teeth, after all.

So Jane sat there, huddled into her corner, watching him, getting all warm and sleepy and wondering if, given his mood earlier, using him as a big comfy pillow on the way to Vegas was out of the question. She found herself nodding off a bit, her head sinking down to the side of the plane, then jerking awake again.

He stood up, got an airline pillow and blanket out of the overhead bin, then sat back down beside her. He pushed the armrest between them up and out of the way, then put the pillow against his side. His arm around her, he invited her to make herself comfortable against him.

She turned her body toward the window, away from him, bent her legs and tucked them half under her on the seat, then leaned back into him, her head on his shoulder. He might nibble on her ear, if he wanted, but she felt fairly safe in this position.

He didn't object at all, merely spread the blanket over her, as she murmured, "Thank you."

Just drifting off to sleep, she felt his hand, under that blanket, palming her leg at the knee and then slowly sliding up her thigh.

Her eyes flew open and locked on his. She felt in an instant that he'd angled his body toward the window. She glanced anxiously toward the aisle and found her view blocked completely by his shoulder. No doubt, his body was now blocking anyone's view of her.

Which was bad.

Very bad.

And in that time she'd nearly fallen asleep, she'd somehow ended up with her back pressed against the front of his body, her bottom tucked firmly against his lap, and he obviously liked it there, because he was thoroughly aroused.

It was a completely involuntary reaction, she reasoned, as she rubbed her hips against him, and it just felt so very good, she had to do it again. She couldn't help it.

He swore softly and started nibbling on her neck, making her squirm all the more, sensations shooting through her body. That hand of his, beneath the blanket he'd so thoughtfully spread over her, sliding even higher on her thigh. His other hand undid the two buttons on her jacket, then settled warm against her belly, eventually sliding up toward her breasts.

He took his nose and nudged her jacket down her shoulder a bit, used his teeth to pull the tiny strap of her camisole aside, and the next thing she knew, his warm mouth settled on her neck, dropping little kisses up and down the line of her neck and shoulder.

She sucked in a breath, his hands all over her, his mouth too, her body tucked firmly against his and turning liquid in his arms.

"Wyatt, we're on a plane," she protested.

"I know."

"And you said you really weren't into doing things like this in public places."

"I said I wasn't into actually having sex in public places. But since you got on this plane that way, I've decided that's not really a firm conviction of mine."

Before she could object, his hand settled, palm flat, against the curve of her hip.

Her breasts got all tingly and full, her nipples bunching up to knots. His hand finally palmed one of her breasts, as well, his thumb rubbing back and forth on one of her nipples.

His hand felt so big and so hot against her, and the camisole was so thin, it was practically nonexistent. His hands were everywhere. So was his mouth.

"Someone will hear us," she protested.

"Only if you get too loud," he claimed. "I didn't take you for a screamer, Jane. Although I'd certainly like to make you scream. Just not here. Not now. Later, okay?"

"Mmm. Okay. Later."

He kissed her neck some more. Lord, she loved it when he kissed her neck. It just made her melt all over, all hot and shivery and boneless with pleasure. He got his hand under her camisole and back on her breast, skin to skin. She rubbed her bottom against him, feeling a pulse throbbing in him, an answering one in her own body.

Could they really have sex on the plane? Would it be that bad? That dangerous? She could shove a pillow in her mouth and just try very hard to move as little as possible, couldn't she?

She wanted to turn around, wanted so badly to touch him, to feel his skin beneath her hands, but he held her fast. She reached back with one hand and held his head down to her shoulder, and with the other, covered his hand on her breast, urging him not to stop tormenting her this way.

Wyatt touching her, kissing her. It felt so good. He was going to drive her crazy. She knew it. But just how far was he going to take this?

"Wyatt?" she whispered urgently. "What are you going to do to me?"

"This," he said, his mouth against her ear, nibbling there as the hand on her hip slid into the curls between her thighs.

She shook her head. "No. You can't. Not here."

"Why not?" he asked.

"Because…you can't."

But even as she said it, her traitorous body had made room for him there, easing her thighs ever so slightly apart. She shuddered as his fingers moved knowingly into the hot wetness of her body, and his thumb…oh, that thumb.

If he hadn't covered her mouth with his, no telling what kind of noise she would have made then. But he'd anticipated that, silencing her with a long, deep, slow kiss, his touch between her legs just as maddeningly slow and sure.

He thrust inside of her with his tongue, with his fingers, and it took nothing and no time, it seemed before she shuddered against him, having to bite down on her lip to keep from crying out in pleasure, the kind of deep, uncontrollable feelings she hadn't been sure she was capable of feeling.

There was no control at all on her part, nothing she was capable of or willing to do to stop this, to hold it back, to contain it in any way. He was completely in charge. She'd given herself fully into his hands, and he was obviously a master at this. Oddly, she felt both out of control and completely safe in his arms, felt no need to protect herself, to maintain any kind of distance. She was his. She might as well have stripped off all her clothes and presented herself to him naked as could be and invited him to do whatever he wanted. She'd given herself to him that completely. Something she'd never felt safe doing with any man, especially one who looked like him, who had the confidence and obvious experience with women that he did.

Jane lay there in his arms, exhausted, spent, gloriously happy. She couldn't believe it. She just couldn't fathom what he'd done to her and how glorious it had felt, how she couldn't wait to do it again, to do anything he wanted, whenever he wanted.

"This is why women make fools of themselves over men," she told him softly, once she could actually think again and form words.

He laughed, the sound so sexy, and thrust gently against her hips once, then again. "You begin to understand how I felt when you told me you weren't wearing any underwear?"

She nodded, then got it. "Payback? This was payback?"

"No, Jane. This is a little thing called foreplay. What do you think?"

"That if the real thing feels any better, I may die."

"And just think, we only have another three hours before we can get off this plane, find a hotel room and get naked," he told her.

Three hours?

She whimpered. "What are we going to do for three hours?"

"Exactly what we've been doing," he promised.

"No. I can't. We can't. Someone will see us. Someone will hear us. Wyatt!"

But he was kissing her again, and she wanted so much for him to kiss her.

She wanted him to do all sorts of things to her, right here on this plane. He couldn't do much more than he already had, could he? She feared she was about to find out.

Chapter Eleven

She felt as if she'd been drugged by the time they landed in Vegas, as if her entire body was utterly exhausted, limp with the aftermath of foreplay like none she'd ever known before and the added fear of trying to stay quiet enough that the whole plane didn't know what they were doing.

Her skirt was all rumpled and up around her waist under the blanket, her legs like jelly. She had no idea where her shoes had gone. Her hair had either all come loose or Wyatt had taken it down, and she wondered if the stubble on his jaw had left faint reddish marks on her neck and her face.

Not that she really cared, as long as he was kissing her.

But they did have to get off this plane somehow, and she might as well be wearing a giant, blinking sign that said, *Nearly had sex on the plane to Vegas.*

"I feel like such a bad girl," she whispered to him, as

she looked out the window, seeing a sea of neon lights below.

He leaned in beside her, looking out the window himself. "You were a deliciously bad girl on this plane, and now, look at all those hotel rooms below us, all those places for you to be bad, Jane."

She grinned. "Are we going to be bad first, or are we going to hunt down our crazy relatives?"

"Well, it is about 4:00 a.m. our time. Surely they've already done whatever it is they wanted to do and are asleep by now. I figure we have some time before they wake up, so what would it hurt to be bad until the sun comes up?"

He dropped a kiss on her shoulder as he said it, and she wondered just how bad Wyatt, in the privacy of his own room, behind a locked door, could be. She didn't want to disappoint him, although in truth, he seemed delighted in anything she was willing to offer him, so far.

The lights in the cabin came up and the pilot announced that they would be landing soon.

Jane groaned and hid her face against Wyatt, afraid that people had to be staring at them. His body was warm and welcoming, his arm around her, hand on the back of her head, holding her against him. He was chuckling softly.

"How terrible is it?" she asked. "Is everyone watching?"

"Jane, they're all still half-asleep. No one really cares."

She peeked out to the side, seeing no one, and then cautiously looked forward.

"See? It's fine."

"I'm all mussed up," she said.

"Yes, you are." He sounded quite pleased by it.

She brushed her hair back with her fingers and then

faced him, embarrassed as could be without the cover of darkness between them. "You have no shame, do you?"

"Not at the moment." He took her chin in his hand. "And you look absolutely gorgeous like this. Someone should always be mussing you up."

He kissed her softly on the lips, and something in her heart turned over, as if she'd gone to the dark side, too, and never wanted to lose this feeling. She wrapped her arms around him and gave him a big, long, deep kiss in the light, just because. He groaned, took her hips in his palms and pulled her onto his lap. She fell back against him, forgetting everything, until a woman cleared her throat somewhere near Jane's ear.

They came up for air to find the stewardess, the gorgeous one who'd been eyeing Wyatt from the moment he stepped onboard, asking them to buckle their seat belts, because the plane would be landing soon.

And she gave Jane a look that said, *What in the world is he doing with someone like you?*

Jane wanted to shoot right back, *Seeing how bad he can make me,* but shook her head and laughed instead.

Once they landed, Wyatt helped her straighten herself up as best he could and guided her off the plane with a hand riding low on her waist, just enough to feel a little devilish. They grabbed the first cab they found and he asked the driver to take them to the Pallazzo.

"Leo's current favorite, I believe," Wyatt said.

Jane leaned back against him, torn between snuggling in the cab and reaching into her briefcase and turning on her phone to see if Gram or Gladdy had answered any of the frantic messages she left for them or if maybe Lainie had tracked them down while Jane and Wyatt were on the plane.

"Don't do it," Wyatt declared. "If you turn on that phone and have a message from them, it might be hours before we sort out their troubles and can be alone."

"I know," she said, but the ultra-responsible, good-girl tendencies were harder to deny now that they were on the ground in the same city as her sweet but maddening grandmother and great aunt.

"We'll be good and responsible when the sun comes up. I promise."

"Okay, but you might have to take my phone away from me and hide it." She pushed her briefcase over to him. "Here. Really. Just find it and take it."

He fished through her briefcase, came up with the phone and slipped it into his pocket. Then he frowned and said, "It's on. You turned it on when I wasn't looking?"

"No," she insisted. "What do you mean, it's on?"

"I mean, it's vibrating, so it must be on."

"I didn't. I swear." She grabbed the phone out of his pocket and saw that it was indeed on, and she had a call coming in. "I must have forgotten to turn it off when we got on the plane, just left it on vibrate."

"Don't answer it, Jane. If you do, I swear, when I finally get you alone, I will make you pay for making me wait even longer."

Responsibility warred with her overwhelming need for him but responsibility won.

"I'm sorry. Really, I am," she said, answering the incoming call. "Hello."

"Jane! Oh, thank God." It was Lainie.

"Did you find them?" Jane asked.

"No, Gladdy called for you here, when you weren't answering your phone."

"Please tell me they didn't get married already?"

"No. They…actually, I don't know. Jane, they're at the hospital. It… I'm sorry. It sounds bad."

Jane froze, the words just not making any sense at first. "Gram?"

"No, Leo."

Lainie told Jane the name of the hospital and insisted she had no other details, though she'd been trying and trying to call the hospital, Gram and Gladdy, with no response. Stunned, Jane thanked her and clicked off the phone.

"What is it?" Wyatt asked.

Jane slipped her hand into his and held on tight, then gave the cab driver the name of the hospital and asked him to take them there.

Wyatt just looked at her, and she could see him trying to make sense of this in his own head. Leo Gray seemed indestructible to her, and she'd only known him a few weeks. How much more invincible he must have seemed to Wyatt.

"All Lainie knew was that they took Leo to the hospital."

Wyatt still didn't move.

"Has he been ill?" Jane asked softly.

"No. Not that I knew. He's always been incredibly healthy."

He grasped her hand like a lifeline, with his other hand pulled out his own phone, went to click it on, but fumbled it, dropping it instead. Jane went to pick it up for him, but he held up a hand to show that he didn't want it. And his hand was shaking.

"How far to the hospital?" she asked.

"Five minutes, tops," the driver responded.

"Okay," she said to Wyatt, still holding his hand, wishing she could somehow protect him from what could come. "Lainie said neither Gram nor Gladdy are answering their phones anyway. We'll find out how he is in a few minutes."

Wyatt knew the doctor was talking to him. Something about a stroke, Leo unconscious since he'd been brought in and on life support. There were questions about Leo's medical history, his doctors' names. Wyatt had that information. Jane handed over his cell phone, and he found the names and numbers. Did Leo have a living will? Did anyone have power of attorney to act on his behalf if he was incapacitated?

"Yes. I do." A power he'd hoped to never exercise.

The papers? They needed the papers. No, Wyatt didn't walk around with Leo's legal papers on him.

Jane stepped in. Jane still by his side, still firmly holding his hand, saying she'd make the calls, get all the papers, so Wyatt wouldn't have to do anything but see Leo.

Wyatt kissed her forehead, said, "Thank you," and then let a nurse lead him through those ominous-looking double doors into the medical nightmare of machines and cubicles and terrified-looking relatives.

Jane's grandmother was seated by Leo's side, holding his hand and crying softly. She looked absolutely heartbroken, and on her left hand—the one holding Leo's—something caught the light with a flash. A big new diamond ring Wyatt didn't remember seeing before.

Wife number five, Wyatt thought, then remembered that Leo had always held out hope that one day he'd be able to say, "Till death do us part," and mean it.

Wyatt feared his uncle was about to get his wish.

He walked to Kathleen's side, took the hand she offered and then helped her to her feet. She threw her arms around him and wept softly, as Gladdy had done outside in the ICU waiting room.

Women, crazy about Leo and fighting over him to the end, Wyatt thought. How perfectly Leo-like. He sincerely hoped the old man hadn't actually married both women. Settling the estate would be a nightmare if Leo had.

"He was so happy," Kathleen said, still crying. "So very happy. We had a grand time, these last few weeks. Some of the best times of his life, he said. I'm grateful for every moment we had together."

Wyatt smiled, despite feeling as if his heart was breaking.

It was exactly what Leo would have wanted. All it was lacking was Kathleen vowing that he'd been the absolute love of her life and that she'd go to her grave remembering the times she spent with Leo Gray. Her and Gladdy both would have been even better, from Leo's perspective.

"He wanted me to tell you," Kathleen said, "that you were the perfect son to him, all the joy and love without all the responsibility that comes with actually being a parent."

Wyatt laughed, despite himself. "He actually put in more time raising me than my father did."

Leo had never had children of his own, although between them, his four wives had given him a dozen or so stepchildren and unknown hordes of grandchildren, almost all of whom adored Leo and still kept in touch with him.

"I'll leave you two alone." Kathleen hugged him once more, kissed his cheek sweetly, then Leo's. "We'll be right outside if you need us."

* * *

By the time they reached Leo's doctor, they knew everything.

Leo had known for weeks that he had an inoperable condition that could cause a stroke, but for reasons Wyatt could not understand, had decided not to tell anyone. He'd just gone about his life, as it had always been until something like this happened. His best hope was to die with a smile on his face in the arms of a beautiful woman, the doctor remembered Leo saying. Wyatt told him that Leo might very well have gotten his wish.

Bleary-eyed and beyond exhaustion two hours later, he walked out of the ICU and found Jane there waiting for him.

She got to her feet, took his hand in her tiny one, and he wondered at how a man could feel instantly better just holding Jane's hand. She stood up on her tiptoes and kissed Wyatt's cheek. He thought there was nothing he wanted more in this world than to collapse into her arms and have her lie to him and tell him everything was going to be fine, when he knew damn well it wasn't. That things would never be the same again.

Leo had been one of the few constants in Wyatt's mixed-up life, one person he'd always counted on and somehow thought he'd always have. Silly given the fact that the man was eighty-six, but he certainly had seemed as if he would live forever.

"The doctors just have to see the power of attorney from my office," he began, "wait a few more hours and repeat the brain scan, and then…"

"I know," Jane said. "The doctor told Gram everything, given the fact that she has a big, new diamond on her finger and claims to have married Leo sometime last night."

Wyatt nodded. "Please tell me he didn't marry Gladdy, too?"

"No, although he bought her a lovely diamond necklace. A consolation prize? A kind of reverse wedding gift? I don't have any idea. But Gram wanted you and I to know that she and Leo did sign some kind of prenup, because they both had promised us they wouldn't marry again without one. So, they were thinking of us. She said they hoped we wouldn't be too mad at them."

Wyatt shook his head, thought about laughing, then felt his eyes flood with uncharacteristic tears. He wouldn't have to worry any more about Leo and his various wives, his love life, his marriages or him getting kicked out of retirement villages.

"Come on," Jane indicated. "The doctor said it's going to be at least noon before they have everything in order and can…"

"Turn off the machines?"

Jane nodded.

"It's what he wanted," Wyatt told her. "What I promised him I'd do if he ever ended up like this."

"Well, you don't have to do any of it right now. There's a hotel across the street. I had Gram and Gladdy get us all rooms there, and you're going to get some sleep—"

"I can't stand to leave him all alone, Jane."

"Gram's coming to sit with him. She or Gladdy will be with him until you get back. There will be dozens of things you have to take care of in the next few days. Take some time to sleep now, while you can."

"I have to find my father and call him," Wyatt argued.

"I left a voice mail for Lucy at your office. She'll get to

work on finding him as soon as she gets in. Leo has four ex-wives somewhere that we'll need to notify?"

Wyatt nodded. "I don't even know if we can find them all."

"Between Lucy, Lainie and I, we can find anyone. But right now, you're going to sleep."

Wyatt did something he never really did. He put himself into Jane's capable hands and let her take care of him and everything else.

She walked him across the street, met her grandmother in the lobby and got key-cards for their rooms, then took him upstairs into a small suite on the fifteenth floor where the darkened sky outside the massive windows told him it was indeed still nighttime somehow and the glow of neon told him he could only be in Vegas.

There was a room service platter of fruit and cheese waiting for them, which he nibbled on while he grabbed a tiny bottle of bourbon from the minibar. Jane pointed out a fresh suit and tie, plus a few other items of clothing from one of the shops downstairs, were hanging in the closet. Gram used to sell men's suits and could tell just by looking that he was indeed a 42 Long. They had stocked the bathroom with toiletries, and anything else he needed, they would find.

"The Carlton women have been busy," he said.

"Yes, we have. Now sit down and eat something. I'm going to take a quick shower. I don't think I'll be able to sleep feeling this grimy."

He sat down with his drink and nibbled on some fruit, feeling curiously empty inside and mostly just…numb. He may have even dozed a bit in his chair, because the next thing he knew, the whole room smelled wonderful and

Jane was standing in front of him in a pretty, flowery silk robe and a nightgown underneath it, her skin a rosy pink, hair down and damp, just brushing her shoulders.

"I must be dreaming," he said at the sight of her.

"Gram and Gladdy shopped for me, too. I'm sure they figured, What's a little tragedy when Jane might still be able to pick up a man out of the deal? And they so seldom have a chance to dress me as they please. I'm afraid to even see what they expect me to wear tomorrow."

Wyatt grinned, despite his exhaustion. Oddly, he felt as if she was the only thing holding him together right now.

She came to stand behind his chair, leaned over the back of it and put her arms around him, kissing the side of his forehead. He turned his face into her shoulder, to her soft, sweet-smelling skin and her welcoming arms. What a kindhearted, comforting woman.

"Was it really just a few hours ago that we were on the plane, driving each other crazy?"

"Yes," she whispered.

"I want to go back there. Isn't it odd, how you can be somewhere, with someone, and be completely happy, and then… Boom, everything just blows up? And you think, I want to go back. I just want to be there again."

"Wyatt, you're exhausted," she whispered. "Come to bed."

"With you?"

"Yes. We'll just sleep. I'm not leaving you alone tonight."

Which implied that he needed her, and he had to admit to himself at least that in this moment, he did. He did not want to be alone. He didn't want to do so much as let go of her hand after they walked into the suite a moment ago. And yet, he had no idea what to say to her decision that they'd be sharing a bed tonight.

She took his hand and led him into the bedroom, pulled the curtains shut tight, flipped off the lights and turned down the bed. He shrugged out of his jacket, loosened his tie. She started unbuttoning his shirt. He put his hands on hers to stop her, feeling he was drowning or choking all of a sudden, as if all he wanted to do was fall into her arms and beg her to never let him go, something the Gray men certainly didn't do.

"I'm going to grab a shower, too," he said, mostly because if he actually did fall apart, he certainly didn't want to do it in front of her. So he slid that pretty robe off her shoulders and tucked her into bed. "Go to sleep. I'll be here in a few minutes."

And then he fled into the bathroom, got rid of the tie, the shirt, splashed water on his face and then leaned over the sink, propped up on his hands and stared at his own reflection in the big mirror. His eyes were heading toward bloodshot. He needed a shave. His hands were shaking again, and he still felt as if he was drowning.

The shower didn't really help, although it felt better to be clean. He dried off, wrapped a towel around his waist, brushed his teeth, even shaved, because he'd already scuffed up Jane's pretty, delicate skin with what he'd done to her on the plane, and if he got anywhere near her in that bed, he'd rough her up even more.

He walked into the bedroom, saw her sleeping quietly on her side. Would he still feel as if he was choking if he climbed into bed with her and pulled her against him? Or would that just make things worse? Make him want her? Want her to help him forget, just for a few moments? None of which was fair to her at all, and besides, he didn't use women that way. He didn't ask them to comfort him or make him forget anything.

But he hadn't asked her to do any of the things she had tonight. She'd just done them, just like she was waiting there in the bed for him, Jane all soft and sweet-smelling and even soothing, as amazing as that was.

He looked down to see that her eyes were open, barely.

"Wyatt, come to bed." She pulled back the covers, and rolled over on the mattress to face the far side of the bed, making room for him.

He dropped the towel around his waist and got into bed. Rolling onto his side, he fit the front of his body to the back of hers, tucking her fully against him ever so carefully, as if she was made of something so fragile she might break.

He'd intended to take good care of her, and arrogant as it was, he knew he could show her things in bed that no other man ever had, taking her places she'd never been before. Somehow, no one had ever taken the time or cared enough to truly please her. It was so obvious from the surprise and sheer delight she'd shown at the least little things he'd done to her on the plane. How she could be that innocent in this day and age, he didn't understand, but he intended to be the one who showed her all the pleasures there could be between a man and a woman. And this certainly wasn't the time or the place for any of it.

Closing his eyes, he knew that.

His body, exhausted as it was, just hadn't quite figured it out yet. Having her cute little fanny pressed up against his groin wasn't helping, either.

He groaned softly but couldn't bring himself to move away. It wouldn't be the first night he'd spent wanting Jane, but it would be the first he'd had to spend in the same bed with her, wanting her but not doing anything about it.

He willed himself to relax, to breathe deeply and evenly, not to thrust ever so gently against the curve of her bottom.

She laughed softly, sleepily, rolled over and looked up at him through the darkness of the night. "Let me guess. Gram and Gladdy left you with nothing to wear to bed?"

"Well, you said that to them, everything's an opportunity to further your love life."

She nodded, placed her palms against his bare chest, running them softly over his skin. He'd been aching for her to touch him this way, to feel those small, soft hands all over his body. It was going to kill him to push her away.

He put his hands on her wrists. "Jane, this is not what I wanted for us. Not at all what I intended."

"I know," she agreed. "But I think it's what you need, and it's what I want to give you."

She pulled her hands free, rolled away from him ever so slightly and then took her nightgown, pulled it up over her head and tossed it onto the floor.

Chapter Twelve

He was too stunned to say anything or to do anything, either.

Jane? Sweet, shy, prim and proper Jane? Peeling off her nightgown, just like that?

When she rolled back into his arms, they were skin to skin, those soft breasts he'd teased mercilessly on the plane nestled against his bare chest, his erection surging against her belly.

She wrapped her arms around him and kissed him softly, gently, and he let her, too shocked to do anything else. He'd always been a man in control in bed, a generous, thoughtful lover, he would have said. He tried to make sure he always gave much more than he ever took.

And here he was with Jane—this was Jane in his bed—shaking like an inexperienced boy, feeling as if he had the same lack of control as one, and yet still wanting to take care of her, to give her more than he'd ever given any woman.

It didn't make any sense. Nothing did tonight.

She kept right on kissing him, her mouth a sweet, shy temptation, her body warm and supple against his. He took control of the kiss, devouring her, grabbing her and crushing her to him with no finesse at all, feeling raw inside and out. That choking feeling was still there, that sensation that nothing in the world made sense, and she was his only lifeline, his only hope.

He kissed her lovely, highly responsive neck, sucked hard on her nipple, slipped a hand between her legs and nearly went insane when he felt how soft and wet and ready she was.

There had to be more, he told himself, something better for her, something to make her want him back in her bed over and over again, but he just couldn't think what that might be. All he could think about was getting inside her, being a part of her, having that connection, at least for a little while.

He went to push her away, to buy himself a moment to think, to take some time with her and show her that she was so very special to him, that she was different. But she only let him push her away long enough to roll onto her back, let her thighs fall open and pull him on top of her.

He didn't so much as take a breath before he was slipping inside of her. And she welcomed him. She had her hands on his hips, pulling him to her, her body rising up to meet his, as if he was the only thing she wanted in this world. It was so easy and felt so good and seemed like everything he needed in that moment. She felt so small beneath him. He was sure he would crush her, and yet, she didn't seem to care. He eased in a bit more, let his forehead fall down to hers.

"Jane," he said, kissing her urgently.

She wrapped her legs around his waist and he sank inside her all the way, her body gripping his in a hot, sweet hold that had him gritting his teeth and ready to beg her to be still, just for a moment. But she showed no mercy, rocking her body against his, her nails sinking into his hips.

Sweet, generous Jane. Taking him.

He lost all control, cried out, rocked hard against her again and again. There was no stopping it. There was nothing. Just her, accepting, urging him on, giving, and him done, just like that, in an instant, a hot, mind-blowing surge of ecstasy and regret.

Once he was capable of the most basic thought, he swore softly at what he'd done. He wasn't even wearing a condom. Sixteen years of scrupulously safe sex, and he didn't even have a damn condom on tonight. With her.

And that choking feeling was back.

As if she'd ripped open wounds deep inside that might never heal, feelings he'd never be able to stuff back inside him.

"It's all right," she told him, kissing his cheek, holding him tightly against her, her body throbbing against his. "Everything's all right."

He didn't even know if he'd managed to bring her to satisfaction, but he doubted it, couldn't remember anything except that exquisite feeling of release, of every thought draining from his head except for how good it felt to be right there inside her, and that it was Jane, and the way she'd just brought him into her, welcomed him, like a man coming home from a long, difficult, lonely journey in the dark.

And what had he done for her? Next to nothing, he feared.

Dammit. What in the hell was wrong with him?

He had his head buried against her neck, lying heavily on top of her and feeling too exhausted to move an inch, and he thought there were tears seeping out of the corners of his eyes.

She had tears, too. He felt them rolling slowly down her cheek.

He managed to lift his head, look down into her glistening eyes. She gave him a sad smile, her hands on his cheek, kissed him sweetly one last time and when he went to say something, anything, pressed her fingers to his lips.

"Go to sleep, Wyatt. Just sleep."

He rolled off her and onto his back, having no idea what to think, what to do. She rolled into his side, draping one leg over his, laid her head against his chest, one hand over his heart.

Regret, bone-deep satisfaction and need warred within him, only to be edged out by complete exhaustion and the kind of all-over relaxation that only came from a night spent with a woman.

Or maybe it was a night spent with Jane, giving herself so sweetly to him and asking for nothing in return. An ease, a sense of peace came over him as he let the feel of her curled up against him fill all the empty spaces inside of him.

He wanted her, still. It was like a low hum of sexual need that he wasn't sure would ever go away, but there was something else, too. Something new and different, completely baffling.

He wanted to just be here with her, hold her, just know she was here, and that he wasn't alone. That choking feeling was easing. It felt as if every muscle in his body relaxed as she lay in his arms and the world finally faded to black.

* * *

He woke from a dead sleep, with no idea what time it was, where he was or how he'd gotten there at first, and then it all came rushing back.

A hotel. Vegas. Leo. Jane.

He rolled over and could still smell her sweet scent on the pillow beside him. He was alone in the bed at… He glanced at the clock. Both hands on the twelve. Noon? Looking at the closed curtains, he saw light bleeding through the edges.

Yes, noon. Not midnight, though he could have slept round the clock. He felt as if he was hung over, his limbs nearly too heavy to move, flashes of the night before moving slowly through his muddled brain.

Leo was dying. They were going to pull the plug today. Wyatt had to sign the papers to let him go.

And Jane…Jane was…taking care of him? Was that how she saw it? Sweet, innocent, giving Jane.

He remembered so clearly the feel of her body beneath his, of her taking him inside her and tears running down her cheeks and his when they were done. The feel of her soft hands and gentle heart, her pretty breasts and the temptation of her mouth.

He swore once again, wishing there was some way to take back what had happened and thinking of how he could make it up to her, and then remembering the condom part.

The no-condom part.

Good God, how could he be so irresponsible?

It was as if he'd woken up and didn't even recognize himself and the way he'd behaved in the dark hours of the night.

He threw back the covers and walked into the shower, hoping the water would help wake him up. Dressing quickly in the suit he found in the closet, he took a few moments to brace himself for facing whomever was on the other side of that door and whatever might have happened in the hours he'd been asleep, and then walked into the living room of the suite.

Jane was there, dressed in a pretty, flowery, silky dress that showed off all her curves, cut high on the thigh and scooped out low on the neckline.

Kathleen and Gladdy's work, no doubt.

She was sitting at the desk, talking on her cell phone, a pad of paper in front of her, pen in hand, taking notes.

She smiled welcomingly when she saw him and pointed to a pot of coffee and some food on a room service cart by the window. He took the coffee and gulped it down, because his brain still felt muddled and slow.

He had no idea what to say to her, how to make up for what he'd done or to thank her for all the things she and her relatives had taken care of last night.

All too soon, before the coffee had done its work, she was off the phone and stood up, list in hand. Coming to him, she put her hand on his arm and got up on her tiptoes to kiss him softly on the cheek.

"Sleep well?" she asked.

"Like the dead," he said, then stopped, realizing what he'd said. *Damn. Leo.* "He's not gone yet, is he?"

"No. Gladdy just called. The doctors have all the paperwork they need on the health care power of attorney and the living will. They should have the results of the last brain scan in an hour or so. They'll be waiting for you, whenever you're ready."

He shook his head and swore softly.

"I'm sorry," Jane said. "I know people are never really

ready, not with someone as full of life and healthy as…well, as he seemed, as we all thought he was."

"I can't understand why he didn't tell me," Wyatt said.

"Maybe he tried, and he just couldn't. Or maybe he thought it would be easier this way. Maybe he thought there would be time. I mean, we always think there'll be time for the things we want to do or the things we don't always say to the people we love. Don't we?"

Wyatt shook his head, lost. "I just never thought of a world without him. It sounds so stupid to say now. I mean, he's eighty-six, but—"

"I know. I never really thought of a world without Gram or Gladdy, either."

"Jane?" He looked down at her, at how pretty she looked this morning, how sweet, and how capable with her list in hand, things checked off neatly one by one. "Last night… I don't even know what to say."

"There's nothing you need to say," she insisted.

"Yes. There is. There's a ton of things I need to say. For God's sake, I wasn't even wearing a condom. It's…inexcusable, I know."

"Wyatt, I'm sure it won't be a problem. I'm on the pill. And I bet you're normally very responsible about these things—"

"Very," he insisted.

"So, I can't imagine there's any need to worry about any of that."

He let out a long, slow breath. *Okay.* One thing down.

"I'm sorry," he began again. "I would never want to hurt you. Never want to take a chance of hurting you—"

"I know that," she said, as if the thought never even entered her mind.

Good. Okay, now for the rest of it. "I don't normally…" he continued. "I mean, I didn't mean for any of that to happen last night. I was just… I…"

"Wyatt, I know." She held on to his hand and gazed at him, a perfect model of acceptance and reassurance and…

He didn't even know what else he saw in her eyes, but it eased some of the feelings of complete chaos inside him, eased that choking feeling that was back. *Dammit.*

"It wasn't at all what I planned for the first time you and I were together," he tried to explain.

"I know that, too. You don't have anything to apologize for. There's nothing you need to do, except get through this day and try to let me help you do it. Okay?"

He frowned. "I don't…"

"Normally let anyone help you? Or take care of you?" she guessed. "Believe me, that's obvious. Neither do I. So I know just how uncomfortable this would make you, because I would just hate it, hate to ever be in the position where I needed anyone's help. But give it your best shot, okay? It's just one of those…awful times and I'm not letting you do this alone."

"Okay," he said, thinking he couldn't imagine what he'd done to deserve her, but so grateful to have her right now.

"Sit down. Have some more coffee. Try to eat something, and I'll tell you what Lucy and I have done so far."

Jane had accomplished all she could think to do. She'd taken care of Wyatt as best she could, done as much on the phone as possible to get all the legal papers and medical records here, gotten a list of Leo's ex-wives and contact information for all of them. Gladdy remembered where

Leo kept his address book, because she'd been in his room one day when he had sent flowers to one of his ex-wives for her birthday, something he always did for all his exes he had told her. So finding them turned out to be easy.

Lucy said Wyatt hadn't seen his mother in at least a decade and that they shouldn't waste time trying to find her now. His father was somewhere on a remote Greek island, last they'd heard. No one knew if they'd be able to get a message to him before the funeral, which it turned out Leo had already arranged himself. So there was very little to do for that except find the funeral home—that number was in Leo's address book also, which Lainie had gone to Remington Park to retrieve for Jane—and tell them they would soon be putting Leo's plans in place.

And by finishing all that, she hadn't had much time to actually think about spending the night in Wyatt's bed, until she found herself watching him walk into the ICU that day, Gladdy walking out a few moments later, looking a bit frail and sad, two words Jane would never have used before to describe Gladdy or Gram.

Gladdy brightened at the sight of her. She came to sit by Jane in the waiting area, taking Jane's hand in both of hers.

"Darling, that dress is absolutely perfect on you. I knew it would be," she said, then whispered. "And unless I've forgotten what it looks like, I do believe I see a little whisker burn on your neck."

"Gladdy, a man is dying in there!" Jane cried out.

"Yes, darling, he is, but the rest of us aren't, and if anything, losing Leo says to me that we really don't have time to waste here. Anything can happen. At any time. And you've been squandering time for too long, Jane."

Jane was taken aback by that. Gladdy thought she'd been wasting time? Jane would never waste anything as precious as time. The great value she placed on organization alone would ensure that she did not waste time.

"Now sit here and tell me what you and that gorgeous boy of Leo's have been doing, because I could tell the first moment I saw you that you've been up to something with him." Gladdy got a little twinkle in her eyes. "Did he like the nightgown Kathleen and I picked out?"

Jane glared at Gladdy for a moment. She'd still been thinking of time and how she didn't waste it, and here was Gladdy quizzing her about her love life. It just seemed wrong. Wrong, wrong, wrong. To talk like this with Leo soon to take his last breath and not fifty feet away.

"Oh, don't look at me like that. It's what Leo wanted," Gladdy claimed.

"What Leo wanted?"

"You and Wyatt. He was so happy about it."

"How could Leo be happy about it? I thought Leo Gray was insane. I nearly assaulted the man at the retirement park—"

"Oh, he didn't mind that. He said Wyatt needed a woman with fire and spirit inside her."

Jane blinked to clear her vision, thinking she must not have understood. "Leo Gray wanted me to get together with Wyatt?"

"Of course. So you have nothing to feel guilty about. Or… I mean, I'm hoping you did something, but you don't have to feel guilty about it. Now tell me. Right now. We don't know how much time Kathleen and I have to look out for you, Jane. None of us ever really knows. You have to let us help you now while we can."

And then Jane just wanted to cry.

She'd been thinking the very same thing since she had heard about Leo and saw how devastated Wyatt was at the idea of losing him, how shocking it was to him. She felt the exact same way about Gram and Gladdy. She simply could not imagine being without them.

"Tell me," Gladdy prompted. "Tell me the good stuff. I need to hear good things today."

So Jane told her. "Yes, he liked the nightgown, although you could have bought him some pajamas. I mean, that was a pretty obvious omission."

"I'm too old to be subtle. Tell me."

"We…we spent the night together—"

"Jane, please. No subtleties, remember. You made love to that gorgeous man?"

"Yes. He was so sad, and I just…couldn't stand the idea of him being so sad or so alone, so lost, and… I wanted to take care of him. I had to. Have you ever wanted to take care of a man, Gladdy? Felt like you couldn't stand the idea of him being in pain or alone, and that you'd do anything you could to stop him from feeling like that?"

A huge smile spread across Gladdy's face. "Oh, Jane, darling!"

"What?"

"You love him," she whispered.

"No!" Jane insisted. "I didn't say anything about love. I don't want to love any man, and he certainly doesn't want a woman to love him. Not on anything other than a temporary basis. I mean, this is Leo Gray's nephew we're talking about. I bet he's had as many women chasing after him as Leo, and he always will. No sane woman could love a man like that! She'd just be begging to get hurt. I know that."

Gladdy shook her head. "Forget that. Tell me more about wanting to take care of him."

"I just… I had to. Given the situation and…" Jane frowned. A little uneasy feeling in the pit of her stomach that had been there most of the night was steadily getting worse.

"Jane, have you ever wanted to take care of a man before?"

"Well…no," she admitted.

"And I'm betting you've never made love to a man because you were worried about him or in an effort to take care of him?"

"Of course not."

Gladdy just smiled and patted Jane's hand. "So, how was it, dear?"

Jane's cheeks positively burned. Sex, to her, more than anything else, had been an awkward thing, a this-is-what-the-big-fuss-is-about kind of thing. She always felt as if she tried so hard, as if it was work, almost, to try to have what other people claimed to have in bed, and should it really be work-like? In the end—what she'd had—certainly hadn't been anything to write home about, nothing to make her blush so furiously, until now.

Wyatt on the plane had been a revelation, a stunner, an absolute delight, and she'd been nervous about how things would actually go, alone in a bedroom with him. About whether the awkwardness that had always plagued her would return or whether she might disappoint him in any way. Although honestly, when they'd stepped off that plane, she'd been ready and eager to do anything he wanted and to let him do anything he wanted to her.

But what it had been, later, after they found out about Leo, was just…

She couldn't really say what it had been, didn't know exactly how, but it had changed things. Maybe everything. It was nothing about finesse or performance or awkwardness or anything sex had ever been for her before.

She simply had to have him in her arms, inside her, holding nothing back, giving him everything she had to give, him as vulnerable as he could be and her feeling just as vulnerable, but unable to put up the barest hint of defenses against him, against what she was feeling.

Jane had cried softly in his arms afterward, and felt as if there was no place else in the world she'd ever been that was as important as being with him last night.

What in the world did that mean?

She had no idea.

"Wow," Gladdy said. "That good?"

The next twenty-four hours were a blur to Wyatt. He'd prepared himself to sign the release for the hospital to discontinue Leo's life support, but Jane's grandmother stepped in, insisting gently that she, as his wife, be allowed to do it, to spare him, he was sure. The doctors were fine with that, as long as they were all in agreement about what had to be done, and Wyatt surprised himself by letting her sign.

She and Gladdy stood on either side of Wyatt by Leo's bedside as he slipped away quietly and peacefully, and then the Carlton women set to work once more, arranging to have the body flown home with the four of them the next day, arranging for the funeral home in Maryland to be ready to meet their plane when it landed. Jane even called all the ex-wives and listened as one by one, they fell apart and proclaimed their undying devotion and love for Leo.

Soon, Wyatt was back on a plane, this time heading home, Jane once again by his side, her grandmother and Gladdy in the row of seats in front of them. He looked down at the armrest between him and Jane, his arm stretched out along it, Jane's small, soft hand resting in his. There'd hardly been a moment since they'd first heard about Leo that he hadn't had Jane's hand tucked into his.

It was a connection that completely baffled him.

Just a hand, just a touch that meant she was by his side, often not saying anything at all, just being there and taking care of things, so he didn't have to.

And both nights they'd been in Vegas, she'd slept in his bed, in his arms. He'd held her. He'd kissed her. He'd made love to her in an act that spoke more of desperation and need than any he'd ever committed before. He simply hadn't been able to help himself or do any better by her, for her. And what had she done? Opened up her arms and welcomed him into her body, as accepting and kind as a woman could be.

Wyatt was baffled by the whole thing.

All he knew was that he was glad she was there, with him, still holding his hand. That it felt as if she understood, that she hurt when he hurt, and that she cared, that she wouldn't leave him.

But all women left, in the end. No one ever really stayed. Wyatt learned that young. His mother walked out on him and his father when he was six, and his father had remarried not long afterward, to a woman who hadn't really wanted Wyatt around all that much. So he'd gone to live with Leo, but even Leo had left now.

Jane would leave, too.

They were headed back to their real lives. They would

put Leo in the ground, and life would go on. This whole thing, this trip, this time out of time, wasn't real. Wyatt knew that. This thing between him and Jane, unsettling as it was, wasn't real.

She didn't believe a man and woman could build a life together that lasted any more than Wyatt did. It had been one of the first things he'd enjoyed about her—that she understood, that they were in absolute agreement on that point.

And here he was, her hand in his, thinking of how different things had been just forty-eight hours ago, the two of them on another plane, him thinking of nothing else but what he planned to do with her once he got her alone in a bed.

Life was so strange sometimes, he thought.

They'd never gotten that time together, not the way he'd wanted it. He'd wanted to dazzle her, shock her, push her to the very limits she'd allow, and then…of course, eventually, it would all turn out to be like any other relationship he'd ever had. He'd leave her or she'd leave him. That was what was supposed to happen.

Not all this baffling loss and sad, needy sex and him feeling as if she simply belonged here, holding his hand. It was wrong. All wrong. And he had to get things back to the way they were supposed to be, to the life he'd always lived. Normal life, just with Leo gone.

He looked down at Jane, in another of those pretty, flirty, silk-print dresses her relatives had provided for her, that stopped halfway up her thigh and showed off her neck and just a hint of her pretty breasts.

"Nice dress," he said.

"You know who to thank for that."

She smiled, sweetly and sadly at the same time, but he

couldn't have any of that. No more sad. No more her taking care of him. It had to end. Then she put her hand on the side of his face, pulled his mouth down to hers and kissed him, more sweetness and sadness and need there.

How could that be such a potent combination?

Need?

He'd needed women before. Dozens of them. But never like this. He felt that choking sensation again. *Dammit.* When was that going to go away?

Jane shifted in her seat, turning her back to him, then almost to face him. She pushed the armrest between them out of the way, and wrapped her arms around him, snuggling against his chest like a woman with a perfect right to be there. Jane, warm and soft and nearly in the same position she'd slept in the night before, practically on top of him.

He'd stayed awake long into the night, despite being exhausted, and had held her, had stroked a hand through her hair, down her back, across that delicious curve of her hips. He had constantly reassured himself that she was there and loved the sensation of all that bare skin of hers beneath his hands.

"Wyatt?" she whispered, her head tucked beneath his chin. "Let it go."

"Let what go?"

"Everything that's running through your head. Just let it go. Let it be. You don't have to figure anything out right now. There'll be plenty of time for that later."

How did she know, he wondered? It was as if she saw inside him. Saw everything? How had that happened? How could he stop it? How could he shove back down all these feelings?

And then she kissed him again.

There was no heat to it, no fire.

Her kiss said, *I'm sorry. I'm here. Let me make it better now.*

Chapter Thirteen

Wyatt wanted the funeral over with, so they'd scheduled it for one o'clock, the day after they got back from Vegas. They'd left his car at the airport, and Wyatt had driven Kathleen and Gladdy back to Remington Park, then found himself alone with Jane, who'd simply turned to him and asked, "My place or yours?"

He'd hesitated just a beat, then said, "Mine."

That was it. She'd come home with him, been naked in his bed, warm and willing once again, and been up long before him the next morning. He found her wearing what had to be another dress supplied by Kathleen and Gladdy, hair up, pen and pad of paper in hand, looking efficient and hardworking as could be.

Except, she was in his apartment, having made herself at home at least enough to make a pot of coffee and have what looked like the remains of an English muffin and peanut butter. Probably hadn't been much to choose from here, Wyatt knew, thinking it didn't sound half-bad.

He had coffee, put a muffin in the toaster for himself and found the peanut butter. He ate standing in the kitchen, looking at her legs as she finished her phone call, came to kiss him good-morning and tell him she needed to go by her apartment before the funeral to put on her black suit.

Wyatt frowned.

Had he missed something? Was this her taking care of him some more, or had there been some agreement he'd completely forgotten about on her moving in here?

"What's wrong?" she asked.

"Nothing," he claimed.

"I checked with the funeral home. Everything's in order. Still no word from your father—"

"I really didn't expect him to make it, Jane."

"Okay. All four ex-wives are coming."

"Great." Wyatt could just imagine fights breaking out over the seating arrangements among the wives.

"I wouldn't normally mention anything to do with the will right now, but Lucy's afraid you might get questions about it at the service. Apparently, some of the exes are quite anxious about… I guess, Leo had been very generous to them and some of their children over the years—"

Wyatt shook his head and laughed. "Yes, he was a very generous man. I'm sure they're all hoping for the same in his will. Honestly, I can't remember exactly what he did in his most recent will, even though I drew it up for him. He changed it a lot."

"Well, I thought I should warn you, that you might want to dodge them today."

"I have a feeling they will not be delayed on any questions about money. God, they want everything they can get from him, right to the end."

"I could do my best to run interference, once I figure out who's who," she offered.

"You're going to protect me from the money-grubbing ex-wives?" He loved that she wanted to try, but she looked like a pixie next to most adult women.

She frowned. "I can do it. I'm not afraid of anybody. Plus, they take one look at me and expect me to be a pushover, so I have the advantage going in. I'm much tougher than I look."

He wanted to come right back with, *Jane, women do not protect me.* But clearly, she thought she needed to, and it was kind of sweet, once he'd gotten used to the idea and as long as it was temporary. Say, until they got Leo in the ground, he supposed.

And since Jane's particular brand of comfort included her sweet, generous, willing body in his bed, was he really going to object? Even if the whole Jane-moving-in feeling left him…uneasy. Grateful, at the moment, but uneasy.

"Okay, tough girl," he said. "Let's see what you can do against the four of them."

He drove her to her townhouse, not surprised to find it neat, efficient, comfortable and without a single thing out of place. This was definitely Jane.

"A great investment," she told him, as they walked in the door.

"I never doubted it for a second," he said, standing in the living room, looking around while she got dressed in the back bedroom.

The walls were a cheery yellow, the old, hardwood floors gleaming, a brick fireplace dominating the room.

And the whole place smelled like her. He wished he could just stay here all day instead of having to face the funeral.

Jane returned a few minutes later in one of her signature power suits, this time in black, but with what he thought might be another camisole underneath it instead of the usual prim, white blouse. This one was a silky-looking, light grayish-blue thing that left her throat and a bit of her chest bare.

"Stepping out of your comfort zone once again?" he teased, because teasing her sounded like a good idea, like a good thing to help him get through the day.

She was so cute when she was being teased, particularly about her clothing. "I just thought, maybe I've been in a rut lately. You don't think it's inappropriate, do you?"

"Not at all. In fact, women have always looked their best for Leo. I'm thinking we're in for something akin to a fashion show in funeral apparel."

"Really? Maybe I should change."

"No. Trust me. This is perfect."

He'd gotten to her side by then, seen that it was indeed a silk camisole, slipped the jacket off one shoulder and seen the tiny little straps that held the camisole up and all that delicious skin of hers underneath. With the jacket on, she looked perfectly professional and even somewhat modest. Perfect for Jane. But underneath was all that skin, and he'd be the only one who knew.

They drove to Remington Park to pick up Kathleen and Gladdy, who were waiting at the curb for them as they arrived.

"Look at them," Jane said. "They look like they've been at the salon all morning. Their hair just so, their best jewelry on, great shoes. Are those gloves? Wyatt, they're wearing gloves. I'm feeling intimidated by the fashion choices of two eighty-something-year-olds."

"You come from a family of good-looking women, Jane. You're going to be gorgeous when you're eighty."

He got out of the car, kissed each of them on the cheek, telling them they looked fabulous and that Leo definitely would have approved. They beamed up at him as he helped them into the car, then, almost in unison, pulled out white lace hankies and dabbed delicately at the corners of their eyes, the perfect vision of class, high fashion and bereavement.

They arrived at the funeral home to find a mob scene, though they were there a full forty-five minutes early. The funeral director met them at the door. Kathleen stepped up and identified herself as the widow, obviously expecting the great respect due to her, even if she and Leo had only been married for a few hours.

Wyatt wondered how that would go over with the four ex-wives.

The director apologized for the lack of space to accommodate the crowd and promised his staff was opening another room and setting up more chairs as they spoke.

"It appears your husband was an extremely well-known and well-loved man, Mrs. Gray," the director told Gram.

"Oh, he was," she said, she and Gladdy clinging to each other, hankies out and at the ready.

Inside, they walked past a large room overflowing with women, just as Wyatt expected. He saw more of the gloves that had so surprised Jane, more white hankies, a few hats here and there, and an abundance of jewelry, especially diamonds.

Jane stopped in her tracks. "There must be five hundred women in there."

"You expected less?" Wyatt asked.

"And you're right. It looks like a funeral-wear fashion show. Like somebody put out a casting call for over-fifty models. I didn't know there were this many gorgeous women of a certain age in this city."

"The Gray men have always been blessed with a gift for finding attractive women," he said.

Speaking of which, he thought he saw more than one ex-girlfriend of his own in the crowd. Just what he needed today. He eased closer to Jane and put a proprietary hand low on her waist, just a touch above her bottom. She all but melted under his touch, easing into his side as if she belonged there. It just felt so good to have her close.

"Look out. Money-grubbing ex-wives ahead," he said, seeing two of them, maybe even three. It had been a long time since he'd seen Number Three and wasn't absolutely sure he'd recognize her anymore.

"Which ones?" she began, then stopped once again at the sight of them, sitting prominently in the front row in the little room reserved for immediate family. "Fur? They're wearing fur? In May?"

"Fashion faux pas?" he asked.

"I don't know. It just seems a bit much."

Both women got up and approached him, each trying to edge out the other to be the first to reach Wyatt.

He was amused to see that Jane took her protective duties seriously. She planted herself firmly in their path, sticking out a hand and introducing herself, then asking if they'd met Leo's widow.

Faces fell at the word *widow,* concerned looks came out, and both women stood a little straighter, shoulders back, chests out, as if they were getting ready for inspection or as if there might soon be an all-out battle for the former affections of Leo Gray.

Kathleen bore their scrutiny with good grace and a hint of steeliness Wyatt couldn't help but admire, launching into an account of her love and devotion to the man.

"Good move, Jane," Wyatt said admiringly, as she came back to his side and tucked her hand into the crook of his elbow.

"That should stall them for a while. Gram and Gladdy can hold their own against anyone, particularly in things concerning a man."

Another ex-wife walked into the room, obviously recognizing Wyatt and making a beeline for him.

"Number Three," Wyatt warned. "She looks like she might step right over you, if you try to get in her way, Jane. Number Three always was kind of mean."

"This is ridiculous," Jane said, taking Wyatt by the arm and leading him away.

He went willingly, following her down the hall and through a door marked Private that turned out to be a walk-in closet with cleaning supplies and paper products. Jane shut the door behind them, plunging the small, windowless space in total darkness. Wyatt felt her reach for him, her hand landing on his arm, then his chest.

His arms closed around her, fitting her body to his, tucking the back of her head against his shoulder, his other hand wandering down until it rested low on her waist. "Distract me, Jane," he whispered, nuzzling her delicious neck.

"In a funeral home?"

"You could do it," he told her, pressing her up against the wall, telling himself he could kiss her here, just for a minute or two. "Leo wouldn't mind a bit. And I don't see any reason to go back out there just yet."

He endured the funeral, mostly by thinking of those few stolen moments in the closet with Jane, kissing her, his hands wandering, her complaining that he'd left her all mussed up.

Just the way he liked her.

Even with the distraction, it was still nearly too much to fathom, being in the same room for the last time with Leo's body, with all these people who knew and loved him, all these women who wanted him and his money, and then Wyatt imagining a world without him.

He did get a kick out of the pretty women there, just the effort they'd obviously made to look their best for Leo one last time, and the over-the-top, downright theatrical mourning. The place was filled with sobs and delicate tears and hankies.

Wyatt held on to Jane's hand and tried to block out the tributes Leo's friends made to him, to his love of life, his energy, his exuberance, the sheer joy with which he approached each and every day.

Someone had insisted on a reception in Leo's honor afterward at Remington Park, something else which Wyatt endured, keeping Jane close to him, allowing her to act as a buffer between him and the rest of the world.

Thankfully, by early evening, he was once again back in his own apartment, alone with Jane. He hadn't asked if she'd wanted to or planned to come back here with him. He'd just brought her and kept her, because that's what he'd wanted.

And now she was standing there, just inside the door, in her little black suit with the pretty gray-blue camisole, looking up at him as if she was ready once again to give him anything he wanted, anything he might need to get through the day.

What kind of man argued with that?

He'd have to be crazy.

"Jane?" he asked, in a warm, sexy tone that had her heartbeat kicking up a notch as he closed the door behind them once they got into his apartment.

"Yes?" she answered, thinking if he had some sort of distraction in mind, if that's what he needed, she was certainly willing.

He claimed her, that big, glorious body of his crowding her until her back was pressed against the wall, and his body settled against hers. She brought her hands up instinctively, not pushing him away, but resting against his chest, on his shoulders, then winding around his neck.

"Seeing you in that little suit reminds me of you on the plane to Vegas."

She grinned. "I liked our plane ride to Vegas."

"Me too."

As he said it, his hands skimmed over her, inside her jacket, down over the curves of her breasts, his mouth dipping into that spot on her neck that made her just crazy. She felt the heat of him seeping into her body, her blood pounding, her breasts heavy and aching, wanting his attention, his hands, his mouth.

He took his hand and palmed her hips through her clothes, pulling her up and to his body, until she could feel he was aroused, as well, a little thrill shooting through her that she had done this to him. Her. Mousy little Jane. The Queen of Awkward Sex Jane.

She'd never felt the least bit awkward with him.

He took her in a flurry of eagerness and need, hands flying over her, taking the time to do nothing but push her camisole up, so he could get his mouth on her breasts, and pulling off her panties and throwing them on the floor behind him.

His hot hands took her hips and lifted them, lifted her, holding her against the wall with his body as he unzipped his pants and down they went, along with his briefs. He started thrusting, teasingly, against the opening of her body, right there without actually being there, sliding along the mouth of that slick opening, sliding in, just a hint, then gone again.

"Wyatt," she begged.

He didn't tease her, didn't make her wait, not in the three nights they'd spent together. He just came to her, filled her, gave himself to her, all need and raw emotion and blinding pleasure. She hadn't known what to think at first, what to say, what to do, and then realized she didn't have to do a thing, just give herself to him, that it was more than enough.

She clutched at his shoulders, loving the feel of his big, hard body, the sheer bulk of the man. Her thighs fell open even wider, her legs clutching his hips, trying to get him where she wanted him, inside her.

He wouldn't let her.

"What?" she asked. "What are you waiting for?"

"You," he muttered, his mouth against hers, making it clear who was in charge here, who was in control.

She let her nails sink into his back, her other hand into his hair. She whimpered, squirmed against him and that maddening, teasing rhythm he'd set, still not even inside her in that aching, empty space in her body.

He shifted his weight and hers, holding her to the wall with one hand, the other slipping between her legs, finding that spot that just made her crazy, the one he'd been merciless with on the plane to Vegas, when she couldn't make a sound for fear of anyone figuring out what they were doing.

Now, pleasure heated and bloomed inside her. She pulled his hair, called out his name. She was completely his in that moment. He demanded absolute control, absolute surrender. She realized it had been his for the taking all along, whenever he decided to claim it as his own. She just hadn't realized the power he held over her, the things he'd demand.

He finally gave in to her, sinking deep inside her, the feeling exquisite. He froze there for a moment, her body throbbing around his, adjusting, making room, gripping. It just felt so good.

He kissed her again, rocked her body ever so slowly against his with those hands that held her hips. She felt helpless, powerless, breathless, crying out, her body quivering with need.

And soon, it was as if the whole world exploded around them, slipped away, leaving nothing but the two of them, their bodies, their pounding hearts, their mouths, every maddening, adoring, confusing thing she felt for him, swelling up inside her and spilling out, along with the tears seeping out her eyes.

She couldn't do anything but cling to him, lie there weakly against him as his body tensed, he called out her name and sank into her one last time.

When she could still barely move, he slipped away from her, eased her down to stand on her own two feet. Which didn't seem possible, as her legs felt like jelly.

But he stayed close, holding her up with his body, as he shrugged completely out of his shirt, his slacks and underwear, even his socks and shoes. Then he scooped her up into his arms and carried her to his bedroom, laying her on the bed, undressing her himself and tossing the rest of her clothes away one by one.

He was so gorgeous, standing there in the dim light of his room, gloriously naked, those tight hips, narrow waist, powerful thighs, broad shoulders, wicked smile.

"That's what you wanted to do to me in Vegas?" she asked.

'That's just the beginning of what I planned to do with you in Vegas," he told her, then got into the bed beside her and pulled her on top of him.

"Wyatt, I can't," she said. Her legs sprawled onto either side of his hips, her body still warm and wet and throbbing from what he'd already done to her. "I don't have the strength to move."

"You don't have to go far," he said, growing aroused again.

He shifted his hips this way and that, shifted her body, until he was once again inside her, then pulled her down on top of him, so that her breasts pressed against his chest, and took her hips in his hand, showing her what he wanted her to do, until she found the strength to take over the movement herself.

He was so deep inside her this way, and the slightest rocking motion of hers just felt…it felt so good.

"There you go, Jane. You like being in control. Remember?"

She laughed weakly, moaned, thinking there were probably a lot of things she could do to him and thoroughly enjoy, things to experience, to learn, to want, to need. Time to explore, pleasures to seek, to discover.

A moment later, any illusion of control she had had was gone once again. He pulled her hard against him and held her there, surging up and into her, taking what he wanted once more, what she was happy to give.

His fingertips dug into her hips, and she ground herself against him, because being close just wasn't enough. She wanted more, needed it, needed to be a part of him, someone who could never be completely separate from him again.

She fell into the pleasure, limply against him, sated, exhausted, his heart pounding beneath her ear, his body still throbbing with pleasure.

So, she thought, drifting off to sleep, this is what she'd wanted all this time, what had been missing, what had seemed completely out of reach.

No wonder it made people crazy, knowing there was pleasure like this to be had in the world. Now that she knew, what would she do to keep it, to make sure she never lost this with him?

Chapter Fourteen

Wyatt sat at his desk the next day, having gone to the office because he hadn't really known what else to do with himself. He'd woken up late, hadn't even turned on his alarm clock last night.

He'd been too preoccupied to think of anything else.

When he'd woken up, Jane had already been gone, leaving him a note in the kitchen saying she'd gone into the office, that she'd see him later.

So he'd shown up at his office, too, only to have Lucy fuss over him, pouring out sympathy and sadness of her own—she'd been a big fan of Leo—and telling him that surely he didn't need to be here today.

He supposed he could go to Remington Park and clean out Leo's room, if the staff hadn't already done that. He could pick up Leo's things and take them… He didn't know where, didn't want to think of that.

There was the will to probate. He could get started on that, but again, really didn't want to. He was putting off the exes as long as he could, and he was just all out of sorts, unsettled, lost.

Lucy walked in, took one look at him gazing out the window, obviously not doing anything, and said, "Go home."

"I don't want to go home," he said.

"Why not?"

"Because… Jane might be there."

Lucy gave him a funny look. "I thought you liked Jane. I like Jane. I like her a lot."

"Of course I like Jane," he said. "I just… Well… I think she might think we're living together."

That took Lucy by complete surprise. "You let her move in? You actually let a woman move in with you? Wyatt, you don't live with women. It's one of your absolute rules."

"I know. I remember. It's just…" He shrugged. What was there to say? "It's Jane."

"So, she just barged in with her things—"

"No things. Just her. And the clothes she brought back from Las Vegas, the ones her grandmother and Gladdy bought her. She looks so sexy in those things."

Lucy sat down in the big, cushy leather chair opposite his desk. Clearly she thought this was going to take a while. "You're saying, the two of you have just been together since you got back from Vegas?"

"Since we went to Vegas," he said. "Four… Is it four? Yeah. Four days. And nights."

"But, you never invited her to live with you? She just—"

"Arranged a single room for us in Vegas, and then when we got back, came home with me. She's been there ever since."

"Did you give her a key?"

"No," he said.

"Did you ask her to stay?"

"No." She just stayed, taking care of him, not wanting him to be alone. Wyatt frowned.

"So, she feels bad that you lost Leo, and she's giving you sympathy sex," Lucy figured out, looking pleased with her deduction.

"Well…yeah. I mean, not just that, but…yeah."

"I bet you've never had to resort to sympathy sex in your life, Wyatt. So it's not surprising you wouldn't understand it."

"No. I really don't understand it," he confessed, hoping Lucy could explain. She loved setting him straight on things he supposedly didn't understand about women, loved reminding him he didn't know everything about the opposite sex, no matter how sure he was that he did.

So maybe she could make sense of this. Mostly, how much he liked it, even if it was sympathy sex. Because it felt…just…like…way more than he ever wanted to feel…about anything. But he liked it, and he sure didn't want to give it up.

He wanted sympathy sex and every other kind of sex there was with Jane. It was just… Did she think they were living together now? Was she going to be there, whenever he got home? In his bed every night, until he asked her to leave?

And could he just ask her to leave? He certainly didn't want to hurt her, and he didn't want anyone else to ever hurt her, either. She was Jane. She was sweet and kind and funny and adorable.

"Okay, here it is," Lucy said. "She feels bad for you. She

likes you. She wants you to feel better, so she gives you sympathy sex."

"I don't think Jane does that," he guessed. That's the part that puzzled him, worried him, gave him an added little thrill at having her in his bed. He doubted Jane had ever given anyone sympathy sex in her life.

"You just said she'd been doing it with you for the last four nights," Lucy reminded him.

"Yeah, but…"

"Wyatt, are you trying to tell me it's different with Jane? That she's different, and that what you have is more?"

"I don't know. How am I supposed to know that?"

Lucy was laughing at him. Not to his face, but he could tell, inside she was laughing. She often did that, too.

"What?" he asked.

"Is she going to be there when you get home today?"

"She said she was."

"Okay, but here's the real question. Do you want her to be there when you get home today?"

"I guess, I've gotten used to having her around." There, he'd admitted it.

"Her, or the sex?"

"Both, I guess."

"You should think about that," Lucy advised. "And I think you're actually going to have to talk to her about this. You do talk every now and then, don't you?"

"Yes."

"But if you do decide to talk to her about this, you can't just ask her what she wants or whether she thinks you're living together. You have to be ready to tell her what you want. Do you have any idea what you want?"

Jane, he thought. *Just Jane.*

The way they were now. Nothing more, nothing less. Just this. Jane in his bed, Jane in his apartment. Sweet, generous, sexy Jane.

"Wow," Lucy said, when he didn't say a word. "We're in brand-new territory here, aren't we?"

Wyatt let himself welcome Jane back into his home that evening. They ate the take-out dinner she'd brought with her, and then hustled off to bed once again. He did his absolute best to make sure she wasn't thinking about how sorry she was for him while they were there. And then, when she was curled up naked and sated by his side, he finally said what he had to say.

"Jane, what are we doing?"

"Sleeping. Wyatt, I have to sleep sometimes."

"I know, but… I mean, us, here, together. What are we doing?"

"Nothing for you to get nervous about," she reassured him.

"Are we…living together?" he asked.

"No. I don't do that. I always tell women they're asking for trouble when they drift into a situation like that, with nothing spelled out up front, no clear expectations, no promises, no agreements. Women have absolutely no protection that way, no security. It's a terrible idea. I would never do that. You don't do that, either. Do you?"

"No. I don't."

"There. See? Neither one of us does that. So we're definitely not living together. We're just…spending some time together. For now. Because things are still hard and people shouldn't be alone in hard times. They should have someone with them, someone to help them."

"And when things…aren't so hard? Then what?"

"Then, we'll do something else," she offered. "We'll sit down and talk about it, and we'll decide. On something else."

"Okay," he agreed.

That made sense. Perfect sense. Jane was such a sensible woman. And it meant they didn't have to decide on anything right then, and they could still keep doing this, Jane here with him, in his bed.

That was perfect for now.

Jane could no longer deny it.

She was in trouble.

And when she was in trouble, she went to Gram and Gladdy. She didn't want to, because Gram had just lost Leo, and even though the relationship was incredibly brief, the man hadn't even been dead for a week, and Gram was in mourning. Maybe Gladdy, too. Jane still didn't understand that whole relationship, except that both women seemed as close as ever, and neither one seemed mad at the other.

How could that be?

If Jane found out Wyatt was seeing someone else, she'd be devastated. She might even resort to violence again, and this time, she wouldn't pull her punches at the last minute, like she had with Leo.

Poor Leo.

If he had truly loved Gram, only to have so little time with her… That would be awful, terrible and so unfair. Why would anyone find someone like that, only to lose him hours after marrying him? It seemed too cruel to even contemplate. If he'd loved her. If the Gray men were even capable of that particular emotion.

Jane got to Gram and Gladdy's cottage. Amy was there at work in the kitchen. She dropped what she was doing and came over to give Jane a big hug.

"It's just so awful," Amy said. "Max is devastated. He's never known anyone who died. I didn't even know he knew Mr. Gray that well, but I guess they'd talked a few times, when Max was with your grandmother or Gladdy, and Max really liked him. And your poor grandmother. She's trying to be so brave, but… I think she really loved him, Jane."

Jane agreed. "I think she must have."

"We cleaned out his room the other day. Your grandmother and Gladdy wanted to do it themselves, but I thought they should have help, so I went, too."

"Thank you, Amy. I should have thought of that myself—his room. I would have helped them."

"It's okay. It was hard, but we got it done. We stored his personal belongings in some boxes in your grandmother's closet. She was hoping you could take them to his nephew."

"Of course," Jane agreed. "I'll do that when I leave today."

Amy said she had to get back to the kitchen. "I'm making raspberry lemon bars. They were Mr. Gray's favorite. You should take some home with you. I've been baking way too much lately. I always bake when I'm sad."

Jane said she would take some lemon bars to Wyatt, then went to find her grandmother and Gladdy. They were in Gram's room, tending to a box in the middle of the floor. Gram was holding up a photo, gazing at it lovingly and adding it to a stack of other things spread out across her bed.

Both women looked up when she came in. She hugged

them tightly, thinking she might never get enough of being close to them this way, especially when faced with the possibility of losing them one day, as Wyatt had lost Leo. Gram wouldn't let Jane go, when Jane would have slipped away from her hug. She took both of Jane's hands in hers and held on.

"Darling, you look like you have something on your mind. Like you need your Gram and Gladdy." She tugged her over to the couch. "Come sit and tell us all about it."

Jane sat between the two women, smiled, took a breath and tried for all the world to play it off like it was nothing, when what she really wanted to do was burst into tears.

"I think," she began. "Well, I'm afraid…maybe… probably…that I'm in love with Wyatt."

And then she did burst into tears.

They fussed over her, held her, patted her back, wiped away her tears, put determined smiles on their faces, which was something they always did, even when life seemed to be most bleak. And she was glad for their comfort, their concern and to have them close now, to still have them in her life. But none of it really changed things.

"I promised myself I wouldn't fall for him," she said. "I promised, and I don't know how it happened. He was just here, and he was nice and so sweet to his uncle. He took care of Leo the way I…well, the way I hope I take care of you both."

"You do, darling," Gram said.

"Of course you do," Gladdy added.

"And he seemed so smart and reasonable and gorgeous and sexy, and it was like the whole thing just sneaked up on me, when I wasn't looking. One minute, we were chasing the three of you to Vegas, and the next, Leo was dying. Wyatt was devastated. Just lost and so sad and alone. I couldn't stand it. I had to help him. I just couldn't leave him like that. And so I…"

"Comforted him?" Gladdy guessed.

"Yes. I did. I mean, I didn't set out to do that, but then… I had to. I had to do something. And not just something. I would have done anything to try to make him feel better, because my heart was breaking for him. I just couldn't leave him. I still haven't left him, not since it happened. I don't think I can."

"You're living together?" Gram asked, while Jane took a breath, finally.

"No. I don't do that. That's really not a good idea. Nothing spelled out, nothing agreed upon, nothing to keep you from getting hurt when things go wrong, and they always go wrong, eventually. But it's…it's…" Jane started bawling again. "Okay, yes, I am. I'm living with him, even through I swore to him that we're not, because I don't do that. And he doesn't do that, either."

Gladdy frowned. "Jane, darling, you're either living with the man or not. I'm not asking a philosophical question."

"Yes, I'm there. With him. I've been with him since we got to Vegas that first night. I knew it wasn't the smartest thing to do, once I got scared and really thought about it. Because we haven't talked about anything—except that we swear we're not living together, which I know is ridiculous, believe me. But we actually said that. We claimed we aren't living together, and yet, we are. It's such a bad idea. I know that. I teach women that all the time. It's just…when it came right down to it, even knowing that, I couldn't leave him alone."

Jane had to stop to breathe and to wipe her eyes with the tissue Gladdy handed her. It was all so awful.

"Gladdy, none of it seemed as important as Wyatt not being alone. He was more important to me than being smart and protecting myself."

"Oh, Jane!" they said together, beaming at her in unison, looking as if she'd given them the world.

"You love him," Gram said.

"Yes, obviously, you do," Gladdy agreed. "This is so wonderful!"

"No, it's not!" she told them. "He doesn't love me! He's just sad and lonely and hurting, and I'm…I'm…I'm afraid that to him, being with me is better than being alone right now."

And then she sobbed some more, not even trying to stop.

"It looks like I'm truly one of the Carlton women after all," Jane cried. "I've fallen in love with a man who's going to break my heart. I know he is."

Wyatt went shopping after work. He normally left this sort of thing—buying presents for women—to Lucy, who had excellent taste. But this he wanted to pick out himself. This was for Jane.

He'd decided she couldn't possibly look any better than she did in a lace camisole, those perfect, small breasts of hers cupped so delicately in the thin satin and lace that hugged her body, covering her but not really covering her. His heart started thudding just thinking about how she looked, how she felt, in those things. And he wanted her to have more of them. Plus, he figured what he bought her, he'd get to take off her, so this was a classic win-win situation.

And it was just lingerie, nothing outrageously expensive, nothing he thought Jane would object to a man purchasing for her. He felt perfectly safe giving her this, and he very much wanted to give her something, some little thing, when she'd given him so much.

So he went to the lingerie store, coming out with a huge black box with a fancy gold ribbon on it, maybe going a tad overboard. But it was for Jane.

He put it on the coffee table back at his apartment, so she'd see it as soon as she came in and sat down, and then waited none-too-patiently.

Where was she?

It was almost seven. She was always here before seven, usually by six. Neither one of them had been working long hours this week.

He felt a little uneasy.

She was coming here, wasn't she? Even if they weren't living together? She wouldn't just *not* show up here without telling him. Would she? Because it wasn't as if they had any kind of agreement about these things, but still… It was Jane. She wouldn't desert him without a word.

Hard as it was to admit, he trusted her. He was starting to count on her, to enjoy knowing that when he got home at night, she would be waiting, or if not, that she would be there soon.

Wyatt drummed his fingertips on the coffee table, right next to the big black box of lingerie, looking at the clock once again, fighting the urge to pace.

He was being ridiculous. He knew it.

She was fine. Everything was fine, and she'd be here any minute. He was worrying about nothing. Old habits, and all. His mother had walked out on him and his father without a word one day. The only stepmother he'd ever let himself get close to had done the same thing. His own father had often walked out the same way, and Wyatt had always ended up with Leo. Leo had been there for him and now Leo was gone.

It didn't mean Jane would go anywhere. Intellectually, he knew that. But old habits died hard. That feeling—of expecting people to just disappear, to be the same as every other person in his life had been—seemed to have a life of its own inside of him.

God, he hated this. Hated it.

He finally heard her at the door at seven-fifteen, pulling it open before she could, telling himself he was being ridiculous, telling himself, of course, she was here, and she was fine.

Except…she wasn't.

Clearly, she'd been crying. Her face was splotchy, her eyes red-rimmed.

"Jane?" He grabbed her hands the moment she set her car keys and her briefcase down on the floor. "What's wrong?"

"Nothing." She sniffled. "I went to see Gram and Gladdy. That's all."

"What's wrong with them?" He'd come to adore them himself, couldn't stand the idea that anything had happened to them.

"Nothing. We just…we talked, that's all. They'd sorted through Leo's room the other day, and Gram sent some of those things with me for you. She said she's kept a few photos, and that she'll have copies made and get the originals to you soon, if that's okay."

"That's fine," he said.

"And she kept his cologne. It smells like him. She loved the way he smelled."

"She can have anything she wants," he stated, still not thinking he was getting the whole story here.

Something was wrong. Why would Jane be upset by anything from Leo's room?

"The first box is just outside the door. I put it down to let myself in."

"I'll get it."

He did, looking at the thing as if something in it might jump out and bite him. It was just a box. Photos of the exes, Wyatt saw, one of him and Leo, one of him and Leo and his father, a few books and some papers.

He'd forgotten about the box he'd brought home, about Jane's present, until she walked into the living room and saw it. He set Leo's things down on the floor by the sofa and then took a seat beside Jane, happy to have something here that he hoped would make her happy, too.

"I got you a present today," he declared.

She sat there, looking surprised and a little apprehensive.

Why would the idea of him bringing her a present leave her uneasy?

He had that tight feeling in his throat again, not the full-blown, awful choking feeling, but something that seemed as if it might turn into that.

"Go ahead," he spoke, while he still could. "Open it."

She smiled, but only with her mouth, not with her eyes, and untied the big gold ribbon, pulling it off the top of the box. Inside were a half-dozen camisoles with matching lacy panties and silk robes of different colors.

"I had trouble making up my mind. So I got all of them," he said, thinking, too late, that he might have done something wrong.

She laughed, barely, and he thought he saw a hint of tears in her eyes, as she reached out and ran her hand along the pale yellow set. "They're beautiful."

"One for every day of the week except Sunday. I thought on Sunday, you could just be naked, all day," he tried, seeing if that would win him a real smile.

No luck.

"Pick a color. See if they fit," he said.

And the minute she did and disappeared into the bathroom in the master bedroom, he started digging through that box of Leo's things, needing to know what the hell was going on.

Chapter Fifteen

There was nothing in the box to bring anyone to tears.

Not that he saw, looking through it quickly.

Photos. Lots of photos. Leo's diplomas from both college and grad school. Marriage licenses. Divorce decrees. Various financial records. An envelope from a lawyer with a Las Vegas address, marked Prenuptial Agreement.

Wyatt didn't think the prenup could have upset her. She already knew Leo and Kathleen had signed one. She'd even wanted her grandmother to have one to protect Kathleen's own assets, so Jane couldn't have been surprised Leo would have wanted one to protect himself, too.

Wyatt opened the big envelope. He was executor of Leo's estate, after all, and he didn't see anything else that might upset anyone in this box.

He pulled out copies of a prenup, standard stuff, both keeping assets they had brought into the marriage, making no claim on the other's assets, agreeing to divide equally any assets they had acquired during the course of the marriage.

Nothing there to be upset about.

The next stack of papers said… Last Will and Testament of Leonardo Thomas Gray, dated the same day as the prenups, the day he and Kathleen went to Las Vegas and got married.

Leo made a new will?

Wyatt sat down, surprised.

He'd drawn up all of Leo's various wills, handled all of his divorces since Wyatt had passed the bar, done all of his prenups. Why would Leo ever make a new will without Wyatt?

He glanced at the cover letter accompanying the will….

Dear Mr. Gray,

Believe I've covered all the changes you asked for…keeping all previous bequests from the most recent will…adding $5,000 in trust for Maxwell Carson, $20,000 for new weight-room equipment at Remington Park and $500,000 in trust for Margaret Jane Carlton….

Leo left Jane a half-million dollars?

That was impossible.

The bathroom door opened and Jane walked out, wrapped in pale yellow silk that fell from her shoulders down to the floor, a hint of the matching lace camisole showing between the folds of the robe.

No wonder she looked so apprehensive when she came home.

He was about to figure out the scheme. That her grandmother and Gladdy hadn't wanted Leo's money. That part was true. They'd gotten it for Jane instead.

"Margaret Jane Carlton?" he asked.

"What?"

She played innocent, and did it very well, he saw, infuriating him all the more. "Is your full name Margaret Jane Carlton?"

"Yes. Wyatt, what's wrong?"

Oh, God, she was really good at it. All innocent and treacherously beautiful and infuriating. He didn't think a woman had ever hurt him as much as she just had.

"I found out about the money, Jane. But then, you knew I was about to. You brought the box with the new will in it. That's why you were so upset when you walked in. Dreading this little scene?"

"What scene? What money? Wyatt, what are you talking about?" she asked, walking toward him.

"The money!" he roared, taking some measure of satisfaction in seeing her jump, startled, stopping in her tracks when he said it.

"What money?" she whispered.

"Leo's money! The half-million dollars you got him to leave you!"

She shook her head. "Why would Leo ever leave me half-a-million dollars?"

"Careful manipulation by three greedy, scheming women, I'd guess."

She took that like a blow, wavering on her feet and clutching the ends of the robe together. "You think my grandmother, Gladdy and I tricked Leo out of a half-million dollars?"

"I know you did. I'm reading his new will. It's all right here in black and white." He smacked the papers against the frame of the door leading to the bedroom.

"You're crazy," she insisted.

"It's right here, Jane! You can't play innocent anymore! God, I should have known all along. I grew up with women like you. My entire life, I saw nothing but women like you, out for all they could get from my father and Leo, even from me. I can't believe this. I can't believe I was this stupid! I was actually starting to trust you, to count on you. I even told someone this week that you were different from the other women I've known." He shook his head, laughed bitterly. "What a crock."

"Wyatt, I have no idea what you're talking about—"

"God, I have no patience for this. Just get out!" he yelled, and when she didn't move, kept right on yelling. "Get out or so help me, God, I will throw you out."

She still didn't budge, just stood there, gaping at him.

He started toward her, angrier than he'd ever been in his life, and she edged away, backing around the perimeter of the room and toward the front door.

"Wyatt, please," she begged.

"None of it was real?" He could still hardly believe it. "None of it?"

"Of course it was. All of it was real!"

"Get out!" he roared.

She grabbed her keys, left there by the door, didn't bother with shoes or clothes or anything else, and fled.

He picked up the nearest thing he could reach, a vase of some kind, and threw it, feeling some sense of satisfaction as it shattered against the front door she'd just slammed shut as she escaped.

* * *

Jane didn't have on any shoes.

She was shaking all over, trying to hold the robe together. She had her car keys, thank goodness, but no shoes.

Walking hurt. The asphalt was grainy, lumpy, and here and there were little pebbles that she stepped on.

It hurt.

But not as much as her heart.

She was still sobbing. One couple passed her and looked scared of her, and another kindhearted older woman asked if she needed help, the police or an ambulance or something. She thanked her and swore she was okay, which was a complete lie, but she just wanted to get away, to get someplace where she could be alone and cry in private, no one looking at her, no one wondering what was wrong.

Why in the world would Leo Gray leave her all that money? She hadn't even liked him, and he'd hardly known her.

Vaguely, she considered that Gram might have asked him to leave Jane some money, but surely Gram knew that Jane was incredibly responsible with money and well on her way to being completely financially secure. She wasn't wealthy, but she earned a good living and had always had a knack for investments that turned out well. She'd been investing in the stock market since she was twelve.

So this didn't make any sense.

And how could Wyatt believe this whole time that she'd been out for nothing but money? That she and her sweet Gram and Gladdy had schemed to get their hands on Leo's money?

She sobbed so hard she dropped her keys, and then

while she wasn't paying attention, she stepped on something that really hurt. At least, she'd made it to her car. She hobbled, mostly on one foot, to the door and got in, her need to just sit there and cry it out warring with her need to get away from here, away from Wyatt.

Wanting to get away won. She dried her tears as best she could, though more fell right away to replace them. Then she headed for her apartment and the blessed solitude to be found there.

It was late before Jane stopped crying, and her brain worked well enough to want to think, logically, about what might have happened. And then, she just couldn't leave all the questions until morning.

She called Gram, apologizing profusely for waking her and likely scaring her. Any phone call at this hour was almost always about something bad.

"Gram, you didn't ask Leo to leave me some money, did you?" she asked, her voice raw from all the crying.

"Jane, darling, what in the world is wrong? What's happened? You sound awful. Are you sick?"

"No. I've just… Wyatt and I had a fight," she admitted, then started to cry again, mad at herself for doing it but unable to stop.

"About what? What did that man do to you?"

"Threw me out of his apartment—"

"Told you to get out? Or actually threw you out, because if he hurt you, Gladdy and I will—"

"Just told me to get out," she rushed on. "Sorry."

"Jane, honey, you're crying your eyes out? Over a man?"

"Yes," she confessed. "Gram, you have to tell me. Did you ask Leo to leave me money in his will?"

"No. Of course not. Why would I? You're doing fine. Aren't you?"

"Yes," she said.

"I never imagined you needed any money from me or Gladdy, and I certainly knew you'd be insulted at the idea of any man giving you money."

"Yes, I would. But Wyatt says he did. He said Leo made a new will in Las Vegas, and he left me a half-million dollars, left some money to Remington Park for a weight room—"

"Now, he did talk about the weight room. That it just wasn't what it should be. Apparently, he liked to lift weights."

"Okay, so that part makes sense. And there was one other thing. $5,000 to someone named…Maxwell. I don't know any Maxwell. Do you? Maxwell Carson, I think."

"That's Amy's last name. Carson. Her son's name is Max. Yes, I bet that's Max. Leo adored him."

"Enough for Leo to leave Max money in his will?"

"Maybe. We kept Max one day, when he had a day off from kindergarten and Amy's babysitter canceled at the last minute. Leo had so much fun with Max. He said it was a shame, how hard Amy worked for so little money, and he worried about her being able to take care of Max."

"Okay, so that makes sense, I guess. But what about me? Why me? He wouldn't just leave me that much money. Would he?"

"I don't know," Gram said. "I'll think about it while Gladdy and I get a cab and come see you."

"No, it's late, and I'm fine—"

"You are most certainly not fine. We'll call a cab. We'll be there in thirty minutes. No arguments. We're taking care of you now."

They arrived in less time than that, letting themselves in with their key, and rushed into Jane's bedroom, fussing and hugging her close and trying to dry her tears, as if she was a little girl again.

It felt so nice, Jane decided. She hardly ever got fussed over, hardly ever allowed it.

"That horrible man!" Gladdy said. "Throwing you out of his apartment? Breaking your poor, dear heart? How dare he?"

She was incensed on Jane's behalf, ready to do battle if necessary, maybe even eager for it, and just knowing that made Jane feel better. They sat on the bed with her, one of them on either side, snuggling close, the three Carlton women, together through good times and bad.

She absolutely adored them.

Gram went to the kitchen eventually, insisting ice cream was in order, that it helped soothe all heartaches, and then nearly had a fit when she found a little blood on Jane's kitchen floor.

"What did that man do to you?" she demanded, looking fierce.

"He didn't hurt me. I told you that. I just… I left his apartment without my shoes, and when I was walking to my car, I stepped on something. I didn't even realize I'd cut my foot until I got back here. I thought I'd wiped all the blood up, but I guess I missed some."

"Let me see what he did! Let me see right now," Gram demanded.

Jane pulled the covers off her foot, which she'd bandaged, hastily and not very well before she'd climbed into her bed. Gram and Gladdy fussed some more, unwrapping it, moving a lamp so they could see it more clearly, then insisting that the cut was deep and might well need stitches.

“It does not. I just stepped on something—”

“Glass, most likely. And if it is glass, it could still be in there, and it has to come out.”

“Gram, I just want to sleep, honestly. I feel so much better that both of you are here, but now, I’m just exhausted.”

Gram frowned, but didn’t argue. “Okay, but I’m not leaving you.”

“Me either,” said Gladdy. “We’ll have a sleepover. We haven’t done that in a long time. It’ll be fun. We’ll see how your foot is in the morning. And decide what we’re going to do with that awful man. He’s not going to get away with treating you like this. We won’t let him.”

Wyatt drank himself into oblivion that night.

It was the only thing that made him not really feel anything, and he needed desperately to not feel anything. Because mostly, he just felt way too much.

Feelings, he thought, snarling. Who needed to feel anything, really? It was all so…messy and upsetting and just came out of nowhere at a man. One minute, he was going along with his life, just fine, and the next… He was flat on the floor, drunk and wishing he couldn’t feel a thing.

Life had to be easier that way.

He’d been just fine until Jane came along. Beautiful, deceitful, lying Jane.

He’d actually thought she was different and had even told her so. That was the most infuriating part. He’d believed her. About everything.

What an idiot he was!

He woke sometime later—in daylight as he could see from the windows of his apartment—to someone pounding on his door. Or was that the pounding in his head? Maybe both, he decided.

Even sitting up, slowly and carefully, the room still did that sickening tilt. And the pounding on the door kept right on going. He wasn't imagining it. It wasn't all in his head.

He finally got to the door, opened it, and Jane's grandmother, who'd worked herself into a full-blown rage, swept inside, looking at him as if he was the devil himself.

Wyatt fought the urge to shield himself from her, thinking she might literally attack at any moment. She fumed at him, bringing her hands up as if she was weighing the value of a good, quick punch or two.

He told himself that surely he could duck the punch of a little old lady, if he had to and stood his ground. He just wished the room would stop its sickening tilt every time he turned his head. He wasn't sure he could duck a punch when the room wasn't even standing still.

"You stupid boy!" she said.

"And you," he shot back. "Ms. I Don't Need Leo Gray's Money. He was dying, and the last days he spent on this earth, he spent with you. You and your granddaughter taking him for half-a-million dollars!"

"I didn't take anything from him!"

"No, you left that part to Jane. What a great scam. I can just hear you, working it on Leo. 'It's not for me, Leo. I don't need anything for myself. But Jane…poor Jane, I worry about her so—"

"Only when it comes to men, not money. Is your view of women so twisted that you can't even fathom the existence of a woman who earns her own money? Is smart and sensible and financially secure on her own? That there might be at least one or two women in this world who didn't want the Gray men for their money?"

"Haven't found one yet," Wyatt retorted.

"Yes, you have. You stupid boy! Where is this will? I want to see it for myself, because I don't believe Leo would have done this. He would have known the quickest way to ruin anything between you and Jane would be for you to think she was after your money. Or his."

"And why would he be so worried about ruining anything between me and Jane?"

"Because this whole thing was a setup. This whole thing between me and Leo and Gladdy, all the trouble we caused. It was us trying to get you and Jane together."

Wyatt laughed. "Oh, please. I don't have any trouble getting women. Leo knows that."

"Not any woman you'd ever want to keep. He knew that very well." She fumed at him, then threw up her hands as if to surrender. "He was dying, Wyatt. Think about it. He knew he was dying, and he said the only regret he had about his life was that he was leaving you so suspicious of women that you might never truly trust one. He couldn't stand the idea of being gone, and you being left all alone."

"Leo knows I can take care of myself—"

"Of course. He just didn't want you to have to do that. He said your father's lousy and always has been, that your mother ran off when you were little, and that he's been the only constant in your life. He loved you like a son, said he always thought you should have been his, and he spent his last days here on earth seeing that you'd be taken care of after he was gone, that you'd have someone to love you."

"And this person I need so much in my life, this great love of mine, is Jane?" He almost choked on the words, but he got them out. "Give-me-half-a-million-and-I'll-love-you Jane? I could find lots of women who'd swear they would love me for a lot less than that."

"Show me the will. Right now. Did you even read the whole thing?" she demanded.

"I read enough—"

"We'll see about that. Give it to me!"

He found the damn thing and shoved it at her.

Him and Jane? Someone to love him once Leo was gone?

Leo knew you couldn't buy love. He'd tried his whole life, and it had never worked. He knew better than anybody.

So did Wyatt.

Chapter Sixteen

"Oh, my God!," Kathleen said a moment later. "This is what you're so upset about? I thought it might be this. It was the only thing I could imagine Leo doing. You object to Jane helping poor women get some kind of education or job training with Leo's money? Honestly, Wyatt, that's—"

"What?" He snatched the papers out of her hand. "Poor women getting an education? He left Jane a half-million. You're trying to convince me that she's going to run some kind of charity with Leo's money? You never quit, do you? It's one scam after another—"

"It's right here in black and white. You didn't even read it? You just glanced at this and jumped to the wrong conclusions and broke her heart? You stupid, stupid boy!"

"What?"

"Leo wanted to leave me some of his money. He wanted to make sure Gladdy and I never wanted for anything, and

I had to work hard to convince him that we never would, that Jane had already seen to that. And he felt bad about how he'd treated her, all the trouble we'd caused trying to force the two of you together. I told him Jane didn't want for anything, either, except a man in her life. Although if I'd known you were like this, I never would have gone along with it—"

"Gone along with what?"

"Setting up you and Jane. Leo and Gladdy and I are old, but we're not stupid. We knew if we caused enough trouble or worried you and Jane enough, that you'd likely end up at Remington Park, hopefully working together to sort out our troubles. And it worked beautifully, I might add, until now!"

"You married him," Wyatt reminded her. "You're telling me, you and Leo got married as a scam to throw Jane and me together?"

"No. We never planned to actually get married, but once we got to Vegas, we were so happy. He was just a delightful person, and he finally told me that he was ill, that he didn't think he had long to live, and… It's silly, I know. I'm not really a romantic, but… He was so sweet, and I just adored him. We thought, why not? And then, he was gone."

"And conveniently left Jane half-a-million dollars in his new will."

"I didn't know he was making a new will. We did the prenup together, and then I went to pick out a dress. I guess he must have gone back and had the will made up then."

"Right," Wyatt said, not believing a word of it.

"Leo kept wanting to do something for Jane, and I told him the only thing Jane really wanted that required money she didn't have was to be able to help women like Max's mother, Amy. Jane can get women like that loans and grants for tuition, but they still have living expenses, and there are only so many hours a day to work, take care of a child and go to school. She wanted to be able to provide grant money to help. I guess Leo thought that was a good idea and a good use of some of his money. Is that really so awful? Is that a reason to break Jane's heart?"

"It doesn't say anything about money for poor women like Amy," he yelled. "It just says money for Jane. A half-million dollars for Jane!"

"I want you to know, I've never seen her cry like that, never seen her so devastated. And to throw her out of your apartment without even her clothes on, without her shoes. She hurt herself getting out of here, you know. She was bleeding. I told Gladdy to take her to the emergency room this morning, while I came over here to straighten you out!"

Wyatt was scanning the papers, looking for the part about Jane getting all that money, to shut up her grandmother, and started to feel a little uneasy, a little sick to his stomach, when he got to the details of the half-million-dollar trust for Jane.

No, not exactly for Jane. For Jane to administer, but for… Women seeking an education or job training, particularly those with children to support while they went back to school. Like Amy. Leo wanted Amy to be able to go back to school, so she could take better care of herself and Max.

Maxwell Carson, from the will, the $5,000 in a trust for his education.

Leo wanted Amy to be the first recipient of a grant from the half million in trust he'd set up, money for Jane to administer as trustee.

Wyatt closed his eyes, felt the most tremendous sense of relief and utter joy he could imagine.

Jane was Jane, the Jane he'd always thought she was, the Jane he'd always adored.

And he'd been an absolute ass to her last night.

"Oh, my God," he muttered.

Kicked her out, screamed at her, frightened her so much, she hadn't even taken the time to get dressed before she ran away from him.

"I'm an idiot," he said.

"Yes, you are," her grandmother agreed.

"Wait… Did you say something about her getting hurt?"

"Yes, idiot boy!"

"Jane got hurt running out of here?"

"Yes!"

"Hurt how? What happened?" He'd been only half listening while he read the details of the trust. "Did you say something about her in the emergency room?"

Kathleen nodded, looking as if he was a man getting what he deserved right now, and she was happy about that, that no one got away with messing with Jane while she was around to stop it.

"What happened to her? Where is she?" He started looking for his keys. Where the hell were his keys? Where was Jane?

"I'm not sure what hospital they took her to," her grandmother said.

"But what happened? What's wrong with her? How badly was she hurt?"

"They hadn't examined her when I left the E.R. Gladdy stayed with her, and I came to find you, to tell you what an idiot you are!"

He stared at the woman. "We have to find her. We have to find out what's wrong with her. We have to make sure she's okay."

Kathleen just nodded.

And then he saw, he was afraid he saw, just how vengeful the Carlton women could be with a man who dared to hurt one of their own.

"You're not going to help me find her? You're not going to tell me where she is?"

"I'm not sure if she'd want you to know where she is." And then the woman just stood there and glared at him.

"Call Gladdy," he demanded.

"She's not answering her phone," Kathleen claimed. "And she's even madder at you than I am. So I don't think she's going to help you, either."

Wyatt raked a hand through his hair, blinked to try to clear his blood-shot eyes.

Jane was out there somewhere, hurt, heartbroken, crying her eyes out over him, thinking he hated her, knowing he didn't trust her at all.

"I have to find her," he said. "I have to tell her how wrong I was. I have to get her to forgive me."

"Good luck with that," Kathleen said, looking as if she could enjoy torturing him like this for days for daring to hurt her beloved Jane.

He went to three emergency rooms, thinking of all the ways a woman could get hurt running out of an apartment building, begging E.R. clerks to tell him if they had a Jane Carlton there, before he finally started thinking halfway clearly.

Once he did, he knew in his heart that if Jane were

really and truly injured, her grandmother would never have left Jane's side, no matter how mad she was at Wyatt.

So this was just about payback, grandmother-style, and Kathleen was really good at it because he'd been terrified, running around town like a crazy man.

Okay. He forced himself to be still, to breathe. If she wasn't badly injured, she was either at her apartment, with Gladdy at Remington Park or they were hiding her somewhere to torture him some more.

Wyatt frowned, thinking he deserved torture, deserved all sorts of despicable acts against his person. He'd been absolutely awful to Jane. Jane who'd been nothing but kind and generous and tender to him.

He decided he'd start at her townhouse and go from there. He got there and pounded on the door until Gladdy opened it, looking every bit as furious as Kathleen's grandmother had been.

"Is she here?" Wyatt begged.

Gladdy just glared at him.

"Kathleen let me have it. I promise. I've been to three emergency rooms already, searching like a mad man. Gladdy, please? Is she here?"

"Three emergency rooms?" Gladdy asked.

Wyatt nodded. "I think I scared the clerks. I'm probably lucky they didn't try to inject me with something to calm me down and put me on a psych hold. Then it might have been days before I could find Jane. Please, Gladdy. I have to find her."

"She cried all night," Gladdy reiterated. "Over you. Jane's never cried like that over a man. She's never cared that much for a man."

And he was grateful to hear it. Not the tears part, but

the caring part. If she was that upset about what he'd done to her, it had to mean she really cared about him, and if she cared that much, he had to be able to get her to forgive him eventually.

"Gladdy, I'm begging you. Tell me where Jane is."

She just stood there, mute, outraged and without a hint of sympathy for him.

Damn. What was he going to do now?

"Sorry," he said, literally picking her up and setting her to the side, to get around her and into the apartment, calling out as he went. "Jane? Are you here? You have to talk to me! I'm not leaving until you do. Jane?"

Jane heard the commotion. She was afraid half the building heard Gladdy yelling at him, Wyatt begging and insisting he had to find Jane.

She braced herself as best she could, but honestly, how could a woman ever truly prepare herself for the reality of Wyatt Gray in the flesh? The things he did to a woman. The things he made her feel, made her wish for, made her come to count on?

No woman could ever be truly prepared against that, Jane decided.

He found her in her bed, wearing a pair of soft cotton pajamas, her eyes still red from crying, and her foot, bandaged and propped up on a pillow.

"You *are* hurt," he said, looking shocked as he came to sit on the side of the bed and inspected her swaddled foot. "I thought Kathleen had to be lying to me—"

"Because all women lie, right?" Jane shot back.

"No, because she wanted to torture me for what I did to you, and she's really good at it," he said, as if he admired a woman who was good at that. "And I deserve to be tortured. I know that. I've been like a crazy man. She just told me you were hurt leaving my apartment last night, and she wouldn't tell me how. She wouldn't even tell me which emergency room you'd been taken to. I've been all over town."

"Emergency room?" Gram told him that? "Wyatt, I'm fine. I got three stitches from stepping on some glass in the parking lot because I didn't take the time to grab my shoes before I ran out. The only reason we went to the emergency room was because my doctor's out of town, and her office couldn't work me in today. They said I really should have a tetanus shot, to not let it wait."

He put his hand on her foot, holding it through the bandages, as if he still couldn't stand the idea that she'd been hurt. What had Gram done? Made it sound as if she'd run out into the street and been plowed down by a car or something?

Jane felt a teensy bit sorry for him.

"I didn't know anything about the money. I swear," she said, still hurt that he could so easily believe she was just like every other woman he'd ever known. "And I won't take it. I'll just refuse. Leo can't make me take his money."

"No, he wanted you to have it. I'm sure of it now. You should have it."

Oh, God, Jane thought, deciding it still hurt more than she would have thought possible. Was that it? The money but not him? Was that what he was trying to say?

She shouldn't be so surprised. She didn't think he'd ever trusted her anyway. Not after what she'd seen last night. And honestly, who could blame him, the way he'd grown up? She understood. She felt like a fool for ever trusting him, too. For putting aside all the lessons she'd learned in her mixed-up childhood. She'd been so smart about protecting herself. Until she had met him.

"Wyatt, there is no way I'm taking that money. Now, would you please go?" She turned to stare at the window, blinking back tears, mad as could be at the idea of them actually falling and him seeing her cry again.

"No," he said. "I won't. I'm an idiot. I'm a mean-tempered ass. I took the least little bit of information and blew up at you. I let years of experience with women—none of whom were you—ruin something beautiful between us."

"If you hadn't ruined it, something else would have," she admitted.

He moved up on the bed until he was right in front of her, leaned down until even with her head hung low, trying to avoid his gaze, she couldn't.

"My only excuse is that I've never felt like that before, Jane. I never thought I would. Hell, I never wanted to. I'm terrified here. I've never really trusted anybody in my life, except Leo, and he's gone. I can't even talk to him to tell him how terrified I am at the idea of loving you."

"You don't love me," she insisted.

"I think I do. God help me, I do. And I think you love me, too. What are we going to do about that?"

"Ignore it. It'll go away. These things never last," she told him.

"I won't go away. In fact, I'm not leaving here. Just try to throw me out. You and Kathleen and Gladdy, give it your best shot. I'm not going."

"Someone always leaves, Wyatt. We both know that."

"I won't. I meant it. I've never found anyone like you.

As smart and funny and sexy and sweet as you. As delightful as you. As adorable as you. And I'm not leaving."

He sat there like a man taking root, content to wait her out, to wait out anything.

"This is ridiculous, Wyatt! You apologize to women by ignoring everything they say and just doing what you want?"

"I'm not leaving."

She felt hot, wet, stupid tears fall down her face then, and she was so mad she could hardly stand it. Crying! She was crying! Over a stupid, stubborn man! He looked panicked at her tears, as if she was fighting dirty or she might have finally found something to use against him that might work.

"Please don't do that," he said.

She stared at him, defiant, her tears still falling.

"Jane, come on. You have a strong sense of fairness, and I'm sure you abhor all sorts of feminine trickery when it comes to dealing with men. Fight fair here."

"I don't want to fight at all!"

"Well, good. Neither do I. I am so sorry. God, I'm sorry. I'll never be able to say it enough. I panicked. That's all there is to it, and I won't do that again, I swear. And I won't leave you. This man is never going to leave you, Jane. How can you *not* accept that there might be one man in the whole entire world who won't ever leave you?"

"One?" she scoffed. "Just one? And you think you're it?"

"I know I am."

"It hurts too much, Wyatt," she sobbed, unable to hold it together at all anymore. God, she hated this! "It's too hard, too big a risk to take. We both know that. We're both so sensible. It's one of the first things I liked about you. We both know better than this."

"No, we were wrong, and you know it. Look at Leo. Eighty-six years he had here, most of them as happy as could be, but in the end, what mattered to him? Just the people who loved him. That's it. The rest was just…details. Details and silly things we use to keep score because we're not smart enough to know any better. I can see that now. You can, too, Jane. I know you can."

"No—"

"You were happy with me. I made you happy, I know I did. And I was terrified with you most of the time, terrified of wanting you too much, loving you too much, and losing you. But I'm done with that. I'm here. I love you, and I'm staying. You couldn't make me leave if you tried."

"Gladdy?" she yelled. "Call the police!"

"Go ahead," he dared her. "They'll let me out of jail eventually, and I'll be right back here. I'm the most stubborn man you will ever meet and the most determined."

"The most unreasonable, you mean."

"That, too," he promised, still sitting there.

She heard Gram and Gladdy whispering at the door to her bedroom.

"How's he doing?" Gram asked.

"Better than I expected," Gladdy admitted.

Wyatt grinned hugely. "You know this was all a setup to get us together, don't you?"

"What?"

"Every bit of it," he told her. "Leo couldn't stand the idea of me being alone once he was gone, and he couldn't have found a more generous, kindhearted, loving woman to be by my side. You blew me away, Jane, the way you took care of me, the way you just gave yourself to me, the way you loved me. I'll do the same for you. I promise. Every day of our lives."

"Oh, do you think they'll go to Vegas to get married?" Gladdy asked. "I want to go back to Vegas! What was the name of the chapel?"

"The Love Me Tender Wedding Chapel. Leo would have loved that. Oh, I almost forgot." Gram hurried to Wyatt's side, pulled the huge diamond ring off her finger and handed it to Wyatt. "Leo wanted you to have this. For Jane."

Gram backed out of the room, grinning hugely herself.

Wyatt looked particularly pleased to have a big, sparkly diamond to hold out to her. "See, they've forgiven me, and I adore them both, too. They're going to be the greatest in-laws a man ever had."

"Oh, yes. We will," Gladdy agreed from the doorway.

They were ganging up on her. She couldn't believe it! And Gram and Gladdy were not quick to forgive, not toward anyone who hurt Jane.

"It's a really nice ring," Gram added. "You always said a woman should never refuse good, quality diamonds from a man, Jane."

Jane rolled her eyes, shook her head. Her foot hurt. Her heart hurt.

Wyatt looked as if he'd spent the night in the gutter, passed out drunk, and woken up to some kind of nightmare. She'd never seen him look anything close to awful, and he probably never would. But he looked truly bad right now. Tortured, he'd said. A crazy man who just had to get to her.

"I'm so scared," she whispered.

"So am I, but I'm more scared of being without you," he explained, sounding as honest as a man could be.

If they were both scared, they were at least being honest and at least halfway smart about this, Jane reasoned.

After all, it was an enormous thing, promising your life to someone, to love, honor and cherish, forever.

"I'll sign any kind of prenup you want," Wyatt added. "Just…you know…because I know you'll want one."

"Well, that would be at least one smart thing to do," she admitted.

"And Vegas sounds good," he said. "I have some very fond memories of being in Vegas with you, even with the awful stuff with Leo. We could go back to Vegas."

"We get to go, too, right?" Gladdy asked, sounding delighted. "We want to go!"

"You want to run off right now and get married in Vegas?" Jane couldn't believe it. Just when he was starting to sound reasonable.

"We could even pack this time."

Gram and Gladdy giggled.

"That's crazy, Wyatt."

"I'm a crazy man, Jane. Crazy about you. What do you say? Vegas?"

"It's crazy. He's crazy," she yelled to Gram and Gladdy.

"We'll start packing right now," Gram said.

Wyatt had her hand in his, was sliding the ring on her finger and she wasn't pulling away.

"Marry me," he said. "Love me tender, I'll love you back the same way."

"Wyatt, it's just nuts!"

But by nightfall, he had her on a plane to Vegas, with her panties on this time, but not for long, Wyatt promised.

* * * * *

VEGAS TWO-STEP

BY
LIZ TALLEY

All the characters in this book have no existence outside the imagination of the author, and have no relation whatsoever to anyone bearing the same name or names. They are not even distantly inspired by any individual known or unknown to the author, and all the incidents are pure invention.

First published in Great Britain 2011
by Mills & Boon, an imprint of Harlequin (UK) Limited,
Eton House, 18-24 Paradise Road, Richmond, Surrey TW9 1SR

ISBN: 978 0 263 88878 2

23-0411

Harlequin (UK) policy is to use papers that are natural, renewable and recyclable products and made from wood grown in sustainable forests. The logging and manufacturing processes conform to the legal environmental regulations of the country of origin.

Printed and bound in Spain
by Blackprint CPI, Barcelona

Dear Reader,

When I tell people I'm a writer, they want to know where I get the ideas for my stories. This one came from an unlikely place—a friend who wore knee-high hosiery with a pair of sandals. I wondered what would happen if I took a small-town, straightlaced librarian who also mixed hosiery and sandals, gave her a makeover and let her get a little wild in Vegas. Thus *Vegas Two-Step*, my mixed-up take on the musical *Grease*, was born.

Of course, I knew my librarian would find love. And Nellie's journey was such fun. I found I'm a lot like my heroine. I know how to transplant day lilies and grow tomatoes, but martinis, limos and gorgeous nightclub owners top my list of Vegas-style fantasy. Like Nellie, I often wonder, *am I stuck in a rut?*

I hope you enjoy Nellie and Jack's journey to discovering the person beneath the wrapping. I loved writing this sassy, Southern story. In fact, I've developed such a tender place in my heart for the fictional town of Oak Stand, Texas, that I often dream of moving there. Since I can't, I plan to visit the small town again in future books.

I would love to hear from my readers either by post at PO Box 5418, Bossier City, LA 71171 or through my website, www.liztalleybooks.com.

Happy reading!

Liz Talley

Thanks to my dad, who taught me to love a good book, my mom for thinking I'm incredible and my husband and boys for sacrificing for my dream.

I especially want to thank my sister-in-law Tafta, who was my first reader, my Thursday lunch group, Keri Ford, Joanne Rock, the NOLA STARS and Wanda. Dreams are possible when someone believes in you…

From devouring the Mills & Boon books on the shelf of her aunt's used bookstore to swiping her grandmother's medical romances, **Liz Talley** has always loved a good romance novel. So it was no surprise to anyone when she started writing a book one day while her infant napped. She soon found writing more exciting than scrubbing hardened cereal off the loveseat. Underneath her baby-food-stained clothes a dream stirred. Liz followed that dream and, after a foray into historical romance and a Golden Heart final, she started her contemporary romance on the same day she met her editor. Coincidence? She prefers to call it fate.

Currently Liz lives in North Louisiana with her high school sweetheart, two beautiful children and a menagerie of animals. Liz loves strawberries, fishing, retail therapy and is always game for a spa day. When not writing contemporary romances for Mills & Boon, she can be found working in the flowerbed, doing laundry or driving carpool.

CHAPTER ONE

Fashion should never be more important than comfort. Coco Chanel never planted ten acres. If she had, she'd have darn sure wore sensible shoes to do it in.

—Grandmother Tucker to a seven-year-old Nellie when she wanted to wear her Sunday shoes to water the garden.

HER EYES CARESSED the barbarian, eating up every inch of his naked torso from the top of his broad shoulders to the sculpted six-pack disappearing tantalizingly into the plaid wool wrapped tight around his waist. Wild, amber locks framed blazing blue eyes, a sensual mouth and a terrifyingly masculine jaw. Muscled arms cradled the buxom blonde straddling his thigh.

Very nice. Nellie Hughes loved rugged Highland lairds. Still, she shoved the book with the yummy cover onto the crowded shelf in the romance section. Scottish boy was tempting, but no more than the lunch—turkey tetrazzini leftovers—waiting for her in the back of the library.

Her stomach rumbled, confirming her thoughts.

She pushed the cart through the romance section of the library toward the break room, swerving around blue-haired Mrs. Davis, who was holding a stack of similarly illustrated books.

A giggle interrupted her pilgrimage.

Nellie inwardly groaned. The high school juniors were at it again. She would nip their chat session in the bud before it escalated into another gigglefest like the day before.

Working on their research papers? She gave a snort as she pushed past the Nonfiction section and headed toward the lone study room in the back. Yeah, right. If the English III teacher knew the girls had been researching the spring's coolest prom dresses rather than Pope's "Rape of the Lock," they'd be back at the high school before they could even bat their heavily made up eyes.

Out and out laughter reached Nellie's ears as she approached the room, but the girls' words stopped her.

"Did you see that librarian's dress? Oh, my God, like my grandmother has the same one."

Wow, way harsh on Rita. Nellie had just placed her hand on the doorjamb when she realized Rita was wearing pants. Surely they couldn't be talking about…her?

She looked down at her flower-print dress. Wait, they *were* talking about her! A little dagger of hurt fishhooked her heart. Grandmother's dress? It wasn't that bad. She'd picked up the dress in the career section of a store two months ago, thinking it was perfect for work. It was totally appropriate, designed to look businesslike. Like a librarian should.

"You'd think someone could help her out," another girl piped up. "She's wearing panty hose with sandals. What the hell was she thinkin'?"

Nellie's gaze slid to her feet.

Okay. Score one for the juveniles. She *was* wearing a pair of knee-high nylons with her peekaboo espadrilles. A good idea that morning when the weatherman predicted above-average temperatures, the combo now seemed a bit dowdy. Big deal. Wearing panty hose was in the uniform code for the county library system. She'd rather be comfortable than fashionable. Early May in Texas could be brutal.

"Well, she's old, Natalie." There was a pause. "That's, like, how old people dress."

Nellie couldn't stop her shoulders from sagging. Old? She was only twenty-nine! Okay…she would be thirty in a couple of months, but that wasn't old.

"Well, if she wants to catch a guy, she needs like a serious spa day and a whole new wardrobe. She has no prospects. I've never even seen her talking to a guy. Plus, I'm getting tired of her bustin' our balls every time I pick up a *Cosmo*."

Someone sniggered. "You don't have balls, Marcie."

Bleats of laughter followed the last statement.

Nellie abandoned the empty cart and strolled into the room. "Excuse me, ladies. You need to hold it down or I *will* put in a call to your teacher this time."

The girls froze, à la deer-in-the-headlights. The room fell silent as all three guiltily raised their eyes to Nellie.

She arched one brow, crossed her arms and pierced each girl with the dreaded librarian stare—the one known to cause death or, at the least, extreme frostbite.

With a roll of her eyes, one girl closed a fashion magazine. Another shuffled paper around, trying desperately to look busy with research, while the ringleader, Marcie Patterson, flashed a mouthful of braces at Nellie.

"Sorry, Miss Hughes. We'll be quiet. Promise."

Nellie frowned. Marcie was just the sort of girl she remembered from her own days at Oak Stand High School. Guileless baby blues that feigned innocence, slim tanned shoulders that shrugged demurely beneath a junior varsity cheerleading uniform, and a vicious tongue designed to slash chubby sophomore girls to shreds. Yeah, she knew the type. Piranha.

"This is your last warning, ladies," she said, leveling her gaze at them.

Then Nellie spun on her heel and stalked past the abandoned cart toward her office. Giggles erupted behind her.

The phone was in her hand before she realized it, and she punched the numbers she knew by heart. Why it had taken her so long, she couldn't fathom. She knew she'd grown set in her ways, pulling out the same old clothes, letting her hair go back to plain brown, spending her nights doing nothing more exciting than watching the Oxygen channel. Stuck in a rut, sure, but she didn't want to make a home there.

Time to do something drastic.

A harried voice answered on the second ring, though raucous laughter shot out from the earpiece so that Nellie couldn't hear the greeting.

The phone clattered. "Sorry. Fantabulous Hair Salon. Can I help you?"

Nellie hesitated. "Kate?"

"Yeah. Who's this?" The voice sounded guarded.

"Nellie."

"Oh, hey girl. I thought it might be Mrs. McNeil. She started complaining this morning to Donna about her hair color. I thought she was callin' for a reschedule. What's up?"

Kate Newman was just what Nellie needed. Hip and edgy, she had been Nellie's best friend since they toddled into Oak Stand Baptist preschool together. Night and day—that's what everyone in their small Texas town had called them. Nellie's light brown hair and quiet disposition contrasted sharply with Kate's wild, dark beauty. Yet they'd been joined at the hip. Kate had moved just outside of Las Vegas two years ago. Nellie missed her audacious friend desperately, especially since she now lived alone in the rambling Victorian house on the town square.

"You know that trip to Vegas you've been bugging me about?"

"The one I can't get you to take?"

Nellie closed her eyes before blurting, "Well, I've changed my mind. I want to come."

"You're kidding?"

Nellie smiled at the incredulity in Kate's voice. She'd been begging Nellie to come on her annual "Girls and Glam" getaway in Vegas ever since she'd moved. And when Nellie's grandmother had died six months ago, Kate had doubled her insistence that Nellie needed a change of scenery.

"Nope. I'm signing on for your crazy weekend."

"I can't believe it! What made you change your mind?"

Nellie hesitated. She didn't want to tell Kate just how frumpy three teenagers had made her feel. That in itself was pathetic. Why should the words of mere high school juniors make her feel so inadequate? But the truth was they'd made her feel as old as the dog-eared Dick and Jane books in the Children's Literature section. And that frightened her.

Because she *was* almost thirty. And she *was* wearing knee-highs. And she hadn't had a date since the town Christmas parade two, no, scratch that, three years ago.

Very sad indeed.

She shouldn't have needed the hurtful words of a few petty cheerleaders to spur her on. All she had to do was take a look at her nonexistent social calendar. "Never mind the why. I just want to do it. Oh, and by the way, let's do that makeover too."

A shout of jubilation erupted from the receiver. Nellie yanked the phone from her ear and held it away.

A flash of blue caught her eye and she pulled her attention from the shrieking phone to see Mrs. Davis standing just outside her door, eyes agog at the screeching coming from the phone.

Nellie put her hand over the mouthpiece. "Just found out the book she wanted came in."

"Must be a damned good book," the old lady groused as she shuffled toward the checkout desk.

The noise at the other end of the line subsided and Nellie held the phone back to her ear. "Kate, calm down."

"Okay, it's just that I've been after you to do that makeover for a while, so I know something's up, but I'm too thrilled to interrogate you now."

"Nothing happened. Really. I just want a change, that's all." She twisted the tassel on the bookmark Grandmother Tucker had given her. Grandmother Tucker. She was part of the reason Nellie had put her life on hold, trimmed her own hair and blown off the few dates that had come her way. Still, she had no regrets. Grandmother Tucker had been the only person who loved her.

"You bet your sweet penny loafers you need a change," Kate drawled, her trademark sultry laugh following.

"I don't own penny loafers."

"Shocking." Kate laughed. Nellie could hear her tapping her ever-present BlackBerry. "When can we get started? Hmm...we're going in...two weeks. That means we don't have much time. My friends Trish and Billie are coming too.

You remember them? Well, they're sharing a room. I think I'll get a suite, so don't worry about any other reservations. Just get your plane ticket. You better call as soon as—"

"Stop. I'll call you tonight and we'll set it up."

Kate ignored her. "I'm gonna clear my books for Thursday. Do you think you can get here then? If we're going to do a makeover, we're going to do it right."

Nellie's stomach plunged at the thought of Kate getting her hands on her overgrown hair, not to mention every other part of her body. God, she'd be waxed, streaked, tattooed and pierced before the petite fireball got through with her. She could end up looking like she belonged in a rap video. A picture of herself in a barely there dress gyrating next to Snoop Dogg popped into her mind. She shuddered.

"Look, Kate, I am up for the makeover, but I need to keep my job, so nothing too outlandish. Okay?" There was no answer. "Kate?"

"Yeah, okay. But you have to be willing to go for something different. I'm thinking sexy, hot and vampy." Kate sounded determined—wouldn't-take-no-for-an-answer determined.

Nellie coughed. "I'm thinking chic, cosmopolitan librarian."

"Like those even exist, Nell," Kate said, disgust in her voice. "But we'll try for something in between."

"Maybe," Nellie conceded, remembering she *was* wearing knee-highs with sensible espadrilles. Perhaps sexy wouldn't be too bad. "Look, I got to go. Talk to you tonight, okay?"

As she hung up, she heard Rita call through her door that she was heading to lunch with her husband and she needed Nellie to cover the front. Nellie hurried to the checkout desk, passing tidy shelves and a display highlighting an East Texas author. Nellie loved the renovated antebellum mansion that served as the library. Located in the heart of the East Texas town of Oak Stand, the 120-year-old mansion stood as a testament that a state-of-the-art facility could be historically charming. Nellie was one of three librarians, and she adored her job. She ran most of the children's programs and also served as an automated systems librarian, planning and operating the library's computer systems. Basically, Nellie was an information architect.

She skirted the heavy oak-paneled counter and tossed a smile to Mrs. Davis, who was clicking her false teeth and puffing out little breaths of frustration.

"Sorry." Nellie pulled the stack of paperbacks toward her, grabbed the scanner and began passing it over the bar code on the well-read books. "These look good. I read this one several years ago. I think you'll enjoy it."

"I'm sure I will, honey. This author writes a hell of a good sex scene. And you're never too old to enjoy good sex," said the elderly lady, a slyness in her voice, though her eyes remained perfectly innocent behind her bifocals.

Nellie choked back a laugh. "Yeah? I wouldn't know."

"Honey, life's too short to miss out on the good stuff."

Nellie handed her the stack of books. "Just what I've been thinking, but sometimes it's hard to find the good stuff. Here you go, Mrs. Davis. Due back on the fifteenth of May."

"Thank you, dear. And if you don't mind my saying, you might have better luck finding the good stuff if you would wear something a bit more youthful. Honey, I have the same dress hanging in my closet and I'm eighty-two."

The blue-haired granny didn't stick around long enough for Nellie's response. Instead, she toddled right out the scarred cypress door. Nellie snapped her mouth closed. Darn it! Score two for the juveniles. They were right about the dress, too.

She sighed and tucked a hank of hair behind her ear as she maneuvered the computer mouse so she could shop for airfare. If she'd any doubts about her girls' weekend, they'd just vanished at the older woman's words.

Okay, Vegas, look out. Time to find the good stuff.

TWO WEEKS LATER Nellie wasn't so sure about looking for the good stuff. She'd be happy with some mediocre stuff. Like her airplane leaving on time or relief from a pounding headache. Or maybe just a clean shirt. So far nothing had gone right and she hadn't even left Texas.

The airport bar was crowded, something that tended to happen when flights were weather-delayed. The smell of cigarettes permeated the place though smoking had been outlawed for several years. Not a great place to wait it out, but at least she could get a drink.

She sipped her wine. A fellow patron to her left jabbed her once more with his meaty elbow, causing her wine to slosh over the rim. Nellie stifled the irritation rising within her and drummed her nails on the scarred bar. She hated the airport, hated waiting, and hated sitting alone at a bar.

As she reached to take another sip of her chardonnay, the man next to her jostled her again. Her hand clipped the goblet of lukewarm wine and it flew off the bar, spilling its contents into the lap of the man to her right. The wineglass bounced off his thigh and smashed to the floor.

Nellie shoved her stool back and, in a belated effort, grabbed for the glass. "Oh! Sorry! Here, let me..."

Everyone in the small bar stopped what they were doing and stared.

Great! Just one more thing to go wrong with this stupid trip. Nellie stared at the mess lying at her feet. Then she looked up and her breath stopped.

Like literally stopped.

All the people around her blurred into the background and the apology she was about to repeat died on her lips.

Good God! He was magnificent.

Not even handsome, or hot, or any of the other words girls used to describe guys. Nope. Just plain magnificent. Like in the "on the front of the romance cover" way.

Her mind took a picture—irritated blue eyes beneath slashing black brows, dark shaggy hair, and a sensual mouth boasting a full lower lip Nellie strangely wanted to slide her tongue over. Magnificent.

"Oh, God! I am so sorry!" she squeaked after finally remembering to take a gulp of air.

The stranger ignored her and busied himself with shaking droplets of wine from his hand.

Nellie grabbed a handful of ridiculously small cocktail napkins from the holder on the bar and held them out to him.

He took them and dabbed at the spreading stain.

Nellie watched him swipe uselessly at the dark patch spreading over his crotch. Lord, it looked like he'd wet himself.

The bartender tossed a towel to the man, giving everyone in the bar permission to go back to whatever they had been doing before the glass shattered. Guilt settled in her stomach. "Sir, I'm terribly sorry. Is there anything I can do?"

He lifted his eyes. Electric blue eyes that pierced the depths of her soul.

She lost her breath. Again.

He said nothing. Just looked down at his ruined pants.

Feeling totally incompetent, Nellie crouched down and began clearing the fragments of glass from the well-worn tile.

"Ouch!" A sliver of glass sliced her index finger. Bright drops of blood popped up.

Suddenly the man was beside her, his grip firm and warm. "Hey, don't bother. Let the barkeep get it."

Nellie totally forgot the cut. Her body was preoccupied with the fact his touch had sent sparks up her arm. Seriously. Shivers right up her arm. Then her heart flopped over.

And for some reason she felt like she wasn't Nellie from Oak Stand. The world slowed down and she became one of those smart women from the black-and-white films they showed on TNT. The shabby bar faded away to lush tropical foliage, piano keys plinking in a smoke-filled room. Suddenly she was Ingrid Bergman, a fair damsel in distress, rescued by the handsome, no, *magnificent,* stranger.

Nellie stared at her dripping finger and then back up at him. Could he feel it too? The frisson of electricity that overshadowed the throb in her finger. Would he sweep her into an embrace and murmur in her ear about having searched the world and finally found her? Oh, and something about "of all the gin joints…"

Reality clicked back into place as the man wrapped a cocktail napkin around her finger and pulled her to her feet. He deposited her onto the abandoned bar stool.

"Hey, Eduardo! Get the lady another glass of wine and put it on my tab. Oh, and a bandage or something for her finger. Wait! Did Pujols just strike out?"

Nellie blinked.

Pujols? Strike out? Was the man more concerned about

baseball? Surely not after what had occurred between them? Didn't he feel it? The electricity? Hello? What did baseball matter at a time like this?

She tried again. "Um…I just wanted you to know I am terribly sorry for spilling my drink like that. I am usually not so…" She trailed off because the man didn't turn toward her. His eyes were riveted on the television mounted above the bar, broadcasting the St. Louis game.

He waved in her direction. "Look, just an accident. No big deal. We all have bad days."

That was it. Nothing more.

Nellie murmured a soft "okay" and picked up the chilled goblet the bartender had set in front of her. She stared at the adhesive bandage lying beside her purse and took a sip of the wine. Her finger wasn't bleeding any longer. It was her pride that needed the bandage.

He had dismissed her.

He'd rocked her world, but she didn't even merit a second glance. Great.

But what did you think, huh? a little voice in her head mocked. *That a gorgeous hunk like that would notice a country mouse like you? You've never turned heads, have you? So why now? Get real, Nellie. Men like him are not for you.*

A voice over the speaker interrupted the spiteful one careening about in her head and announced her flight was boarding.

Thank God. She could escape, tail tucked and all that. She grabbed the bandage from the bar, jabbed it into her purse, and took a last swig of the crisp chardonnay, trying to forget how rotten her day had been. Time to move on. Go to Vegas. Forget Texas for a few days.

Not to be as easily dismissed, El Magnificent drew the eye of every lady under ninety when he stood and settled his tab. Sure, it still looked like he'd wet himself, but he didn't try to hide the embarrassing stain. Confidently, he picked up his attaché and strolled out into the terminal. Normally, Nellie would have insisted on paying for her second glass of wine, but tall, dark and dismissive had obviously picked up the tab. She tossed a couple of one-dollar bills on the bar instead. She'd pay her own tip, darn it.

Nellie shouldered her carry-on and hurried out the open doorway, blinking against the harsh lights of the main terminal and the moisture that blurred her vision for no good reason. She caught her reflection in the shiny partition of a closed fast-food vendor and winced.

Ouch! No wonder Mr. Magnificent hadn't given her a second glance.

She'd been in such a hurry to get out of the library that she hadn't taken the time to change her clothes. Her navy cotton skirt was rumpled and her once smartly ironed linen sailor-top blouse was stained with grape juice, thanks to a certain raucous seven-year-old at the Read for Summer launch. Her brown hair was swept back into a disheveled ponytail from which several tendrils escaped to frizz unbecomingly around her pale cheeks. To make matters worse, her eyes appeared bloodshot from the seldom-used contact lenses.

Heck, she'd probably frightened half the people in the bar.

Well, she huffed as she hurried through the terminal, who cared? She was getting a makeover, wasn't she? And though she'd fallen more than a little head over heels for the God-like creature in the bar, he still was just a man in a bar. No one truly fell in love at first sight.

Over a man. In a bar. At the Dallas airport.

That happened in movies, to the Ingrid Bergmans of the world. Not to silly, plain daydreamers.

God, she really was pathetic.

Nellie dug out her boarding pass and handed it to the trim, smartly dressed attendant.

Forget Mr. Magnificent. She would never see him again. He would be a memory, fading just like the throb in her finger.

CHAPTER TWO

You ever see a God-fearin' woman with a tattoo? Nope. You know why? Because if God had wanted you to have a picture of Daffy Duck on your backside, he would've given it to you before you popped out of your momma.

—Grandmother Tucker to Nellie when she won a tattoo from the gumball machine.

"OWWWW!" NELLIE YELPED as the straightening iron brushed the top of her ear. "That hurt."

"Sorry," her friend Kate said, running practiced fingers through Nellie's newly highlighted hair, giving it a tousle. "It hurts to be beautiful."

"Another reason to forgo all of this torture." Nellie tucked a hank of golden hair behind her now pink ear before turning her attention to the spidery faux eyelashes on the granite before her. "I mean, is it worth all of this trouble?"

"Are you really asking that question after that guy hit on you last night?"

Nellie tossed her a contrite look. "Sorry about that. You were talking to him first, and I—"

"That's okay." Kate smiled. "I'm not into personal trainers anyway. They're always talking about protein and ways to define your abs. No thanks."

Nellie picked up one of the eyelashes and practiced lining it up on her lid before giving up and tossing it beside the makeup kit sitting on the hotel room vanity. "He wasn't quite the guy I thought he was."

Kate rolled her blue eyes before applying mascara. "They never are."

She picked up the abandoned eyelash and turned Nellie's head toward her. "So what about this trainer guy? Is he gonna meet up with you tonight?"

"Not a chance." Nellie watched as her best friend expertly set the lash into place. Kate's forehead furrowed as she contemplated her work. She was a perfectionist. Always had been. Nellie had first noticed the trait in second grade when she'd watched her dress and redress her Barbie twenty times before the outfit was acceptable for dinner with Ken.

"Good, he was a total loser," Kate concurred, handing her a tube of lip gloss. "I didn't drag you here for losers. Tonight we find you a winner."

Nellie swiped her lips with apricot lip gloss and smacked them before sliding from the stool centered in front of the vanity. As she rose, she almost did a double take at the sight of herself in the mirror. She looked like a stranger, so not herself. "I'm not here for guys, Kate. I came because I needed to get away—a little pick-me-up. Not a pickup."

"Whatever. I say you need a dude, a seriously hot, make-your-knees-knock dude." Kate's voice followed her as she entered the bedroom. "And you ain't gonna get that in Oak Stand, Texas. I know firsthand."

Nellie sighed. She really didn't want to worry about fending off prowling single men. The personal trainer had taught her that much last night on her first sojourn into Las

Vegas nightlife. Boyish, blond and charming, he had made her feel like she used to feel back in college—young and free. But she'd found out pretty quickly what kind of slimeball he was. Seems he thought buying drinks equated with free sex in the back corner of the club.

Did she really look like that kind of girl?

She headed for the huge window showcasing the twinkling Vegas nightlife and pressed her forehead to the cool glass. The fountains danced beneath her. Vegas nights were incredible. Sheer, hot, pulsing energy. A far cry from the peaceful Texas nights she enjoyed from the front porch of her Oak Stand home.

Tonight she stood, a whole new Nellie, designed to make men drool. Kate had accomplished her mission. Maybe Nellie *did* look like that kind of girl.

"You look hot, Nell." Kate confirmed her thoughts.

She spun around as her friend sank into an overstuffed chair with a huff. Kate bent over and fastened the straps of the mile-high sandals she'd bought that afternoon. Nellie had no idea how her friend would walk in them, much less dance in them at the clubs they'd visit that night.

"All thanks to you."

Kate flashed a quick smile. "Yeah, I'm good."

"And humble." Nellie laughed.

"Well, you've got those good Tucker bones. Not to mention big tatas." Kate bounced invisible breasts in front of her own small chest. "Seriously, you've always been pretty, Nell. You just never accentuate it."

"There was never much of a need."

Kate opened her mouth to impart more Kateisms, but the connecting door opened and Trish leaned in and asked, "Where we headed tonight, girls?"

Kate stood up and smoothed the short black skirt over her toned thighs. She wore her hair spiked around her angelic face. The cobalt streaks in her ebony hair matched the blue of her eyes. She looked like a Gothic Tinkerbell. "Down to Fontana. Friend of mine got us into a pharmaceutical party. Table service and everything. Then I was thinking about Agave Blue. I know one of the bouncers."

Nellie's stomach tilted south. Agave Blue. The hottest club in town. Owned by the guy she'd spilled her wine on in the airport bar.

Jack Darby.

When she'd seen him staring back at her from the cover of the *Las Vegas Life* magazine sitting on the nightstand in their hotel room, she'd nearly dropped the cocktail Kate had shoved in her hand. The man who'd made her pulse race leaned against a low-slung sports car with his arms crossed and a sensual grin curving his mouth. The words beside him read Sultan of the Strip, and the nightclub owner looked every inch of the moniker with a billowing linen shirt and harem girl at each elbow.

Of course, it was stupid to worry about Jack Darby. It wasn't as if she'd run into the man again. And if she did, he wouldn't recognize her. Kate had made sure by turning Nellie into a five-day, alter-ego party girl ready to take Vegas by storm.

"Here. I got you a little something to complete your small-town-girl-gone-bad image." Kate rummaged through a bag.

"What, taking a fake name wasn't good enough? I need more intrigue?" Her friend spun her around so she was facing the window again.

"Whoa! What are you doing?" Nellie squealed as something wet slapped against her bare shoulder—the shoulder just above the scandalous bustier Kate insisted she wear because it "rocked" the designer jeans dipping low on her hips. Kate started counting. "Wait! Are you putting a tattoo on me?"

"Just a temporary one. It'll come off with baby oil."

"No, Kate. Tattoos are trashy," Nellie said, protesting but remaining still nevertheless. She didn't want to mess it up.

"Says little 'Miss Nelda Rae Tucker,'" Kate drawled. "I've got three permanent ones, Nellie."

"My name's not Tucker. It's Hughes. And I didn't mean on you. Just me," Nellie finished lamely. Kate was different. Free. Able to live as she pleased. Nellie would always be a Tucker, no matter what her last name was. And Tuckers didn't have tattoos. Tuckers didn't wear bustiers, thongs or strappy, impractical sandals. Tuckers didn't make out with virtual strangers in dark corners of dance clubs. Nope, Tuckers were dignified. Practical. Sensible.

But "Elle," the identity Kate had insisted Nellie assume for her extended weekend, was anything but a boring Tucker. She was supposed to be a single, twenty-something Dallas interior designer with layered caramel hair and sexy new clothes. "Elle" was her naughty side.

Nellie sighed, "Okay. But it will come off, won't it?"

"Heaven's sake, Nell. Yes. It will come off."

Nellie waited while Kate peeled off the backing and dusted her shoulder with baby powder before hurrying to the bathroom mirror to see the tattoo her friend had put on her shoulder. Nellie supposed it was tasteful as far as tattoos went—a small red heart with a crack creeping from the bottom. A blue tear leaked from the crack. It looked odd upon her shoulder.

"A heart?" Nellie called back at Kate.

"Not a heart. A heartbreaker. That's what you are."

"Okay. Enough drama. Let's roll." Kate's friend Trish sauntered into the room. The Clark County assistant district attorney was followed by Billie Nader, a local artist. "I need a beer and some music."

Kate handed Nellie a hotel key card. "Just in case you hook up with someone tonight."

Nellie shoved it into her pocket. "Don't worry. I'm not that kind of girl."

Billie tossed Nellie a know-it-all smile. "Honey, everyone's that type of girl."

"Nellie's not, but maybe Elle is," Nellie laughed as they headed toward the elevators. Even as she said the words she didn't believe herself. Elle might be her alter ego, but she wasn't stupid. One-night stands were for true cosmopolitan girls of the world, not small-town librarians who had the town square named after their great-grandfather. Nellie couldn't risk being so irresponsible even as the sultry Elle Hughes.

Or…could she?

Rule number one for Kate's girlfriend getaways was "Be whoever you want to be." Assume a name, an identity, or a whole new life. It was part of the game. Part of escaping the mundane of one's normal life and embracing the freedom of being a hot, single girl in the most sinful city in the world.

Nellie caught a glimpse of herself in the mirrored elevators just before she stepped inside.

Damn, but after her makeover she looked the part. Could she forget everything she'd ever been taught so she could play the part too?

THE MUSIC THROBBED, heavy and sensual in the dimness of the club. Blue lights swirled over the bodies packed within every square inch of Agave Blue. As far as Nellie could tell it lived up to the image of hottest club in Vegas. Mirrors blanketed the deep blue walls and refracted the spinning light, throwing it on the sophisticated crowd.

Perspiration trickling down her back, Nellie moved with the crowd toward the promise of a cool cocktail. She was out of breath and needed a break. She hadn't danced to "Vanilla Ice" since the eighth grade Halloween dance when she was decked out in a pumpkin costume. Tonight she was far from a plump pumpkin. More like Cinderella. No, screw that, she looked like a wicked stepsister.

Nellie twisted her hand from the grasp of her dance partner as she finally spied Kate. She stood next to the bar talking to a cute guy in a tight tee, hands fluttering against his chest, teasing him as she flashed him her trademark come-hither smile.

"Let's go dance some more," toothy, twenty-something hottie said.

"No, thanks. I see a friend." Nellie gave him a little apologetic shrug. He looked crushed, but brightened as a petite redhead crooked her finger at him, urging him to join her on the dance floor as a song by Akon cranked up.

Nellie skirted a grouping of chairs occupied by several trendy, martini-wielding club goers. Suddenly an arm snaked around her, tipping her into the lap of a tanned Pro-Am golfer. Mitch had introduced her to the mojito and taught her how to do the old-school, but always fun, electric slide a mere hour ago.

"Come 'ere, sexy lady," he slurred. "Tell Jace here that I got the moves."

She laughed, removing the overly friendly Mitch's wandering hands from her waist as she stood. She gave him a sassy smile. "Well, yeah, if your moves consist of trying to grab my ass every time I get within a foot of you."

The others laughed and she walked off wondering who in the world she had become.

Oh, yeah. Elle Hughes. And Elle tossed back fruity little cocktails, danced with unbelievably hot guys, and flirted with cute golf pros. Being her alter ego felt weird. As if she was totally someone else. She waded through the throngs of people, knowing the men she passed raked her slim form from head to high heels. And it didn't matter whether the guys were barely legal or fighting a receding hairline, they all looked.

Embarrassing, yes, but powerful all the same. She could see why some women fed off it.

Kate dangled a frosted martini glass in her direction, handing it off without taking her eyes away from the piece of eye candy murmuring low in her ear.

Nellie didn't really want to be introduced, so she swung her hips to the rhythm of the music and sipped the sweet concoction. The rum slid smoothly down her throat and uncoiled in the pit of her stomach. Dangerous. She took a bigger sip and licked the sugar off the rim of the glass.

Her sensual move caught the attention of the man flirting with Kate. His cool gray eyes undressed her, assessing her with practiced ease. The guy was a pro. Kate picked up his obvious interest in her friend, so Nellie smiled, lifted her glass in salute and headed to find Billie and Trish, who had table service somewhere in the crush. Maybe she could take a break with them for a minute. Her feet were starting to hurt.

But the place was packed, the music booming, and the dizzying lights had her turned around. She couldn't remember where Trish said they'd be sitting. She stood for a minute, searching the throbbing crowd, but she had no luck. Her eyes lighted on a lone bar stool at the end of the packed bar. It had her name written all over it, or so her toes shouted. She needed reprieve from the torturous high-heeled sandals, so she headed for the stool and sank onto it with a sigh.

Her toes thanked her.

And no one took notice of her, which was good, because she didn't want to fight off any random guys or feel obligated to smile and laugh. She just needed a break from the "fun." It had been years since she'd gone out to clubs, and doing it two nights in a row had her missing the comfy couch in her living room and reruns of *Seinfeld.*

But that was stupid. She'd come to Vegas to party. To live it up a little.

Still, she missed home.

And she hoped Mr. McIvy remembered to feed her cat.

JACK DARBY HAD BEEN WATCHING the blonde for the past hour from his office behind the two-story DJ booth.

He'd first seen her on his way to give Rick Newhouse, his weeknight manager, the keys to the safe. He'd tried to catch her eye, but she was busy pulling some guy's hands off her ass. He watched her, amused and somewhat irritated by the behavior of the too-tan dude in tight clothes. And he knew immediately the woman did not belong in a meat market nightclub, no matter how much she tried to pretend she did.

He'd sneaked another look at her as she gyrated on the dance floor, watching the lights catch her, enjoying the expression on her face. He'd been intrigued. Mesmerized. Like a child watching a kaleidoscope, the pretty colors drawing him in. But he'd moved on, back to the confines of his office. This was his place of business and his policy was never to date at work.

But he couldn't seem to help himself. Was it the way she moved, unsure and wobbly in her high-heeled sandals? Or maybe just the way she seemed surprised at the attention paid to her by every male she walked past?

"Hey, Jack. Didn't know you were up here," Rick said, entering the office and pulling him from the distraction of the sexy woman moving her hips to the beat of the music. "The margarita machine's down again."

Jack didn't have to turn around. Rick had slipped in for a smoke. Jack suspected his manager had been ducking into the office bathroom and blowing his smoke into the vent rather than taking it outside to the smoking patio. "Did you call Vinnie?"

"Yeah, but it's the second time this week. Still freezin' up even though he said he fixed it. Want me to call him again?"

Irritation burned in Jack's gut. He turned toward Rick. "What do you think? You're the mana—"

"Whoa, dude. Just askin'." Rick shoved the pack of cigarettes into his back pocket and lifted his hands defensively.

"Sorry, I'm just…I've got things on my mind," Jack said, setting the half-filled beer he held onto the desk. Normally, he dropped everything for a problem at the club. But tonight, he just didn't want to deal with the place that had brought him Vegas-style fame and fortune.

Which was so unlike him.

Maybe it was the way his gut churned like a stormy sea. Or the thought of another sleepless night. Or the way he felt so out of control, as if he'd screwed up by agreeing to sell the club and build a dream with his father. Tonight, he wanted to be anywhere but where he stood. "I'll call Vinnie in the morning."

Rick saluted and spun back toward the door that led to the loft-style VIP rooms situated above the frenzied dance floor.

Jack felt guilty. He should be taking care of business and not wallowing in his beer, watching some woman like a pervert. "Hell, I'll just go take a look at it. Maybe I can figure something out."

He headed down the stairs, sliding past an overweight guy reeking of ten-dollar cologne. The lummox stepped on his foot, causing a bolt of pain to zip up his leg. The man shouted "sorry partner" before lumbering up the stairs balancing four longnecks. Jack grimaced and jogged down to the bottom floor, sidestepping lithe ladies and overeager dudes looking for action. The music sounded louder than normal. Lady Gaga was getting on his nerves. They were playing her way too much.

Jack blew out an exasperated breath. He needed to get out of Agave. Fast. It felt as if the walls were closing in on him.

He made his way to the bar and slid behind the massive neon-lined counter. The frozen drink machines sat like boulders anchoring the ends of the bar. A pitcher of half-melted drink mixture sat to the side, an accident waiting to happen.

"Hey, Jack, the marguerita machine's down again," Lewis hollered, popping the lids on three beers before handing them to a guy in a cowboy hat. Quarters hit the tip bottle. Lewis lined up eight shot glasses and started pouring. The club was almost too busy tonight.

"I know. I'm gonna take a look," Jack yelled, opening a cabinet under the machines and searching for a screwdriver. He knew the action would probably be fruitless. The bartenders never put anything back where it was supposed to go.

He lifted his head to ask Lewis where the screwdriver might possibly be and his eyes landed on the blonde.

She sat directly above him at the end of the bar. Alone. And she seemed to be making some kind of mental list because her eyes were fixed on a bottle of Wild Turkey and her lips silently moved.

A half-finished drink sat in front of her.

He shut the cabinet door and moved towards her. She didn't look at him. Just kept moving her lips.

"Get you another drink?" he said, bending toward her so she could hear him over the noise of the music.

She couldn't. Her green eyes didn't even blink.

He leaned in a bit farther and shouted, "Get you another drink?"

The blonde jumped half a foot off the bar stool and clipped the handle of the pitcher sitting just to his left.

Melted margueritas flew into the air, slopping onto the bar and splashing onto the woman. Her luscious lips fell open and the cleavage spilling out of her bustier jiggled as she leaped upright—an action he couldn't help but appreciate even though he knew he shouldn't.

"Ack!" she cried, shoving her stool back into a group of people.

He righted the pitcher and grabbed a white bar towel from the stack sitting beside the register. "Here!"

He tossed the towel to her, but she missed. Instead it landed on the head of a skinny, bald guy before sliding immediately to the floor.

"Sorry," Jack said to the guy, then widened his gaze to take in the blonde, who was shaking droplets from her bare arms.

The bald guy gave him a "go to hell" look and turned his back, reentering the conversation in which he'd previously been engaged. The man didn't bother to pick up the towel.

"Oops," the blonde said, and then started laughing.

Her green eyes met his and he swore his world tilted just a bit. And then an incredible thing happened. For the first time in weeks, Jack laughed.

CHAPTER THREE

If a stranger tries to get you into his car, scream and run away. He may try to bribe you with candy. But don't you ever get in the car with a strange man. Ever.

—Grandmother Tucker to Nellie after watching *America's Most Wanted.*

NELLIE CHOKED on her laughter when she realized just who had spilled the pitcher of margaritas on her.

Jack Darby.

The irony of the situation didn't escape her.

But from where she was standing, he had no clue she was the person who'd recently baptized him with her chardonnay. And why should he? She looked way different.

She stooped to pick up the towel just as he slid around the bar and pushed through the crowd surrounding her.

"Here, let me help you," he shouted, his mouth so close to her ear she could feel the heat of his breath on her bare neck. Her senses sprang to life just as they had at the airport bar. Something about this man made her knees feel like Jell-O and her belly jump as if it were full of frogs.

"No, no, I'm fine—it barely splashed on me," she called out over the music, dragging the towel along her arm and shoulder, wiping away the remainder of the liquid.

He grasped her elbow, sending a frisson of heat up her arm, and helped her to stand. He shouted some words at her. Something that sounded like "I'm sorry" and then he kept talking, but the music was so loud she couldn't understand what he was saying.

"What?" she shouted.

He shook his head and leaned closer. To do so, he placed one hand on her hip and tugged her to him. Leaning close, he spoke in her ear. "I'm sorry. I was trying to buy you a drink."

The heat of his hand seared the flesh that peeked out from between the bustier and low-slung jeans. She flinched, but he didn't seem to notice.

She inhaled his scent. He smelled faintly like beer, but there was another scent, so masculine and tempting she longed to bury her nose in his trendy blue shirt.

She lifted up on her tiptoes and shouted into his ear, "It's fine. Don't worry about it."

"Do you want another drink?"

Nellie shook her head. "No, I'm done."

He pulled back and studied her.

For a moment, she wished she hadn't come to Vegas. Because standing there talking to this guy was just a fantasy. He was so out of her league. The way he looked at her, with desire radiating from the depths of his blue eyes, was only because she was trussed up like some bimbo Barbie doll. His sudden interest didn't come from a feeling that could ever be real. It was all pretense, a mirage in the desert sand.

She watched as his eyes moved from hers to her mouth and then dropping lower. Suddenly he looked hungry and it made her stomach feel prickly. He leaned closer and whispered against the sensitive shell of her ear.

"Wanna get out of here?"

She caught her breath.

Did that mean what she thought it meant?

Sex?

She shook her head.

He pulled her to him again. "No. Just outside."

Just outside? A flare of anticipation died within her. For some reason the thought of him wanting to take her home had excited her. But that was stupid because she was not that kind of girl. No matter what Kate said.

But she needed a breath of fresh air and she couldn't keep shouting at him. She looked over her shoulder for Kate, but her friend was nowhere to be found. She'd likely gone off with the guy she'd been accidentally brushing against all night.

Jack took the towel from her, tossed it onto the bar and gave her a wolfish smile. She felt his sexy grin right down to her French manicured toes. Her heart leaped in her chest.

Whoa, easy girl, her mind said, though her body tightened in response.

She nodded to Jack. He grabbed her hand and headed toward the entrance of the club while she tried to wrap her mind around the fact that sex with the nightclub owner had automatically popped into her head. Was she insane? Why would she jump to that conclusion? Sex might not even be on his mind. But he was a guy…sex was always on men's minds, wasn't it? So many questions rambled around in her head. She decided to stop thinking and focus on the backside of the man tugging her toward the stainless-steel doors. And his backside was a rather nice view.

Before she could blink or change her mind, they reached the lobby foyer and tumbled into the night.

The hot night air sucked the breath from Nellie's body, not to mention that as soon as the doors closed behind them, Jack spun her into a kiss.

At the touch of his lips on hers, Nellie forgot to breathe. In fact, she forgot who she really was and who she was supposed to be.

All that existed was the man wrapping his arms around her. There was nothing tentative in his kiss. It was demanding, passionate, and all things Nellie had ever dreamed of in a kiss.

He threaded one hand in her hair and tugged her head back, allowing him to deepen the kiss. His tongue stroked her bottom lip just once before he broke the kiss.

He pulled back and stared down at her, his sapphire eyes a mixture of passion and perplexity. He blinked and gave her a lopsided smile. "Sorry, I couldn't help myself."

Nellie looked up at him and croaked, "That's okay."

He released her and stepped back, nearly clipping the loafer of a fat guy in a Hawaiian shirt pulling on the hand of a frizzy-haired woman.

"Watch it," the man said.

Jack didn't say anything. Just stared at her. "I will."

The street on which they stood was not dark. Not in Vegas. The whole strip lit the night like a department store Christmas tree. Festivity permeated the air. The sidewalks were busy, papered with flyers and discarded cigarettes. Shouts of laughter came from the people lined up behind the red velvet rope to the left of them.

Jack ignored them. Instead his focus was on Nellie. "My name's Jack. Jack Darby."

Nellie started to extend her hand, but that felt wrong. They'd just lip-locked in front of all of Vegas. She shoved her hand into her back pocket. "Uh, my name's Elle." God, the bogus name felt awkward on her tongue. Elle. What an impostor.

He curled his arm around her, his fingers briefly dipping into the waist of her jeans, stroking her bare hip and causing her stomach to contract as he murmured low in her ear, "Nice to meet you, Elle."

Nellie swallowed hard. This guy was a professional, just like the one Kate had been with. And as much as the idea of a random hookup appealed to a part of her, she really had no business playing with the fire that was Jack Darby. Plus, the man had ignored her the last time they'd seen each other. He was shallow. Not worthy of the black lace thong she wore.

"Uh, maybe I should go back. I'm with friends and I'm not the kind…" She snapped her mouth shut. What was she saying? Wasn't this what she wanted when those snippy cheerleaders made fun of her in the library study room? To be different? To open herself up to possibilities? The man with his arm curled around her had to be all the things she'd never experienced, even if he was as shallow as certain gene pools.

So why not?

Carpe diem, right?

"Let me call my friend and tell her I'm with you." Nellie swallowed again. Mostly because she'd just issued an invitation. Or thought she had. She slid the slim cell phone from the pocket of her jeans. The message screen popped up on her phone. Kate had already texted she would catch up with her at the hotel.

"Get your friend?"

"What? Oh, yeah. I'm gonna meet her later, I guess."

He smiled. "Much later."

Nellie swallowed, hesitation rearing its head at his comment. Why was she going off with some guy just because his kiss turned her to pudding? She knew nothing about him.

Well, okay, she knew a lot of stuff from the magazine article. He had a couple of sisters, had gone to USC on a baseball scholarship, and had worked his way up from busboy to owner of three separate multimillion-dollar nightclubs. He had an MBA, a dog named Dutch, one house in Malibu and another in Vegas. He was thirty-two, single and loved taking his nephew to Cardinal games.

So he wasn't a garden-variety serial killer. She should ignore "Nellie" and instead listen to "Elle."

Shouldn't she?

"So now we've been introduced, what should we do?" he asked, his fingers still aimlessly stroking the bare flesh between the tight bustier and her jeans. His touch was seriously driving her crazy, making heat flare in strange regions of her body.

What did she want to do? Was it a trick question?

"Um, I don't know. I'm not from here. Well, I assumed we were going to…your place?"

His eyes widened. "Really?"

Nellie could feel her cheeks redden. Shit. He didn't want sex. She felt as dumb as a cow. "Oh, I meant…I'm sorry, it's just you kissed me and…I assumed you wanted…"

Jack smiled at her loss of words. "Well, I can't lie. I've been thinking about getting you naked all night." He paused, as if he wasn't sure himself. "But, as much as I want to introduce you to my new sheets, I assumed you wouldn't be up for that."

Nellie didn't know what to say. Had he sensed her inner struggle? "I…"

His eyes found hers. They looked almost tender in the glittering city lights. "I like the thought of getting to know you, Elle."

"Seriously?" Jack Darby, the consummate Vegas playboy, didn't want sex? He wanted to get to know her better?

Jack shrugged. "Don't you ever want to do things a little different?"

Different? She almost laughed. If only he really knew how different she was being. Or maybe he did. "Okay. So what do you want to do? Go to the casino? Grab a drink?"

A funny light appeared in Jack's eyes. "I've got the perfect place." He looked over at a valet lolling at his stand. "Hey, Sammy, get my car."

"You got it, Jack," the valet said, hurrying into the fluorescent-lit garage to their left.

Before Nellie could blink, the red car from the magazine spread appeared in front of them. She had no idea what kind of car it was, but it looked sexy and fast. Kind of like the man beside her.

The valet hopped out, leaving the car roaring. Jack handed him a crisp bill and pulled open the low-slung door for her. She slid into the leather interior, noting the car humming beneath her, a sensual reminder of the power of the man sliding behind the wheel. Before she could blink, they pulled away from the curb and onto the busy Vegas strip.

She sneaked a glance at Jack Darby. He had one hand draped over the steering wheel, his dark hair ruffled by the breeze. He looked like a movie star, had that sort of luminous quality that made her long to reach out and touch him, just get close to him. She shivered despite the warm air blowing through the open windows.

Even though she thought she knew the kind of man Jack

Darby was, she realized she'd just done something her grandmother had told her to never do.

She'd just gotten into a car with a strange man.

ALL JACK DARBY COULD think about was why he'd turned down sex with the lady sitting next to him.

What in the hell was he doing?

Okay, obviously she was hot. But his fascination with her wasn't because she looked drop-dead gorgeous in some black halter top thing and tight jeans. It was something altogether different, something he couldn't quite put his finger on.

Maybe she simply reminded him of the girls he'd known back home. Wholesome, pure, with an audacious side begging to get out. Still, it didn't explain why she sat next to him, her face conflicted, her hair brushing the tops of her delectable shoulders.

His mind drifted to her lips pressed against his. She'd tasted like heaven—minty mojito and honey. Just brushing his tongue over her lower lip had ignited something more than a flame of passion.

And that shook him. He hadn't felt this way since… well, it had been a long time.

And he hadn't taken her up on her halfhearted proposition to go back to his place?

That decision was not like him.

But her suggestion *had* been halfhearted. Elle didn't seem like the kind of girl who went home with random guys. He'd bet her temporary tattoo on that.

The gearstick vibrated in his hand as he shifted gears. Her gaze skittered to his. And then darted quickly away.

Jack couldn't stop the twitch of his lips. "We're almost there, Elle."

"Almost where?"

He chuckled at the squeak in her voice. "Look, I'm not a psycho. I'm not taking you to some hidden lair to torture you till you scream. Okay?"

Elle bit her lip and stared out at the dry cleaners and nail salons they were zipping past. "I know. Sorry I'm acting so weird." She fell silent for a moment. "But I wanted to be…" Her words fell off and she bit her bottom lip again. Her cheeks pinked and shadows crossed her eyes.

Something told him not to push it. And he always trusted his gut instinct.

"You like pancakes?"

Elle made a funny face. "Pancakes?"

"Yeah, I'm in the mood for pancakes."

A wrinkle furrowed her smooth forehead. "This is seriously getting weird."

CHAPTER FOUR

Pancakes will make you fat. But let's have some anyway.

—Grandmother Tucker to a plump thirteen-year-old Nellie right after Thomas Wynn broke up with her.

"WHAT'S THIS PLACE? A gas station?" Nellie asked as they pulled up to the well-lit center.

"It's the best place in world to get a two-a.m. meal," Jack said, putting the car into Park and shutting off the ignition. "I'd seriously cook you breakfast, but I don't think I can be alone with you right now and still uphold my promise of not whisking you to my lair and making you scream."

Nellie giggled. She couldn't help it. She sat in a fire-red sports car at 2:12 a.m. with one of the hottest guys in Nevada…and instead of having no-strings-attached sex, they were about to eat pancakes. It was absurd.

Of course the only thing nuttier was if she'd actually gone to Jack's house, stripped off her clothes, jumped into the center of his bed and screamed, "Take me now, you big strong stud!"

Maybe eating pancakes wasn't crazy. Maybe she was. Because she knew if she'd pressed it, she could be having indulgent sex with the man sitting next to her. What kind of woman passed up an opportunity with a man like Jack?

But she already knew the answer. One who knew how to knit, how to grow the biggest tomatoes in Howard County, and how to make a toddler stop crying over the wrong sucker flavor during story time.

He turned to her and smiled, reinforcing the thought she was the nutso. His smile was warm butter. She felt it to her toes. "The parking lot isn't full for nothing. Be prepared to eat the best pancakes in the whole U.S. of A."

Nellie opened the door before Jack could get around and do it for her. "Okay, I'm prepared, but I'm not dressed to eat too much. I'd need my stretchy pants for that."

His eyes swept over her, stoking the embers that still burned within her. "Don't remind me how great you look in those tight-assed jeans."

Nellie wagged her finger. "You wanted a change of scenery."

"I like the scenery fine. Now hurry up and get inside before I change my mind and introduce you to those sheets."

Nellie scurried around to meet him. He latched his hand on to hers and suddenly, for the first time that night, she felt she was on a date. Her ardor cooled; her heart squeezed. Bad sign.

When they entered the small restaurant, smells assaulted them—bacon sizzling, coffee brewed and warm vanilla pancakes waiting on the warmer. Her stomach growled and she realized the few chips she'd munched on before she'd downed the martinis had long since vanished.

A straw-haired waitress waved them toward an empty booth near the back of the place. Other couples huddled over laminate tables, a few college kids cracked jokes and a businessman in a suit tapped at a laptop.

"Diverse," she commented as she slid onto the cushioned bench. The waitress wiped the table, slapped a couple of menus down and winked at Jack before sauntering away.

"Yeah, I love this place. Big Earl runs it. He ran a café in one of the casinos, but the economy forced him to close. His brother-in-law owns this gas station and they dreamed this up. It's doing well."

Nellie looked around. "I can see that. I like the nostalgia."

Framed records from long-ago artists dotted the walls along with neon signs declaring, Eat at Joe's or Dine-in Here. It reminded her of the local diner in her hometown where she sometimes sipped old-fashioned malts and savored grilled patty melts.

"Me, too," he said and picked up the menu. "So what do you want? The waffles are good, the biscuits and gravy are good, but personally I'd recommend the pancakes."

"I'll have what you're having," she said, not even bothering with the menu. She wasn't picky and felt she could eat a moose.

He lifted his eyebrows. "Is this a pancake challenge?"

Nellie nodded. "Bring it on."

"Stop talking dirty," he said. His blue eyes radiated mischief. Her heart pinged again. And that was even more troublesome than her libido. But, really, it had to be because she hadn't been on a date in forever. Who fell in love at a gas station diner over pancakes with a guy she'd just picked up at a club?

Okay. Plenty of people. But she wasn't going to think about it.

"Bring. It. On." She flashed her own naughty smile as she repeated herself.

"You are a bad girl, Elle." Jack waved the waitress over and she jotted down the colossal order. Nellie gulped. She admitted to being hungry, but who could eat four pancakes with sausage? "Still want to take me on?"

His words sounded innocent, but they were tinged with hidden meaning. Did she still want to take him on? Yeah, she did. But did that mean him? Or just the pancakes?

"Bring. It—"

"I got it the second time," he laughed, tearing the paper ring from the napkin-wrapped silverware. "And I'm glad you're up for a challenge. I like challenges."

She couldn't read his eyes this time. No glint of devilment. No gentle teasing.

She studied him in the bright fluorescent light. At two-thirty in the morning, he should look tired. But he didn't. His skin only showed faint smile lines around his brilliant blue eyes. His hair looked rumpled, and his mouth made her feel tingly just looking at it.

She searched about for something to say that was clever or profound, but she was saved by Ruby, the aptly named waitress who plopped a huge plate in front of her and smirked, "You won't be fittin' in those jeans if you eat all that, missy."

Nellie tossed the sassy waitress a smile. The woman looked about seventy, but she likely wasn't past sixty. Cigarettes, big-bellied truckers and unpaid bills hadn't done Ruby any favors. Nellie forgave her the attitude. "Oh, don't be so sure. I do love a challenge."

"I like a gal with fire," she cackled, reminding Nellie of the witches chanting around the cauldron in *Macbeth*.

Ruby gave Jack a lighthearted punch on the shoulder before heading back toward the register. "Be careful with this one, Jack."

Nellie picked up her fork. "You know her?"

He shrugged and then focused all his attention on the buttery, syrupy stack in front of him. "I come here a lot."

And then it was on. But not in the way she had expected when they had pulled away from Agave less than an hour ago.

It was good. It was sweet. And there were several moans of pleasure. And when it was over, both Nellie and Jack sank back, exhausted. And very, very full.

"Oh, my Lord, I think I'm gonna throw up," Nellie groaned.

"That would be so attractive," Jack said, patting a stomach that actually looked distended beneath his fitted shirt.

"Shut it," Nellie said, unbuttoning her jeans.

Jack laughed. "You really don't like to lose, do you?"

She smiled. "Figured that out, did you?"

He looked down at her plate. It looked as though it had been licked clean. She stared down at it too.

"Lady, I don't think I've ever said anything like this before, but you eat like a man. I gotta say I'm impressed."

"Well, it's nice to know my appetite impresses."

He grinned. "More than your appetite impresses me. I could give you a list."

Nellie tried to stop the blush. She so wanted to be flirty, experienced, accustomed to men giving her backhand compliments. But she wasn't. So she changed the subject. "So, you want to tell me about yourself?"

He sat up a bit. "Oh, serious now, are you?"

She shrugged.

"I like crossword puzzles, the smell of cut grass and fuzzy kittens. Your turn."

Nellie giggled. "I like blackberries, Hugh Grant movies, and the color of sweet gum trees in the fall."

"Hugh Grant?" He lifted a brow.

"The accent," she said, shrugging. Her explanation launched into a discussion of their favorite movies.

Finally, after arguing whether *Lord of the Rings* or *Star Wars* was the best trilogy, Jack buttoned his jeans. "Okay, I think I can move now."

Nellie laughed and refastened hers too. "Honestly, I've never eaten like that before. And never on a date. I'm appalled at myself."

"I'm appalled for you," he teased, taking the check from Ruby as she sashayed by their table.

The waitress stopped midstride, backed up and cast an eye on Nellie's plate. "You better marry this one."

And then she was gone.

Nellie wanted to laugh off the remark, but she felt awkward. Ruby's comment was meant to be playful, but it was a mood killer. Even Jack had little to say about that zinger.

"We'd better get going. It's already after three, and I have to work in the morning."

"Sure." Nellie smiled, hoping her one date with the handsome club owner wouldn't end on a sour note. She didn't think that kind of goodbye would sit well with her tummy or her ego.

Out of habit, she looked around for her purse before realizing she had left it in the hotel room. She still had a twenty in her pocket. Her grandmother had raised her to let the gentleman pay on a date, but she wasn't in Oak

Stand now and she wasn't Nellie. Elle would likely insist on paying her own way.

"Ready?" Jack asked as he peeled off several bills and tossed them on the table.

"Thanks for buying breakfast. I would have been glad to—"

Jack pressed his finger to her lips. "My treat."

He pulled his finger away and smiled, holding out his hand to indicate she should rise and head to the swinging door. Nellie scooted from the bench and rose, her nose nearly brushing his chin.

"You've got syrup on your neck," he said, eyeing an area above her collarbone.

"I do? Where?"

Jack grabbed her hand. "Leave it. I'll take care of it in the car."

"But I can just go to the ladies' room and wash it off. I don't want to get it on your car seats." Nellie tried to turn toward the door in the back marked "Dames," but Jack tugged her toward the entrance.

"I'll take care of it. Trust me. I'm looking forward to it."

Then he threw her the same wolfish look he'd given her earlier as he'd tugged her from the bar into the Vegas night. It was the same look that had curled her toes and made her heart beat faster. She liked that look.

"Ever make out in a GT-R?" he said, pulling out his keys and pressing the unlock button. The car perked up, illuminating the lonely parking spot.

Nellie giggled. "Nope."

"Let's give it a whirl."

CHAPTER FIVE

Root hog or die.

—Grandmother Tucker to Nellie when she asked how she would get a prom date.

"NELL, YOU'VE GOT TO stop with the 'I shouldn't have given him my info' stuff. It's ridiculous." Kate shoved another blouse into Nellie's hand.

"Why?" Nellie asked, squinting critically at the sheer top and putting it back on the rack.

"Because you want to see him again. You've got the biggest guilt complex of anyone I know. Your grandmother did a real number on you." Kate pulled the blouse from the rack and pushed it at her insistently. "Here. Try this on."

"No. Too revealing." Nellie shoved the blouse back with its other too-revealing friends. The boutique was full of outlandish snips of clothing that barely covered all the right parts. "And don't bring my Grandmother Tucker into this. I know I'm what she made me. I can't change who I am."

"Bullshit." Kate turned on her. "You hide beneath that small-town Tucker girl shield like she taught you. I know the real you, Nellie. I grew up with you. The real Nellie would wear this shirt without a bra."

"Yeah, right," Nellie snorted. "I've grown up, Kate."

"I know. It shows." Kate nudged her hand with the hanger. "You need some excitement in your life. Some sexiness. Something more than baking blueberry muffins for the Ladies Auxiliary's fashion brunch. I think you found that last night, right?"

True, Nellie thought, finally taking the wispy shirt from Kate's outstretched hand. It *was* a nice shade of cranberry. With a similarly colored camisole underneath, it would probably complement her golden-streaked hair nicely. She turned her attention back to Kate, who was jerking hangers across the rack with unfettered frustration. Nellie noted her friend's expression—resolute determination, absolute annoyance. Not a good combination. Kate furrowed her raven eyebrows beneath her spiky cobalt-streaked hair and pulled out a clingy yellow shirt. She held it up in front of Nellie, shook her head and returned it to the rack.

"You do know me better than anyone, Kate." She and Kate had bought their first bras together, smoked their first cigarettes together and taken their first college exam together. "That being said, you know I cannot help who I am."

"Wrong. I know you can." Kate shoved her toward the dressing room, sweeping a huge assortment of clothing over her arm and following behind.

Nellie plodded into the dressing room, wishing they had stayed out on the main floor of the chic boutique. In the privacy of the fitting room, Kate would unleash on her. And Nellie didn't want to hear about what a total dud she was. How boring she was. How dowdy she'd become while existing in Oak Stand. How predictable…blah, blah, blah. She knew who she was. And she liked who she was. Well, most of the time.

"Look, Kate. I like my life. Sure, sometimes it bores me.

Sometimes I need to feel different—that's why I came to Vegas for your glam weekend. But I am not you. When I wake up after a night out, I sometimes have regrets."

Kate flounced toward the chair in the corner of the posh dressing room and plopped down with a flourish. "Okay, listen, Nellie. I get you. I know you were raised to be ashamed of every passionate impulse you have. But I know who you are under all those layers your grandmother wrapped around you. I know the girl who snuck out for the Pearl Jam concert is still in there somewhere."

Nellie rolled her eyes. "That was you who snuck out. I stayed home and did my math homework, remember?"

"I thought you came with us?"

"No," Nellie said, shrugging out of her T-shirt and hanging it on the hook.

"Oh, my God! Is that a hickey?"

Nellie's color went past red and stopped at purple. She shot her friend a murderous do-not-go-there look.

Kate merely smiled. "*Nice!*"

Nellie chose to ignore Kate's comment. She had been shocked enough to find the small passion mark on her neck that morning in the hotel mirror. Jack had done an amazing job of getting the syrup off her neck.

Kate tucked the gloating smile away and continued on her original mission. "I remember the first time I saw you, Nellie. Mostly 'cause I really liked how I could see my reflection in your shoes. You had your hair pulled back, a smocked dress with lacy socks and shiny patent leather shoes. You said 'yes, ma'am' and 'please' and 'thank you,' and that was it. You were like a doll all dressed up. I tried to pinch you to see if you were real."

"I distinctly remember," Nellie said, glancing at her

friend in the mirror as she shimmied out of the capris she wore. Kate looked as if she was just getting started.

"And when you got dirty, remember how upset you would get? You knew what your grandmother expected. You knew from day one you were a Tucker and that meant something in Oak Stand. You were different."

Nellie sighed as she pulled on a silky sleeveless sweater dress in a tawny gold. It felt like the touch of a butterfly's wings. She would definitely purchase it. She caught the price from the dangling tag in the reflection of the mirror. Maybe not.

"Nellie, she made you think you had to be a certain way. That's probably why you're a stodgy librarian. She picked the job out for you. It's genteel. Acceptable."

Nellie held up one finger. "Now, stop right there. *I* chose to be a librarian. And it's not stodgy. Being a librarian today is different than it was twenty years ago. We don't even call ourselves librarians. I am an archive specialist."

Kate rolled her eyes. "I know. They have computers and little scanner thingies."

"Yeah, little scanner thingies. That's the absolute correct term." Nellie grimaced. "Look, I love my job, Kate. That has nothing to do with being a Tucker or with my grandmother's expectations about what I was supposed to do with my life. It has to do with me being realistic."

"Whatever, but still—"

"Grandmother Tucker had her good points." Nellie didn't want to endure another tirade about her grandmother. "She raised me the way she was raised. She didn't know any other way."

"But that doesn't mean you have to continue on that path. That very narrow path."

"Most of the time I like that path, Kate," Nellie said, stepping into a pair of raw silk pants that complemented the sweater. They looked magnificent on her. She glanced at the price tag. $380.00! No way. For pants?

"See." Kate motioned to the price tag with disgust. "Just what I'm talking about. You have a buttload of money and won't spend it. Your grandmother had millions and still saved aluminum foil for a second use."

Nellie tossed Kate her own look of disgust. "Money is not the issue. Why would anyone pay over three hundred dollars for a pair of pants?"

"Because they make your ass look great," Kate said.

Nellie rolled her eyes, but still spun around to check out her derriere. Sure enough, her butt did look great. Maybe a splurge? Surely a girl was justified when the pants made her look so tiny, so curvy and so splendid all at the same time?

"Nell, you have a ton of money and insist on living like a pauper."

"I don't live like a pauper. I just know the value of money."

"Sensible," Kate drawled, as though it was the worst word ever invented.

"Exactly." Nellie smiled.

"Is that what you were last night, Nellie 'I'm such a good girl' Hughes?" Kate pointed to her own neck—the same area where Nellie had her hickey.

Damn, Nellie thought. Why did Kate have to be so perceptive? "I was a good girl."

"Yeah, right," Kate snorted, separating the clothes she liked from the ones she wouldn't be caught dead in.

Jack Darby. Nellie sighed. She loved his magnetic blue eyes and the slight cleft in his chin. Oh, and the way he sipped black coffee and teased her about her empty plate.

If only Kate knew her "good girl gone bad" had actually remained good. Well, for the most part anyway.

"I shouldn't have gone with him," Nellie muttered, jerking a turtleneck over her head and tossing it on the settee. "It was totally irresponsible. A safety issue."

"Are you kidding me?" Kate ranted. "Seriously? Isn't letting loose what you came here for?"

"I came here for a girls' weekend. Shopping, talking, coffee...." Nellie rolled her hand with each word. Kate frowned and handed her another two-hundred-dollar top.

"That's *not* what this weekend is about. It's about losing yourself, finding your inner party girl, playing around, daring yourself to be something other than what you are."

"So for you that means…what? Doing what you do every weekend?"

"For your information, Miss Smarty-pants, I don't party every weekend." Kate crossed her arms and sank back into the antique chair. Nellie grinned at the contrast. MTV meets Victorian charm school. "What I meant is that this weekend we get the chance to be whoever we want to be. Like a free pass."

"There are no free passes in life." Nellie pulled a pair of low-slung jeans from the clips on the hanger. They were dark indigo with tan stitching. Very trendy. So unlike her. But Nellie tried them on anyway.

"Spoken like a true Tucker." Kate pushed bloodred nails through her spiked hair. "Give yourself a break. You're twenty-nine-years old. Not sixty. You can buy some hot clothes and have a fling with an even hotter guy. I'd kill to be in your shoes right now."

Nellie glanced down at her old ballet flats. She'd had them since the late eighties and had dragged them out when she heard they were back in style. She arched a newly shaped eyebrow at Kate and drawled, "Really?"

"Well, not those." Kate glanced down at the old black flats in horror. "I was speaking metaphorically and I was referring to Jack Darby."

Nellie's heart pinged at his name.

"Oh, is someone blushing?" Kate teased. "Come on, Nell. Tell me what he was like. I gotta know."

Nellie caught sight of her face in the mirror. She matched the cranberry blouse. "I don't kiss and tell."

"Bullshit!" Kate exclaimed. "Remember that fraternity party? I heard all about Skip Jordan."

"That was seven years ago, Kate."

"How big was his—"

"Enough, Kate!" Nellie shrieked, throwing the jeans at her dearest friend. "You are bad."

"I know." Kate smiled, deftly catching the expensive denim. "That's why all the guys like me."

"And for your information, I enjoyed last night."

"I bet you did." Kate gave her a sly smile.

"We didn't have sex."

Kate's eyes bulged. "Why the hell not?"

"Because I wasn't…I don't really know. But we just didn't. Okay?"

She wanted to say she liked Jack, but that sounded so high school. How could she make Kate understand how comfortable she felt with Jack, how natural it felt to ride beside him in his sports car, to sit across from him and cram pancakes in her mouth, to respect the fact he drew a line and didn't cross it. It made her sound lovesick. "He was a gentleman."

Kate slapped a hand to her forehead. "Don't do this, Nell. This isn't about love. It's about sex."

"Love?" Nellie whirled around. "I am not in *love* with Jack Darby. I don't even know him."

"Exactly!" Kate pointed a finger at her. "This is about you being something other than who you normally are. This is about being Elle. This is about having mind-blowing sex and letting go of who you think you are supposed to be."

"Why is everything about sex with you? I *am* letting go. When have I met a guy in a bar and gone off with him?"

"I thought you said you didn't have sex?" Kate cocked her head. Nellie wanted to kick her, but she didn't want to split the too-tight pants she'd just pulled on.

"We didn't!" Nellie yelled.

"But you just said—"

"We. Didn't. Have. Sex." Nellie propped her hands on her hips and stared at Kate as if she'd just brought back a torn library book.

A knock sounded on the dressing room door. Both Kate and Nellie jumped. A saleslady called out, "Is everything all right in there?"

Kate and Nellie's eyes met; they both stifled a giggle.

"No problems," Kate called out, her violet eyes dancing. "Just trying to decide which outfit will get Nellie laid."

Nellie clapped a hand over her mouth and shot Kate a dirty look. Silence met Kate's naughty comment.

Nellie laughed lightly, just in case the saleswoman lingered in the fitting rooms. "You're a nut."

Kate gave her the same smile she'd given Nellie countless times throughout their misadventures. It squeezed Nellie's heart because she loved her wild, crazy and, apparently, nymphomaniac friend.

"Kate, I'm having a good time." Nellie swept a manicured hand down her trim length. "And this is not the old Nellie. For goodness sake, I ran into Jack Darby at the Dallas airport. He barely looked at me, and I spilled a whole damned glass of chardonnay in his lap. You think I don't know what this is?"

Kate looked confused. "Huh?"

"Never mind, it's not important. I get who Jack Darby is. I get who Nellie Hughes is. If I didn't look so good in these damn jeans and if you hadn't made me look like a flippin' Hollywood movie star, he wouldn't even give me the time of day. So, I don't have fantasies of love with this man."

Nellie knew as she made the statement that she was lying through her Crest Whitestrips-whitened teeth. After Jack had dropped her off with a sweet kiss, she'd lain awake reliving their impromptu date. Then when she'd awoken that morning, she'd lolled in the hotel's colossal tub wondering when he would call or if he even would. She felt like a teenager with her first crush.

So? She was a liar. And, so, her heart galloped when she thought about Jack. Big deal. It wasn't going anywhere. She was here for a few more days. She'd given him her number thinking it would be fun seeing him again. Fun to hang out with him, laugh with him, kiss him. He embodied every man she'd ever dreamed up in Oak Stand while lying in her lonely bed in the wee small hours of the morning. Why shouldn't she embrace the opportunity to be with a guy like him? For even a short time?

It would be a weekend romance she'd always remember. After all, what would it hurt? She would deal with any letdown when she got back to Oak Stand. When she went back to being the real Nellie Hughes. For a few more days she would take her friend's advice and play the consummate, sophisticated Texas party girl Elle Hughes.

A knock on the dressing room door interrupted Nellie's mental pep talk. The door opened a crack and in swung a sexy blue strapless dress.

"May I suggest this for procuring his interest? I've been told it inspires 'getting laid.'" The saleslady's twinkling brown eyes appeared over the top of the dress. She swayed the garment back and forth like a Delhi street vendor tempting tourists with his wares.

Nellie laughed while Kate pulled a credit card from Nellie's purse and held it up. "I assume we're gonna need this?"

The saleslady's eyes glossed over. "Oh, yeah."

JACK DARBY TAPPED his pen against the ink blotter on his massive walnut desk and glanced back out the squeaky clean window for the umpteenth time that day. He felt antsy and he couldn't focus on the work he needed to be doing. Elle Hughes kept intruding with her flashing green eyes and generous lips. He couldn't stop thinking about the sweetness of her neck or the way her cold hand had pressed to his as they sprinted to the car like love-struck teenagers.

He rolled her name on his tongue, saying it out loud. "Elle Hughes."

"Huh?"

Jack ripped himself from his vivid daydream of Miss Hughes's lips beneath his own and looked up at his business partner, Dave O'Shea. Dave had just popped his balding head into Jack's office.

"Uh, nothing," Jack muttered, picking up the contracts from his desk, stacking them together and shoving them into a thick file folder. "I can't really get to these today, Dave. I have to talk to Rudy about a few clauses before I sign."

"You gotta problem with 'em, Jack?" Dave's bulldozer frame filled the doorway as he shifted from one motorcycle boot to the other. For a big mountain of a guy, he looked nervous.

"No, no. Just some personal stuff on my plate. Don't worry. We've finally got the numbers right on this. I'll have them complete before next week." Jack hated putting the deal off, but it was important and needed his full attention. At the moment, he couldn't give that. Why, he had no clue, but he was pretty sure it had to do with a certain sassy Texas beauty and her mysterious effect on him, which was crazy. A woman had never caused him to lose focus on a business deal.

The intercom on his desk buzzed and his secretary droned, "Jack, your father's on line one."

Jack shrugged at Dave. "Got to take this."

Dave threw Jack his own shrug and shuffled back out the door. "Let's get going, Jack. I've been patient, dude, but I'm starting to run low on the stuff. Sign the damned papers already."

Jack released a pent-up breath, not really wanting to talk to his father, but grateful for the call so he could get rid of Dave. Selling his business to O'Shea made him feel queasy.

Not because Dave wasn't good. The hulking man had a shrewd business mind lurking beneath his construction worker demeanor. But Trojan Works, Inc. had been Jack's baby since its conception. He would still own stock in the company, but not the majority. And he would no longer run the nightclubs. The idea of not being in the clubs, especially Agave Blue, made him twitchy. A little scared.

Agave was his identity.

Jack jerked the phone to his ear and pressed the blinking button. “Hey, Dad.”

“I just got the new horse, and by God, he is a big son of a bitch!”

Jack smiled at his father’s enthusiasm. “Everything go all right?”

Tom Darby launched into details of the horse’s ride from California, giving Jack no room for any other questions about the stallion they’d just purchased from a top-notch breeder. The mustang, a proven producer of strong broncs, would serve as the stud for their horse-breeding business. Despite the fact that his father was talking about their newest venture, Jack couldn’t stop the visions of Elle from invading his thoughts.

“So what do you think?” His father sounded impatient.

“Huh?” Jack asked, ripping himself away from memories of last night.

“I said, what do you think?” Tom Darby growled, obviously perturbed at his son’s lack of attention.

“About what?” Jack kicked his chair away from the desk and stared out at the world churning beneath him.

“Why the hell weren’t you listening in the first place? This is important, son. I am too old to do this by myself. You said you’d do this with me. I need you, Jack.”

Jack closed his eyes. “I know, Dad. I’m in this thing. Didn’t I just spend three days in Texas scouting out locations? But I have a lot on my mind with this buyout.”

The line grew quiet. Jack could almost hear his father chewing on his thoughts, measuring his words, trying to rein in his excitement over the horse and be a supportive father at the same time. “Understandable, son.”

"Listen, I'll try to get out next weekend to take a look at the stallion. I've been reading a couple of articles on breeding techniques we may want to try. By the way, have you broken the news to Mom?"

The line was silent again.

"Dad?"

"We've discussed it. As much as she wants to see her grandbabies, she can't tolerate the thought of leaving the dairy."

Jack could hear the frustration in his father's voice. Tom had given up his career in the rodeo for the sweet Lila and her family dairy with the promise that one day he could pursue his dream of raising broncs. His mom just hadn't realized her sixty-three-year-old husband would remember the promise or that it would involve moving to Texas, where her husband had been raised and where, ironically, both her daughters lived. Lila could be a mule.

"Don't worry," Tom said. "And your mother'll be looking forward to seeing you. It's been a couple of months and it'll give Lila an excuse to try some of those new recipes she's been downloading off the computer. I can hardly find the keyboard under all these papers she's been printing."

Jack hung up and rubbed his churning gut. God, what had he gotten himself into? Breeding tough-ass rodeo broncs?

Why had he agreed to do this?

He was Jack Darby.

Love-'em-and-leave-'em Jack.

Bright-lights, big-city Jack.

Wonder-boy-of-the-strip Jack.

Not shoveling-horseshit Jack.

Hell, he'd only been to a rodeo once. He spun his chair around and faced the huge window. Cars were crawling down Flamingo Road, little beetles going to battle, streaming toward the setting sun like sacrificial soldiers.

Jack rubbed his hand over his face, allowing a heavy sigh to erupt. He just wasn't himself. Wasn't that devil-may-care playboy with the killer smile and Midas touch. And he hadn't been that man in several months.

It wasn't just that he had agreed to go into partnership with his old man. He could have done that without too much risk and still pacified his father. Jack had the capital; he could have easily been a silent partner. But when his father put all the figures together and asked, "Will you do this with me?" Jack found himself nodding.

The decision still stunned him. Yet, he knew it was the right thing to do. His heart wasn't in running the business anymore. Wasn't fair to the guys who'd bought into the business or to the patrons who'd come to expect superior service and atmosphere from the nightclubs.

And his behavior in the business world wasn't the only thing puzzling him. Just last week he had turned down Greta Palmer, the flavor of the month in starlets, when she had blatantly propositioned him during a celebrity poker game. What man turned down lips like that?

Then to further bewilder himself, he had gone to church last Sunday. To church! Why? He had no idea. He hadn't been to a church since he wore short pants, but he'd been looking for answers to why his life had suddenly become so dissatisfying. And then on the street someone had handed him a flyer. It read Is your life empty?

And it was, so he went.

Frankly, he'd been surprised the whole place hadn't caved in as he walked up the aisle. He sat down, looked up at the cross affixed to the wall, and then got up and left before they could hand him a visitor tag. He felt like a hypocrite, wanting God to give him answers when he'd done nothing worthy to merit them.

Jack was stumped by his own sense of confusion. He felt lost, floating around, unanchored and unfulfilled. Lonely.

Until last night.

Until he met Elle.

Something about her felt right. The way his father said it would when the right girl came along. The way it had been with his parents.

Jack snorted when he thought about his parents and his dad's conviction that love could slam into you like a two-ton truck.

He could still remember scoffing as a teenager when his father first told the tale of falling in love with his mother. The two of them had been sitting in his father's old farm truck, waiting for Miss Kitty, their best milk cow, to deliver her second calf.

"Mark my words, Jackie boy, one day she will come in and, whoosh, it will hit you like a ton of bricks."

"What will hit me?" A fourteen-year-old Jack scowled, peeling the price tag off the side of his root beer bottle.

"*L-O-V-E,* that's what. Just like it was with your mother."

"Aw, Dad, please, this is just lame," Jack moaned, rolling the sticker into a cylindrical sticky projectile. He flicked it out the open window. Crickets chirped in the warm California night air, and Jack wondered why he was stuck in the musty cab of the Ford with his father instead of playing Sega at his best friend's house.

Tom Darby chuckled. "One day you won't find anything lame about girls or about love."

Jack had thought about Christie Jenkins and the way her

wrap shirt pulled against her breasts when she leaned over to slip her calculator into her backpack. Did his dad think he was a dweeb? Or worse? Oblivious to girls? Shit, he'd already been to third base with Courtney Arnold. Or at least he thought it was third base.

"Yep, your mama walked into the co-op, and I about dropped that thirty-pound bag of seed I was loading. She was as pretty as a buttercup. My whole body just kinda froze up. Couldn't decide whether I wanted to run laps around the store or just throw up. But I knew it. Knew it like I knew the sky was blue or the grass was green."

"Well, sometimes the sky is gray, Dad. And grass turns yellow in the winter." Jack knew he was being a smart-ass, but what could he do? His old man was loopy.

His dad just chuckled. "Good point, son. Never said it was a cakewalk. There were hard times, times where the clouds grew mean and the grass got beat down, but it's always been worth it." He rubbed his Levi's-clad thigh and then reached for his thermos of coffee. "I knew Lila was the one for me the first time I saw her. And one day it will happen to you. You'll take one look and that'll be it."

Jack had watched his father take three long gulps of coffee, his strong muscles moving in his massive neck, and wondered if he ever wanted to feel that way. Love? Sounded kinda stupid. Sex, well, that sounded good. Way good. But love? That Romeo-Juliet-till-the-death crap? Stupid.

As a teen, Jack had been convinced love was for the weak, the poets, the guys who couldn't get laid. Even if his old man was one of them.

But at thirty-two, Jack wondered if his old man hadn't been right. Was Elle his blue sky? His green grass? The breath of air he'd been searching for these many months?

Or was it just that everything else in his life felt so topsy-turvy? Maybe she was just a diversion—someone to prevent him from thinking about the road ahead?

Not sure.

But he was damned sure going to find out.

Jack reached for the cellphone he'd left on the edge of the desk. Elle had given him her number last night right before he'd pulled away from the hotel. He'd tried to be casual about it. Gave her the old "let me get your number and maybe we can get together again before you leave town" routine, knowing all the while he'd call her. Her eyes said yes even though she'd dropped the phone twice while trying to peck her info into his phone.

He pressed the button on his desk.

"Yes, Jack?"

"Marie, call Marcelle at L'Esperer and get me a table. Tell him I want the best. And a limo. Don't forget a bottle of Cristal."

"Of course, Jack." Marie responded in her normal tone, but he could hear the question in her voice. It had been months since he had been to the trendy French restaurant, months since he had ordered flowers, months since he'd even thought about a date.

Jack leaned back and folded his hands behind his head. Tonight he wanted the best for Elle. He wanted to see if the feeling was still there or if it was just something conjured up by the full moon and a belly full of Earl's pancakes.

The knot in his stomach loosened.

Elle Hughes.

Was she his match?

CHAPTER SIX

There's only one way to learn how. You gotta just dig right in. They ain't gonna bite you, girl.

—Grandmother Tucker to Nellie as she contemplated the foam worm tub on their first fishing trip.

NELLIE STOOD at the hotel lobby bar, agog at the exotic atmosphere. Huge, chunky Oriental bar, delicate lotus blossoms, swanky leather chairs—all designed to help patrons achieve their perfect Zen. Man, Vegas did everything bigger and better, yet she had to admit the smooth elegance of the hotel bar could not capture the energetic vibe of Agave Blue. Jack Darby knew what he was doing.

At the thought of the man she was awaiting, Nellie's stomach plummeted. She was as nervous as a pet coon. For the twentieth time that evening she wondered if she'd done the right thing in agreeing to this date.

What if last night had been a fluke? What if the ease between them was a sham made possible only by the three deadly cocktails she had swilled? Had it all been an illusion? Would she see him and stammer? Forget the sophisticated woman she was supposed to be? Fall flat?

The questions went unanswered.

Nellie slid onto the sleek bar stool trying to affect an air of remoteness. She'd been hit on twice already and turned down several drinks sent her way. Nervously, she glanced yet again at the glowing numbers on her cell phone.

Seven-ten.

He was late.

Maybe he wasn't coming. She'd received his message on her phone and texted the meeting place back. What if he hadn't received it? What if he had just changed his mind?

A movement behind her pulled her back into the present. Lips brushed her shoulder.

Nellie spun around and met impish blue eyes.

Before she could say hello, his lips were on hers, soft, yet branding her as his. Nellie didn't resist. She surrendered, melting into the kiss.

Jack.

He tasted as good as she remembered. Mmm. Better.

He eased back, his eyes unfathomable in the low light of the bar, and it struck Nellie that this was the third time she'd been at a bar with him. She glanced at her drink. Not a chance of a spill this time.

"Ready?" Jack queried, his minty-fresh breath stirring the wisps of hair framing her face.

"Of course," Nellie responded, scooping up her beaded evening bag and placing her hand in his.

"By the way, you look delicious tonight," Jack drawled, flipping her hand and bringing it to his lips.

He bestowed a gentlemanly kiss on her hand, and she couldn't stop the delicate shiver that ran up her spine at the heat in his touch. She wanted to go slow, but wasn't sure if she could. She felt all coiled up, ready to leap out of her skin, excited to be with Jack, at what the night might hold.

"Thank you," she said, glad she'd taken the saleslady's advice and bought the strapless dress. The deep blue cotton hugged her body, hitting all the right points before stopping mid-thigh. Simple, revealing and oh, so sexy, the sheath needed no adornment. Silver Grecian sandals graced her feet and dangling earrings brushed the tops of her shoulders. The only spot of color was the cherry-red of her lips and matching red heart tattooed on her shoulder. Coincidently, the teardrop matched the blue dress. She looked so sinful she was certain if she'd been back home, the Ladies' Christian Book Club would have thrown her into the back of a minivan and whisked her down to Larson's Creek for a forced baptism.

Nellie Hughes looked hot. In a dangerous, not so innocent way.

And if the book club ladies knew she wore nothing but a barely there satin thong beneath the sinful dress, well, that might have involved an exorcism.

Easy girl, she thought, trying to control the naughtiness rising within her. It was a second date, and even though there probably wouldn't be a third or fourth, she didn't need to throw herself at the man.

Jack placed his hand on her hip, steering her through the crowded bar. As hot as a cattle iron, his grip burned through the thin material, pressing into her sensitive flesh. She tried to take her mind off the way he made her feel but couldn't seem to stop.

As they entered the lobby, Jack dropped his hand from her hip and picked up her hand. The move was sweet, very second-date-like. And, just like that, Nellie swung from visions of twisted sheets to the novelty of going on a date. Not counting last night's impromptu dash for pancakes, it had been too long since she had gotten dolled up and been taken out to dinner.

They exited the posh lobby and a long stretch limousine materialized outside the revolving door. A uniformed driver opened the limo door with a little flourish. "Madam. Mr. Darby."

Nellie turned to Jack with a smile. "You're joking! What fun!"

She sank into the plush seats, feeling much like Cinderella must have felt en route to the ball. Except her prince was with her. And she didn't have on a fluffy dress and loads of underclothes.

Jack gave the driver a smile as he climbed in beside her. "Thanks, Jeff."

The driver closed the door and the overhead lights dimmed. She gulped as Jack pushed a button, raising the darkened partition between the passenger area and driver.

"Really?" she squeaked, not knowing whether she should put on a show of maidenly modesty or just go ahead and kiss Jack as soon as the window slid into place.

"What?" he said innocently.

"Oh," she muttered, motioning toward the dark glass now separating them from their driver. "I mean…uh, nothing."

"What? Did you think I wanted to take advantage of the situation, Elle?"

"I didn't mean to imply…I mean—oh!" Nellie cried as his hand brushed her breast when he reached across the seat toward the bar. He picked up a crystal glass and handed it to her.

"Champagne," he said, taking his own glass from the drink holder set into the faux wood.

Nellie took a sip. "Wow, that's…um, good. And very bubbly." She sneezed.

Jack laughed. "It's Cristal…only the best."

She sneezed again. Then she felt incredibly gauche. Jeez. One sip of champagne and sophistication sailed out the window. "I don't usually drink champagne. It gives me a headache in the morning."

He grinned. "Me, too. I got it because I was trying to impress you with a romantic gesture."

Nellie's heart thumped at his words. Jack didn't see her pleased smile; he had turned and started digging through a small refrigerator set into the side of the long car.

"Voilà!" He held two beers aloft. "Would a beer suit you better?"

She clapped her hands together. "Now you're talking. I'm from Texas. We don't drink girly champagne."

He smiled and popped the tops, handing her one and keeping the other for himself. She watched him take a long draw off his beer, enjoying the way he tipped his head back and savored the taste. He'd dressed in charcoal slacks with a light gray button-down shirt opened at the throat. He looked what he was—sexy, charming and urbane.

Nellie took a sip of the beer. It tasted way better than the champagne. And no sneezing.

Jack held his beer bottle toward her. "To us. To our second date."

Nellie clinked her bottle against his. "To our second date. And to Earl's pancakes."

That made him laugh. She decided she liked making him laugh.

"SO WHERE DO YOU LIVE in Dallas, Elle?"

Nellie took a huge gulp of wine, certain someone was about to jump out from behind the lush foliage beside the table and yell, *Liar!*

"Well, I have an old house in the center of town. Very trendy area."

Jack smiled. "Must be nice. Which area? University? Or near the West End—what's the new place? Victory…"

"Park," Nellie finished for him, thankful she'd read an article about the artsy community near the American Airlines Center. "No, I live in an older neighborhood."

"Do you like living there?"

Nellie hardly ever went to Dallas, but she remembered the shady streets in the heart of Dallas and the pricey homes there. She couldn't be too rich, or could she? Jack didn't know her from Adam so she could be anything she wanted to be, right? Yet it would probably be better to stick closer to the truth—less chance of screwing her story up.

"I love living there. Um…it's the city, of course, but at times it's quiet, simple." Nellie smiled and raised a forkful of chicken to her mouth.

"I've been to Dallas several times. I have two sisters who live in Texas. Houston and San Antonio."

Well, that probably explained his being in Texas when she'd sloshed her drink on him the first time. The time he blew her off. "Really? Older or younger?"

"Hmm? Oh, older. I'm the baby of the family. The only boy. How 'bout you?"

"I have a younger half sister, Anne Marie. She's fifteen and lives in Tyler with my father and his wife. My mother's not really in the picture. She's mentally ill." *God, why had she volunteered that information? What a downer.*

"Sorry." Jack shot Nellie a compassionate look. "That must be hard."

Nellie nodded. What could she say? It *had* been hard, but she'd been loved by her feisty grandmother, the same woman who would have padlocked her in her room if she'd known Nellie had gone off with a virtual stranger and then made out with him in the parking lot of a pancake house.

They both took a sip of wine. She could see Jack searching for something to say, something not so personal as a parent being off her rocker.

"Well, I know what you mean about enjoying the simplicity of a quiet neighborhood. I like to escape from the hubbub of the city myself. That's why I bought a place out in Henderson. Most find it odd that a guy like me would prefer suburbia, but I need a retreat every now and then. Sometimes all of this gets to me." Jack gestured toward the awesome view afforded by the open balcony doors of the French restaurant perched on the side of the Forty Palms Hotel, twenty-two flights up. Vegas nightlife winked below them, unceasing and tireless.

"I totally get it," Nellie said. "Everyone needs some peace, huh?"

Peace. Exactly, Jack thought. And that was what he felt with Elle. Along with excitement, joy and wonder. Lord, he hadn't felt like this in forever. And it felt good.

It felt good to be himself. To not have to be so slick, so witty and "in the know." He felt relaxed, better than he had in months, maybe years.

And at the same time there was an undercurrent, a sort

of hum of sexual tension. He wanted her, that much was true, but it felt good to let things run their course.

Yet with Elle studying his mouth, her own lips parted, her eyes reflecting something deeply mysterious, he wanted to rush her through dinner. And through this mini-courtship.

Shit. Was that what he was doing? Dating a girl who would be leaving in a day or two? Setting himself up for failure?

No. Again, he reminded himself to trust his gut.

"Sir, is there anything else I can get you? Dessert, perhaps? A cordial?" The snooty waiter cleared the remains of their dinner. Jack noted his pencil-thin mustache, regal manner and affected French accent.

"I don't think so. We prefer pancakes with lots of syrup." Jack waggled his eyebrows at Elle, delighting in the pink kissing her cheeks.

The waiter frowned, obviously not pleased they would choose such an inferior food over his cherries jubilee. "Very well then, sir." He placed the bill on the table with a flourish and spun away.

Jack shook his head. "If he'd had syrup like I had last night, he'd no doubt know why pancakes trump any dessert ever known to man."

Elle giggled, involuntarily touching the mark still faintly visible on her collarbone.

And Jack found himself inordinately pleased with the sound. Honestly, he'd never had a woman giggle with him. Laugh, sure. Snicker, certainly. But giggle? Nope. The sophisticated, world-weary Jack would not have tolerated it. That Jack demanded urbane, experienced women. Women who would have sipped the Cristal champagne just because it cost more than a hard day's wage. Women who would have blanched at the thought of eating pancakes.

Elle Hughes was beautiful and sexy, but she'd never be in the same category as the women Jack had dated in the past. And, surprisingly, that's what drew him to her.

"Did you happen to rub any hollandaise sauce behind your ear?"

Elle's eyes sparkled. "No, but I could dab some wine."

"Don't bother. I don't need an excuse this time." He jammed the appropriate amount of cash into the bill jacket and rose, graciously pulling out Elle's chair, all the while using it as an excuse to brush against the curve of her shoulder, to stroke her inner elbow. He felt her tremble and it pleased him to know she desired him too.

They left the restaurant, not bothering to hide their longing to escape the confines of polite society. Jack pushed the elevator button and draped one arm around Elle. She tucked her head against his shoulder.

"Have you ever made out in an elevator?" he whispered into the shell of her ear.

She shook her head.

"Wanna give it a whirl?"

This time she nodded.

His mouth found hers, demanding and insistent. He wanted to consume her right in the foyer of the most exclusive eatery in Vegas. And he didn't give a damn who saw him acting like a sophomore about to get some action for the first time.

The elevator doors swooshed open and someone jostled them as several people exited the car. He never stopped kissing Elle. Couldn't stop. Not even when the gentleman muttered, "Excuse me," and a woman out and out laughed.

Finally Jack lifted his head. Elle's lips were wet and tempting.

"I think we better go downstairs to the casino," he said, trying to pull away from her so she couldn't feel how much he wanted her. It took all his energy to step back.

Elle walked into the empty elevator car. "Okay, we'll go to the casino. You can teach me all the games. But first you said we'd make out in the elevator."

He laughed. "So I did."

"Well, we didn't make it to the elevator."

"I can't be responsible for what I might do to you in that elevator."

Elle smiled and crooked one finger.

He went as willing as a lamb to slaughter.

CHAPTER SEVEN

The only good thing about baseball is the way the men look in their pants. I may be old, but I ain't dead yet.

—Grandmother Tucker to Nellie during the Texas Rangers game they won tickets to.

NELLIE SLID onto the newly painted bleacher and tried to look like she wasn't having heart palpitations at the sight of Jack standing on the pitching mound hugging a cute blonde in a seriously short pair of athletic shorts.

"Who's the whore?" Kate drawled, plopping her Prada purse onto the bleacher in front of them and pushing her almost too obnoxious sunglasses into place on her nose.

"Don't say things like that," Nellie reprimanded, trying not to sound like the librarian she was.

"Bullshit. That's your man, isn't it?"

Nellie felt her heart flinch. "No. This is a fling. Remember?"

Kate slid her glasses down and met her eyes. "Oh, I remember. Do you?"

"Of course I do," Nellie snapped.

Kate smiled as she refocused on the field. "Still, he invited you. Miss Look-at-my-tight-ass needs to know her place. Go out there and claim him, Nell."

"Are you insane?" Nellie ripped her eyes off the blonde in Jack's arms and turned to her friend. "I will do no such thing. We shouldn't have come. I don't know why—"

"Don't worry. You look classy compared to that." Kate gestured toward the blonde before her attention was stolen by a player sitting on the bottom bleacher unlacing his cleats.

She and Kate had headed out to Henderson after she'd mentioned to the girls that Jack had invited her to watch him play softball. Trish had elected to follow up on a deposition, which had pissed Kate off, and Billie had napped. Only Kate had wanted to go with her. Nellie was certain it had something to do with guys in tight baseball pants who might potentially rip their shirts off. She was just glad to have her friend with her.

She crossed her legs, tossed her hair over her shoulder and leaned back, propping her elbows on the bleacher behind them. She liked her outfit—clingy white sleeveless shirt that buttoned only so far down, white shorts that made her legs look tanned, plucky leather thong sandals and a chunky gold bracelet she'd borrowed from Billie. It was a good look, a look that said, No big deal.

"Elle." Jack's voice interrupted her mental playing-it-cool checklist.

"Good God, I'd like to lick his stomach," Kate whispered.

"You are so sick," Nellie returned out of the corner of her mouth.

But she knew what Kate meant. Jack had shrugged off the blonde and headed toward the bleachers. He looked like every woman's dream. It was everything she could do to not leap from the bleachers, tackle him and have her way with him. When had sweat become sexy?

"You came," Jack said, propping his arms on the fence.

"I'll bet," Kate whispered.

Nellie tried not to laugh. Or turn red. "Yeah, I told you I would try to make it. Sorry we missed the game. We got lost."

His eyes slid over her and made her tingly. Then he smiled and her heart raced. Nellie knew she was falling for him. Hell, she'd already fallen. It was more Game Over, Love wins.

She licked her lips. "Jack, this is—"

But Kate wasn't beside her any longer.

"Where'd she go?" Nellie asked, shocked she hadn't felt her friend slip away.

Jack's eyes crinkled as he smiled. He jerked his head toward the dugout. "Hamm took off his shirt."

Nellie glanced at the dugout. Sure enough, Kate stood next to the Adonis who'd been unlacing his shoes. He no longer wore a shirt. "What the—"

"Don't worry. They all do that when he takes off his shirt. Girls can't resist his six-pack." Jack's ball cap perched backward on his head and the faded Texas Longhorn shirt molded itself to his body like a second glove. He looked sweaty, hot and ready to grace the cover of a fitness magazine.

"I resisted," Nellie said.

"And I appreciate that, Elle." His gaze met hers and held. They remained that way for a full minute. Just holding each other's smile, content to have no words mar the moment.

"Wanna get out of here?" Jack asked.

"Yeah, but I came with Kate."

"Kate looks busy. I don't think she'll mind."

She looked over at Kate. Her friend had waylaid Adonis

with a smile of invitation. Then she cocked her head to the side and walked her fingers up the man's chest. Kate. She was nothing if not obvious.

"Still, let me talk to her a minute."

Nellie slid from the bleacher, grabbing Kate's ridiculously expensive handbag. She tried to move slowly, as if she weren't in a hurry to escape the sunny ballpark full of good-natured people packing away equipment and making plans for beer and pizza. She didn't want everyone to know that all she could think about was being alone with Jack.

"Kate?"

Her friend ripped her eyes from the man in front of her. "Mmm?"

"Uh, Jack wants—"

"You to wash his back?" Kate finished, lustily eyeing Jack's teammate, who was shrugging into a dry shirt.

"Not necessarily," Nellie said. "I thought I would go with him and then meet you and the girls later for the show."

"Don't worry about the show. I got the tickets for free. Don't know why you wanted to see those blue guys anyway. Freaky." As she spoke, Kate kept brushing against the unsuspecting Hamm or whatever his name was.

"Blue Man Group?" the Brad Pitt look-alike asked. "I love those guys."

"Really?" Kate drawled the word. It sounded like honey pooling. "'Cause now I have an extra ticket."

And just like that, Nellie was free. Free to go with Jack. To spend a few more precious hours with him. Or maybe more. If she didn't have to go to the Blue Man show then she could spend the whole evening with him.

Or maybe the whole night.

Her stomach flopped over at the thought.

"See you," Nellie called out as she turned back toward Jack.

Jack had grabbed his bag while Nellie talked with Kate. Keys dangled from his hand.

"All set?"

"Yeah, I'm yours for the night," she said, sliding her arm into the crook of his, all the while tossing the blonde who'd draped herself on him a few minutes ago a sunny smile. It was tacky. Low. But Nellie enjoyed every moment of it.

She had staked her claim.

"Mine for the night, huh?" Jack murmured against her ear. "I like the sound of that."

"Me, too," Nellie said.

As they strolled toward the sleek sports car, Nellie wondered why she had allowed herself to get so tangled up in Jack Darby. Okay, she knew the motto for the Girls and Glam getaway. Indulge. Create a fantasy. Live for the moment.

But this had grown into more than that. Now it felt dangerous. Not as in "take a risk" dangerous. More like "eat a carton of ice cream and go through a box of tissues" dangerous. Like this one was going to hurt. Bad.

But what could she do? Blow him off and go back to the hotel? Go watch the blue men bang on drums? She only had a couple of days left. Could she really spend them without Jack?

No. She would take what she could. Continue being Elle. Pretend he wasn't anything more than what she intended him to be.

Jack opened her door. "Whew. It's getting hot. I could really use a cold one."

"I'll second that," Nellie quipped, hopping into the bucket seat.

Jack clasped a hand to his chest and staggered back. "I am in love."

Nellie watched as Jack jogged in front of the car to the other side, wondering if he knew what a chord his words had struck within her. So silly of her, but a little part of her wanted to believe he meant what he said.

But that was stupid, because he didn't know her, really. He didn't know her name, where she lived, what she did, or anything much else about her. What would he think if he knew she could embroider tablecloths and transplant heirloom roses? What would sexy Jack Darby say if he saw her in her library jumper with the books appliquéd to the pockets, or in her Coke-bottle glasses?

She really didn't want to know.

So wishing for something that wasn't going to happen was unrealistic.

And Nellie was never unrealistic.

CHAPTER EIGHT

Good sex only happens between a man and woman who love each other. And to be honest, Nellie, I could only label it "good" about a tenth of the time.

—Grandmother Tucker, upon delivering the "birds and bees" talk to Nellie on her fifteenth birthday, just two weeks after Nellie had let Clive Sikes get to second base.

NELLIE WALKED AROUND the infinity edge pool, admiring a backyard that could have been featured on HGTV. Sunlight glittered on the surface of the water, seductively inviting a plunge into the aqua depths. She momentarily wished she'd brought the bikini Kate insisted she buy. The thought of parading around in front of Jack with just two strips of glittery hot pink made her shivery inside. Shivery hot.

"You want to take a swim?" Jack's voice came from behind her. He handed her a bottle of beer then clinked his against hers before lifting it to his mouth.

"I don't have a suit," she said, knowing her words invited suggestion.

Sure enough, he lifted one eyebrow and tossed her his trademark wolfish grin. "No one can see you. The only neighbors who might are in Costa Rica canopy gliding, or whatever they call it."

"I don't know," she hedged, eyeing the perimeter of the

backyard. The space did seem fairly hidden, but she'd never actually skinny-dipped. It seemed like total wild abandonment.

Jack snapped his fingers. "Know what? I think my sister left a suit in the cabana the last time she and Drew were up. Let me check. You can change while I grab a shower and my suit. Then we can cool off in the pool."

Nellie nodded then took a big gulp of the beer. Icy cold, it slid down smooth and felt like liquid courage. She knew everything had been leading to this moment and was extremely glad they had not made love the first time they'd met. Correction. The second time they'd met. The first time hadn't counted because she'd been just plain ol' Nellie Hughes.

Jack returned from the cabana off the side of his pool holding a bright green swatch of cloth.

"Here you go. You two are about the same size, so I think it'll do. Go ahead and change in the cabana. I'm gonna grab a shower and put some chicken in to marinate. We can grill tonight if that is okay with you."

Nellie took the suit from him. Her stomach felt like bats had taken up residence, but she delivered a breezy smile. "Sounds great."

Jack entered the house, leaving her to the intimate beauty of his backyard. She didn't fail to notice it had been professionally landscaped. Fragrant hibiscus dominated urns while tropical palms provided a leafy background for the climbing Mandevilla and windmill jasmine. Trumpet flowers and bird of paradise dotted the beds surrounding the pool, and gentle bamboo swayed against the privacy fence.

Nellie entered the cabana and slipped out of her clothes, folding them neatly, even the white wisp of a lace thong. She slid into the bright green suit, noting there were a lot of cutouts revealing a lot of flesh. Thank goodness Kate had talked her into the spray-on tan and bikini wax. She turned to check out her backside, just to make sure the cellulite wasn't too bad and the suit was in place. She caught sight of herself in the mirror.

The suit flattered her, dipping low between her generous breasts and skimming the lower part of her back. The heart tattoo looked bold on her tanned shoulder, and once again Nellie marveled at how different she looked. Yep, totally Elle.

She took her white sleeveless shirt from the neatly folded pile, pulled it on and left the cabana.

Jack wasn't back yet, so she made her way to the steps and dipped one toe into the pool. The water wasn't too cold, just refreshing. The sun glared down, making a small bead of sweat roll down her back. Now she felt stupid for keeping her shirt on. He'd still be seeing her in the bathing suit.

But before she could slip the shirt off and toss it on a lounge chair, something swept her from her feet and lobbed her into the pool.

She came up sputtering.

Jack grinned from above her, wearing a red suit and looking way too fine without a shirt.

"No fair!" she cried, wiping the rivulets of water from her eyes while trying to tread water. She didn't have time to complain much longer.

All she heard was a cry of "Cannonball" and a wave of water rushed toward her.

Jack emerged next to her, grinning like a twelve-year-old prankster.

"Jack!" She went to splash him but his head disappeared. She turned in a circle looking for him. Then she felt his hand on her foot, tugging her down into the depths of the pool.

She went willingly.

His arms wrapped around her, slipping beneath the open shirt. They felt so warm in the coolness of the water. His naked chest felt splendid next to her skin as she bumped against him. Their legs tangled and he pulled her close to him and kicked toward the surface. They both emerged with a gasp.

His smile, so teasing before, didn't seem playful now. And his hands were busy, traveling the length of her body.

"Elle, I've tried to wait, but you look so damn good and you feel so damn good, I don't think I can just make out this time. I'll stop if you insist, but…"

His words trailed off even as his hands stayed busy. She looked into blue eyes that flamed with passion. She knew they mirrored her own.

"I don't want to stop this time," she said.

And that was all it took.

Jack seemed to send up a silent prayer of thanks, pulled her tighter to him and swam toward the steps. His eyes remained on hers, but when he felt the edge of the step bump them, he lowered his head and kissed her sweet, wet lips. This time she tasted yeasty like beer, with a hint of cinnamon. She tasted of all things good. All things sexy and right.

Elle gave a moan of surrender. Her bottom sank onto the step as she angled her head so he could deepen the kiss. Her arms curled about his neck, pulling him to her. He went eagerly, his dripping chest pressing against the delicious softness of her breasts.

He tore his mouth from hers and whispered against her ear, "Take this shirt off so I can touch you, Elle."

He went back to exploring the sensitive curve of her neck as she shrugged out of the sodden shirt. It hit the edge of the pool with a slap.

"Oh, good girl," he growled, dotting small wet kisses along the edge of her breasts where they swelled against the neckline of the borrowed suit. He tugged the edge of the suit with his teeth and one rosy nipple emerged.

Sweet Lord.

Nellie couldn't believe the liquid pool of pleasure spreading within her. She felt like she was watching herself do these naughty things with Jack. She saw his eyes darken at the sight of her nipple. Boldly, she slid her fingers to the halter of the bathing suit and tugged it down.

Jack smiled.

And all of her reservations fled as she watched him take her in. His eyes made love to her just before his mouth descended. Oh, dear God. His mouth was hot. Her breasts were tight and heavy, almost painful with the need to be touched. And at the first tug of his teeth on one hard peak, she bucked against the stone steps.

"Mmm," she groaned, rocking her hips against the erection straining his swim trunks. She needed to feel him inside her.

The heat uncoiling in her pelvis settled low, throbbing and hungry as Jack moved his head to her other breast and gave it the same dedicated attention.

"Mmm, Jack!" she panted, running her nails down his back and moving her thigh so it rubbed against his crotch.

Jack's only response was a heated groan. He shifted his hips, splaying her legs, leaving her open to the friction he created by moving against her. Her need for him rose to a fevered pitch.

Tired of the barrier between them, she pulled his head back from her breasts and shimmied out of the suit. Jack grinned and pulled his trunks off too. It joined her suit with another heavy plop.

Nellie peered up at him, framed against the sun. He was as good as she imagined. He looked like David, carved and molded in masculine beauty. Well, except for one notable exception—that part was a whole lot bigger where it counted.

It was her turn to have her mouth water.

She wanted to touch every inch of him, to marvel at the smooth planes and deep hollows of his body, to feel the crisp hair sprinkled over his muscled chest, to drag her nails down the firm flanks of his backside. She wanted to taste him, the saltiness of his neck, the water droplets clinging to his shoulders. She felt insane by the desire to have Jack Darby.

He lowered himself to her, covering her once again with the heat of his body. She rejoiced in the feel of him. His lips moved on hers and she opened her mouth to him. Her arms twined round his neck as she pulled him even closer, grinding her hips up into his, allowing his erection to slide against the slickness at the juncture of her thighs. Jack's hardness hovered just at the entrance, enticing with sweet friction. She couldn't take it any longer. She pushed at his chest and slid her hand down in an effort to touch him, to wrap her hand round the pulsing silken length of him.

But his hand stilled her.

"Please, Jack."

"Please, what? What do you want, Elle?" He brushed his lips down her neck, lingering on the delicate curve of her collarbone, tasting the sweet slope of her breast.

She bucked against him, hooking one leg over his, pulling her body as close as she could to his, reveling in the crisp hair of his chest against the hardness of her nipples, the jutting erection rubbing against her.

She felt out of her mind with passion, flooded by the sheer lust raging within her. She wanted him inside her. Now.

Jack seemed to sense her frustration, her need.

"Just a minute, baby."

He left her for a minute before he came back, lifting her from where she sagged against the pool steps. Water sluiced off her body and the air chilled her briefly before he swept her into his arms and carried her to a cushioned double lounger beneath a pergola covered with blooming jasmine.

He reached toward the small table and grabbed the condom lying there.

"Pretty sure of yourself?" Nellie muttered.

He just smiled and ripped the package with his teeth. She squirmed beneath him, willing him to hurry up. He must have felt the same way for, in the blink of an eye, he settled back between her thighs. He caught her mouth with his and with one thrust he entered her, filling her, causing her to gasp with pleasure.

"Oh, Jack, that feels…so good," she panted, her hips rising from the lounger to meet his thrusts, her body a slave to its need. She didn't have to think about not being good or not knowing what to do. Her thoughts fled and her body took over.

"Yes," Jack agreed, wanting to go slow and savor the feel of Elle's tightness around him but not able to stop himself from plunging inside her over and over. He was lost, and the woman beneath him seemed to be his only salvation.

"Sorry, babe. I can't last much longer." He clenched his teeth, trying to hold back the oncoming orgasm. He wanted to take her to her peak, but wasn't sure if he would make it.

Just then he felt her tighten around him, tiny spasms shaking her body, jiggling the fullness of her breasts. Her head bucked against the cushion as she shattered against him. Her body convulsed and a small groan of pleasure escaped her lips.

He let go, exploding, pumping into her, wishing it hadn't ended so quickly. He collapsed on top of her, utterly depleted, unable to lift himself from her soft body.

She wound her arms around him and they lay there, their heavy breathing mingling with the chirping of birds.

Finally, Jack rolled off Elle, leaving one arm behind her to pillow her head. He studied the vines snaking through the arbor above them.

Words would not come. None needed to be spoken. What had just occurred seemed magical, a melding of bodies so in tune, so connected, words might destroy it.

So they lay there silently, Elle stroking his arm and he twisting her hair. He felt completely at peace with this woman, as if he'd made love to her a hundred times. God help him, but the past few days had felt so right.

"Jack?"

"Yes?" He propped himself up on one hand and studied the woman lying beside him. She was lovely even in the harsh afternoon light. Her skin glowed, her cheeks flushed, and her green eyes still held a glimmer of passion. Lovely wasn't the word for her. His heart actually skipped a beat when she smiled at him.

"That was wonderful."

"Yes," he agreed. "Absolutely wonderful."

CHAPTER NINE

Go on and have your fantasies, Nellie. Life's about as hard as the stone laying over your grandpapa. So you just pretend yourself into happiness, girl.

—Grandmother Tucker when she saw Nellie dressed in her wedding veil, holding a clutch of her prized irises.

NELLIE TRIED TO WIGGLE her toes but found them buried beneath a warm, hairy lump.

"Eh!" she shrieked, her eyes flying open just in time to see a long pink tongue swoop out.

"Ew!" she groaned, pushing away the huge black Labrador retriever wriggling playfully in the twisted bedding. The dog's eyes laughed at her and he reared up to deliver another determined kiss. Nellie blocked him, wiping away the evidence of the first kiss from her cheek.

"Dutch, down!" Jack commanded from the bedroom doorway. Dutch ducked his head and slunk off the plush bed as if he'd been beaten rather than reprimanded. "Sorry. He knows he's not supposed to get on the bed. Guess he found you as irresistible as I do."

Nellie couldn't stop the pleasure flooding her heart, though by now she should have been used to his honeyed words. Lord knows he'd whispered more than a few into her ear last night. And again in the wee hours of the morning.

She smiled. "No problem. I like dogs. I guess I'm just not used to them waking me up with such an enthusiastic greeting."

Dutch stared adoringly at his master. The dog's tail thumped on the golden Berber rug, creating a tempo that matched Nellie's heart. Did she look at Jack with such adoration? Was she turning into a lovesick puppy?

The only genuine canine in the room made another move toward the bed. Jack caught him by the collar and pulled him toward the open door. "Come on down. I got breakfast."

Breakfast? He could cook? Jackpot. Of course, it might be nothing fancier than Lucky Charms or buttered toast, but Nellie couldn't remember any man ever cooking anything for her, not even her own father when she went to visit him as a child. Where Nellie came from, the kitchen belonged to the women. The men could have the barbeque for steaks and such, but real cooking was done by the fairer sex.

She snorted at the thought. When it came to "fairer," Jack Darby would have to be included. Damned if the man wasn't as pretty as a Texas bluebonnet. Okay, not pretty, but definitely easy on the eyes.

She slid languidly out of the bed thinking her initial impression of the room last night was spot on. Modern, chic and elegant. The chocolate-and-gold-striped walls and billowing curtains were masculine without the gross special effects often found in Texas bachelor pads—beer signs, trophy bucks and pictures of fish. Modern furniture furnished the room and was personalized by framed family photos.

Nellie padded into the kitchen, wearing nothing but an old T-shirt of Jack's emblazoned with Fishermen Use Their Poles across the faded front. She propped her fists on her hips and studied Jack as he raced from the six-burner stovetop to the Sub-zero fridge, balancing a carton of eggs and a quart of milk atop a huge tub of butter.

The carton of eggs popped open and two brown bombs hit the stone floor in rapid succession.

"Shit!" he muttered under his breath, trying to toe open the fridge door and close the carton at the same time. Nellie wanted to laugh, but the smoke rolling up from the frying pan atop the stove set her in motion.

"Ah, hell!" Jack said, slamming the tub and carton on the granite countertop. Before he could reach for the handle of the pan, Nellie beat him to it, setting it on a back burner and turning the flame off.

They both stared at the blackened lumps still smoking in the pan.

She couldn't stop the giggle that escaped. "What was that supposed to be?"

Jack ran a hand through his dark hair, unintentionally ruffling it and making him appear bed-rumpled sexy. He sighed. "Well, it was supposed to be French toast."

Nellie slipped her arms about his middle and gave him a squeeze. "Nice try."

"Look, I really can make French toast. Any idiot can. It's just been a while since I had anybody over. You know, since I needed to fix something like breakfast."

Nellie smiled. Well, that said something. Perhaps Mr. Playboy Vegas wasn't the Lothario she thought him to be. Suddenly she felt like dancing. Or singing. Or maybe just fixing breakfast.

"That's okay. Tell you what. You go clean up those eggs and I'll whip us up some breakfast."

Jack crossed his arms and cocked his head. His blue eyes twinkled despite the frown he shot her way. "Why do I get cleanup duty?"

"'Cause you made the mess," she quipped, scooping up the sizzling pan and looking for the trash disposal. "Plus, after you clean up the eggs, you can go relax with the paper or something."

"Deal," Jack declared, dropping a kiss on her hair.

Nellie set to work, keenly aware of how good it felt to be cooking breakfast in Jack's kitchen. It surprised her at how comfortable she was. She could almost pretend it was a normal day—that she poured coffee for him every morning, fussed over the burnt mess stuck in the frying pan, and arranged his eggs and bacon into a smiley face and delivered it to him with a kiss.

Nellie shook her head. *Stop with the fantasies, Nell. Are you deranged? Remember, this is a fling! What you feel is not real. You're Elle, not Nellie. Get real, sister.*

Shoving her dreams of domestic bliss aside, she assembled a simple but yummy breakfast. She found cream-colored stoneware in the cupboard, dished up steaming scrambled eggs with sausage, wheat toast and sliced cantaloupe she found in a plastic container in the fridge, and delivered it to Jack with a kiss.

She added the kiss just to spite herself.

He slid one hand under her T-shirt and gave her naked bottom a squeeze. "This looks almost as good as you. Where did a Dallas businesswoman like you learn to cook like this?"

Nellie ignored the fact she wasn't a businesswoman and

drawled, "Why, I'm a Southern girl, sugar. We live to serve our men. And put meat on their bones."

Jack pulled her into his lap. "Oh, you live to serve your man, do you?" He nuzzled the side of her neck, nipping his way up to the sensitive shell of her ear.

She laughed. "You're a bad boy, Jack Darby."

He kissed along her jawline. "You're damn right."

He gave her a smacking kiss and set her on her feet. "Now let me get to my breakfast, woman."

With an exaggerated sigh, she fetched her own plate and filled her coffee mug, then returned to the table to watch Jack enjoy the breakfast she'd made him. He ate with gusto, not that she'd expect any less. After all, in her limited experience, he seemed to do everything with intent, enthusiasm and passion. And since that included the bedroom, she considered herself pretty lucky. At least for two more days.

Jack munched his toast thoughtfully, watching Elle as she shoveled the steaming eggs into her mouth.

God, he was lucky. Not only was Elle hotter than a two-dollar pistol, but she could cook.

She had toppled into his life like a sexy Texas angel, delivering him from his self-imposed funk. Making him want to smile, want to live big, want to sneak kisses in elevators, dream about wide-open skies. Making him feel that love was possible.

He wondered yet again about his father's declaration about the right woman coming along and slamming into him like an out-of-control freight train.

Would his world ever be the same?

Was Elle the right girl?

She looked at him with eyes that were windows into

her soul. It was as if he could see her every thought—the longing, the hope, the excitement, the fear, the resignation. Was she as scared as he was? Did she feel the same way?

He needed to play this cool. No need to rush her, scare her. They had time. These past few days were only the beginning. Dallas wasn't far, and he had plenty of frequent-flier miles. He'd be in Texas on a regular basis with the ranch venture, anyway. He knew their blossoming relationship was meant to be.

"What do you want to do today?"

A furrow emerged between Elle's eyes. "Gosh, I hadn't really thought about it. I mean, I probably need to get going. I'm sure Kate's got something planned. She always does, and since I've been…occupied lately, I should hang out with her."

"Oh, so that's what you call this…occupying time?"

Elle's cheeks flushed yet again. She did that so easily. Man, she was cute. Jack wanted her for himself. All day. All night. And every moment in between. But he understood. Maybe he could figure out a way to share her. "Well, if you have plans…"

Elle set her coffee mug down. Her eyes focused on the swirls of cream clouding the surface. "Let me call Kate and we'll go from there."

"Wait—why don't you see if your friends want to come over here?"

"Over here?" Elle jerked her cup, causing coffee to slosh over the rim. She darted to the counter and ripped a few paper towels off the roll.

"We could have a get-together…a cookout," Jack said, lifting one shoulder to send a "no big deal" vibe even as he silently prayed for her to agree.

"A cookout?" Elle swiped the spill from the glass table.

"Are you a parrot?" Jack laughed. "I thought maybe we could grill the chicken we never got around to grilling last night. Then maybe swim, drink Coronas, or whatever."

Jack watched Elle's wheels turn. He could see her weighing the pros and cons, wanting to be fair to her friends but still be with him. Jack thought the cookout was a pretty good idea. He would be able to finally meet Kate, learn more about the real Elle Hughes. That was, if she agreed to it.

"Okay, that sounds fun. Let me call Kate and make sure she doesn't have some big deal planned for today. She's usually up for a good time."

Jack lifted his hand and gestured her to go ahead.

"My phone's upstairs." Elle slid from the chair and he tried not to watch her as she walked out of the room. Shit. If she happened to glance back, she would see the naked hope in his eyes. Jack smacked his head as she disappeared around the corner. When had he become such a putz?

He cleared the dishes, loaded them into the washer, and poured himself another cup of coffee. He stared out at his back patio to see Dutch digging in a flower bed.

"Okay."

Jack jumped at the sound of Elle's voice behind him.

"Sorry, did I scare you?" she asked, rubbing his shoulder tentatively as if she were unsure about touching him in such a possessive manner.

"You don't know the half of it," he muttered.

"Huh?" she asked as he turned and took her in his arms.

"Nothing," he answered, hauling her against him and

delivering a kiss on her delicious lips. She tasted like coffee and sex so he deepened the kiss. When he finally lifted his head, they were both breathing heavily.

"Let's not start something we can't finish," she said against his shoulder.

"Who says we can't finish it?"

"Me." She gave him a playful push. "I've got to go back to the hotel, change, grab my suit and stuff."

Jack allowed himself to be pushed back, but not before he caught her hand and brought it to his lips. "I've been having a good time, Elle."

"Me, too," she whispered, watching his hand cradling hers. "I didn't know I would feel so… I mean…"

Her eyes caught his, held his gaze. He could see her searching for the right words. The moment was so tender, so poignant, yet he knew the words would be left unsaid, hovering just out of reach. It was all too strange for both of them.

Elle laughed. "I can't even remember what I was going to say."

He returned her laugh, wanting to tell her he felt the same way, that his life was spinning out of control. But the moment had been broken. "So, just how many friends are you bringing this afternoon?

"Three others to be exact. Is that okay?"

"Absolutely," he said as he steered her from the kitchen toward the stairway. "I'll ask a few friends over to even out the numbers."

"Good. I told Kate there'd be some hot guys. I have to dangle a carrot."

Jack tugged her up the stairs. "Hello. Hot guy? What am I? Chopped liver?"

She scampered a few steps ahead of him and turned, jutting her hip out. “And so humble too.”

He leered. He could see straight up the T-shirt that brushed her mid-thigh. The view was awesome.

Elle squealed and scrambled to the top of the stairway. He was right behind her. He figured she probably needed help getting dressed. Or something.

CHAPTER TEN

A fool and his liquor are soon parted.

—Grandmother Tucker after Uncle Vergie upchucked his bourbon onto the kitchen floor at the family reunion.

"ARE YOU ABSOLUTELY CERTAIN there are going to be hot guys here?" Kate inquired, bouncing up the steps to Jack's Mediterranean-style house. Her short ebony locks curled around her face—a nice change from the jarring blue-streaked spikes the day before.

"Well, coming from someone who snagged a guy from Jack's softball game and couldn't stop raving about the way he scorched her eyes, I would say there's a good chance," Nellie replied, juggling the bottles Kate had insisted on bringing.

"Here, girl. Let me help you." Trish took two of the bottles containing bright liquids. Kate had been adamant they bring the makings for martinis. Several different kinds of martinis.

"Thanks, Trish," Nellie said, smiling at the willowy attorney who looked as if she'd leaped from the pages of a high fashion magazine. Nellie wished she had Trish's earthy, sophisticated vibe. She always seemed in control.

"And why do we need all these drinks?" Billie complained as she chugged up the stairs carrying a plate of brownies she'd bought at a gourmet supermarket and then placed on a plate so they'd look homemade. Dressed in an odd combination of parachute shorts, a tiny tank top and chunky silver rope necklaces, Billie cast grumpy brown eyes at the front door.

"Uh, 'cause it's like a party, Billie," Kate drawled, not able to hide the disgust in her voice. Kate's impatience with Billie was as perpetual as Billie's complaining. Kate spun around dramatically and pressed the buzzer beside the enormous oak door.

Billie rolled her eyes. "You'd think she was supplying a frat party. I'm only going halfsies on what I drink. I'm not paying for all of this stuff."

Nellie stifled the urge to chuckle. Billie had pieces displayed at various museums around the country, not to mention commissioned work for five-figure sums. Even Madonna had a Billie Nader. The thought of her being so stingy with her money was amusing. Of course, Nellie could understand it. She felt the same way and she had plenty of old Texas oil money in the bank.

Before she could reply, the door swung open.

Damn, but Jack Darby knew how to fill up a doorway.

"Ladies," Jack said, bestowing a smile on each of the women. "Welcome."

"Jack." Kate nodded, doing her best imperious-lady-of-the-manor impression. "Thank you."

Typical Kate. Nellie shot Jack a smile and shrugged. Her over-the-top friend hated to be grandstanded by anyone, much less a mere man. Even one as sexy as Jack.

His lips twitched at the cheekiness in Kate's voice. "Ah, the slippery Kate. We meet at last. And I've heard so much about you." His eyes caught Nellie's. They twinkled like waves on a lake in summer.

"I hope she didn't tell you the truth," Kate drawled. "You probably wouldn't let me in if she did." She raked her eyes over Jack with practiced ease. Kate loved to shock, loved to defy, loved to make people just a tad bit uncomfortable.

Jack ignored the bait. "Well, come on in."

"We brought drinks, lots of booze," Billie said, sliding by and turning to offer her hand. "I'm Billie Nader. I met you at Marilyn Turner's benefit last year."

"Of course." Jack smiled, taking her hand. "Nice to see you again. And you too, Trish."

"Jack." Trish nodded, as elegant as a Nubian queen.

All three women sauntered into the huge living area just past the open foyer, leaving Nellie alone with Jack.

"Hi." She smiled, unable to keep her sudden nervousness at bay.

Jack leaned one tanned arm against the doorjamb, preventing her from slipping by. "Hi, yourself, pretty lady."

Nellie tried to shrug off her tenseness. Lord, she'd been naked on the stairs with him just five hours before. She forced a breezy smile. "Am I invited to this shindig or not?"

"There's a price for entering."

"Oh, really? No one else paid."

"They don't have the right qualities." Jack reached up and tucked a hank of hair behind her ear. His actions were tender, his words heavy with meaning. She swallowed.

"What's the price?" she asked.

"Just a kiss."

"Oh, that doesn't seem like so much." She rose up on tiptoe and brushed a kiss across his mouth. "There."

"Nope." He wagged a finger. "That will get, uh, maybe a toe in."

Nellie laughed. "A toe? Come on. It was worth more than that."

"Try again." He leaned back against the wall and crossed his arms.

She wanted to run her hands under his trendy little T-shirt and then let her tongue trace the bottom curve of his lower lip, but her hands were full of bottles of appletini mixers and the foyer could easily be seen from the warehouse of a living area where the others had gathered.

Nellie sighed and pressed her mouth to his again, allowing her tongue to flick out and taste his lips teasingly. Jack let her take control of the kiss, seeming to satisfy himself with a passive role. She could feel herself slipping under his spell, entering that place where all else ceased to exist—a most wonderful place.

Jack grabbed the bottles from her hands, simultaneously breaking the kiss. "Come on in, then."

Nellie fell back to earth and followed him into the living room.

Trish and Billie lounged on the large sectional couch while Kate busied herself unloading the booze at the bar. Four guys ranging from hulking to lithe were also in the room. Two were engaged in a heated discussion about illegal recruiting practices, whatever that was, one stabbed his BlackBerry with a small black pen, and the other brooded at the end of the bar. All of them turned and stared at Nellie as she followed Jack into the room.

"Guys, this lovely woman is Elle Hughes."

A chorus of "hey" shot her way. Nellie tried to paste a smile on her face, but she felt damned awkward, no way around it. She wasn't used to being center of attention. Plus, she prayed both Trish and Billie remembered her pretend name. They'd practiced in the car on the way over.

"Elle, the two guys by the window are Jay Busby and Nick Jones," Jack said. "Both are assistant coaches for UNLV. Tim Heyward, the guy checking his e-mail, is my best friend from college." He rebuked the slightly nerdy looking guy with a hard look. The man slid the BlackBerry into his pocket with an apologetic smile.

"And that mountain over there is my business partner, Dave O'Shea," Jack finished.

"Nice to meet y'all." Nellie nodded, purposely making eye contact with each of Jack's friends. She looked at her own friends. Kate was ignoring everyone, plunking down glasses and wrenching lids from the bottles she'd brought. Trish and Billie cast uncertain glances at each other. Were they wishing they had made other plans?

"Has everyone else been introduced?" Jack asked.

Mumbled introductions were made, none overly friendly. Nellie cast a doubtful glance Jack's way. He looked stymied. He gave a shrug and pulled Nellie into the kitchen.

"Good Lord," Nellie groaned, setting the bottles of liquor on the countertop. "This feels like a junior high dance. Girls on one side, boys on the other. We shouldn't have done this. It's too hard to have an intimate get-together with people who don't know each other."

Jack started pulling the steaks from the fridge. "Hey, chill. They're grown-ups. Liquor will loosen them up. Looks like your friend Kate brought enough for an army."

Nellie sighed. "Yeah, I know."

"Here, help me with these. I'll get them on the grill and then we'll go make nice with the boys and girls."

Nellie hesitated. It didn't feel right abandoning her friends in uncharted territory. After all, weren't she and Jack the hosts? Wouldn't it be totally rude to just leave the guests to their own devices? Nellie decided that maybe she was thinking too hard. They *were* all adults.

She followed Jack out the door and helped him put the foil-wrapped potatoes on the grill. He placed the marinating steaks and chicken on the side plate, and lit the tiki torches around the pool.

When she and Jack returned to the living room, it was as if the good-time fairy had waved her wand over the group. Nellie sent Jack an incredulous look. Music boomed through unseen speakers, Kate passed out mixed drinks while cracking jokes, and Dave and Trish held hands.

"Told you," said Jack as he took a martini glass from Kate's hand.

"Told her what?" Kate asked, shoving a glass into Nellie's hand.

"Nothing." Nellie nodded toward the glass. "What's this?"

"A cosmopolitan. Your favorite drink." Kate's eyes communicated more than her words. Oh, right, Nellie thought, *be* the name of the drink. She took a sip. Not bad, she mused, not bad at all.

Before Nellie knew it, she'd done two shots of tequila, learning "lick it, shoot it, suck it," and was on her third drink, a delicious appletini. She sipped the fluorescent concoction and watched Jack flip the sizzling steaks on the built-in grill next to the pool. Earlier she'd slipped into the pink bikini, covering it with a silky cover-up that brushed the top of her knees. The other girls had put on their suits and joined the guys in the pool for a game of volleyball. Kate had tried to talk her into playing, but Nellie knew she'd be no use to the girls' team. To be honest, her ears felt flaming hot, her teeth absolutely numb, and the whole world seemed to be rocking more than a bit. Perhaps she shouldn't have tried those tequila shots.

"Elle, maybe you'd better slow down on those martinis," Jack said, taking a swig of his beer and pushing her shoulder so she sat upright on the stool. "You're kinda listing."

"I'm fine." Nellie waved a hand in his direction. "I drink these all the time."

He quirked an unbelieving brow. "Really? 'Cause I'm pretty sure you're drunk."

"No, I'm not," she huffed, sliding off the stool. Her feet hit the stone pavers below but her body kept moving. She righted herself before her knees connected with the stone. "See. I'm fine."

"Right," he said, removing the tilted glass from her hand. "Slow down, okay? I don't want you to get sick. You mixed this with tequila so we could be in for a real show."

She couldn't stop the annoyance from burgeoning even though she knew he was probably right. "Don't worry, Jack. I'm a big girl."

Nellie tottered toward the lip of the pool, intending to dip a toe into the water. She tried to glide gracefully, but the horizon rocked a bit. The Nevada sky blazed with color as the sun sank below the terracotta horizon. Peach clouds streaked the deepening sky, framing the golden orb fading away like an old warrior. A dry breeze filtered through the palms flanking the backyard oasis and tousled Nellie's layered hair.

Trying for the sophistication of a fifties starlet, she allowed her cover-up to slide from her shoulders to the natural stone below. She sucked in her belly, straightening her spine. She'd never worn a two-piece swimsuit before and didn't feel comfortable strutting around in it. Perhaps she should play volleyball with the others. At least she'd be half-hidden by the water. Shrieks drew her attention to the middle of the kidney-shaped pool.

"Whose team am I on?" Nellie called out above the whooping.

Out of nowhere a ball hurtled in her direction and conked her right on the head.

Off balance from the three drinks she'd downed, she fell gracelessly into the shallow part of the pool.

Cool water closed over her and she flailed about, trying to gain her footing. Panicking, she couldn't find the bottom of the pool. Her feet finally hit the hard surface, but not before she inhaled what felt like a gallon of water. Chlorine blasted a path through her nostrils and she emerged sputtering. For a moment she couldn't suck in any air. She slapped the water, feeling as helpless as a baby in a bathtub. Everyone else in the pool stood staring at her, seemingly frozen in place. Finally, huge racking coughs shook her frame. Water spewed from her nose.

God, it hurt. Burned. Her lungs were on fire.

"Elle!" Nellie heard a splash and then Jack scooped her into his arms. She didn't have time to appreciate the security he offered. She could feel the contents of her stomach churning. She was about to vomit.

"Out," she moaned, motioning frantically for him to get her out of the pool.

Jack lifted her like a child and climbed the steps. As soon as her feet hit the patio, she bolted for the nearest greenery and emptied her stomach of the assorted alcoholic beverages she'd drunk, plus a good deal of Jack's pool.

"Oh my God," she groaned, sinking to her knees. Her

whole body trembled as she clasped the nearest planter to keep from falling over. She hadn't been sick since she was in high school. She'd forgotten how much she hated to throw up.

Nellie felt a cloth on her forehead. Jack. "Here, babe."

She grabbed the napkin and wiped her mouth. She kept her head down. She didn't want to look at Jack. Or any of the others, who were bound to be watching the melodrama.

"Are you okay?"

She cringed. She could read the reproach in his words. His concern veiled his real intent—to say "I told you so."

"Yeah," she mumbled, still afraid to meet the censure in his eyes.

"Come on. Let's get you upstairs. We can dry off and you can slide back into your jeans. Then we'll tackle those steaks. Okay?"

What? No lecture. No tough love, stew in your own juices, fix your own problems? Nellie knew she was still under the influence of the tequila, but surely Jack wasn't that cool. She'd just barfed in his oleander bushes.

"Nell? You okay?" Kate called from behind her.

"Yeah. Just swallowed half the pool. I was never much of a swimmer, you know."

"Yeah, I remember. You need some help? I mean, you want me to help you…"

"I got it," Jack said, lifting Nellie from beneath her arms. She allowed him to pull her to her feet and finally stood like a kitten caught in a rainstorm, tremulous and half-drowned. She turned to Kate and Jack, wishing she could just slink away, but neither was looking at her. They were staring at each other. Nellie could almost hear the lines being scratched between them on the stone terrace.

Kate crossed her arms over her tiny bikini top as she studied Jack like a territorial terrier. Her eyes narrowed as she probed, weighed, measured. Nellie knew Kate. She didn't give control to anyone. Ever. She trusted very few people, and none of them were men.

Jack wrapped one arm about Nellie's waist and withstood Kate's scrutiny. Nellie wouldn't have been surprised if the man nonchalantly inspected his fingernails just to annoy her overprotective friend. But he wasn't budging; she could feel his claim as he squeezed her hip.

"All right," Kate said. "It's my turn to serve, anyway. N…Elle, if you need me, holler."

Nellie sank against Jack as he maneuvered her toward the house. He grabbed a couple of fluffy towels from a basket on the patio and toweled her off. Her teeth chattered despite the warmth of the night. Jack peeled off his jeans, revealing a bright turquoise pair of swim trunks. His shirt followed. He wrapped both Nellie and himself in a towel and pulled her into the house.

Suddenly, she wanted to tear herself away. Tell him she didn't need anyone to take care of her. Not Kate, not him, not even her Grandmother Tucker—not that the poor woman could anymore. She knew she was irrational, but she was tired of pretending. Tired of being something she wasn't. Tired of everybody telling her what to do.

But she couldn't. She wanted Jack's strength, wanted him to touch her, heal her, make her feel she was worth something more than the winner of the Oak Stand jelly contest. She wanted to be something more than Nellie Tucker.

Nellie Tucker. The girl with homemade dresses, owllike glasses and shiny shoes. Poor little Nellie Tucker, lonely little rich girl whose mother overdosed on heroin because she couldn't take being who she was. Poor little Nellie Tucker who lived with her crazy grandmother, who spent all day in the garden, who missed her senior prom because she couldn't find anyone Grandma Tucker approved of to take her, who sat at home when other girls sneaked out to shack up with guys, who came back to Oak Stand, Texas, to be another eccentric Tucker.

But she wasn't that girl anymore. Would never be that girl again. And Jack was part of the reason. She no longer wanted this to be just a fling. She wanted something more.

But everything was based on a lie.

She looked at him as they climbed the stairs. Her hand fit in his perfectly, like a key into the lock. He was made for loving her, for making her more than she ever thought she could be.

Perhaps it was the alcohol whispering this into her mind, but she didn't think so.

Everything had been leading up to this point. She had to come clean. Then she would see where it took her.

"Now I've got you alone," Jack growled playfully against her ear, jarring her out of her silent contemplation. They were in his bedroom. His hands cupped her bottom and pulled her against him. She could feel his erection pressing against her stomach, and though she'd just been sick as a dog, she couldn't stop the warmth from creeping through her abdomen, spiraling down, delighting with its heavy need.

"Jack—" Nellie swatted at his hands. "Our friends are down there."

"So?" he said, rubbing against her.

"We can't."

"Why not? I have it on the best authority that my parents

conceived my sister in the bathroom at their neighbor's Christmas party."

"Conceived!" Nellie bleated, pulling his hands from underneath her bikini bottom.

"Well, I got us covered on that, but we can practice procreation, right?" He walked toward his bedside table, laughing.

"But first I need to brush my teeth," she said, more to herself than to Jack. She turned toward the bathroom. Her opened bag sat inside, spilling her clothes onto the floor. "Wait. Jack, we can't have sex while everyone else is down there. That's weird."

"You still don't feel good, do you? Shit. I'm sorry, Elle. I'm a complete pig." He closed the drawer and turned to her, his swimming trunks tented. Nellie had never seen a guy like that. Jack looked silly.

She giggled.

"What? Are you laughing at this?" he said in mock outrage, gesturing toward his erection. "'Cause look, lady, you did this to me."

She stopped laughing. "Sorry. I've just never seen that before. It's comical."

His expression softened. "That's what I like about you. You bring fresh perspective to everything."

She swallowed and turned to the bathroom. "I'm gonna change and then we can go salvage dinner."

Nellie closed the door, though she knew it was silly to do so. It wasn't as if Jack hadn't seen her in all her splendor. The man had explored every square inch of her body, for Pete's sake. But she needed a moment to center herself. Jack had her more than off balance and it had nothing to do with the potent drinks she'd consumed.

"HEY, ELLE?" Jack called at the door a few moments later. He gave a soft knock before pushing it open. Elle had already donned her jeans and sequined tank. Her hair was starting to curl around her face. Bare feet peeked out beneath the faded denim. She stood framed in the seductive light of the bathroom, vulnerable and sweet. He wanted to eat her up, consume her innocence, let her fill him with wonder, awe, joy. Because he knew she could do that. She made him feel that life was beautiful again.

Jack could feel the smile curve his lips. Good Lord, he could feel his heart thrum. This was it. Time to make it real.

"Elle, I wanted to talk to you. I mean, now might not be the best time, but since I can't talk you out of your clothes…"

Elle's lips twitched, but she refused to make eye contact with him. Instead, she rooted around in a cosmetic case and pulled out her hairbrush.

"These past few days have been incredible."

Still no eye contact.

"Since you're going back to Texas soon, I wanted to tell you how much this has meant to me. To be with you even when you hadn't planned on it. Thank you for giving me a part of you."

Elle's hand curled around the hairbrush. He could see the white of her knuckles and the tension in her mouth as she pressed her lips together. Tears glossed her lovely green eyes.

"Elle?"

She finally turned to him. "Yeah, it has been great. I…" She struggled for the words. Her voice was tremulous, heavy with emotion. "It has been good."

She tore her gaze from his and spun back toward the mirror, pulling the brush through her damp hair.

"I wanted to talk about continuing this—this thing we've got going," he said, walking toward her.

His gaze met hers in the mirror and he could see the surprise in her eyes. She wasn't expecting that. She thought he was going to end it all. Jack could see it, feel it radiate off her. Damn, didn't she know she'd captured him? Couldn't she see it in his every move?

"Continue this?" she asked, spinning around. He caught her hips and pulled her to him.

"If you want to," he said, lowering his eyes to study her lips. Lord, they were luscious. He could kiss them every single day. "I want you to want to, Elle."

"You do?" she said, reaching out to stroke his hair. "How are we going to do that? I mean, I thought this was just a fling?"

"Is that what you want it to be?"

"I…don't know. I guess I never thought about it. I mean, I thought about more than just this, but I didn't think it would happen."

"Why?" Jack asked, watching her closely.

"You are you. I know about you—your lifestyle, your women." She stepped away from him, putting space between them.

"You think I'm just playing you?" he asked. He couldn't stop the annoyance from creeping into his voice. Was that what everyone thought about him? He was some shallow playboy who lived with no repercussions? Did Elle think he tossed women away like yesterday's newspaper?

"No, I don't mean that." She rubbed her eyes with one hand. Her French manicure stood out against her tanned hands, and the small heart tattoo winked from beneath her tank. It was fading.

He crossed his arms. "All I'm asking is for you to be part of a relationship, Elle. What does that have to do with my image?"

Elle flinched. He couldn't stop the anger in his voice. This wasn't going according to plan. In his vision, she was supposed to fall into his arms, declare she felt something more too.

"I guess I didn't think you would want a relationship. I thought it was understood that this was just a fling. You know, one of those 'what happens in Vegas' things."

He didn't move. He couldn't believe it, but Elle was blowing him off. She didn't want him. She was the one who wanted a brief love affair and nothing more. He thought she'd felt the way he did. That what they had was a beginning, not an end.

"So this is it? You don't want to continue?"

She lifted her head. Her eyes were full of pain. "I never said that. I just didn't expect this, didn't think you would want me."

He felt himself reel. Not want her? Was she crazy? How could she not know how much he wanted her? "My God, Elle, don't you know how I feel? I knew you were something special when you walked through the door of my club. I took one look at you and you had me, lady."

She whirled around. The hairbrush clattered to the floor. "You can't be serious."

"Why?" He didn't understand her reaction. He'd basically told her she had him in the palm of her hand, that he was totally under her control, that she was The One. What kind of whack job was this woman? How could she question him?

He studied her. An incredible array of emotions danced

across her face. Shock, incredulity, irritation, hope, and then the most unexpected of all—amusement. Before Jack could scoop the hairbrush from the floor or Elle into his arms, the crazy, beautiful woman threw back her head and laughed.

CHAPTER ELEVEN

Be careful what you wish for—you just might get it.

—Grandmother Tucker to Nellie when her new baby sister Anne Marie spit up formula on Nellie's new wrap skirt.

"OH? YOU'RE LAUGHING? I'm spilling my guts and you're laughing, Elle." Jack sounded as if he were addressing a three-year-old. Nellie wondered if he'd send her to a time-out. That made her laugh harder.

Oh, God, the irony of the situation. A song could be written about it. In fact, a song *had* been written about it, but that wasn't relevant at the moment. Nothing seemed to be except the fact Jack thought he was falling for the woman standing in front of him.

And he couldn't be. Because she wasn't real.

She felt his hands on her arms. He shook her lightly. "Stop laughing."

Nellie clasped a hand over her mouth partly because she was still a bit nauseated and partly because she couldn't believe the situation she found herself in. One look at Jack's wounded expression and she sobered.

"You don't know me, Jack."

"Of course I know you. I know you pretty well if you remember." He ground out the words between nearly clenched teeth, unconsciously jerking his head toward the bedroom. Nellie met his eyes. He was pissed. Nice. Anger and hurt would pair perfectly with the humiliation Nellie was about to go through.

She shook her head. "You knew I was 'the one' the first time you saw me? So what do you mean by 'the one'?"

He blew out his breath. "Look. Just forget about this. You're drunk. This whole conversation is bad timing. We've got guests downstairs."

"Wait!" she cried as he spun toward the open doorway. "I'm not that drunk. We need to finish this."

Jack turned and cocked one eyebrow. Damn, but he still looked sexy when he was perturbed. Oddly, she wanted to reach out and soothe his brow, kiss the stubble beginning to sprout along his jawline, put her arms around him and pretend nothing needed to be said between them.

Just keep pretending.

But she knew she couldn't.

"So what did you think when you saw me, Jack?"

He threw her a dubious look. But finally he sighed and settled against the doorjamb with a loose-limbed elegance that belied his obvious annoyance. Silence hung over them like a wet paper towel. Nellie watched Jack try to figure out her game.

Finally he spoke. "I thought you were the sexiest woman I'd ever seen in my entire life."

"Yeah?" She felt her heart leap despite what she knew was coming.

"Yeah, and I felt something right here kinda break loose." Jack placed one hand against his chest. "And I knew I had to meet you. See if there was something to it."

Damn, those were powerful words. But they were a lie.

She slowly shook her head. "No, that's not what you felt when you first saw me."

He frowned. "So you're a psychic or something? You know what people think?"

A little piece of her heart broke off. "I'm pretty sure the word 'sexy' didn't come to mind the first time you saw me."

"Oh, yeah?" He shifted so he was no longer leaning against the doorjamb. He loomed before her, crowding the bathroom with righteous male ego.

Nellie squirmed; the tile beneath her feet felt like a slab of ice. She wiggled her bare toes, trying to generate warmth. Her hands trembled so she shoved them into the back pocket of her jeans, still twitching under his scrutiny.

Jack's eyes bored into hers, pinning her to the floor like an ant beneath a torturous magnifying glass. "So what's the deal, Elle? What are you not saying?"

She longed to summon some anger, some outrage that this man was so shallow, so obtuse he didn't know he'd met her before the night in Agave Blue. But she could feel only complete and utter sadness. He'd just verified what she'd known all along—their relationship was as fake as the tattoo on her shoulder.

"You remember when we went out to dinner?"

"Yeah, it was only two nights ago."

Nellie blinked. Two nights ago? Seemed like ages. "Okay, yes. But…we talked about ourselves."

He nodded, his eyebrows lifted in an "I'm waiting" look.

"Well, I lied."

"You lied."

"I don't live in Dallas. I'm not some fancy interior designer. I let you believe I was."

"Really?" His lips turned up. He looked almost relieved.

"Well, I kind of figured that out when I said I had a cypress ceiling and you didn't call me on it."

She ignored his flippancy. "I'm nothing you think I am. I live in a small town. I'm a librarian. I don't even date."

His eyes narrowed. "What does that mean?"

"It means I don't date. I sit home on Friday nights. I play online poker. Eat ice cream. I can knit. I make fig preserves from my tree out back." She couldn't stop her voice from rising. "I don't drink martinis and I don't wear stupid bikinis. I go to church and make the costumes for the Christmas pageant every year. I have brown hair and glasses. Don't you see, Jack?"

She started pacing. She didn't even look at him or expect an answer to her question.

"I'm not this!" she yelled, sweeping her hands down her body. "This is fake! From my nails—" she held her hands up "—to my hair, to my tan, to this stupid tattoo! I'm completely made to look like something I'm not!"

"Which is?" he drawled from his corner.

"Sexy! I'm not sexy or chic or sophisticated!"

"Your boobs are real."

She spun around. "What! Are you kidding? That's your response?"

Jack shrugged. "Just an observation."

Nellie was speechless. For the moment.

"Look, so what you're saying is you got a…what do you women call it?…a makeover? That's what this is about, sweetheart? Because it totally worked. I mean, when I first saw you, you were beyond hot."

She knew she looked like a fish. She opened and closed her mouth without any sound issuing forth.

Jack continued before she could say anything intelligible. "But it's not just that. You are beautiful, Elle, in every way. And I don't really care what your job is. Hey, I dig librarians."

He walked to her and gently chucked her chin to close her gaping mouth. "Babe, I felt it the moment I first saw you. It seared across my heart. No kidding. I know it sounds hokey, but I watched you walking through the bar, flirting and laughing, and I was a goner."

She peered up at him. Though his words were tender, she couldn't stop the anger burgeoning within her, welling up, simmering beneath the surface. "You're an idiot!"

Jack flinched and dropped his arms. "That's nice, Elle. I lay my heart out there and you stomp on it. Nice."

She pushed him back. "Yeah? Well, guess what, buster? The first time you saw me was not in Agave Blue. It was in the airport! So what you felt is as much a lie as my hair color!"

"What?" he shouted. "I'm sick of this bullshit! What in the hell are you talking about?"

"The airport, Jack. At the bar. I spilled chardonnay in your lap. Remember?"

"The airport bar? That wasn't you. That was some… wait." Dawning registered in his eyes. He peered at her, his forehead crinkling. "That was you?"

Her heart slammed against her rib cage and broke into a million little pieces.

Jack looked like she had hit him in the head with a shovel. She felt as though he'd returned the favor.

She bit her lip. She wouldn't break down. Not in front of him. She had to get out, but he was blocking the door. Instead, she dropped her cosmetic bag into her Vera Bradley duffel and zipped it. "Yeah, that was me. Hard to believe what highlights can do for a girl, huh?"

No answer came from Jack. He just stood there.

"Can I get by? I need to get my sandals."

Her question seemed to jar him from his contemplation. "Wait a minute. Why didn't you just tell me in the first place?"

She ignored him and tried to slink by. He grabbed her arm. "Look, Elle. You're not leaving until we finish this."

"Don't call me 'Elle.' It's not even my real name. Everything was fabricated. Everything. So, yeah, this is finished, Jack."

"The hell it is. You drop something like that on me and want to waltz out?" He pushed his hand through still damp hair. It stuck up in effrontery. "No way, lady. You're the one who lied."

Her head snapped up. "So I lied. Big deal. This was supposed to be a fling. I didn't want to have a relationship with you, Jack. I just wanted to sleep with you."

His hand slipped from her arm and he stepped back. Pain flashed in his eyes. For a moment, she wanted to reach out and take the words back, but she was a wounded animal, hurt too badly to care what damage she'd inflicted on him.

Nellie couldn't believe the words tumbling so easily from her mouth. She'd never been one for confrontation, but she was angrier than she'd ever been in her life. She wished she'd never become "Elle." She wouldn't be going through all this drama. And she wanted to punch Jack. Bloody his nose for making her love him, for saying she was the one. All of it based on a lie.

"Oh, I see. Double standard. Seems like I'm not the only one to judge a book by its cover, Miss Librarian."

She shrank at the sneer in his voice, but she was pissed enough to mutter, "Screw you, Jack."

"You already did, Elle." His voice was low. Wounded. "Or whatever your name is."

"Move!" She swung her bag onto her shoulder, shoving past him into his bedroom. Just before she exited she spun around. "And just so you know, my name is Nellie. Yeah, plain, old-fashioned Nellie."

"Well, thanks for clearing that up for me. Anything else you're hiding? A husband maybe?" he called as she stalked out the door and down the stairs they'd made love on that morning.

Jack's voice sounded mean. He was as angry as she was. She knew she was out of control, would regret her actions tomorrow, but she was powerless to stop herself.

The party had moved back into the huge family room and everyone turned their eyes toward Nellie.

"Did you need help dressing, Elle?" Kate teased. "Took you a little while." She set down her soda and popped up from the accountant's lap where she'd been sitting.

"Let's go." Nellie turned toward the kitchen. She'd left her sandals by the back door.

She ignored Dutch's soft woof from the laundry room and tugged on her shoes. She wanted to scream "shut up" at the stupid dog just because he belonged to Jack, but that would be moronic.

"What's going on, Elle?" Kate had followed her into the kitchen.

She angrily wiped her cheek. "You can stop calling me that stupid name. And I don't want to talk about it. I just want to get the hell out of here."

"Whoa, Nellie. You're cussing."

"And you're stating the obvious. You want to get the others or should I just call a cab?"

"Whoa! Chill, Nell. I'll grab my purse." Kate cast a puzzled look at her before spinning on one foot and flouncing back into the family room. Nellie could hear her cajoling the other two. Obviously things had gotten pretty cozy pretty fast for the single ladies swilling martinis. Nellie was pretty sure Billie was going to have to go more than halfsies on the drinks. Masculine protests joined the feminine ones.

Kate emerged from the living room. "Okay, Nell. Trish and Billie are gonna hitch a ride with O'Shea when he goes back to close Agave. It's just me and you, sista."

"Fine. Where's Jack? I don't want to see him when I go back out there."

"He didn't come down."

"Good." Nellie picked her bag up and headed back toward the foyer. Everyone in the living room stared at her, but she was too much of a chicken to meet their eyes, or maybe she was just too afraid she would start sobbing. Part of her wanted to run back up the stairs, throw herself into Jack's arms and beg his forgiveness. He'd wanted a relationship, something more than just a memory of a woman and a weekend. She'd ruined everything.

It was over.

But the other part of Nellie, the stubborn Tucker part, marched forward, telling herself she'd been nothing but a damned fool.

She marched through the front door and down the steps before finally dropping into Kate's powder-blue VW bug. Kate turned the key and the car revved to life. Finally, Nellie allowed the tears to fall.

"Don't, Nellie. He's just a stupid guy. Plus, I told you not to..."

"Don't. Don't say 'I told you so.' You know that's the last thing I want to hear."

Kate clamped her mouth shut. "Right. Let's go get a cheeseburger."

Nellie's only response was to lean forward and hide her face in her hands.

"And cheese fries." Kate lightly touched her back. Nellie couldn't stop the sobs that shook her body. She wanted to pretend she was strong and could care less about Jack Darby, but she'd never been a good actress. Plus, this was Kate.

Her friend sighed, "Okay, and a double fudge brownie sundae."

Nellie threw her head back against the headrest, ignoring the tears dripping from her chin. "With extra whipped cream?"

"Damn straight."

CHAPTER TWELVE

Spit in one hand and cry in the other and see which one fills up the fastest.

—Grandmother Tucker when Nellie didn't get invited to Clay Peterson's sixth grade dance.

THE MOMENT Nellie arrived in Oak Stand, she called in sick. Selfish, true, but she couldn't face shelving romance books or making nice with snobby little cheerleaders. Give it a couple days, she told herself. So she did. She hadn't been off the phone with her supervisor Cathy ten minutes before she tossed the suitcase full of outrageously priced clothes on her bed, pulled out her ugliest old shirt and shorts and headed to the side yard for some therapeutic gardening to heal her heart.

And two days later, the damned thing still hadn't stopped hurting.

Nellie tilted her bowl and watched the ice cream pool in the bottom. Then she flipped through the channels on her old TV.

Nothing on.

She sighed and swirled the melted clump of chocolate cherry blast. She really should go put in another load of laundry, but she couldn't summon the energy to get off the couch. She'd felt this way for two whole days. Depressed. Angry. Sad. And every other emotion in between.

She tucked her stocking feet under her. She'd finally settled on her favorite station. On the screen, a girl and her mother schemed to kill the head cheerleader who had stolen the jock boyfriend. Oh, please, Nellie thought, clicking the TV off. Was a guy really worth it?

At that thought, she threw the remote against the wall. It landed with a satisfying clatter on the worn wood floor beside the overgrown houseplant Nellie had tried to kill twice since her grandmother's death.

"Screw men," she called out to the empty house. She sounded angry, but all she really wanted to do was crawl under her quilt. She supposed this was how someone got over a broken heart.

But then again, she was tired of feeling sorry for herself, of wearing old ratty clothes and eating enough transfats to clog her arteries for life. So she'd finally pulled one of her new outfits from the suitcase, tried to fix herself up, and had ventured out to the grocery store to get some healthier alternatives to ice cream and cookies. She had survived.

And tomorrow she would return to work and show Oak Stand the new Nellie. Because she wasn't going back to frumpy clothes, frizzy brown hair and stubby fingernails.

Tomorrow morning she'd sashay down the square, confident and classy, and then waltz into the library ready to take control of her destiny.

Except she wasn't confident or classy. She *was* screwed up. Thanks to being Elle for five days. And thanks to Jack.

She felt a stab of pain in her chest at the thought of Jack, but she tried to shrug it off. She needed to stop thinking about her broken heart and find the damned under-eye concealer she'd paid a small fortune for. Then she'd be fine.

Brokenhearted… Nellie laughed. Ha. Ha. Joke's on her. She'd come away as broken as that little heart tattoo on her shoulder but with way more tears than the single one leaking from its crack.

The first night after her gardening adventure, Nellie had hopped into the shower and scrubbed the damned tattoo off. It had taken her a good hard attack with the loofah but finally no trace remained. Too bad it wasn't as easy to erase Jack.

Ignoring the remote on the floor, she uncurled and padded toward the kitchen. En route, she trailed her finger in the dust on her great-aunt Sophie's antique sideboard and then again on her great-grandmother's polished piano. The floorboards creaked and the fluorescent light hummed when she flipped the switch. Her kitchen materialized out of the darkness, a relic from the sixties, a temple to her late Grandmother Tucker. Nellie dumped the bowl into the large farmhouse sink, not caring that it fell from the stack already there, chipping the edge. It was an ugly bowl purchased with green stamps back in the seventies.

Nellie turned and looked at the kitchen she'd grown up in. The tired linoleum sported cracks around the ancient oven, the tiled countertops were avocado-green, and the lighting cast a pall that made everything look sickly. Though it was familiar, cozy even, with the red teapot and hand-embroidered kitchen towels, she was calling a contractor tomorrow. If she wanted to change, it meant reassessing all facets of her life. No more living by her grandmother's rules.

That meant a new kitchen with stainless-steel appliances, gleaming granite countertops and ceramic floors. Nellie imagined the double ovens mounted beside the six-burner stove. And an espresso machine. There might not be a Starbucks in tiny Oak Stand, but Nellie would be damned if she couldn't make her own lattes.

She felt better. A project. That was what she needed to take her mind off Vegas.

She reached for the light switch just as the phone jangled on the wall.

"Hello."

"Hey, girl. Just thought I'd call. How's the asshole of the world?"

Kate. She'd been calling Oak Stand the "asshole of the world" for as long as Nellie could remember, or at least since she'd learned the naughty word. It always offended Nellie, because even though Oak Stand was small-town backward at times, it was a great little place—a Texas Norman Rockwell painting. Just because Kate had chosen to see it in a rearview mirror didn't mean everyone felt that way.

"Same as always," she sighed, plopping down on the same straight-backed chair she'd sat in as a teenager. Grandma Tucker had never allowed her a phone in her room, so all conversations took place in the kitchen. It had taken the fun out of gossiping, cussing and talking about cute boys.

"So what did you do today? Watch grass grow?"

Nellie smiled because it was close to the truth. She had finished pulling up the dandelions and nut grass that had covered all her beds. "Not quite, but I did see Brent Hamilton at the grocery store."

Kate snorted. A hulking football player and no Einstein, Brent had been Kate's first. She'd been nuts for the rippling abs and chiseled jaw of the all-district quarterback. Nellie had never found Brent to be much of a conversationalist, but then again, Kate hadn't used him to practice social chitchat…

"Yeah, he nearly ran into a display of Cheerios when he saw me." Nellie laughed. "I decided to try out the halter top thing with the crop pants. I even put on the cute wedges even though they kind of hurt my feet."

"Figures. He always loved a hot bod, and since he's never seen yours, I'm betting he salivated like a Pavlovian dog."

"Yeah, he looked long and hard. I have to say there's something thrilling about that kind of power. Very weird, but addictive."

"Ah…you are learning, my child," Kate said, using her "Confucius says" accent. "So? You okay?"

"I think so. I'm heading back to work tomorrow. Look, I know I was a mess, but it was what it was. A fling destined to end badly. You know me. I don't do things lightly. I wasn't going to be able to be all cool about it, shake hands as though spending that time with him and making love to him was no big deal."

"I know, but, Nellie, you gotta realize the world's not like Oak Stand. People don't grow up and marry their high school sweetheart, stay in the same small town, do the same things they've always done. And they don't say 'making love.' It just doesn't exist anymore."

Nellie frowned. "Why not? Because I've got to tell you, Kate, that whole sex and the single girl thing just ain't happening for me. I can't go to clubs, drink martinis and pick up single guys for a fun night of sex. I'm just not wired that way. See? Look what happened. The first guy I pick up in a club, I fall in love."

Kate sighed. It sounded sad, resigned. "Yeah. I know, Nellie. You can't change a leopard's spots, but I think we did a hell of a job rearranging them. And, little leopard, you've stretched your legs and sharpened your claws. I hope one day you can look back and not regret it."

"Me, too," Nellie murmured. "But, hey, I do like my new image, Kate. I tried the straightening iron and actually got my hair looking pretty good. My hand is getting steadier with the eyeliner, and I painted my toenails bright pink to match the outfit I'm wearing tomorrow."

Her friend laughed. "I've created a fashion diva. Just promise me no more discount chain outlet stores. Use the catalogues I sent home with you."

"Will do, sister." Nellie threw in a little half salute for good measure even though Kate couldn't see her.

"Well, I got to run. Billie hooked up with one of those coaches at he-who-must-not-be-named's house and now we've got to go to some UNLV basketball recruiting thingy. Ciao!"

Nellie placed the phone in the cradle.

She hit the lights and padded up the stairs to her bedroom. Her suitcase still lay open on the floor, spilling out her new clothes in a waterfall of colors and textures. Nellie started pulling them out, sorting and stacking. Lord, she'd spent a bloody fortune on herself this past week, but it was worth it.

She hung a pair of white linen pants over the overstuffed bedside chair, placing a curve-hugging magenta blouse atop it. She'd wear the beaded sandals with it, sans the knee-highs. Forget the rule book. Nellie Hughes—Oak Stand rebel.

She tugged off her ratty robe, turned out the light and slipped into bed. She felt as though she didn't even belong to herself, had left herself back in Vegas. The person now lying in the bed was one of those doubles the aliens made when they took the real person up into their spaceship to do weird experiments on them. She was a duplicate—a duplicate who looked better than the original but was still a hollow mold.

Jack Darby had done a number on her.

Stupid cheerleaders.

JACK HATED green-bean casserole, so why his mother made it for dinner was beyond him.

It could be he was just grumpy as an old bear dragged from hibernation, because usually her oversight wouldn't have bothered him.

It was just that he seldom went home. And when he did, she always fixed his favorites.

But green-bean casserole with that nasty gray muck on it? Nowhere near his favorite.

"Don't you like the dinner, Jack?" his mother asked, taking a sip of her overpriced chardonnay. "You haven't eaten very much."

"It's fine, Mom," he said, scooting the green-bean casserole around, camouflaging his lack of interest in the dish just as he had when he'd been a boy.

"Oh, that's right. You're the one who doesn't like green beans. Sorry, Jackie, I forgot. I am getting old."

Now he felt like a first-class jerk.

"It's all right, Mom. It's good." Jack flashed his trademark make-'em-melt smile. Except he forgot it didn't work on the woman who'd once wiped his bottom.

His father, forever in his own world, set down his fork. "Who doesn't like green beans? Jack?"

Jack shook his head. "Not my favorite, but it's not a big deal."

His mom lifted a shoulder in a feeble shrug. "Well, I do try. You know, I try to please everyone. Of course, no one cares about me. About what pleases me anymore."

Lila Darby looked at his father. Pointedly. Jack knew she hadn't accepted the fact the ranch would be in Texas. She would miss her garden club, tennis with friends, and the Historic Society, where she chaired some project or other. She hated the thought her brother would continue running the dairy—the dairy her father had established in the small town of Downey Mills over fifty years ago. Lila was certain Downey Mills couldn't run without her at the helm.

Jack rubbed his face. *Here we go.* His mother, the drama queen, was the perpetual tragic figure in every family quarrel from green beans to his sister's teen pregnancy. She loved being the victim, and right now with his father chomping at the bit over the fruition of his dream and with Jack rudely shoving off the date she'd "arranged" for him, Lila Darby played Desdemona to the hilt.

"Now, Lila," his father started, "no one is criticizing supper. This is a fine dinner, honey."

Jack wiped his mouth and pushed his chair back. "I've gotta run. I told Charlie I'd stop over and look at a couple of mares he's been holding for us. Thanks for dinner, Mom."

He didn't ask to be dismissed. Hell, he was a full-grown man, no matter how his mother wanted to treat him.

"But what about dessert? I made a cheesecake. It's got caramel-banana sauce. You love cheesecake, darling." Lila kept speaking as he disappeared through the dining room door.

Jack heard her complaining about his lack of manners all the way out to his car. Lila didn't mince words. She called through the open screen window at him, tempering her fussing with an offer to wrap him up a piece for later.

He didn't answer. Just hopped into the roadster and took satisfaction in the roar that drowned out his adoring, yet annoying, mother.

Women.

He was sick of them.

All of them.

And he was a liar.

Because there was one who haunted him, whispering over his shoulder, reminding him he'd had some peace with her. Elle. Or Nellie. Or whatever the hell her name was. She'd filled the void and made him think love was possible.

Right before she ripped his heart out, stomped on it and then waltzed out the door, giving him no chance to defend himself.

Women.

Dust boiled up around his car as he tore down the dirt driveway of his parents' farmhouse. His foot hit extra heavy on the accelerator, causing the car to fishtail as he reached the pavement of the main road. The peel of the tires announced his anger to the world.

Good. He was pissed because she'd ruined him.

Ruined him for women like Therese Montoya, who had slunk into the country club bar wearing sexual promise like a Hermès scarf, fabulous and worth every single penny. He'd stared at his mother's pick from across the table, watching her eyes issue invitations in the flickering candlelight. He'd studied the way her hands cupped the goblet of Pinot, the huskiness in her low laughter, the sinful plumpness of her lips. And felt nothing. Absolutely nothing.

Hell. Before Elle and before this strange stage he was

going through, he'd have had Therese buck naked underneath him before the ink was dry on the check. Instead, he'd dropped her off with an offhand "I'm bushed" comment before promising to call her another time. She'd pursed her lips and given him the "when hell freezes over" look. It hadn't mattered because Jack wouldn't call.

He shifted the stick, allowing the car to surge forward and hug the curves of the road he'd driven since he'd gotten his license sixteen years before. The needle climbed past ninety, but he didn't slow. His car was made to eat the road, tame it, power over the miles of asphalt like an emperor bending subjects to his will.

He passed the turn to Charlie's ranch. He was in no mood for company. He needed to think.

The road stretched before him, a blank page to work out the tangle of his life. To figure out how he'd get back to normal.

But he knew the answer. He wouldn't. Until he found Nellie. The real Nellie.

It started in Texas. It would end in Texas.

CHAPTER THIRTEEN

It'll feel better when it quits hurtin'.

—Grandmother Tucker to Nellie when she stubbed her toe on the top step of the porch.

WHEN NELLIE WALTZED into the library wearing her clingy pink shirt, linen cropped pants and heeled sandals that clacked when she walked across the wood floor, Rita Frasier dropped the scanner. The flabbergasted look on her face might have been worth it if Nellie hadn't seen the invoice for the new scanner. Who would've thought one measly piece of equipment could cost as much as Rhode Island?

"Holy cow! What did you do in Vegas?"

She wanted to flippantly say something like, *screwed the finest man west of the Rio Grande,* but that seemed a little crass.

Plus it was Friday. Rita always went to Bible study luncheon on Friday, and she would be damned if she would have the whole Oak Stand Baptist Church gossiping about her.

"I got a makeover," said Nellie, dumping her new purse on the counter and setting down a stack of books she'd meant to bring in before she left for Vegas.

"You look incredible." Rita's eyes swept her form from

her razored caramel layers to her bada-bing cherry pink toes. "I mean, you don't even look like yourself. I heard Angela Hill saying something about seeing you at the grocery and how great you looked, but I thought she just meant rested or something. You look awesome."

Nellie couldn't stop the warm glow of pleasure that rose in her cheeks. She didn't have time to reply before Cathy came plowing into the office behind a cart laden with what looked like every reference book in the library.

"Oh Lordy, I'm so tired I could—" Cathy yawned and glanced at Nellie. "What happened to you?"

Nellie shrugged. "I got a makeover."

Cathy rubbed her weary brown eyes. "Damn it. Just what I need. Nellie going all babe-a-licious on me when I still got twenty-five pounds of baby weight sagging around my middle. Great. Now I'll have to stand six feet away from you."

Normally, Nellie would have thought Cathy was kidding, but the woman glared at her as if Nellie's blow-drying her hair that morning was some kind of plot to make Cathy look like a heavy milk cow. Nellie could do nothing but shrug. "You look good, Cathy. How's the baby?"

She knew when to change the subject. She'd had plenty of practice with her eagle-eyed grandmother.

Cathy forgot all about her puffy middle and the towering stacks of books and whipped out a brag book. "He's the sweetest thing you ever saw. See, this is his first bath. And here's Paul feeding him a bottle."

Nellie angled her head so that she could see the brag book, which she was certain contained about a hundred photos of little Logan Reed Brown who, according to his mother, was the cutest baby to ever be born in Oak Stand. Ever.

Luckily, on about picture forty-three, the door opened,

signaling the first patron. Nellie wanted to shout an amen because she felt a mean neck cramp coming on.

"Bubba?" Nellie's head shot up at Rita's incredulous voice.

Sure enough, lingering in front of the check-out desk and looking about as comfortable as an ass-load of clowns in a Yugo was Big Bubba Malone, the only man to never set foot in the Howard County Library.

Stovepipe legs clad in Dickies work pants were stuffed into lace-up construction boots caked with red clay. Bubba's head sprouted from massive cement truck shoulders covered in a plaid shirt converted to sleeveless by careless scissors. Furry red beard, bulbous nose and dainty ears graced the bowling ball that Bubba placed a beat-up Longhorns cap on daily. He made Larry the Cable Guy look like George Clooney.

"Hey, gals." He swiped the ball cap off his head, nearly blinding them with his sweating pate. "Uh, Miss Nellie, I seen you over at the grocery store and I said to myself, 'Dang, that gal's looking mighty good these days.'"

No. Oh, no. Nellie felt a load of rocks drop into the pit of her stomach. She could also feel her cheeks beginning to glow.

"And I said, heck, I need to just go on and ask Nellie to go over to the stockyards with me in Fort Worth to see them cattle run." Bubba stopped and swiped a massive paw over his sweating brow before continuing. "Any of y'all ever seen them cattle runnin'?"

Both Rita and Cathy shook their heads. Their eyes were riveted to the sight of Bubba sweating and squirming on the hundred-fifty-year-old cypress floor. Nellie thought they looked like her aunt Clarice the first time she watched popcorn pop in the microwave—amazed and hungry.

"Well, anyhow, how 'bout it, Nellie? Want to go with me and see them cows haul ass through downtown Fort Worth?"

Bubba Malone asking her out. Dear God. Nellie prayed she stood on a trapdoor that would open and allow her to whoosh through the floor. Or perhaps the tower of books on the cart could shift and collapse, rendering her unconscious. And for heaven's sake, why weren't there earthquakes in Texas? She could use one right now.

But nothing moved. No one came to her rescue.

Everyone just stood still as Oak Stand at midnight.

"Well, Bubba, that sounds, um, nice, but I'm allergic to cows." Okay, she'd just told a whopper of a lie. She knew it, Rita knew it and Cathy was probably too tired from two-o'clock feedings to clue in.

"Really?" Cathy tore her eyes from poor Bubba to Nellie. "You can be allergic to cows?"

Nellie coughed. "It's called 'bovine intolerance.' It's hereditary."

"Really?" Cathy said. "Hmm."

Bubba said nothing, just shifted from one leg to the other.

"How about we just go for an ice cream sometime?" Nellie asked. God, why did she always have to be so nice? But, really, Bubba might be a scary mountain of a redneck, but he was okay. He drank Budweiser like it was mother's milk, chewed Red Man by the box and scored a thirteen on the ACT, but Nellie couldn't shoot him down in front of Rita, the biggest gossip in Howard County, who just happened to be going to Bible study that day. She knew how it felt to be on the short end of the stick.

"So you're allergic to cows but not their milk?" Cathy bobbed her head back and forth from Bubba to Nellie.

"Uh, yeah, it's, um, something in their dander." Nellie

turned her hands over in that vague "I don't know" manner. She darted a quick look at the plaster ceiling above her head, pretty sure the wrath of God was about to smite her down right there in the library. In the past week she'd not only had illicit sex in the swimming pool of Nevada's answer to Hugh Jackman, but was now lying through her teeth about having a disease she'd made up. Bovine Intolerance—well, at least it sounded like a disease.

"Uh, yeah, I like ice cream. I guess we could go over to the Dairy Barn sometime. When ya wanna go?"

Nellie really didn't want to set up an ice cream social with Bubba Malone in front of her two co-workers. "How about I walk you out and we can talk about it?"

Nellie scooted from around the desk, and Bubba stepped back toward the door. Nellie wasn't sure if he was being gentlemanly or just checking out her butt. She was kind of sure it was the latter when she turned to wait on him and caught the general direction of his eyes.

And he didn't even have the decency to look sheepish.

"You want to go tonight or maybe tomorrow?" Nellie asked. "I could just meet you there."

"Well, tonight's my poker night. Tomorrow I'm goin' bass fishin' with Talton, but I guess I could clean up and meet you that night." Bubba hooked his ball cap over the fat roll on the back of his neck and settled it onto his bald head.

Nellie stepped onto the wide-planked porch of the library. The porch wrapped around the antebellum house, boasting cheerful red rockers that creaked on the worn painted floors. The surrounding oaks cast shifting shadows on the freshly painted railing, while Boston ferns swayed from chains, rocking to and fro in the late May breeze.

The town square sat just off to her right. She could

glimpse the fountain pouring water over the walls surrounding the statue of her great-great-grandfather Rufus Tucker. She'd stood on that porch hundreds of times. First as a toddler clutching the hand of Grandmother Tucker as they climbed up the stairs with her storybooks, soon after as a long-limbed, berry-brown girl holding stacks of Nancy Drew books, and finally as a librarian juggling file folders and a briefcase.

But she never thought she'd be standing on the porch arranging a date with Bubba Malone.

"Okay, Bubba, I'll meet you on Friday, say, at seven?"

"Yep. That'll work."

"Um, Bubba. You know, I'm not really looking to get into a relationship or anything. Um, this is just a friend thing, huh?" Nellie felt awkward asking, but she didn't want to leave Bubba with any misconceptions. Just a friendly ice cream on Friday night. Not a date.

Bubba looked like a worm crossing hot pavement. "Sure, I mean, yeah, we're friends. We've always been friends."

She nodded.

"It's just I saw you and you looked so pretty," he continued. "And, I mean, I always liked you. You're so smart and nice. I just thought to myself, 'That Nellie, well, she's always been a gem in the rough. Now she's shinin' like a new diamond.' I had to take a shot."

An awkward pause hung over them for a moment before Bubba cleared his throat. "Hey, Nellie, you remember that time you told those Godwin kids off who were makin' fun of me and my momma?"

A smile curved her lips. Bubba was good at shifting topics too. "Yeah, those kids were plum rotten, weren't they?"

"Never seen such a sweet girl get so mad. Man, you was

like a wet hen, all ruffed up and ready to peck their eyes out." He laughed and it sounded like pieces of rusty metal rubbing together. "I always did like you, Nellie. You're good people."

"So are you, Bubba," she said, punching him on his massive arm. "I'll see you Friday night at seven sharp. Don't be late. You know us librarians, we don't take to dawdlers."

Bubba delivered a sloppy salute and stomped off the porch toward his gargantuan pickup truck with the dual exhaust pipes that roared when the engine was cranked. She knew. She'd once dropped a dozen eggs onto the pavement outside the grocery store when he fired up and bellowed out of the parking lot.

Nellie walked back into the library. Rita leaned over the counter, her eyes ablaze. "Well, I'll be. Who'd a thunk old Bubba had it in him? How'd you get out of that one?"

"Well, I guess I didn't. We're going for ice cream tomorrow night."

"Really?" Cathy arched her pencil-thin eyebrows. "You and Bubba? That's like eating saltines with filet mignon."

"Which one am I?" she asked, picking up the stack of books she'd set down along with her purse and starting for the small office at the back of the library.

The last thing she heard was Cathy giggle at something Rita said. Nellie didn't want to know what it was.

She entered the office and shoved the books onto the folding chair in the corner. Her office could really use a makeover too—every nook and cranny was stuffed with books, papers and files. The desk squatted in the middle, battle-scarred and weary but still serviceable. The mustard-yellow walls had dings and scratches. The space would have been grim if not for the framed Georgia O'Keeffe pictures, cheerful potted houseplants, and obnoxious pencil cup sporting an uptight librarian on it that said Librarians have tight buns.

Kate had a twisted sense of humor.

Nellie slid behind her desk and switched on her computer. Being out of town for even a few days had put her behind. She had tons of summaries to prepare for the database, not to mention several dozen book reviews to read. Cathy wanted a list of possible acquisitions before the next board meeting, and she also needed to get a compilation of genealogical resources available to present to the Senior Citizens' Center next Friday. Nellie would be swamped for several days.

The hours flew by as quickly as her fingers flew over the keyboard, entering the required information in the database. Before she knew it, Cathy knocked on her door and told her to grab lunch.

Because she'd forgotten her lunch, Nellie strolled home. She had an hour so she took her time and meandered through the small garden in the center of the town square. Her house towered on the corner of the square, overseeing town operations just the way her great-grandfather Joseph Tucker intended it to. Birds sang, the fountain gurgled, and Bernie the weenie dog barked a greeting as she passed his fenced-in yard. By the time Nellie reached the walk of the stately colonial she'd called home since she was in diapers, she'd forgotten just how much she hated men.

Until she saw the brooding hunk sitting on her porch swing, just as comfortable as if he'd been born lord of the manor. What was he doing here and how did he know she'd come home for lunch?

"Afternoon, Nellie."

"Hello, Brent. I guess you've taken to making yourself at home on my porch." She pulled her keys from her pocket.

"I figured you wouldn't mind too much."

"I guess I don't," she said, climbing the stairs to the door. She could feel Brent's eyes on her and she didn't like it. It felt foreign, and she'd rather he didn't visually undress her as if she was one of those girls at the gentlemen's bars he frequented.

"It's weird. I still think about it being your grandmother's porch. She made some good lemonade."

Nellie just grunted an affirmative. She stuck the key into the dead bolt. Hearing it click, she swung the beveled glass door wide, allowing her cat Beau to slide out and curve around her legs. She could already see his stray hairs clinging to her white pants but didn't care.

She scooped Beau up and deposited him on the top of the porch railing. "Did you need something, Brent?"

Brent Hamilton, all-state quarterback and Oak Stand's answer to Tom Cruise, flashed his best blinding smile and lowered his lids to sultry. He slowly stood up, allowing the porch swing to bump against the back of his knees. He took a few steps toward Nellie, and she caught a whiff of his spicy aftershave. "Why? You asking for something, Nellie?"

Lord, was this how he flirted? And she thought she was pathetic. She folded her arms and shot him her best no-nonsense glare. "No. You're the one standing on my porch. Not the other way around."

Something cruel flashed in Brent's Nordic eyes. "You a lesbo or something, Nellie? I mean, there's been rumors and all."

She flinched at his words. Lesbian? Just because she didn't spread her legs for every man in Oak Stand? Nellie wanted to throw something at Brent. Beau would probably work. He'd scratch those perfectly tanned cheeks. But who hurled a cat at a man? Part of her wanted to slink inside and close the door, hurt and embarrassed, typical Nellie. But she did neither.

Instead, she allowed her lips to curve upward then she casually caught her lower lip with her teeth. She raked Brent with her eyes, not once but twice. Then she reached out and laid her hand flat on his muscled chest. "Why? You want to watch, Brent?"

She had never seen Brent Hamilton at a loss for words, but damned if he didn't look shocked. His eyes shifted from conniving to confused. Poor Brent. She'd rocked his delicate sensibilities.

Nellie allowed a low laugh to escape and she walked her fingers up to his shoulder. "Just kidding, Brent. I don't do girls, anyway. And if I did, I wouldn't let you watch."

She pressed one finger into the cleft in Brent's chin before stepping away. She threw him a sunny smile.

His only response was to blink.

"You never did tell me why you're on my porch," she said, grabbing the doorknob and turning expectantly toward the man still gathering his wits.

"Uh, yeah, Bob McEvoy told me you were looking for a contractor. I saw you heading this way and thought I would come by and offer my services." Brent still looked shell-shocked. She wondered if anyone had ever provoked the town hero before.

"I plan on remodeling my kitchen. I put in a couple of

calls this morning, so I could go ahead and get the quote process rolling. You want to give me an estimate?"

He nodded his head. "Look, I'll just give you a call and we'll set up a consult. I gotta get going anyway." He seemed to be in a big rush all of a sudden. Self-satisfaction burgeoned inside Nellie. She'd turned the tables on someone. She'd made a man so uncomfortable he wanted to slink off her porch like a whipped pup.

"Sure," she drawled with a hint of come-hither in her voice. "You just give me a call anytime."

Nellie couldn't say Brent actually scrambled off her porch, but he sure didn't waste much time hustling toward the truck parked just around the corner. It had Hamilton Construction written on the side of it, along with his phone number. She could jot the number down, but she was almost certain Mr. Football would be calling her. His eyes may have gone all befuddled, but they'd definitely shown interest. Brent would be back.

She picked Beau up and nestled him in the crook of her arm. His lawn-mower purr cranked up and she dropped a kiss on his heart-shaped nose. "Well, Beau, I've gone two years without a date and darned if two men didn't pop up today. Too bad neither is the one I want. Too damn bad."

She dropped the cat back onto the gray boards of the roomy porch and checked the antique mailbox beside the front door. Nothing but the electric bill, a tanning bed flyer, and a brochure advertising a free weekend in Las Vegas.

She wanted to laugh, but the pain flashed so hard and fast she couldn't even smile at the irony.

"Get Wild In Vegas." Big, bold letters, flashing signs, bright lights.

Been there. Done that.

Nellie crumpled the brochure into a giant multicolored ball just the perfect size to fling into the wastebasket.

"Screw men," she said as she stomped into her house. They could all go to hell.

CHAPTER FOURTEEN

"Homemade, flaky crust" my butt. I caught her buying those pie crusts from the grocery store. She ain't foolin' nobody. See, just goes to show you, you can't tell with some people. They put on a flag-waving, God-fearin', homemade pie-making show, but underneath they're just like the rest of the world. Frauds!

—Grandmother Tucker after she lost the pie contest to Lula Mae Bradford, her archrival.

JUST AS JACK crossed the Oak Stand city limits sign—population 3249—he felt the tire go flat.

Not the best introduction to Nellie's hometown. Scratch that, *his* new hometown. One he'd hadn't even laid eyes on before putting his Vegas house on the market, settling the nightclub deal with O'Shea, and purchasing a run-down farm he'd only glimpsed on an Internet site. It had taken him almost a month to get his affairs in order. And now he was in Oak Stand. The least the town could do was offer him a lukewarm welcome.

That was obviously not in the cards, Jack thought as he angled his new Ford F-250 to the side of the road in front of a ramshackle building called The Bait Shack.

The truck rolled to a stop and Jack thumped the steering

wheel with his head. He was exhausted, hungry and cranky. Two days driving across the arid southwest in the blistering sun made for a giant headache.

The only bright spot in his trip was the gleaming new truck he drove. A fiery red beauty, it purred over the highway, eating the miles, cradling his body in plush leather seats, and providing him song after song on the satellite radio. The only thing it couldn't do was reinflate its own tire.

He slipped from the truck, noting the door to the bait shop opening at the same time. He walked around to the passenger side and, sure enough, the tire was flat. It caused his fine-looking truck to tip like a drunken sailor on shore leave.

"Man, that's some truck." Jack heard the voice from behind him. "You got a flat or somethin'?"

Jack wanted to turn around and say, "Nah, I just overinflated the other three for the hell of it…"

Of course, he wasn't quite sure of the size of the fellow behind him, so he didn't. They grew them big in Texas. He wasn't going to risk a black eye.

Jack turned around. "Looks like it."

The man staring back at him was skinny as a beanpole, blacker than tar and gap-toothed to boot. A friendly smile lit his grizzled face. "Reckon we'd better get to changin' it then."

Jack raised his eyebrows at the stranger's words. For one, the man didn't even ask if he could lend a hand. Jack had experienced his share of kind strangers, but this one seemed pragmatic in his approach. He was going to help; that's what he was supposed to do. Second, he was about seventy, perhaps even eighty, yet there he was, shuffling around behind the truck, wiping his brow with a worn bandanna.

"Woo, sure is hot," the man commented. "We're in for a rough summer, I do believe."

Jack followed the man, who turned and stuck out a papery hand. “My name’s Willie Turner. This here’s my store.”

“Pleased to meet you,” Jack said, taking the man’s hand. It felt fragile in his larger one. “Name’s Jack Darby. I appreciate your help.”

Willie’s rheumy eyes danced. “That’s what neighbors are for.”

Jack didn’t know how the man figured he was a neighbor. No one in Oak Stand knew him or his name. He’d bought the horse farm in the name of his newly established corporation, Sonar Caballo, so the man’s words puzzled Jack.

“Neighbors?” Jack asked.

“Ain’t we all neighbors in this ol’ world?” The old man bent and peered underneath the truck. “Your spare sittin’ under here?”

Jack launched into action, locating the jack and the spare. Before he could blink, he and Willie had the deflated tire off and the spare on with a minimum of groaning and sweating. He wiped his hands on a towel he’d tucked in the door of the truck before he set out.

“Come on in and get yourself a cold drink,” Willie said, turning and heading for his tiny store. He didn’t leave room for a refusal.

Jack pulled the screened door open and felt the cool rush of air-conditioning as he tried to adjust his eyes to the dim room. It smelled of earthworms, hummed with crickets and rattling coolers, and felt like he’d stepped back thirty years in time. There was even a 1977 Dallas Cowboys calendar on the wall behind the cash register.

“Go on and grab a soda,” Willie said from behind the counter. “Get me one of those orange ones if you don’t mind." He rifled underneath the counter and Jack stepped toward the cooler, pulling out a Nehi Orange and a Dr Pepper. He shut the case just as Willie flopped a dog-eared phone book onto the counter.

"I can't rightly remember Old Bill Fuller's number. He's got a tire store in town, and I know he could patch that tire right up. You got time for that?"

Jack popped the top on his soda and handed Willie the orange can. "Yes sir. I'm going to be staying over at the Henderson place. I mean, well, I just bought the place."

"Know it well," Willie said, thumbing through the few yellow pages in the book. "My mama used to work for Mrs. Henderson back in the fifties. They was good people. Their boy dying over there in Vietnam liked to kilt them."

Jack took a big gulp of soda, enjoying the way the icy beverage coasted down his throat and settled in his belly. He had no clue why he'd told Willie he'd bought the farm. He wasn't ready to reveal himself to the town, at least not until he saw Nellie.

Willie shoved the phone book toward him, handing him a tiny notepad and pen brandishing a bank logo.

He obediently jotted down the info, folded the paper and shoved it into his back pocket. "I thank you, Mr. Turner, for helping me. It was a kindness I hope to repay someday."

Willie waved his gratitude away. "The good Lord put us here to serve."

Jack finished his soda and reached into his back pocket for his wallet. "My thanks anyway. How much do I owe you for the drink?"

"Not a thing. Just make sure you come see me when you want to go fishing on that pond you got out there. I got every kind of bait you need and some you don't," the old man added, settling himself into a folding lawn chair behind the counter.

Jack smiled. “I’ll do that. It’s been awhile since I’ve been fishing. Perhaps you’ll join me and help me catch a mess of fish to fry.”

Willie pointed one crooked finger at him. “Name the place and time.”

“I’ll do that, Mr. Turner.” Jack waved as he walked out the door.

Blinking against the brilliance of the afternoon sun, he walked back to his truck. Gravel crunched beneath the old work boots he’d found in the back of his closet. He’d been in town but half an hour and already had a date. Okay, so it wasn’t with Nellie, but fishing with an old-timer who knew his way around a rod and reel was a close second.

Now he just had to figure out how to present himself to Nellie. His plan had gotten him this far, but what next?

Most people would’ve called him crazy. Hell, at times he thought rolling the dice on Nellie sounded like the stupidest stunt ever. Chuck everything and go after some woman who’d lied to him like a snake-oil salesman? Maybe he’d swallowed a stupid pill the night Elle—wait, Nellie—had shown up.

But, no, he knew. He hadn’t even been surprised when a horse farm popped up for sale right outside her hometown. Serendipity. Fate. Kismet. Divine intervention. Put any name to it, but Jack knew what he had with Nellie was real.

He slid behind the wheel and fumbled for the air-conditioning button. Damn, but Texas was hot in late June. The air was so thick he felt he couldn’t even breathe. Rivulets of sweat coasted down his back.

He fired the AC on high.

Sweet, cool air poured out as he pulled away from the bait shop. Willie had come out front and stood waving goodbye.

Not such a bad welcome after all.

AVOIDING THE BLACK HOLES dotting the gravel-deprived driveway, Jack bumped up to the Henderson place. Maybe he'd been too optimistic about his welcome. The house loomed in the distance, large, domineering and in want of a good coat of paint. For some reason, it made him recall the Amityville house. Spooky. Oaks draped the front yard, and in the gloom, he could just make out an old greenhouse with plastic flapping ghostlike in the Texas breeze.

Jack stomped the brake to avoid hitting a cat that sprang from beneath the sagging porch. The truck skidded to a stop.

"Hell," he muttered. "Just what I need—a run-down, piece-of-crap house. Can't wait to see the barn."

He didn't make a habit of talking to himself, yet in a setting such as this, black cat included, he felt it perfectly logical.

Jack opened the truck door, slid out from behind the wheel, and pulled his cell phone from his pocket. He needed help.

Someone answered on the fourth ring.

"Wuz up, J.D.?"

"Hey, Drew. Not much. Where's your mom?"

The phone clattered and he heard his nephew call for his mother before asking his favorite question. "When you comin' down for a game?"

"I'll try and make it soon. I got to get your mom's help first." He hated putting Drew off. Lord knows he didn't make his nephew's baseball games often enough. Maybe if things worked out with Nellie—and they would work out—he could take her to watch his nephew pitch.

"I had to ice my shoulder after every game. It's been sore a lot."

"You using that liniment I sent you?"

"That stuff smells like horseshit. How am I supposed to ever get laid smelling like that?"

Jack heard his sister pick up another line. "Andrew Taggart! You watch your dirty mouth!"

"Sorry, Mom. Bye, J.D., gotta get to practice."

He heard his nephew hang up. "Hey, sis."

"What am I gonna do with him? His father doesn't take a bit of interest. Getting laid. He just turned seventeen, for goodness' sake."

He smiled, kicking a stone into the overgrown grass beside the front walk. "Well, that's when I first got laid."

"Don't tell me that," Dawn said. Jack could hear resignation in her voice. "I can't believe he's old enough to brush his own teeth, much less want to have sex."

Silence hung on the line.

"I'm getting old," his sister sighed.

"Yeah, getting old sucks," he said.

"What's up?" Dawn asked. Jack could hear dishes being dumped into the sink. His sister was a legendary multitasker.

"I need your help." He looked up at the house. It had good bones, but needed some major sprucing up. He was going to spend a buttload to get the place in shape. He could only hope his Vegas house sold soon and for above asking price.

"You? Wait. You? Jack Darby? You need help?" Dawn was not only a multitasker, but a typical older sister.

"You want to be a smart-ass, or do you want to put your skills to use?"

She stopped taunting. He could hear her nearly salivate over the phone. "Skills?"

"Yeah, this place I bought needs work. A lot of work." He walked up and surveyed the porch. A couple of slats were missing. The front door looked to be in good shape, but the windows were fifty years old with cracking paint.

"What do you mean? Like a remodel? Because I don't do remodels. I own a furniture redesign shop."

"Uh, like I know that." He started to add that he'd helped her finance it, but she didn't need to be reminded of her little brother's success. She was doing fine on her own.

"Just saying," she said. He heard glasses clink and a cabinet door slam. "You want me to come up and take a look?"

"I'm calling," Jack said, pulling a set of keys from his pocket. He was almost afraid to open the door. He wished he had brought Dutch. At least the dog would protect him. Or maybe not. Dutch was afraid of the wind if it blew too hard.

"Hmm." Dawn was thinking. He could hear the cogwheels turning in her head. She was visualizing her calendar—Andrew's games, consultant appointments, meetings at the church. "I guess I can come up this weekend. Larry has Drew. Next week's out because of tournament ball. I could at least help you get a game plan for what needs to be done."

"That's great, Dawn. I could really use you." He knew the words that would lock Dawn into coming. Need and appreciation. His sweet sister was so predictable. God, he loved her.

"Okay, okay, you already have me. No need to pour on the sugar, Jackie."

He rolled his eyes and noticed an enormous spiderweb lacing the beams of the porch. He put the key in the lock and gave it a twist. The bolt slid home with a loud click. Jack pushed the door open. The creak wasn't as bad as he'd expected.

Sunlight followed him into the foyer. First impression: The Waltons meet the Brady Bunch. Dusty oak floors made a worn path into the large living room. Groovy striped wallpaper lined the single wall to his right.

"Wow."

He heard crystal clinking before Dawn said, "What?"

"This living room is really orange." He stepped into the room. A tired gold sectional filled one half. A shag rug centered in front of a bay window harbored a forest of dust bunnies or maybe Texas tumbleweeds. A macramé basket hung drunkenly from a lone hook in the corner. A few tables were scattered about, as if they'd missed the burn pile by a splinter. In the corner squatted a wood-burning stove.

"Like how? Russet or tangerine? Or maybe a melon?"

He snorted. "Like orange. Um, Tennessee-orange."

"Tennessee-orange? What kind of…oh, yeah, you're a guy. Tennessee-orange. That's like bright."

"Yeah. No shit, Sherlock," Jack quipped, walking toward the kitchen tucked to the right of the living area.

"You want me to come or not?" she snipped. He forgot how much she hated "potty" words, no matter that she used them herself every time she stubbed a toe or broke a nail.

"Sorry," he said, peering through the gloom of the small kitchen. It looked very green, like that sixties' green. Puke.

"Okay, listen. I gotta run. Drew has practice. He's already started my car and is honking the horn. I'll come on Friday. Until then, hire somebody to do some cleaning and start salvaging anything you think you can use. I'll bring catalogues so we can order the basics." Dawn didn't ask. She commanded. It was the benefit of being the oldest.

"Aye-aye, captain." He closed his phone. Thank God for sisters like Dawn. He never could have called Cheryl to help. She was constantly on deadline. Forgetful, lovely and committed to writing those God-awful romance books, his sister Cheryl would have gladly pitched in to help and then promptly forgotten she had. She'd remember at Christmas.

Dawn took charge. Newly single after thirteen years of a rotten marriage, she held her vulnerability in her hand like a repulsive beetle, refusing to look at it even as it scuttled about her palm. She balanced raising her son Andrew with launching a new business, taking Internet classes, and avoiding her creep of an ex-husband and all his legal troubles.

She was a classy lady.

He trudged through the dining room, kicking old empty boxes to the side along with dusty newsprint. Depressing. Up the stairs. Rickety. Into the first bedroom. Moldy. Second bedroom. Musty. Master bedroom. Not so bad.

He was afraid to peek into the bathrooms—they couldn't be good—so he whipped out his cell phone and started calling the utility companies. He needed to get someone out here ASAP. He could rough it for a few days, but Jack Darby had been no Boy Scout. And he wasn't starting anytime soon.

CHAPTER FIFTEEN

The grass may be greener on the other side, but you still gotta mow it.

—Grandmother Tucker to Nellie when Nellie complained about being a Tucker.

ALL THROUGH THE MONTH of June, Nellie had tried to avoid thinking about Jack. Okay, that was a lie. She thought about him every night as she lay in her double bed, staring at the curvy mirror just above the old-fashioned washstand. The night shadows flickered in the mirror, begging contemplation, so she would grow philosophic about all things great and small.

She thought about Grandmother Tucker with her iron will and soft smiles, about her own failure to achieve her dream of being married and raising kids, and the spark in Jack's eyes just before he slid his body into hers. The way he cupped her face, peering into the depths of her eyes, searching for who she truly was. That raw, tender moment of sheer nakedness. Not of the body, but of the soul.

She'd had that with Jack. A perfect stranger she'd met in a bar. Emphasis on the perfect.

But the other stuff got in the way. Her own insecurities about who she was, who she should be. Part of her loved the way she'd felt in Vegas; the other part wagged her finger at the wild half, reminding her who she was, how she was supposed to act, what was expected.

She was Nelda Rae Hughes. And she was a Tucker. Tuckers stood straight, combed their hair before they left the house, served on charity boards, gave benevolently, but spent wisely. Grandmother Dorothy Rivers Tucker made sure her granddaughter understood this. It was her birthright. Her destiny.

And unlike her own mother, Nellie never rebelled. Probably because she didn't want to end up like her mother. Pregnant, forced into a miserable marriage, and then strung out on whatever drugs she could beg, borrow or steal, Grace had been a tragic figure destined for a bad end. Nellie's father had thought he could get his hands on the Tucker millions through Grace, but that was before he got to know Dorothy Tucker. Before he realized how stupid he had been. Before he realized living off the Tuckers was as hopeless as Grace's sanity.

When Grandmother Tucker found Nellie, she'd been lying in an overloaded diaper, listless and lifeless, way past the wailing stage. Her mother, strung out on bad stuff, had driven away two days before, leaving her baby behind. Grace had never even looked back. Or so Uncle Teddy had told her.

Of course, at eleven years old, Nellie had soaked this up, a willing sponge to her alcoholic uncle's tale. Grandmother Tucker had come into the parlor, heard Uncle Teddy and promptly hit him in the head with the fireplace broom.

Then Grandmother Tucker had stepped over Uncle Teddy as he lay moaning on the floor, lifted Nellie into her arms even though she weighed a hundred pounds, and told her Uncle Teddy was an idiot. Nellie believed her because ever since Grandmother Tucker had scooped Nellie up off the floor where she lay in that house just south of Tyler, abandoned by her own parents, she'd belonged to Grandmother Tucker.

And Grandmother Tucker had been a hell of a strong woman. How Nellie had both loved and hated her. Yet love triumphed. It always did. Or maybe not. Take her and Jack. Her only course of action was to leave Grandmother Tucker in the past. And leave Jack there, too.

That had been her mantra for a whole month. Leave the past and look to the future.

So she worked and she got busy on the kitchen renovation. She'd hired Brent Hamilton and had no clue when he did any work. Every time she saw him, he was on the phone. It never sounded work-related, but the kitchen showed progress so she couldn't complain.

She'd step inside, and Brent would shout a hello, rake her up and down with his eyes and lift his eyebrows appreciatively. It both flattered and repulsed.

"When you going out with me, Nellie baby?" he would ask.

She gave the same answer every day. "When hell freezes over."

It drove Brent crazy. He couldn't stand being turned down. Especially by the former nerdy town librarian.

"We'll see about that. I've got plans for you, and they'll drive those women from your mind." He would wink playfully, trying to establish some intimacy based on his lame lesbian comment.

She ignored him. No doubt, he was good in bed. He'd

had plenty of practice. But he didn't intrigue her as he once had. Two months ago, she would have tripped over herself to get to Brent. Of course, two months ago, he wouldn't have asked.

He asked now because of the way she looked. Shallow. She was the same person she'd always been. Except now she wore expensive, formfitting clothes, straightened her frizzy hair so it shone like satin, curled her eyelashes and polished her toenails. She'd always held her shoulders back—Tucker rule—but now her breasts were headliners instead of two-bit extras. It was all icing, window dressing. The real Nellie still wore her comfy panties under the kick-ass jeans. Well, most of the time anyway. The pretty silk ones were sometimes hard to ignore.

Brent approved of her new look. So she wasn't surprised when she came home one Saturday, wearing a silk sleeveless sweater in pale blue with a white handkerchief skirt and backless sandals, to see him come out of the kitchen looking for her.

He stomped out, covered in dust, but looking pretty darned good despite the debris peppering his wavy hair.

"So you went out again with that redneck Bubba Malone but you won't go with me?" Incredulous. The idea of her having an ice cream with Bubba Malone had baffled more intelligent people than Brent. And when she'd gone with him a couple of days ago to the Jupiter Steakhouse, well, that just stunned her handsome contractor. Especially after he'd asked her out for the same night.

"Bubba and I are friends," Nellie snapped. "He's a nice guy, Brent. I'm not looking for a relationship right now." She tossed her bag onto the coffee table.

"Right," he drawled, folding his arms over the tight T-shirt he wore. "You're a woman. You're all looking for relationships."

Her head shot up. "No. Sometimes we're just looking for a good time. Sometimes we don't want any strings attached." Nellie knew it was herself she wanted to convince. Vegas was about an affair. Just sex. Nothing to do with love. Nothing to do with wanting to have Jack Darby's babies and fold his underwear for the rest of her life.

"Well, let me go upstairs and grab a shower. 'Cause, baby, I'm all about pleasure without strings." He gave her the same half-lidded look he'd given her before, rubbing his hands down his massive torso and stretching like a cat who anticipated a bowl of cream.

"While you're up there, make sure you don't go through my underwear drawer again." She suspected the man had rifled through her stuff while she was at work. Which was downright freaky.

Brett didn't even look ashamed. "I like the little red ones."

"You're sick!" Nellie said, prepared to fire him. "You're not supposed to go through your customer's things."

"Don't get those panties in a wad, Nellie." He moved her way and her mouth went dry. Brent was a full-grown man with full-grown needs. He wasn't like Bubba, all sweet despite his obvious maleness. He stopped in front of her, towering, smelling like sawdust and sexy male.

She licked her lips. Stupid. Men always liked that. It was an invitation, so she stepped away, nervous at being alone in the house with him.

"Don't worry, Nellie," he said, giving her a knowing smile, "I don't beg women to go out with me."

He laughed low and tromped toward the front door, his big work boots rattling the glass in the china cabinet. She dropped her arms to her sides wondering why she'd hired the man. He was seriously twisted.

Nellie shoved all thoughts about men to the back of her mind and walked into the kitchen. Fresh-cut plywood was perched atop sawhorses; cappuccino-colored tiles were scattered round the room; and a stainless sink leaned up against the wall. It looked like a tornado had hit.

The screen door opened again. "Hey, Nellie. You home?"

Bubba.

"I'm in here," she called.

Heavy footfalls gave way to a gravelly voice. "Whoa! He's a tearin' it up in here, ain't he?"

Nellie spun around. Bubba had just squeezed into the kitchen. He cradled his ball cap in his hands. Ever the gentleman. He might spit tobacco into an old pea can, but his momma had raised him right.

"Yep. But that means progress, right?"

"I reckon," he conceded, studying the dismantled kitchen with appraising brown eyes. They were puppy dog eyes, odd in such a large doughy face. "Brent Hamilton's pretty good. I seen some of his work over at the McFarlands'. Solid."

She turned her own critical eye on the progress. "He's a pervert. I should have gotten more estimates, I guess, but I just wanted to get started."

Bubba stiffened. "Is he botherin' you?"

"Nothing I can't handle," she said.

"Well, good, 'cause I ain't gonna be around much. I got a job."

"A job? That's fantastic, Bubba. Where are you working?"

"Oh, some fellow's up and bought the old Henderson place. It's been sittin' there for years. He wants to make it into a horse farm and needs someone to help with the cleanup and such. It's gonna take a pretty penny and plenty o' sweat to bring that ol' place up to snuff."

"So Hattie finally sold it?"

"Yeah, wasn't nobody who wanted it. I guess she figured it was time. This fellow seems okay. Little green, but he damned sure could run a tractor."

Nellie grinned. Knowing how to handle a John Deere was on par with a master's degree around these parts. "Well, that's great, Bubba."

She stepped around him and headed out of the kitchen.

Bubba followed her. She pushed out the front door onto the porch. The sun was hovering over the horizon, ready to sink down and blanket the little town in gentle darkness. Her favorite time. Sunset.

"You hungry, Bubba? I'm in the mood for a burger."

Her mountainous friend grinned. "You buyin'? I ain't started this job yet."

"Absolutely. And you tell Mr.…wait. Who's the guy who bought the Henderson place?"

Bubba squinched up his face. "Shoot. I've done gone and forgot his last name. Plum forgot it. But his first name's Jack."

Nellie's stomach flopped. "Jack?"

"Uh, yeah. He's got some horse, I don't know, corporation. Gonna raise racehorses or show horses. No, wait. Rodeo horses." Bubba snapped his fingers, making a crack loud enough to cause a person to hit the floor.

Nellie jumped. Then she felt stupid. Not her Jack. Her Jack was a city-slick club owner. A fancy-pants urban fantasy of a man. She couldn't imagine him covered in dust, sweating on a tractor, shoveling horse manure. No way. Didn't fit. And why would Jack show up here? He didn't even know where she lived. And with the way she'd left, why would he bother? Plus, to buy a horse farm? Ridiculous. Just a coincidence.

"Well, you make him pay you what you're worth," she said, turning back into the house. "Let me get my purse."

"Shoot, Nellie," Bubba called through the screened door. "You know I ain't worth a plug nickel. This guy don't know what he's getting. I may be big and strong, but I'm as lazy as a Louisiana bayou."

She came out with her purse hanging from her shoulder. "Don't sell yourself short, Bubba. You're way more than meets the eye."

"Just like you, Nellie. I always knew you were somethin'. I'm glad we're friends. I get tired of tryin' to talk to Woodley and Jimbo about things. They're just liable to grunt at me, that's all."

"I'm glad we're friends, too," she said, trotting down the porch steps. She tried to visualize Bubba holding a serious conversation with his cousins. It baffled the mind.

"Let's get double cheese fries," he called out behind her. "I'm starvin'."

Yeah. She'd just use extra cheese to get Jack out of her mind.

Who would have thought Bubba Malone would be her new "Kate"? Bubba Malone, confidant and girlfriend. That made her giggle. Which felt good. "Hey, let's get the brownie sundae they've been advertising too. I love Dairy Barn sundaes."

"Deal," Bubba said, rubbing his meaty hands together. "I need to bulk up for my new job. It's damned hot and I'll be sweatin' like a preacher on revival night."

Darkness descended as they took off through the freshly cut lawn toward the other side of the town square. Nellie slid off her sandals and squished her bare feet through the lush Saint Augustine. She loved the way the grass felt between her toes. Summer decadence.

She put her shoes back on when she got to the sidewalk. Bubba was ten feet ahead of her, plowing through town, a man on a mission. Double cheese fries were so good she wasn't offended by his failure to wait.

Her walk took her past typical small-town businesses—a nail place, the barbershop where her grandfather had received his first haircut, the vacant green stamp store, and the antique store where she'd bought a Tiffany lamp. Finally, she reached the Dairy Barn. Rusty-red, it was reminiscent of a time when girls with swinging ponytails huddled under their boyfriends' letter jackets while Charlie Mac served up shakes and fries. It had been an Oak Stand fixture since 1956.

She pulled the door open and the familiar smell of onion rings and bleach assaulted her. Hundreds of eyes swung their way. It was Saturday night in Oak Stand. Nearly everyone was there.

Brent Hamilton dropped the hand he had on Livy Wheeler's ass and smiled.

What a snake, Nellie thought, noticing Brent had changed his shirt and combed the drywall bits from his shaggy brown hair. She ignored him and sauntered to the counter, throwing the stooped Charlie Mac a smile. "Two double cheeseburgers, an order of cheese fries—"

"Double order," Bubba called over her shoulder.

She nodded to Charlie Mac as his blue-veined fingers scratched out the order on his pad. "Diet Coke, root beer, and a double brownie sundae."

As she dug the money out of her wallet, Brent sauntered over.

"What's up, Nellie? Bubba?" He still wore his dusty jeans and boots. Guess Livy didn't mind him talking to Nellie because she followed him over.

Bubba grabbed his diet coke and shoved past, giving Brent a hard glance. Nellie smiled at Livy. "Hey, Brent. Livy, how's your momma?"

"She's doin' better." Livy Wheeler glowed with youth. Curvy, brunette—she was a sweet kid, way too sweet for Mr. "Grabby Hands" Hamilton. Her mother had recently undergone a mastectomy and her prognosis was good, unlike Bubba's mother, who had stage three breast cancer.

"That's great," Nellie said. Bubba inclined his head at Livy but said nothing.

Livy averted her eyes briefly before turning back to Nellie with a smile. "Hey, you hear about the new guy who bought the Henderson place? Oh, my gosh, he's like so hot." She cast an apologetic glance toward Brent. He looked perturbed. "Sorry, Brent."

"Really?" Nellie wanted to smile at Livy's offhanded comment, but something gnawed at her. A hot guy named Jack at the Henderson place. Maybe she could get a description. "You saw him?"

"Only at a distance. At the grocery store." Livy turned a full-wattage smile on Brent. "But he's not as hot as Brent."

Livy's voice turned singsong. Brent leered. Nellie snorted. Charlie Mac shoved a plastic number her way.

She felt stupid. No way it could be her Jack. Just a coincidence. Coincidences happened all the time.

"Well, gotta go. Y'all enjoy your night." She slid past both Brent and Livy, glad she'd hadn't talked herself into going out with her contractor. He was a slimeball.

Nellie wound through the dining section, heading to

the large table Bubba anchored—no doubt to hold the vast amount of food she'd just ordered.

"Hey, Nellie," Hannah Bloom called as she walked by. "You hear about the Henderson place being sold? Ted's gonna put up a new barn for the guy who bought it."

Nellie paused at Hannah's table. Hannah came into the library almost weekly. She was a mystery junkie, eating up Sue Grafton and Elizabeth Peters books like a guilty dieter. Hannah had been worried about her husband Ted, who'd experienced a business slump after he'd broken his leg on a job. "That's terrific, Hannah. I know Ted must be happy about the job. Probably be a big one if the guy's raising horses."

"Yep." Hannah popped a fry into her mouth. "He's celebrating with a chocolate milk shake."

Ted Bloom came up behind Nellie. She'd known him since he'd peed on her front lawn when he was six. "Hiya, Nell. I see you're with Bubba again. Y'all datin'?"

She shook her head. "Nope. Just friends."

Lord, she thought. Couldn't two single people go out and about without people wanting to know where they'd registered their china pattern? She changed the subject. "Hannah told me about your job over at the Henderson place. You'll be seeing Bubba over there. He was hired to do cleanup."

"Yeah, that fellow's hired a couple of folks. Gonna be a big operation, I reckon."

Nellie caught one of the diner workers weaving her way. She motioned him over to the back of the diner where Bubba sat. "There's my order. Y'all have a good evening. Congrats on that job, Ted."

She waved to a few other patrons as she made her way over to her table. She could hear snippets of conversation peppered with "Bubba" and "Henderson place." When she got to the table she saw Bubba had waited on her like one dog waits on another. His mouth was full of cheeseburger. He pushed out a chair with his foot. "Mfff. What took you so long? Everybody's lookin' at me just like at Jupiter."

Nellie tucked her skirt under her and wiped a smear of ketchup from the laminate table. Nothing like fine Oak Stand dining. "Sorry. Ted's going to be working out at the Henderson place too."

"Oh." He took another bite of the colossal cheeseburger. "I swear it's got everybody talking as much as when Mrs. Holtzclaw got her niece to do the chairs in the choir loft and Mrs. Monk fell off and everyone saw her girdle."

Nellie chuckled as she pulled the pickles off her burger. "It's not that bad surely. Wait. Me and you hanging out or the new guy coming to town?"

"Both, I guess." Bubba shrugged and attacked the cheese fries.

Nellie guessed a dowdy librarian turned sex goddess going around town with a backwoods Bubba and the news of a "hot" guy moving to Oak Stand definitely called for unchecked gossip.

As she ate her hamburger, she glanced around the busy diner. She knew just about all the customers. Everyone, from her second-grade teacher to the guy who sold her honey, thought they'd known the simple Nellie Hughes.

But she had surprised them. In Oak Stand, each person had a slot. Nellie had slid out of hers when she came back highlighted, plumped and, well, different. All the townsfolk whispered, wondering what happened to the not necessarily homely, but certainly not fabulous Nellie Hughes.

"People's lookin' at us again," Bubba mumbled, tearing

her from her contemplation of the room and reminding her that if she wanted some brownie sundae, she'd better grab a spoon.

"Maybe because you have chocolate sauce smeared on your cheek," Nellie said. Bubba took a swipe at it with a wadded-up napkin. "Besides, as my grandmother always said, 'Let 'em look.' "

"Your grandmama sure was somethin'. She thought the sun rose and set on you." He blocked her spoon with his and stole the cherry off the whipped cream.

Nellie blew out an exasperated breath. "You think so?"

"I know so." Bubba shoved what was left of the sundae toward her. "She was hard on you, sure, but she loved you somethin' fierce. She wanted lots of things for you. I could see that. I mowed your yard every week, so I saw what you couldn't."

She tilted her head. "What do you mean? She barely let me go to college."

"Yeah, but she was just scared, is all. Everybody left her."

Nellie had never thought about it in that light. From the loss of her first child to her husband falling down an abandoned well to Nellie's mother going crazy, Grandmother Tucker had cause to squeeze Nellie tightly. "Bubba, you're much smarter than you look."

"That ain't exactly a compliment, is it?" He leaned back, folding his arms over his generous stomach.

"It's a compliment."

Nellie plopped the last fry into her mouth. The diner was still crowded. Every now and then a couple of people would chance a peek at Nellie and Bubba and look quickly away. She thought it was amusing. And annoying.

She had just reached for her purse when near silence descended on the restaurant. She glanced up. And that's when the room rocked, tilted, and turned upside down like a roller coaster. She didn't know whether to scream or throw up.

Because Jack Darby was standing in the doorway.

CHAPTER SIXTEEN

Forget having clean underwear. There ain't nothing important about clean underwear when you're in a car wreck. I always thought that was the stupidest of sayings. If you really want to be prepared, don't leave home without combing your hair and wearing your pearls. You never know when you might run into an ex-boyfriend.

—Grandmother Tucker to Nellie after she'd had her only fender-bender.

NELLIE COULDN'T BELIEVE her eyes. Jack Darby standing in the freakin' Dairy Barn. Jack Darby in Oak Stand, Texas. Jack Darby with another woman.

Nellie fell back into her chair.

She thought about grabbing a menu and hiding behind it, but there were no menus on the table. The Dairy Barn was strictly counter service.

She felt panicky, sick, confused and every other feeling ever known. All at the same time. It was a kind of drowning feeling, like her head going under water. Now everyone would know. She'd gone to Vegas, and what had happened there hadn't stayed there the way it was supposed to.

"Well, I'll be. There's the fellow that hired me. You can meet him." Bubba waved one hand in Jack's direction.

"Stop that!" she hissed, tugging at her friend's arm.

"What?" He looked at her, confused. "Don't you want to meet my new boss? He's a nice guy, even if he is a Cardinals fan."

Nellie closed her eyes. Maybe Jack hadn't seen Bubba. Surely he hadn't. The place was packed. But then again, Mount Bubba was hard to miss.

Oh, shit. Why was he here?

And more importantly, why was he here with a beautiful woman?

"What's wrong? You look kinda sick." Bubba leaned forward, his expression concerned. "Was your hamburger bad?"

She felt the cheese fries backing up on her. Bathroom. She needed to get to the bathroom. Unfortunately, it was at the front of the diner. Just to the left of Jack.

Oh, God! What was he doing here? She couldn't have been more surprised if the Queen Mother had strolled into the Dairy Barn.

"Nell? Hey? You okay?" Bubba rose and headed around the table.

She waved him off. "Nothing. It's nothing. I'm okay."

But then she saw Jack heading her way, pulling the brunette behind him.

Oh. No.

She actually contemplated running. Leaping over the table and making a beeline for the door. But there were too many people. Too many obstacles. Plus, she'd never been athletic. She was liable to fall and break her neck.

"Hey!" Bubba crowed, waving again toward the door before dropping back into his chair. "Jack, over here."

Jack met Nellie's gaze and held it. His blue eyes seared her, piercing her skin and razoring right to her heart. She tore her eyes from his. She didn't want to see what lurked in their blue depths. She wanted to pretend this was not happening. That Jack wasn't here, moving toward her.

And yet at the same time, she felt a bit like the Grinch, as if her heart had grown three times its size. *Jack was here.* If she wanted to, she could reach out and touch him. He would be warm, alive, not just a wispy ghost of a dream, haunting her with silky laughter and sensual kisses. And what had happened in Vegas hadn't stayed in Vegas. He was here. Her heart leaped.

Nellie watched his progress as he prowled across the room, yanking the woman with him. He ignored the other people in the diner. No one else called out to him other than Bubba. Jack stopped right beside Nellie's chair. She could feel the heat from him, smell the citrus cologne mixed with fabric softener, and see the worn cowboy boots beneath the faded hem of his jeans.

Bubba extended a hand. "Hey, buddy. You found the hangout okay, huh?"

Nellie lifted her eyes. Jack stared at her even as Bubba pumped his hand. "No problem, Bubba. Don't think I would have missed it."

His voice sent shivers down her spine. Half of her wanted to throw her arms around him and cry like a child. The other half of her just sat there, kind of like her cold hamburger.

"Jack, this here's my friend Nellie," Bubba said, nodding toward Nellie. "She's about the smartest, prettiest girl in Oak Stand."

At this, she should have blushed and looked pleased, but she was too busy concentrating on breathing. Jack stretched a hand toward her. "Can't say that I've had the pleasure of meeting *Nellie.*"

Bubba looked confused. The woman with Jack lifted one perfectly shaped eyebrow.

Nellie stared at his hand before slipping her own into his. She felt disconnected until she touched him. A jolt of electricity raced up the length of her arm. She blinked. This was not happening. She wasn't shaking the hand of the man she'd fallen so hard for. She wasn't shaking the hand of the man who'd made her burn. She wasn't shaking the hand of the man who'd…come after her? Wait. Was he here for her?

She glanced up. His expression was guarded. "Uh, nice to meet you—"

"Darby. Jack Darby." He sounded like James Bond, though he looked much better than 007. His striped button-down shirt made his shoulders outrageously broad. The faded jeans hung from his hips, and his sunburned cheeks made his eyes turn cobalt. No wonder Livy Wheeler had dubbed him *hot.* He could have burned up half of Oak Stand with his tight buns and sexy smile. Not that he was smiling. Nor could Nellie see his buns. But she remembered. Man, did she remember.

She pulled her hand from his.

"Y'all gettin' something to eat?" Bubba blurted, breaking the uncomfortable silence.

An "ahem" sounded from behind Jack. He snapped awake. "Oh, right. Uh, this is—"

The woman behind Jack stepped forward. She looked like Salma Hayek—golden skin, loose wavy brown hair and soft luminous eyes. "Hi, I'm Jack's sister, Dawn. I'm helping him get his house in order. You know bachelors. They can't pull it together without a woman."

Nellie felt the question in Dawn's eyes. Only Bubba seemed oblivious to the awkward exchange between Jack and her.

"I beg to differ." Bubba grinned, shoving a toothpick in his mouth. "I like my milk crate bedside table and beanbag chairs."

Dawn snorted. "I suppose you have one of those wooden spool things from the phone company as your coffee table, too?"

"How'd ya know?" he said.

Dawn laughed. Jack forced a smile. Nellie sat there like a puddle in the road. Doing nothing except being.

"Well, we'd better get to the counter," Jack said. "Looks like business is picking up." Nellie could feel his eyes on her. He waited for her to say something, to show she knew him. But all she could do was stare at the ketchup squeeze bottle. Her tongue wouldn't move, so she pressed her lips together and studied Dawn's cute cork-wedge sandals.

"Yep. It's Saturday night in Oak Stand." Bubba stretched back in his chair. Nellie thought she heard the legs groan.

Dawn took that as a cue to make the standard "nice to meet you" platitudes. Jack said nothing, just lasered her with his eyes. Nellie sat stone still, managing only a smile. That was all.

As they walked away, she slumped against the vinyl chair. She felt like crying but knew it would draw more attention. But maybe not. Everyone with the exception of Beverly Tyner, who was fussing at three of her kids, stared at the two newcomers as they wound their way through the diner, stopping to chat and shake hands with many of the locals. They looked like movie stars, benevolently bestowing their glow on each individual, but they were totally unaware of the power of their presence.

Bubba wasn't watching Jack and Dawn. He stared at her as if she'd suddenly grown two heads. He wisely didn't ask any question other than, "You ready to go?"

She nodded and reached for her purse. She felt numb, shocked and outraged this was happening to her. She headed for the exit, stiff and proud. At that moment, she was exceedingly glad she was a Tucker. No one could throw their shoulders back and go through the motions like one of her clan.

Nellie shoved the swinging glass door open, and took several gulps of the humid night air.

Bubba trudged along behind her, holding the door for a couple of teenagers who'd just walked up.

"What the hell?"

The voice came from behind her. It wasn't Bubba. It was Jack.

She tried to pretend she didn't hear him. Maybe he would go away. Everything would go away.

"Nellie!" Wish not granted.

She turned around. Jack stood in front of the Dairy Barn, hands on his hips like an irate parent. Bubba stood behind him looking confused.

"What?"

"That's what I get? A total brush-off?"

She couldn't see his eyes clearly in the shadows of the night, which made her uneasy. "I…uh…what are you doing here?"

He didn't move closer to her, just folded his arms across his chest. "What do you think?"

She could feel emotion tightening her throat. She needed to get home before she lost it in front of the people looking out the plate glass windows of the Dairy Barn. Before she made a spectacle of herself in front of everyone she knew. "I really don't know."

He shook his head. She couldn't tell if he was disappointed or perturbed. "I guess you'll find out."

She waited for him to say more, but he didn't. Just nodded to Bubba and went back into the diner.

She turned around and started walking. What else could she do? Go back and confront him? People had already seen him beeline for their table and then follow them outside. She could only hope they'd think he wanted to speak with Bubba, not her.

So she headed back around the square toward home. Bubba followed, kicking a small stone the whole way like a schoolboy. The scuff of his boot and the resulting tumble of the rock were the only sounds in the darkness, but she could tell he was waiting for her answer.

Nellie stepped onto her front walk. "I know Jack."

Bubba parked a big boot on her porch. "Figured that out. I'm smarter than I look, remember?"

She walked to the porch swing, kicked off her sandals and tucked one foot underneath her. The swing creaked as she set it in motion. "I met him in Vegas."

"Why's he here?" Bubba asked, eyeing the small rockers lining the porch before sinking down onto the steps.

She shrugged. "Don't know. I never even told him my real name."

"Why?"

Hell. Bubba was no Kate. Kate ranted, filled in blanks. She didn't ask open-ended questions that required the rehashing of one's motives. Nor would she have waited as patiently as he had. "Because I wanted to be someone else for the weekend. Someone glamorous, free, uninhibited. I made up a name and had an affair."

"With him?"

She swallowed hard. "Yeah."

"Shoot," Bubba said. "That sounds like something Kate would do."

"Yeah. It does, doesn't it?" She managed a smile.

"Well, whatcha gonna do?"

She shrugged. That was the million-dollar question, wasn't it? And the answer? "Nothing. I don't know why he's here. I guess it could be coincidence. He's starting a horse farm or something, right?"

"Un-uh." Bubba shook his head. "He came here 'cause you was here."

That ill-spoken observation nearly shook her from the swing. Jack had come for her?

"But that doesn't make sense, Bubba. Why not just pick up the phone? Call me and talk to me? I don't know what to think. The way we ended…"

"I guess I don't know how you left it. But that man thinks he's got somethin' to prove. That's how we are, I mean, as a breed. If we want something, we want it. I guess ol' Jack didn't think a phone call would do it. He's got a plan, I reckon."

Nellie stared at the sweet olive bush beside the porch. It made the summer night sweeter with its fragrance. Stars winked from under the moss-decked oak branches each time the swing arced back. Crickets chirruped and june bugs thumped against the screened windows. She should have been at peace.

"A plan," Nellie echoed, allowing her toe to drag against the faded boards beneath her, her stomach churning at the portent of two simple words.

"Mmm." Bubba lurched, stiff legged, off the porch stairs. "I guess I gotta get. I told Momma I'd watch the news with her tonight. She's havin' one of her good days."

He pulled his cap out of his pocket and shoved it onto his head.

"You're leaving? We're just figuring this out. I need a man's opinion." Nellie wrapped her arms around herself and threw him her best puppy-dog look. It didn't seem to work because he started digging his truck keys out of his pocket.

"You ain't gotta do nothing. Just wait."

"Wait?"

"Well, it's like this, Nellie. You know when you go fishin'?" Nellie nodded. "Well, you know there's fish there, right? In your case, it's a big one. You gotta sit back and see if he's gonna nibble or just take the whole thing in one big gulp. Then I guess you gotta decide if he's a keeper."

Kate would have never talked in fish analogies, but Nellie totally got where he was going. She just had to watch the cork. Of course that made her bait. It was a bit disgusting to think about herself as a wriggling worm on the end of a hook.

"See ya," Bubba called en route to his truck.

"Bye, Bubba—thanks," she called over the chirrups of the cicadas. He lifted one hand.

Not a man of many words. But those few words made sense… She sighed.

Bubba's big truck roared to life, interrupting the tranquility of the night. Nellie swore she could feel the swing vibrate. He backed out and hit the curb. The truck lurched as he gave it gas before shooting off down the street.

Bubba Malone. How had an ice cream sundae bestowed out of charity led to such a friendship? And she really liked him, felt totally comfortable around him even if his eyes often dipped to her chest.

But he was a man, after all.

Men. Who could understand them? She had such little experience with them. Was Bubba right? Did Jack have a plan? And did it involve wanting her?

Time to cast her line and see what happened.

JACK DIDN'T HAVE A PLAN. Not one single idea of what to do. He'd just walked into the Dairy Barn on a Saturday night and there sat Nellie.

And what was her reaction?

Nothing.

She'd sat there like a wart on a toad. Okay, she looked better than a wart on a toad, way better. And she did seem a little panicked. But he saw no affection, no sign of gratitude, no glimmer of love. Shouldn't she have done *something?* Acknowledged they knew each other? Marvel he was there? Nope, she sat like a corpse, pressing her lips together in a tight-assed smile. And then when he'd confronted her, she'd been so perturbed. Not what he'd expected at all.

"Okay, what the devil's going on?" Dawn slid into the truck with two greasy bags. Damn, he knew the awkward exchange wouldn't go right over his sister's head. She had eagle eyes and a nose for trouble. Lord knows she'd gotten herself in a good bit of it over the years.

He glared at her. "Nothing's going on."

"The hell it isn't," she said, returning the glare and slamming the truck door. She stabbed one finger at the Dairy Barn. "That in there was something going on."

He said nothing, just fired up the engine and pulled away from the diner. He didn't have to explain anything to Dawn. He wanted her here to help him with the house, not repair his love life. After all, she'd done a bang-up job on her own, marrying the ass who'd knocked her up then spending the next thirteen years of her life pretending he wasn't a worthless excuse for skin.

He could feel his sister studying him. Women. They just couldn't let it go.

"She's why you're here," Dawn said. He could hear the astonishment in her voice. "Oh. My. God. You're in love with her!"

Jack swung around the square, switching lanes so he could turn north. He shot Dawn a don't-go-there look and gritted his teeth. She thought this was amusing.

Case in point—she started laughing. "I wondered why you picked this town. I thought you and Dad had settled on somewhere closer to Houston. Now I get it."

He remained silent.

She stopped laughing. Jack could tell she was chewing on the situation. A few seconds passed.

"She didn't know you were coming," she said at last. "I mean, I could tell she was stunned. You came here and didn't even call her?" Dawn's mouth fell open as she studied him in the scant light of the streetlamps. "Oh, wow. You don't have a plan, do you? I mean, that was awkward."

He gripped the steering wheel so hard he thought it might shatter. He wanted to tell Dawn to shut her mouth and get out of his truck, but she was right. Man, did he hate it when his sister was right. So he simply nodded his head.

"Oh, Jack, what have you done?"

"What have I done? I rearranged my whole life for her.

I left Vegas and moved to a town I don't know squat about for her. I rolled the dice for her." Jack spit the words out. Even as he said them, Dawn shook her head.

"Now what?" she asked, rooting through the paper bag and snagging an onion ring. She popped it in her mouth and then offered him one.

He took it. "I don't know. Something."

"Good plan. I always thought 'something' was underrated."

"Don't be a smart-ass."

She laughed. "Can't help it. I am my mother's daughter."

"Amen," he said.

"Well, I'll tell you this, Jack. I would give my right arm for a man to do for me what you've done for her. She'd be the stupidest woman in the world to turn down someone like you. And I don't say that because you are my yucky little brother." She leaned over and smacked a kiss on his cheek.

"Bluck! Sister germs."

She laughed. "Don't wipe it away or I'll give you another."

A comfortable silence settled as he tore through the city limits sign heading for his new place. Andrew, who hadn't made it to his dad's for the weekend, waited on them, probably not patiently, to deliver his chicken sandwich and Tater Tots. Jack and Dawn had agreed to leave him so he could program the newly installed satellite system. God willing, Jack would be able to catch Sports Center that night. Thank goodness for teenagers and their vast knowledge of all things electronic.

Jack made the turn into his pitiful excuse for a driveway. He had to think about how he would handle Nellie. How did someone shake things up in this town? Climb the water tower and spray paint I love Nellie onto the side? Throw rocks at her window until she appeared like some celestial creature? Of course, he had the perfect weapon tucked deep in the pocket of his suitcase, but that would be sophomoric.

Yet it would provoke a response.

Jack looked over at Dawn. She looked like a bobble-head. He had to get those potholes fixed. He'd get Bubba on that Monday before he shattered every tooth in his head. And he wasn't paying for his sister's dental work.

"I may have a plan."

"Heaven help that girl" was Dawn's only response.

CHAPTER SEVENTEEN

Pay attention. You never know when the Lord might be trying to tell you something.

—Grandmother Tucker to Nellie when she caught her writing notes to Kate in church.

THE NEXT MORNING when Nellie walked into the sanctuary of the Oak Stand Baptist Church, she nearly tripped over Perla Hightower's walker.

And it wasn't because Perla stuck the contraption with a horn and tennis ball feet into the aisle. And it wasn't the sunlight pouring through the beautiful stained glass windows temporarily blinding her.

It was because the devil himself, along with his sister and a teenage boy, sat in the second pew. In her spot. The spot where the Tuckers had sat for generations.

Didn't he know visitors sat in the back of the church?

Nellie tried to tamp down her grumpiness. It wasn't very Christian after all. But where in the devil was she supposed to sit? She couldn't sit next to him. And what about Cousin Ned? Her cousin only came twice a year—Christmas and Easter—but if he did get a sudden case of religion, he was out of luck too.

Nellie glanced around. Several people gave her a shrug.

It wasn't as if they could explain to a visitor that the second pew belonged to the Tucker family. Because it really didn't. It was just an unspoken rule.

Nellie slid into the back pew next to Shirley Fisher, who had bladder problems.

As the service began, she tried to focus on the announcements and prayer requests, but it was difficult with Jack's head in her line of vision. The man had been on her mind all night and she hadn't gotten much sleep. Fortunately the dark circles beneath her eyes happened to match her gray dress.

Not only had the man invaded her thoughts and dreams, he'd invaded her world.

And just to prove the point, he turned around as everyone stood to sing "Holy, Holy, Holy" and winked at her.

He might as well have been holding a pitchfork.

The action didn't escape the notice of a few members in the congregation. Virgil Walker turned and raised his bushy eyebrows at her. She shrugged, tore her gaze from Jack Darby and focused on the lyrics to the hymn.

During the actual sermon on "Resisting Temptation Thrown in the Path of Righteousness," she'd wriggled more than the three-year-old in the pew in front of her. Talk about hitting below the belt. At one point during the impassioned sermon, Nellie expected someone in the congregation to hop onto a pew, point at Jack, and scream, "That's him right there. The devil's temptation!"

Then turn a finger on Nellie and shout, "And she hath partaken!"

But that wouldn't happen.

Because Oak Stand Bapist was genteel and didn't stand for caterwaulin' by its congregation. And Oak Stand wasn't

Salem. Though at times, for Nellie, the town had felt that way.

And it wasn't Jack's fault he was so tempting. Just to prove the point, Mary Jo Danvers, who sat right behind him, fanned herself…and Nellie knew it wasn't because the preschool teacher was overdressed or the sanctuary was warm.

Try as she may, Nellie couldn't focus on much of anything, so when the benediction came, she grabbed her purse and headed for the double doors. One of the ushers frowned at her, but she kept going. Even when she heard her name.

"Nellie." She knew it was Jack. The man had gotten up and let everyone see him follow her out of church. Great.

She hurried down the wooden steps as if she had the hounds of hell on her high heels. On the last step, she felt his hand on her elbow.

"Wait a sec," he said.

Nellie spun around. "You were sitting in my spot."

His forehead wrinkled. "What?"

"My spot," she said, gesturing at the church. A few people had slipped out, and one or two threw them an interested look. "That's my regular spot. Second pew."

"You could've sat with us," he said, shoving his hands into his khaki trousers. He wore an orange golf shirt with an alligator on the pocket. His hair had been moussed and his loafers probably cost more than the pastor's weekly salary. Jack Darby looked exactly like what he was. Out of place.

The church bells tolled and the doors flew open, spilling forth chattering women, screeching children and men calling out tee times.

"I'm sorry," he said, waving over her shoulder at someone. She heard a giggle but refused to turn around.

"No problem." Nellie saw Dawn and Andrew trot down the steps toward them. She really didn't want to make small talk, especially with Jack's family. She wanted to heat up her Lean Cuisine and pretend everything was as it used to be.

Before Vegas.

Before Jack Darby.

Before she fell in love.

Because the Vegas playboy coming to Oak Stand had scared her. The thought of him lurking around every corner made her skin itch and feel too small for her body. She hadn't asked him to come. He was supposed to stay behind. Be her one indiscretion. Her one fantasy come true. Why had he assumed she would want him here when he so obviously didn't belong?

"What is wrong with you?" he asked.

Nellie shook her head. "I don't know."

She felt moisture in her eyes so she turned on one heel and walked away.

WHEN NELLIE GOT HOME, she skipped the frozen dinner, pulled out her oldest T-shirt and shorts, and headed to the side yard for some therapeutic gardening.

The sun shone hotly and it didn't take long before sweat poured down her face. The flower bed still had a serious case of nut grass, and she needed to plant the irises she'd left near the potting shed.

She set to work, only stopping when a stubborn root blocked the hole she'd just dug. The darned thing wouldn't come loose. She tugged, but instead of ripping it from the ground, she lost her grip, sprayed herself with loose soil and plopped onto her bottom in the damp grass.

"Great," she said, blowing an errant piece of hair from her sweaty forehead. She dropped her head to her arms. Besides dealing with Jack around every corner, the Oak Stand Garden Club's Tour of Homes was a week away. She still needed to weed the bed beside the brick path out back, wash the outer windows and replace the perennials in the side bed.

"Hey."

Nellie looked up.

Hunter Todd Avery stood in front of her, his bare toes wiggling in the grass. "Mom said I could come over. Whatcha doin'? Your hair looks pretty. Want me to help?"

Nellie smiled. The last time Hunter Todd had "helped," he'd trampled a couple of daylilies. "Nope. This can wait. What color do you want?"

"Blue!"

She scrambled to her feet and brushed her hands off. "Okay. Wait for me on the porch. No swinging till I get there."

Nellie headed around to the front of the house, trotted up the steps, washed her hands and fetched Hunter Todd's favorite color. The front door hadn't closed before he held out one abysmally dirty hand, demanding his treat. Nellie started to make him go wash up, but then mentally shook her head. She wasn't the child's mother.

"Here you go. One blue Popsicle."

The treat hit the child's mouth before he could mutter "Thank you." He did, of course, say thanks, or at least she thought he did. It came out garbled.

Nellie peeled her own Popsicle and joined the child on the porch swing, kicking them into motion. Nothing like orange sugar and the chatter of a four-year-old to make her feel better. The swing creaked as they sailed as high as it would allow. The porch groaned a bit, but Nellie knew the sturdy beams would hold. Her great-grandfather had made sure of it.

"Why don't you have any kids?"

Nellie sighed. "I told you already. I'm not married."

Hunter Todd's earnest brown eyes met hers. "You ain't got to be married to have kids. My aunt Stacy has one and she ain't married. It throws up all over everything. Gross."

Nellie laughed and wondered why it felt rusty to do so. "You're right, I guess."

Hunter stuck his Popsicle back into his mouth, which by now had a nice blue ring around it. His little feet dangled, brushing against hers as the swing slowed to a gentler rhythm. Something about the way he leaned trustingly into her warmed her, like her grandmother blowing on a scraped knee after putting on Mercurochrome.

"So, you gonna get married then?"

Nellie stopped an orange rivulet of syrup from trailing down her hand. The direct question felt like a solid punch. Kids. They didn't hold back.

"I don't know."

"My uncle Jimmy can be your husband. He's got a tattoo. It's real cool—a skeleton head. And he rides a motorcycle. My mawmaw says he shouldn't 'cause the last time he had a crash and got a suit. Now he lives with Mawmaw. He ain't got a wife."

Nellie stifled a smile. Jimmy Newsom had gotten drunk, hit a seventy-three-year-old-postal worker who had promptly gotten out of her Buick and beaten him senseless with her umbrella, then he'd spent the weekend in a correctional facility. After a nasty lawsuit, he'd been forced to sell his house and move in with his mother. No thanks. "He sounds like a prince, Hunter."

"He ain't a stupid prince. I hate those dumb guys. I like Transformers. They're awesome."

Nellie stopped the swing with the toe of her shoe. "So true. Look, I gotta get back to my flower bed. You can stay here and swing. Just don't let Beau out of the house. Okay?"

"Okay, but he likes to play with me." Hunter Todd held the conviction her cat Beau loved to play chase with him. Beau did not like Hunter Todd, and he darned sure didn't want the four-year-old to chase him.

Nellie patted the boy's leg and rose. She brushed some dirt from her old denim shorts—shorts that had definitely seen better days. The hem had fallen out on one side and bleach spots dotted the front. The T-shirt she wore had a faded heart on it. She'd pulled her hair back, but it had come loose, falling in bedraggled clumps around her face. Her spare set of glasses perched on her nose, because as soon as she'd gotten home, she'd longed to go back to her former self.

Nellie picked up the trowel she'd dropped earlier. She had a lot to get done before the sun sank into the East Texas horizon.

So she set to work.

But before too long, she heard Hunter Todd carrying on a conversation. Dang. He'd let Beau out.

Nellie struggled to her feet and headed back around the corner. But Hunter Todd wasn't talking to Beau. He was talking to Jack.

She nearly skidded to a stop and lunged behind the sweet olive bush. But she didn't. She just took in the sight of Jack sitting on the top step, holding an action figure and listening to the four-year-old explain how the slime would come out of its eyes.

Hunter Todd spied her. "Hey, Nellie. Look—I found you a husband!"

JACK'S EYES MET HERS. Then took her in. Tangled hair, ugly glasses, dirt on one cheek and orange droplets down the front of a shirt that had likely been pulled from a rag bag. Bare toes wiggled in healthy Saint Augustine grass.

Nellie had never looked cuter.

She shook her head. "Who said I was looking, Hunter Todd?"

"You gotta get married, Nellie." Hunter Todd jumped down the steps with both feet and grinned up at Jack. "This guy ain't got a wife neither."

Jack laughed.

She didn't.

"What're you doing here?" she asked, pulling the gardening gloves from her hands.

"You ask that a lot," he said.

"I have good reason," she responded.

"Actually, Dawn needed me to pick up some shampoo from the store and I saw the kid alone on your porch." Not the best explanation, but he couldn't tell her that the confrontation at church had him worried. She'd looked like a cat in a room full of rocking chairs searching for a way out. Not good. But then again, it had been a better reaction than her sitting there ignoring him.

The kid hopped around like a tree frog while he and Nellie stared at each other. At one point Jack put a hand out to prevent the kid from toppling off the steps.

"Oh," she said, rubbing her hands on her dirty shorts. "That's Hunter Todd. He's my neighbor."

Well, hell. She wasn't going to make it easy.

"Besides, I wanted to see your house. It's nice by the way."

She cocked her head and the ugly glasses slid down her nose. "You did."

"Yes, I did."

"So?" she said, propping her hands on her hips. It pulled the ratty T-shirt tight against her breasts and momentarily he forgot he was standing on her front porch in plain view of the nosy neighbors. He wanted to haul her against him and kiss her prickly demeanor away. Something crackled between them and he wondered if she thought the same. He clenched his hands and shoved them into his jean pockets.

"I—"

A horrific scream split the air.

"Hunter Todd!" Nellie cried, leaping forward to grab the child, who'd just crashed onto the porch and conked his head on a heavy rocking chair.

Jack reached him first, scooping the wailing boy into his arms.

"Hush, and let me see," Jack said, dropping the kid's legs and rooting through his unkempt hair looking for blood and carnage. He didn't see anything but a growing lump.

Hunter Todd just shrieked louder.

"Okay," Jack said, sinking onto the rocking chair and settling the child into his lap. "Come on, buddy. It's just a little bump. Nellie will get some ice for it."

Hunter Todd stopped wailing, but the tears didn't cease. The child sniffled. "Okay."

Jack looked up. Nellie stood staring at him as if he'd stripped naked and danced the hula.

"What?" Jack said, shifting Hunter Todd so he could sit up a bit.

She blinked. "Oh. Nothing."

"The ice?"

Her body jerked. "Oh, of course. I'll be right back."

While Jack waited on Nellie, he rocked Hunter Todd,

who still emitted a periodic whine or sniffle. Nellie emerged from the house with a bag of frozen peas and an embroidered hand towel. She wrapped the bag in the towel and pressed it against the child's head.

"That's cold," Hunter Todd whined.

"It's supposed to be," Jack said, loosening his hand so he could take the bag from Nellie and hold it in place. His hand brushed hers and she pulled away as if it were a hot poker.

Nellie gave him a shaky smile and retreated to the porch rail.

Silence fell as mockingbirds called out from branches and the occasional car whirred around the town square. As Jack sat there in a rocking chair on Nellie's front porch holding the child, it struck him that perhaps she hadn't wanted him here in Oak Stand. He had driven the For Sale sign in his lawn back in Nevada and never even thought of the possibility that he might strike out.

Sometimes his own arrogance overwhelmed him.

So now he felt scared. Afraid he'd risked everything and pressured Nellie without considering her feelings.

Nellie looked back at him and Hunter Todd. "He's asleep."

Jack slid his eyes down to the child in his lap. Sure enough. He removed the bag of veggies and shifted the boy into a more comfortable position. "You want me to take him home?"

She nodded and took the mushy bag.

Then she did something unexpected. She bent and dropped a light kiss on Hunter Todd's head. Then she looked right into Jack's eyes and brushed his forehead with her lips. His heart literally fluttered. A poetic, girly reaction. But, hey, nothing had been the same since she'd eaten the last bite of those pancakes back at Earl's place.

And more importantly, it was just what he needed. Like summer rain on parched earth, her kiss gave him hope.

"But let me go explain to Maude. I doubt she'd take to a stranger showing up with her child in his arms."

Jack stood, careful to not wake the boy. Blue stains ringed his mouth. Still, there was nothing more beautiful than a sleeping child. He followed Nellie through the flowery-looking bushes, noting how worn the path was. Hunter Todd was likely a regular visitor.

With a smile and question in her eyes, Maude Avery took Hunter Todd from him. He and Nellie walked the path back to her house in silence.

"I've got to be getting back," he said. He didn't want to go, but something told him he should. That old gut instinct.

"You've got dried snot on your shirt," Nellie said, leaning back against the big cement planter flanking the front door steps.

He looked down at his orange shirt. Yep. Dried snot. "It'll wash."

Her eyes softened. Or was it the sun glinting off her glasses? "Thank you for helping with Hunter Todd. It was very…nice of you."

He shrugged. Who did she think he was? An ogre who couldn't deal with kids or emergencies or his out-of-control feelings? "Sure."

He turned toward his truck, which he'd parked out on the street.

"Jack?"

He spun back toward her. "Yeah?"

"What do you think about my glasses? You didn't say anything earlier." Her voice sounded funny.

"I don't think anything about them. They're not the

most attractive frames. They kind of hide your eyes, but they're—"

"Not me?" she finished for him.

"They're functional," he said. He didn't wait for her to say anything else. Just climbed into his truck and pulled away

CHAPTER EIGHTEEN

Thongs! Why the devil would anyone want to wear one of those things? Of course, I always was a bit bottom heavy.

—Grandmother Tucker after Twyla Peters bent down to pick up her car keys, revealing a bright turquoise strip of satin.

"HEY, MR. MCIVY. Nice morning, isn't it?" Nellie had to shout over the chatter of the goldfinches on her feeder.

"Sure is, but it's gonna get hot." Mr. McIvy lived next door to her in a little Craftsman bungalow. He and his wife grew prized roses, so he was up every morning spraying and clipping.

Nellie put Beau back in the house and trotted down the front steps. She fetched her oversize sunglasses from her bag and headed down the walk toward the library. She wore a short piqué skirt and a sleeveless boatneck blouse in soft grass-green. Her higher-than-normal Kate Spade sandals clacked a merry rhythm on the walk. She had painted her nails lilac and brushed an extra coat of mascara over her lashes. Shiny gloss on just her lower lip made her mouth look plump and kissable.

Just in case.

Monday was usually busy at the library, especially

during the summer months. Would Jack drop by? The man seemed determined to invade her world, and she still wasn't sure what to do about it. But after yesterday, something had changed. Something had broken loose inside her when he'd gathered Hunter Todd into his lap and rocked the child. It had made her wonder if she'd done what he accused her of back in Vegas. Had she committed the cardinal sin of librarians? Had she judged a book by its cover?

Maybe Jack *could* belong in Oak Stand. And maybe what they'd had in Vegas wasn't pretend at all. Maybe he felt the same love she felt. The thought made her belly quiver.

Because he had seen her at her worst. Just the way the people in Oak Stand had seen her for the past few years. Plain ol' Nellie. And the man hadn't run for the city limits. In fact, she could've sworn he'd almost kissed her.

She sighed. No time to analyze it.

Nellie crested the hill and noticed a crowd gathered in front of the library. Rita and Cathy shook their heads and gestured wildly. Fred Lillie, the local paper's photographer, snapped pictures. Almost everyone else, about seven total, stood shielding their eyes against the bright morning sun and looked up at the flagpole.

Nellie looked up.

Well, the flag wasn't there. But something flapped in the faint morning breeze.

"Nellie! Can you believe someone would do something so juvenile?" Rita called out.

"What?" she asked, coming up on the group. Her sunglasses shielded her eyes, but she still could not make out the item causing such sensation.

"Boys! I swear!" Cathy declared. "Logan will be pulling these kinds of stunts before I can blink."

Nellie headed closer to the flagpole where everyone stood peering up.

At her thong. Blowing in the Texas wind.

Dear God. That bastard. He had run her white lace thong with the cute ribbon ties up the library flagpole. She'd known Jack had her wispy thong; she'd left it in the cabana the day they went swimming and had dropped it when she'd fetched her clothes. He had even made funny jokes about how he'd found it floating in the pool and thought it was a jellyfish. He'd said he would return it to her the night they had the cookout. But she had stormed out, left it. Tried to forget about the white lace thong and all it signified.

Now here it flew—a blatant reminder of her night of sin.

Right in her face.

Hadn't the man ever heard of sending flowers?

She stared at her thong. "Well, I guess it's not exactly patriotic."

Rita giggled. "Not unless it was red, white and blue."

Fred just clicked with his camera. Of course, there was no way Max Settler would let him put any such photo in the *Oak Stand Gazette.*

"Who do you think did it?" Miss Taylor asked in a near whisper. She lived next to the library and studied the comings and goings of the town as if it was a full-time job. "Is it aimed at you, Nellie?"

"Why would it be aimed at me?" Nellie hoped she didn't look guilty.

"Well, you've gone and gotten…well, you know."

"Hot as a firecracker!" Mr. Harp, the eighty-two-year-old retired mail carrier cackled. "Nellie's looking good."

"Well, what's that supposed to mean?" Cathy propped

her hands on her hips. "Does that mean Rita and I are chopped liver?"

Mr. Harp's mustache twitched. "Well, I didn't mean to offend."

Nellie ignored Cathy and started lowering the thong. Everyone's eyes followed its descent until she finally tugged it free. There was no note, but Jack didn't need one to get his message across, did he?

Except she wasn't really certain of the message. What did a guy mean when he strung your thong up a flagpole for everyone to see?

"What size is it?" Rita asked, peering down at the wisp of lace in her hand.

"What does that matter?" Cathy huffed. "You think it can't be mine just because I'm still fat? I could have worn that before I had a baby."

Rita rolled her eyes. "No. I thought I'd wear it tonight for Bill."

Everyone laughed and finally started moving on. Nellie wanted to tuck the thong in her purse but was afraid doing so would show ownership. She really didn't want Cathy or Rita knowing it belonged to her, so she just let it dangle at her side as she climbed the steps of the library.

Rita and Cathy tagged behind, concocting crazy scenarios about who the thong belonged to and who had strung it up the pole.

"Yeah, it could be aliens, but it's probably just some high school boy who got laid for the first time and wanted all his friends to know about it." Cathy laughed. Nellie glanced down at the scrap of material still dangling from her hand. If only it were as simple as aliens.

"Well, if those teenagers would just go to church," Rita said. "I mean, there's just too much premarital sex in this world. People don't give a fig whether they're married or not and don't get me started on the teenagers. They're like rabbits to hear Jolene tell it." She slid behind the checkout desk and powered up the computer.

Nellie rolled her eyes. Rita's sister-in-law was a counselor at Oak Stand High. Her tales could curl toes, according to Rita, who was sworn to secrecy and couldn't reveal anything Jolene told her. Rita reveled in the secret knowledge and dropped hints like bread crumbs.

"What are you going to do with it?" asked Rita.

Nellie tried to deliver a nonchalant shrug. "Throw it out, I guess."

"Oh," said Rita.

"Why? Did you really want it?" She couldn't imagine Rita wearing such a sexy piece of clothing. Her coworker was a nervous little bird of a woman whose idea of sexy involved a turtleneck.

"Of course not." Rita's fingers flew across the keyboard. "Gross. It belonged to someone else. Plus, I'm a Christian."

Nellie laughed. "I'm pretty sure you can be a Christian and wear a thong. I don't think there's a commandment, 'Thou shalt not wear a thong.'"

Rita frowned. Cathy smirked and disappeared into her office. Nellie followed suit, unlocking the door to her own office and placing the thong on her desk.

What now?

Was the next move hers?

Should she be the girl he'd met in Vegas? Bold, sassy and uninhibited? Put on the thong, slip on some stilettos and parade in front of Jack, daring him to take her? Sounded right for the girl she'd pretended to be in Vegas. But she wasn't that girl. Not really.

Or should she just ignore his gesture?

No.

Jack wasn't going away.

And it was time she stopped trying to wish her Vegas escapade away. The man would likely show up sometime today. She'd deal with him then.

But before she could face Jack, she had children to take care of. Nellie tucked a few strands of hair behind her ears and stood. She pressed the creases from her skirt and dug her lip gloss from her bag.

The children's section of the Howard County Library never failed to thrill her. Formerly the mansion's conservatory, the area contained a huge wall of amazing beveled windows that allowed sunshine to tumble inside. Huge prints inspired by A.A. Milne and Lewis Carroll hung along the honey-oak-paneled walls. Comfy, kid-friendly chairs dotted the Wedgwood-blue carpet, creating an elegant, magical gathering spot. Nellie always felt as if she were stepping into the world of Lemony Snicket or perhaps just falling down the rabbit hole.

"Miss Hughes!" shrieked Lucy Reeves, leaping from her mother's lap as Nellie entered the children's section. Lucy pirouetted. "Look at my piggy tails. Mommy did them special just like Pippi Longstocking."

Nellie squatted and studied the four-year-old. Lucy never stayed still. "Wow. You look just like Pippi. If I didn't know you were Lucy, I'd say you were Pippi!"

Lucy glowed.

"You wook piddy," said Jefferson Hyde, the three-year-old with enviably long lashes and a perpetually runny nose.

"Thank you, Jefferson." She smiled at him and then turned her attention to the other children waiting for story time. "Is everyone ready to hear a story?"

A chorus of yays rang out. They were always ready.

She herded all of the children towards the rug. Five minutes later after they'd shaken the wiggles out and sung the book song, she began reading *Skippyjon Jones.* The giggles and whispers never bothered her; most of the children listened with rapture at the tale of the kitten turned sword-swinging Chihuahua. After she finished the story, she passed out small bags of jelly beans. Since Skippy had saved the beans, the children might as well share in the bounty.

Nellie mingled with the parents and children, making recommendations for books the children might enjoy. Her neighbor Hunter Todd had insisted she show everyone the purpling lump on his forehead and little Mary Grace sounded out the word *cat* four times to Nellie's delight. She loved all the children and made a huge fuss over them, but she couldn't stop her eyes wandering to the entrance of the room, looking for Jack. Surely, after sending such a flagrant signal, he'd show up.

By four o'clock she had started growing annoyed. She had waited nearly all day. Where was he?

She'd looked up so often, seeking a pair of gorgeous blue eyes, that Cathy had finally asked, "What's up with you? You expecting someone?"

"No," said Nellie. "No one."

But she lied.

"Well, you're making me dizzy. Wanna shelve some of these books?"

She didn't, but she took them anyway. She had plenty of work to do in her office, but didn't want to be holed up back there. Just in case.

Romance books. Great. She sighed. Just what she needed—to be surrounded by illustrated covers of half-dressed beauties cradled by strapping earls and knights. She already felt keyed up. If he would just appear, she could confront him. Figure out what she should do.

But as five o'clock struck on the massive grandfather clock in the center of the library, he hadn't come.

Cathy locked the front door and snapped her fingers. "Oh, Nellie. I almost forgot!"

"What?" Nellie said.

"I have something here for you…." She disappeared behind the main desk, rummaging around before finally pulling a brown paper sack from the depths of the shelves. "Here it is. That good-looking guy who bought the Henderson place came by and left it for you while you were reading to the children. Do you know him?"

She handed it to Nellie.

It was flat and very obviously a book.

Rita stood behind her. "Is it a donation to the library?"

Nellie didn't want to open it in front of the two women. After the thong, what else would the man come up with?

"Open it," Rita said, moving closer.

"Maybe I better save this for later." Nellie dropped the bag to her side.

"Why? You think it's something more perverted than the thong this morning?" Cathy asked, maneuvering the mouse on the computer in order to shut it down. Nellie frowned. It might very well be. Visions of the Kama Sutra danced in her head.

Rita pulled the bag from her fingers before she could grab it back. Which was really rude for a Bible study leader.

Rita tore open the bag. "A book on baseball?"

Nellie looked at the book in Rita's hands. *My first Book of Baseball: The St. Louis Cardinals.* Her mind flashed back to the airport bar and the game he'd chosen over noticing her.

For some reason tears pricked her eyes.

Rita flipped open the book. "It's for kids. Why would he give you a kids' book on baseball?"

Cathy narrowed her eyes, noting the dampness in Nellie's eyes. Her mom radar had already kicked in. "Wait. Who's this guy to you, Nellie?"

"Did you meet him in Vegas?" Rita asked.

Nellie just stared at the book Rita held. He'd given her a book on the Cardinals. And it meant….what? He was sorry about ignoring her in the airport bar? Or he wanted her to learn to love what he loved?

She swallowed and took the book from Rita. "Yes."

She walked away from them. She really didn't have anything else to say. They could think what they wanted.

Because she didn't know what to think herself. At first she wondered if Jack had come to punish her. Showing up at the Dairy Barn, then her church, as if he meant to embarrass her, needle her into admitting what she'd done in Vegas. The panties up the flagpole seemed like a slap in the face. She might have thought his motives a bit spiteful if not for the incident with Hunter Todd, and now the book.

The book was very subtle. Very Jack.

Made her think about Bubba and his fishing analogy. Definite nibbles.

Time to find out exactly why the hell Jack had come to Oak Stand, Texas. She just wasn't sure if she needed a knife to cut bait or a net.

"WHOA!" Jack yelled to Bubba over the chug of the old John Deere. "That ought to do it."

The tractor lurched to a stop and Bubba twisted himself in the seat. "Man, I didn't think we'd do it. I guess nothing does stop a Deere."

Jack grinned, sweat pouring down his face. Damn, but it felt good to work. He hadn't done so much manual labor since…well, honestly, he didn't think he'd ever done as much work as he had today. At first, he thought the job would be easy—hell, the barn looked like a good wind could bring it down. But those big beams supporting the rotten timber were a bitch to topple. Last one and the tractor had pushed it down steadily till it fell with an ear-splitting crash.

The tractor's engine died with a belch and a fart.

"'Scuse me," Bubba said, hopping down. Jack swore he could feel the ground vibrate as the man landed. It was as if another beam had fallen. He and Bubba grabbed the chains lying by the metal gate and latched them to the chain encircling the beam. They'd learned the hard way to place the chain around the beam before they pulled it down. Each beam weighed over 700 pounds. Jack took the other end of the chain and hooked it to the tractor.

Bubba strolled over to the ice chest and brought out a cold beer, popped the tab and took four big gulps. He tossed Jack one of the icy cans.

Man, nothing tasted better than an ice-cold beer after a long day's work. Of course the day wasn't over. They still needed to maneuver the last beam over to the pile. He would salvage them for the new barn being raised on the other side of the house. Plus, debris needed to be hauled away.

"With the burn ban in effect, we can't burn none of this. Gonna have to haul it over to Linden. I got some fellows that can help us out. They'll work for pretty cheap."

Jack wiped the sweat dripping in his eyes. His shirt was sopping wet, so he peeled it off and dropped it over the scrawny bush beside the metal corral. "Good. I appreciate your finding some folks for me."

Bubba nodded. "I'm gonna haul this last beam over to the new site. We need to get started by next Monday."

Jack nodded and Bubba clambered up the side of the tractor. Jack took another swig of his beer.

"Uh-oh. Here comes Nellie." Bubba pointed toward a cloud of dust coming up the driveway.

Jack blinked against the setting sun. Sure enough, an ugly silver car bumped up the driveway.

"You're on your own, bud." Bubba cranked the old tractor. It burbled and coughed, and finally started crawling. The time-scarred beam bounced behind it.

Nellie.

Well, he'd gotten a reaction. Wonder what she thought about her panties flying over great-granddaddy's statue? Or the book he'd left her? He knew she'd be unhappy about the thong, but what about the book? He'd find out. No more pleasantries or polite little smiles. It was time to get it on. But not in the way he wanted.

He didn't bother with his shirt. He was a man who knew how to choose his weapons. Instead he grabbed another beer, popped the top off and waited. Liquid fortification.

He didn't have to wait long.

Nellie came along the path like an eagle swooping down on a defenseless mouse—direct and with purpose. As best he could tell, she carried the thong, balled up in her hand. Perspiration glistened on her forehead. She skidded to a halt in front of him and launched the scrap of lace his way.

The thong hit him square in the chest and stuck there.

Jack peeled the flimsy fabric off his sweaty chest and dangled it between two fingers. “Guess you got your thong. Sorry it took me so long to get it back to you.”

CHAPTER NINETEEN

I swear men do the damnedest things.

—Grandmother Tucker to Nellie as she watched grown men race lawn mowers around a track on TV.

NELLIE WATCHED as a slow, sexy smile crept across Jack's face. He looked so damned good leaning up against the rusted railing of the livestock pen, one foot perched on the lower rail, chest glistening like a model for *Playgirl.* Not that she'd ever seen that particular magazine. Okay, once at a bachelorette party. But Jack Darby could've posed in it. His muscles gleamed as the softening sunlight sculpted him against the dusty backdrop. Tight, worn jeans and work boots only heightened the fantasy.

Her mouth went dry and her eyes ate him up.

Jack waited. Damn him. He knew what he was doing to her. She tried to remember what he'd just said. Oh, yeah. The thong. He still held it aloft, looking even naughtier with the wisp of lingerie in his hand.

He cocked his head. "You didn't want this back?"

She forgot all about how sexy he was. What a smart-ass! "Okay, time to talk. What are you doing here, Jack?"

He tucked the thong into his back pocket and dropped his foot from the rail. "Well, now let's see. We just knocked this barn down. We're going to move it—"

"You know damned well I don't mean out here," Nellie interrupted, waving one hand around the nearly barren site. "I mean in Oak Stand. Are you playing games with me?"

His aw-shucks smile disappeared. His eyes darkened. "No games, Nellie."

She propped her hands on her hips. "You invade my town without asking, sit in my pew, run my underwear up the town flagpole and don't call it 'playing games'?"

He took a step toward her. "Just wanted to see if the passionate woman I met in Vegas is still under that stiff exterior you've built around yourself here. Since you're here and pissed, I'd say she is."

She shot him her best go-to-hell look. "Really? And I thought I was just another notch on your bedpost."

A shutter closed in his eyes, but not before she saw the glimmer of pain.

"Oh, so you've figured it all out, have you? Figured me all out too, huh?" he said, a little too flippantly.

"Go back to Vegas and stop playing cowboy."

His eyes flickered. Was it hurt? She wasn't sure. The man was probably a crackerjack poker player. He didn't give much away. "I'm not playing cowboy. I'm building a horse farm, little Miss Tight-Assed Librarian. I'd already been looking in Texas *before* you dumped your drink in my lap. This was happening *before* you tore apart my life with your lies."

"Tore apart your life? With lies? You must be joking. Everything in Vegas was a lie."

Jack stared hard. "So that's what you think?"

Nellie hesitated. She knew what she'd felt when they were together—the actual friendship and the incredible sex were as real as her grandmother's three-carat diamond ring. "I don't know what to think."

They stared at each other.

"Jack, everything I thought about myself…I mean, ugh…I don't even know what I mean." She fell silent. She'd never been good in an argument, always thought about what she should have said three days later.

Jack folded his arms. "I'm angry with you, Nellie. You made me hope, made me believe true love was possible. Then you just threw it away. Tossed it out like last week's garbage. And when I came here, you ignored me."

"I didn't ask you to come," she said. "And I didn't throw anything away. What we had wasn't real. You said so yourself. Remember? The first time you saw me, you barely spared me a glance."

He shook his head, a wry smile touching his lips. "Lady, the real Elle—Elle Macpherson—could have sat down naked in my lap in that airport, and I would have shoved her off to watch a tied game in the ninth."

He acted like that explained everything. "That's not true," said Nellie.

His eyes glittered. "Don't call me a liar."

She crossed her arms. "You're trying to justify the fact you didn't think I was 'the one' the actual first time you saw me. Don't you think finding your soul mate is more important than a stupid baseball game?"

He lifted one brow but said nothing.

"I felt it."

"Felt what?" Jack asked.

"Felt that feeling. The first time you touched me. In the airport. It was like sparks shooting up my arm, making my heart feel funny. I couldn't believe you didn't feel it too." She shook her head. God, how stupid that sounded now. Why had she told him?

His eyes softened. "I'm sorry. I honestly don't remember touching you. My pants were wet, the Cardinals were at bat, and I had an assload of problems on my plate. I wasn't looking for anything but a base hit from Pujols."

She rolled her eyes. "But if I had walked into Agave Blue looking like I had in the airport, would you have noticed me?"

He shrugged. "That's a question I can't really answer. Why ask it?"

"Because it's at the heart of the matter." Nellie couldn't stop the pain from ripping through her at his words, yet she knew them to be true. Neither of them would ever know the answer to that question.

"I don't think it's the heart of the matter. I think my not being interested in you before you had the makeover thing gives you an out, a way to avoid the prospect of a relationship. What are you so scared of?" He let the words fall like books tumbling from a desk, each one smacking her with its own truth.

"Scared? I'm not scared. I'm confused."

"Yeah, you are. You're running from me just as hard as you ran that night in Vegas. You're not fighting. Is what we have just not worth it to you?"

That really slammed into her. He thought she didn't think him worth fighting for? How had he suddenly turned the tables on her? Why did she now feel everything was her fault?

"Wait a minute. What is 'it'? Do you even know? Are you talking about love? Or sex? You can't accuse me of something when I don't know what you are accusing me of."

Jack stared off in the distance, his eyes seemingly measuring the horizon. His jaw tightened. "I'm talking about love."

"Oh, God, Jack. How could that be love—*this* be love—when you don't even know who I am?" Her heart was breaking into itty-bitty pieces. He couldn't love someone who wasn't even a person, who was just a piece of a person. And his words—oh, how she craved them, but they were false. Just like the night of the party. Illusion.

"You are so wrong. I know who you are, Nellie." Jack smiled. It was a tender smile, one that reached inside her and twisted her heart. "I see straight inside you. Even at the airport, I could tell who you were. I could see the warm woman, the unsure way you moved, the sweetness in your eyes."

His words trailed off, but his eyes caressed her. Silence yawned between them. She turned away and drew circles in the sand with the toe of her sandal.

"I know who you are," he said, his voice smooth as river stones. "The problem is you don't know who you are."

Nellie felt as if he'd slapped her. Of course she knew who she was; she'd been in this body for thirty years come August twelfth.

"I know who I am," she sputtered.

He moved forward. She tilted her head back and looked into his eyes. She could see none of the former irritation. Quiet acceptance had taken its place. "Baby, I came here because I believe what we had in Vegas is real. I believe you walked into Agave Blue for a reason, and that reason is me."

He placed his hands on her shoulders. Nellie could feel moisture gathering in her eyes. "But, Nell, you've got to decide who you are and what you really want. I believe inside that luscious body there are two people—sweet, small-town librarian and hot, loving seductress. Baby, those two just need to meet and get to know one another."

She couldn't stop the tears. They slid down her cheeks. He wiped them away.

"I'm here to stay, Nellie, but just like that night we met in Vegas, I'm not going to push you to do something you don't want to do. Where we go from here is up to you."

"That's not fair," Nellie moaned, stepping back and wiping her cheeks. "You turned the tables. Made this my fault. My problem."

"No, I didn't." Jack shook his head, a bemused smile on his face. "I know where I stand. You gotta find out where you stand."

He leaned forward and brushed a soft kiss on her lips, so light and tender it made her heart hurt.

"I got to get back to work." Jack yanked his shirt from the bush and pulled it over his head. An ancient-looking USC cap followed. She stood watching, not believing he was ending the conversation, leaving everything up to her.

He headed past her toward the other side of the house. Just before he disappeared over the hill, he turned and patted his back pocket. "Oh, and, Nellie, if you change your mind about the thong, just give me a call. I'm as good at puttin' them on as I am at takin' 'em off."

He threw her a typical Jack Darby devilish grin then strolled out of sight, leaving her standing in front of a huge pile of rotted timber and a couple of rusted-out animal pens. She felt a bit confused. More than slightly dazed.

Not know who she was?

The hell she didn't.

She stomped up the embankment, trampling the scraggly dry grass, ready to tell Jack just exactly who she was. But then she stopped. Maybe he was right. Maybe she was threatened by his being in Oak Stand, because when she was with Jack she was different. It had been easy to let her "Elle" side free in Vegas. But not here in the town her great-great-grandfather had built.

Was she afraid of that part of herself?

The thought made her knees weak.

"Hey, Nellie, want some tea?" Dawn stood on the front porch holding a glass.

She really just wanted to get in the old Buick and leave. Crazy mixed-up was how she felt, and making small talk with Jack's sister over a glass of iced tea wasn't exactly what she needed right now.

Her shoulders sagged. "Yeah, that sounds nice." She couldn't help good breeding—things like that never wore off. Plus she'd been rude yesterday at the church. No sense in not rectifying that.

She strolled up the cracked walk and took the frosty glass from Dawn.

And then broke into tears.

"Aw, no. What's wrong?" Dawn grabbed her arm and pulled her the rest of the way up the creaky stairs. Two Texas Longhorn camping chairs sat on the newly scraped porch. Dawn shoved her into one.

"N-n-nothing," said Nellie when she could manage. "He said…he said…oh, nothing."

Nellie couldn't vocalize just why she was sobbing. Maybe because Jack was right. Or maybe because she was in love. Or maybe because it simply felt good to let it out.

Dawn didn't say a thing. She sank down into the adjoining chair, scooped up her own tumbler of tea and let Nellie cry.

Finally Nellie subsided into sniffles with an occasional hiccup. She wiped her eyes with the hem of her shirt, not even caring it was the first time she'd worn it, or that the price tag she'd cut off had read $120.00.

"Sometimes there's nothing like a good cry, huh?" Dawn murmured. "If I don't do it at least once a month, I break a good piece of china or run someone off the road. It's like required."

Nellie managed a laugh. "Yeah, but it sucks when you do it in front of your boyfriend's sister. Well, except he's not even my boyfriend. Uh, so stupid."

"Yep, and being around men makes you stupider."

Nellie nodded and stared out at the darkening shadows on the lawn. The Bermuda grass showed signs of dying. Huge oak trees lined the driveway to the house, their gnarled branches at once grotesque and elegant. The azalea bushes needed water and the flower beds were so choked with weeds it was hard to tell flower from dandelion. The old Henderson place needed plenty of work.

"You know, when I was little, I hated Jack," Dawn said, setting her tea in the cup holder of the chair. "He was so stinkin' cute. Little cherub lips, dark curly hair and those incredible lashes around those baby blues. Everyone thought he was the cutest thing they'd ever seen." Dawn gave a depreciating laugh. "And I was the opposite."

Nellie shot her a puzzled look. Where was she going with this?

"I was eleven. You know, braces, those little bumps before breasts, not to mention about thirty pounds overweight. I was plain miserable. So I took it out on cute Jack."

"Why?" asked Nellie.

"'Cause he got all the attention. All the oohs and aahs. I hated it. Made me feel like crap, so I would pinch him, torment him, push him down when Mom wasn't looking."

"Wow."

"Yeah, I'm not proud of it or anything." She laughed. "Anyway, one day, Jack was out on his trike. We lived on a dairy, you know."

"You grew up on a dairy? Jack grew up on a dairy?"

Dawn looked startled. "Yeah, a real dairy with cows and everything."

"Hmm." Jack milking cows? There had been nothing about rural life in his Vegas bio. Nellie couldn't imagine using "cow" and "Jack" in the same sentence.

"So, anyway, it had been raining and Jack was racing up and down the driveway on his trike. I'll never forget it. He was wearing these red boots, probably pretending to be a fireman or something, and mud flew up and splattered his legs and arms. Mom and Dad had left us with Frannie—she helped Mom out. She never really watched us very well, so I could pretty much do what I wanted. Cheryl, our other sister, was always reading. Even at seven, she was a big ol' nerd. I was bored, so I decided that I would crank up the old tractor and drive it around."

Nellie could almost see where this was heading but was too enthralled to stop her.

"That old tractor was stubborn as a mule, and I had no business driving it. But I thought I was big enough. I cranked Bertie—that's what my dad called the tractor—and started windmilling around the property. I remember pretending I was in a convertible going over to meet my boyfriend. Well, I came around the corner, and there was Jack. I didn't see him until Bertie was on him."

Dawn's eyes glazed over as she stared out at the swaying branches. Long shadows reached for the porch and gloom descended as if it were lending itself to her tale.

"I remember his little face. And the feeling that shot through me. The emptiness, the sheer acceptance that I was about to kill my little brother. It was weird, you know, that kind of disconnect. But I swerved at the last minute. That big wheel came about a half inch of crushing the tricycle and pulling Jack underneath."

Nellie shivered despite the suffocating humidity.

"I don't remember much else. How I turned off the tractor, how I climbed down. How Frannie came out screaming at me at the top of her lungs. But I remember Jack. I sprinted over to him. He just sat there on that dumb tricycle. He looked up at me and gave the biggest grin."

Dawn's wistful eyes were chocolate soft in the waning light.

"You know what he said?"

Nellie shook her head.

"He said, 'Hey, Dondee, you can drive a tractor.' That sweet little boy I sometimes hated was proud of me because I could drive a tractor."

Poignant silence fell around the two women who were strangers yet had one simple thing in common: they loved Jack.

Dawn shot her a small, sad smile, but her voice held an edge. "So you see, it's very hard for me to sit here and comfort you, give you tea and sympathy."

"Why?" Nellie squirmed, a bit uncomfortable at the change in Dawn's tone.

"Because that day as I held that squirming little boy, bawling my eyes out, I swore I wouldn't let anyone hurt him. And you have."

She pierced Nellie with eyes that were no longer velvety and welcoming, but hard as the nails sticking up out of the loose porch boards. "That man gave up his life for you, bought this dump and moved halfway across the country. You need to think long and hard about that, about what he did, and what it says about the way he feels about you."

Nellie couldn't stop her own anger from rising. Dawn wanted to lecture her, make her think about Jack? She couldn't get him out of her mind. Couldn't get anything about their relationship out of her mind. And his sister wanted to preach to her? "So what are you going to do if I hurt him more?"

Dawn shrugged and flashed a quasi-grin. "Whatever it takes."

Nellie struggled up from the camping chair, setting her half-full glass of tea on the rickety porch rail. "Look, Dawn, I admire your sisterly concern, but I didn't ask Jack to show up here. Besides, surely you realize you can't control what happens to another person's heart.

"And what about what I feel? What I want?" Nellie was far from finished. "You'd rather I lie to Jack so he could be happy? Don't you know how those relationships end?"

Dawn flinched at her words. Her mouth opened but no sound came out.

Nellie shook her head and walked down the stairs. Off in the distance she could see Bubba and Jack stacking random pieces of wood in a pile. Bubba was laughing. She waved.

She opened the door to her Buick and looked back at Dawn. Jack's sister sat, stony and silent. Nellie felt a bit sorry for her. She had been trying to protect Jack.

"Thanks for the tea, Dawn," Nellie called, sliding behind the wheel. Dawn managed a small wave. She seemed lost in thought.

Nellie cranked the car. It purred to life. Fifteen years old and only 25,632 miles on the odometer. Grandmother Tucker had hardly ever gone any farther than the town square. Nellie had sold her small convertible just after her Grandmother had died. Driving it had seemed impractical. Now she wished she'd kept it.

As she set off down the lane, she glanced back at Jack. He stood in the field watching her drive away.

He looked lonely. Hopeful. Sexy.

She wanted him. And she loved him.

But he'd been right. First, she needed to do some hard thinking. She loved her job, loved her town, loved the fact she could cook up a pot of butter beans and batch of corn bread without dragging out a recipe. But she also despised much about her life. Okay, *despised* was a strong word, but she had to face a few issues about herself.

Jack's words held truth. She needed to figure out who she was.

Was she Elle or Nellie? But maybe they weren't separate entities? Sure, playing the part of Elle in Vegas had been liberating, but Nellie had still been herself. Nothing about Elle had been forced. Nellie had allowed herself to be what she sometimes longed to be. She wasn't two people in one body. Elle was just another facet of herself.

Jack hadn't fallen in love with Elle, he'd fallen in love with Nellie.

Changing her name hadn't changed who she really was.

Nor had highlighting her hair, or buying new clothes or wearing a fake tattoo on her shoulder.

By the time she'd pulled out of the bumpy driveway, Nellie knew what she wanted. It was time to show Jack he'd come to Oak Stand for all the right reasons.

CHAPTER TWENTY

They say the way to a man's heart is through his stomach. There are other ways, trust me. But they are a bit more dangerous and could get you pregnant.

—Grandmother Tucker after watching *The Barefoot Contessa* one afternoon.

JACK SPENT the next several days trying not to think about Nellie, but it was easier said than done. For one thing, the town had been founded by her family. From streets to statues, he ran across the Tucker name almost daily in one context or another. And though Nellie technically was a Hughes, everyone called her a Tucker. He understood. He'd grown up in a rural area where people still called his sisters "those Darby girls" though they'd been off and married for over ten or so years.

Still, Nellie's name came up often, thanks to Bubba Malone, who mentioned her at least once every hour. Usually it was in regard to her cooking. Seems she'd been over at Bubba's taking care of his momma. Bubba reaped the benefits, bringing leftovers every day and making annoying "mmm" noises. Jack wasn't pleased Bubba got to spend time with Nellie while he sat at home fantasizing about tumbling the long-limbed, hot woman in the sweet-smelling pasture out back. Country living did have its benefits—no neighbors for miles.

Not that he hadn't met his neighbors. They'd come out of the woodwork trying to catch a bite or two of gossip. After seeing him follow Nellie out of church, everyone had suspicions. He was from Vegas. Nellie had just been to Vegas. Small-town people were a lot smarter than all the big-city people portrayed them to be. To them, "if it smells dead, it mostly likely is dead."

So he got lots of information on Miss Nellie Hughes, along with a watermelon, a lemon pound cake and a fruit basket.

He had to give them credit for lacking big-city bluntness. The conversation seemed to go something like this.

"Welcome to our little town, Mr. Darby."

"You can call me Jack."

"Oh, Jack then. We hope you like living in Oak Stand. It's a fine town. Did you know our town was founded by Rufus Tucker? His great-great-granddaughter still lives here, can you believe? Her name is Nellie. Have you met her by chance?" Eyes slide to his, gauging a reaction, studying him, waiting for his answer like a spider waits on the hapless mosquito.

Or sometimes like this.

"From Vegas, huh? I sure would like to go there. Do a little gambling, see that big dam, and those topless showgirls. You know who just went out to Vegas? Nellie Hughes. You know her? Meet her in Vegas? That'd be a coincidence, wouldn't it?"

"Yeah, it would."

"So…"

Silence.

"So you gonna raise horses, huh? What kind? I know a man over in Marshall that raises them paints for show."

Or sometimes there were no questions. Just a rundown on Nellie's life.

"You know someone else who makes good pound cake? Nellie Hughes. Why, her grandmother made the lightest cake. Gotta sift the flour three times. That's the key. Well, Nellie was raised by her grandmother. Nellie's momma went plumb crazy, strung out on drugs, you know. And her daddy… Well, if you ask me, that's a man who was just lookin' for a meal ticket. Went off to work on oil rigs and didn't come back. Left that baby with her crazy mother and took up with a piece of trash down in Mississippi. He divorced Grace—that's Nellie's momma—as soon as the poor woman was committed. He's remarried now, but Nellie's momma is over in Longview in a home. She don't know nobody. Shame, ain't it? But of course, I'm not a gossip. By the way, who's doing your painting?"

That particular conversation had been a doozy. It took Jack a good thirty minutes before he could make an excuse to get back to work.

And he had worked. Hard. And his sister and Andrew had helped him. Which was why, as he sat slurping his cereal, he dreaded having to tell Dawn and Andrew goodbye. They were leaving the next day. But his dad would be in town the following week. Tom was wrapping things up in California and still trying to placate Lila.

"Hey, here's the mail from yesterday. You worked so late I went to bed and forgot to give it to you." Dawn padded across the kitchen in her bare feet and tossed the bundle on the table. "I need to go over the schedule with you before I leave."

"Schedule?" he said, popping the rubber band and separating the junk mail from the bills. His forwarded mail had finally caught up with him.

Dawn plopped a calendar agenda in front of him. "I have all your appointments for the house highlighted in blue. All appointments pertaining to the buildings and property are in pink. Meetings with local officials for permits and licenses are yellow. Over to the side, you will see a list of numbers. Those are the invoice numbers for the furniture companies along with contact info."

He felt as though he'd climbed on a Tilt-A-Whirl "Whoa. Wait a sec. I have all these people coming out today?"

"I'll handle everything today. After that, you're on your own." Dawn stole a frosted bran flake from the side of his bowl and popped it in her mouth. Her eyes sparked mischievously. "Flooring people will be here in half an hour. I need to shower and get coffee. Don't forget to call Dad. Something about the horse trailer registration and bringing Dutch down when he comes."

Dawn left and Drew walked in.

He shuffled about the kitchen banging cabinets and rattling drawers. Finally he parked himself at the table with a salad bowl and a gallon of milk. He poured half the box of sugar snappies into the massive bowl and added a good portion of the milk. Then he started slurping away.

Jack shoved back from the table, pulling Dawn's "calendar from hell" away from the fray. He didn't want his blues mixing with his yellows or he'd have too many greens. Drew kept right on attacking the cereal.

"I'll meet you outside in ten minutes. We're pouring cement today and then going to town for fencing."

"Mmmfff..." was all he heard. He'd just reached the door to the back porch when Drew called out, "You missed one."

Jack spun around and snatched the vellum envelope from his nephew's outstretched hand. He stomped onto the screened back porch and plunked down on an ancient rocking chair. He'd be damned if he sat and listened to Drew smack his way through a second bowl of cereal.

He squinted at the envelope he held. It was addressed to him in fine, clear strokes. No return address, but an Oak Stand postmark.

He slid a finger under the flap and pulled out...an invitation? The front was monogrammed with the initials NRH. He opened it.

Jack—
Please come to dinner so we may continue our discussion. Friday night, 7:30 at 401 Fort Street. Thong optional.
Nellie

He allowed the note to fall into his lap. A dinner invitation? And what did she mean by thong optional? Was that a double entendre? Or did she just want it back?

He stared at the back end of his property as he thought about the implications. The fig tree had been picked clean by the birds. Two pear trees bore spotted fruit. Some clumpy purple flowers grew unchecked at the base of several trees and pampas grass puffed against a dilapidated shed. At one time, the place had been well loved, carefully tended, not sad and scraggly.

Yet Jack could feel nothing but satisfaction. Friday he would know one way or the other. He leaned toward a happy ending, but did he really know Nellie the way he thought he did?

A mockingbird landed in the fig tree and warbled a joyful tune. She was a spot of beauty in the jumble of the overgrown, yellowed yard, and her song gave him faith. Faith that everything would fall into place. Everything would be right.

He hoped.

NELLIE PORED over the cookbooks shoved willy-nilly into a box in the dining room, looking for something impressive to serve Jack. She wanted this dinner to be fabulous. Tenderloin with cracked-pepper crust, braised lamb chops with traditional mint sauce, shrimp and scallop pasta in a lemon sauce—one by one she discarded each choice. Nothing seemed right. Finally, she settled on the epitome of Southern cuisine—fried chicken, mashed potatoes, purple hull peas, corn bread, fresh sliced tomatoes and Texas chocolate sheet cake. No man could resist.

Pleased with her choice, she had but one problem. Her kitchen was still in shambles. Brent had made good progress, but on the day she'd issued the invitation, she lacked an actual cooktop and the ovens weren't installed. She'd done some cooking over at Bubba's since his momma had been feeling the effects of chemotherapy. It gave her time to think. No therapy like dicing onion and tenderizing flank steak. But she needed her own kitchen.

So she offered Brent a bribe of an extra five percent profit on the project if he could finish the kitchen in a few days, not the expected week or two. Lacking a mind for math and anything better to do, he agreed. By Friday morning, the kitchen was complete. For just a thousand dollars extra.

Nellie had nearly tripped over the plumber on his way out the front door. As she turned to watch him go, she realized her house was quiet. Very quiet.

For the past several weeks, she'd heard saws buzzing, hammers banging, tiles crashing and lots of colorful phrasing. She'd grown so used to having other people in the house, moving, toting, painting and repairing, it felt odd for it to be silent.

She dropped her purse on the dining room table, rounded the corner and stared at her completed kitchen.

Wow. It was awesome. Stone floors, newly stained cabinets with pewter hardware, gleaming appliances, granite countertops and caramel walls. Lovely, beautiful, magnificent—all three. She swore she could feel a lump in her throat.

Before she could stop herself, she was fast at work restoring order. She pulled out pots and hung them on the rack hanging above the farmhouse table that served as the kitchen island. New canisters went on the gleaming counters, her grandmother's cheerful red kettle on the stove, and her ivy planter in the corner. As Nellie set her kitchen right, she stopped to marvel at the new stainless-steel microwave, the built-in desk for bill paying, and the clever corner panel that hid her small TV. By the time she'd hung her hand-embroidered towels on the small bar by the sink, several hours had passed.

Cripes! She had to get to the store. She'd shelled the peas last night, so she poured them in the sink to rinse once more. She placed freshly picked big boy tomatoes in the window for the sun to warm and then scooped up her new Prada bag and headed out to the car.

By the time she'd shopped, then stopped for fresh

flowers and some vanilla candles from the Enchanted Garden Gift Shop, it was nearly two o'clock.

By five, she'd fried the chicken crisp and set it in the warming drawer, and the potatoes were peeled and ready to boil. The peas had a good scald on them, and the corn bread was baking. Nellie pulled the sheet cake out to cool. She'd frost it just before Jack got there. Everything turned out beautifully. Nellie sent up a prayer of thanks and then headed upstairs for a much needed shower.

By six-thirty, she had butterflies in her stomach and chocolate icing all over her. She'd inserted the damn beaters incorrectly and gotten a huge surprise when she'd turned on the mixer. Chocolate splattered the front of her shirt and face. Nellie grabbed a paper towel just as the doorbell rang.

Crap. She swiped the paper towel across her face and scrambled to find the matches. She tapped her way across the kitchen to the dining room in her new Manolos and lit the candles on the table, blowing the flame out just as it singed her fingers.

"Damn!" She waved her hand as if she could shake off the pain. She had to stop cursing; she sounded like the workmen who'd traipsed through her house daily.

The doorbell sounded again. Her plan to greet Jack at the door, cool and calm and unruffled, disintegrated. She hit the button on the new satellite radio, filling the dining room with traditional jazz, and ducked into the kitchen.

Time for a backup plan. She shrugged off her shirt, unhooked her lacy bra and reached for the old-fashioned frilly apron in her cupboard. Jack had wanted her to meld her two personalities. Well, tonight he would meet the woman she'd always been.

JACK RANG the doorbell again and wondered if he'd gotten the wrong night. No, couldn't be.

He pressed the buzzer yet again. He was just about to peep in the window when he heard Nellie call out, "It's open."

He twisted the brass doorknob and stuck his head in. "Hello?"

"Come in. I'm just finishing up in the kitchen." She sounded out of breath.

Jack stepped inside and shut the door behind him. He was immediately assaulted by the sheer rightness of the room before him. Tiffany lamps flanked an overstuffed couch while warm golden walls highlighted a staircase arching above a built-in bookcase—it was the sort of room that made him want to sink into the squat chair in the corner and pull out the day's paper. Perhaps Dutch at his feet and squabbling kids upstairs rattling the floor. Nellie would come out of the kitchen and call them down for supper.

He shook the image from his head and closed the door behind him. Stop being a moron. He was here for dinner, not eternity.

Across the cozy living room sat a grand dining room table covered in a lacy white cloth complete with flickering candles. Soft jazz played in the background. Nice.

And then the smells hit him—warm buttery cake along with something fried. He thought about Bubba's leftover lunches and his stomach growled. Jack headed for the kitchen like a guided missile toward its target.

"Smells good," he said as he stepped into the kitchen.

Nellie glanced up. She had a spatula in one hand and a huge half-iced cake in front of her. Chocolate frosting smudged one cheek. He forgot about food.

"Right on time," she said, scooping more frosting from

the bowl and smearing it on the cake. "I appreciate a man who's punctual."

He took her in as she went back to work. She'd pulled her hair into a bun. It might have looked severe except a few tendrils had escaped to curl around her flushed cheeks. Perched on her nose were the hideous glasses, thick as a magnifying glass and rimmed in gunmetal gray. Her lips were pink and glossy above a horrible ruffled yellow apron that disappeared beneath the table.

"Oh, hello. I'm looking for Nellie Hughes. Is she here?" Jack tried for a straight face, but failed miserably.

She dropped the spoon in the bowl and stuck her hands on her hips. "Oh, very funny."

That's when he noticed her shoulders and arms were bare beneath the apron and he could see the outline of her nipples.

His mouth went dry. Was she naked under the apron?

Nellie turned around and reached for a paper towel.

Hello. He'd never encountered a better sight than her bare derriere beneath the limp yellow bow around her waist.

She turned around, lips twitching and eyes gleaming. "Would you like a glass of wine?"

Jack couldn't seem to make his mouth work. His tongue was glued to his teeth. He couldn't even swallow. His mind was trying to wrap itself around the fact that Miss Nellie Hughes stood in her kitchen naked beneath a ruffled old-fashioned apron, calmly asking him if he'd like a glass of wine.

"Jack?" she said. "Wine?"

"Hmm? Yeah." He nodded.

She spun around and leaned over to the small wine rack resting in the corner of the cabinet. One foot came off the floor and the curve of her breast strained against the bib of the apron. He had to clench his fists to stop from reaching for her. Hell, he needed to find some control, some cool, some of the unflappable Jack Darby who'd existed long ago.

"So you decided against the thong?" Jack said, finally finding his voice.

"Huh?" Nellie said, standing on tiptoe and pulling down two crystal goblets.

"I said I see you've decided to go without the thong. Your invite said it was optional."

"Oh." She set the goblets next to the cake pan. Her forehead wrinkled. "Yeah, I decided against it. They're really uncomfortable."

"I know. Mine's killing me." He grinned.

Nellie's eyes widened. "You're wearing a thong?"

"You said it was optional, so I decided to give it a whirl. I hope you really didn't want yours back. It was a tight fit."

She laughed. "You're kidding."

"Wanna find out?" he asked, moving around the table toward the vixen who seemed determined to drive him wild and enjoy every moment of doing so.

She stuck one hand in the middle of his chest, effectively stopping him from closing the distance between them. "Nope. I want some wine. Will you open it? The corkscrew's in the drawer behind you, I think."

He tucked his hands in his pockets to keep from hauling her up against him. So, it was her turn to play games. Okay, he was willing as long as she didn't cover that beautiful ass. He opened the drawer and found the opener.

Nellie completed icing the cake. She offered him a frosting-covered beater. He shook his head and handed her a glass of chardonnay. She set the wine on the counter and then looked him directly in the eye before raising a beater to her lips. He wanted to shout, *Stop. Don't do it,* but couldn't bring himself to prevent the kinky torture of Nellie licking every drop of chocolate frosting from the beater. He even flinched when she moaned, "Mmm."

She spun around and dropped both beaters into the soapy dishwater, presenting him once again with the loveliest of views. Jack decided he'd never seen an ass as fine as hers. She looked over her shoulder and gave him the biggest come-hither smile. "Ready to eat?"

Jack nearly came undone. Nearly.

"It looks delicious." He returned her smile with one of his own, one dripping with sexual promise. Every naughty thing he'd ever considered doing to her flitted through his head. He could tell she recognized the lewd thoughts—she looked both anxious and turned-on. Good.

"Oh, it is," she promised. "Go ahead and sit. I'll serve you."

"Every man's dream," he said, not moving one inch. He pretty much had her blocked. Penned in. Right where he wanted her.

Nellie eyed the pots sitting on the stove. "Go ahead. It's getting cold."

"From where I'm standing, it looks pretty hot. Burning hot." Jack lifted one brow.

She seemed unaffected, because she shoved right by him, scooting out of reach, and pulled the warming drawer open. A platter of golden fried chicken appeared in her hand. She spun around and sauntered to the dining room table.

"Damn," he muttered beneath his breath. He wasn't sure he could do it. He felt like a junkie who hadn't had his smack in weeks. He damn near shook with the need to throw her onto the table and do away with the niceties. To hell with talking it out, coming to a decision. Miss Hughes was playing with fire.

He wiped the sweat dotting his forehead, snatched the two goblets of wine and headed to the dining room. He'd do his best, but he wouldn't be held responsible if he couldn't finish dinner.

Nellie smiled at him as he sat down in the cushioned Chippendale chair as if she was Miss Suzy Homemaker and not the very bad girl she truly was. "Here we go. I'll just go get the corn bread and we can get started."

He watched as she spun around, thinking it was time to finish rather than start. Things had started a long time ago. Of course, Nellie knew exactly what she was doing, clacking back and forth bare-assed. It wasn't until she leaned over to ladle peas on his plate that he figured out two could play at this game.

He reached for his wine, brushing the outline of her nipple. Satisfied at hearing the intake of her breath, he murmured, "Oops. Sorry."

Nellie jerked back. "No problem."

Jack let his napkin slip from his lap, revealing his raging erection. He bent to retrieve it, allowing his hand to slide under her apron and squeeze one sweet cheek.

She swatted his hand. "Hey!"

He gave her a sheepish look. "Sorry. I always wanted to do that."

"To me or to someone else?"

He shrugged. "Just waiting for the opportunity to present itself."

Her eyes narrowed. She slung a heap of mashed potatoes onto his plate. "The gravy is in the gravy boat."

He wondered what in the hell a gravy boat was.

Nellie strutted back into the kitchen, bottom swaying, breasts jiggling enough to tempt a saint. Jack clenched his teeth. He picked up the wineglass and downed it in one motion. She came back with a pan of corn bread. Red mitts covered her hands. She looked pretty cute in her yellow apron and tight bun. Ugly glasses aside, he thought he could really get into the nerdy-librarian-gone-wild scenario. Definitely a turn-on.

Nellie popped the mitts off her hands and sat down opposite him. "I hope you like it. It's about as traditional Southern as I could get. Here." She thrust some type of genie lamp at him.

He took it and then wondered what the hell he was supposed to do with it.

"It's the gravy," she said, sticking a fork in a small tray of sliced tomatoes and dishing a few onto her plate.

"Oh." He ladled the creamy country-style gravy over his potatoes and selected a piece of chicken from the platter in the center of the table. He loved fried chicken but didn't indulge in such artery-hardening food very often. Having Nellie cook for him was a big treat. And if it tasted as good as it looked, and if he had a shot at being the man she cooked such fabulous dinners for all the time, he needed to buy bigger jeans.

He picked up his fork and scooped up some peas. She smiled as if anticipating his response. Then he felt her foot snaking up the leg of his pants, sliding higher and higher until it reached his knee.

"Fire," Jack whispered after swallowing the first bite.

Nellie took a sip of wine, her eyes as innocent as a schoolmarm's. "Pardon?"

"You're playing with fire."

She smiled brightly but her foot didn't budge, just moved back and forth beneath his pant leg, stroking the fire raging within him.

"I always liked playing with fire. Fascinating to see what would happen."

Jack leaned forward and blew out the candles on the table. The room darkened, but he could still see the sparkle in Nellie's eyes.

"Why'd you do that?" she asked.

"Because I don't want the house to burn down while I teach you why you shouldn't play with fire."

CHAPTER TWENTY-ONE

Don't you worry none, Nellie, my darlin'. One day you'll find love and it won't leave you, won't fall down a damned well and take your heart with him. He'll be just the thing. I know it 'cause I pray it for you every night.

—Grandmother Tucker to a sleeping four-year-old Nellie.

NELLIE SCREECHED when Jack scooped her into his arms. He pulled the glasses from her nose and tossed them onto the table. Really. She'd spent all day cooking the meal. Or at least part of the day. Of course, Jack sweeping her off her feet and taking her upstairs to the down-filled bed was what she wanted. Planned for. But she couldn't give in so easily, could she?

"Jack! Wait! What about supper? I worked—"

"It'll keep." He leered at her. Her apron gaped, allowing him to see straight down to her belly. He licked his lips. Her nipples tightened in response.

"No, it won't. Have you ever had cold mashed potatoes?" She wrapped her arms around his neck and nuzzled into his citrusy, scratchy neck. He smelled good—like hot, sexy man with something to prove.

His lips descended and all thoughts of lumpy potatoes

and cold gravy fled. His mouth was demanding and tasted like wine. Delicious.

She pulled back. "Okay. I like cold fried chicken anyway."

He grinned and nipped one shoulder. "Upstairs?"

She nodded. "But you can put me down. I don't want to be responsible for throwing your back out. That would take the romance out of it, huh?"

Jack silenced her with a kiss. "Baby, I could tote you to Vegas and back and still want to carry you up those stairs."

"Get goin' then. I've been ready for this since you walked in the door."

He took the steps nearly two at a time. Her hip bounced against the evidence of his arousal, and by the time she'd pointed him toward her bedroom, she was nearly crazy with desire. He stormed in, dropped her on the bed and then covered her with his body. He felt better than chocolate, better than a stack of brand-new crisp novels, better than a half-price shoe sale.

Really good.

So Nellie relished it—the feel of his body against hers, so hard, so heavy, so absolutely right. He slid his hands to frame her face and peered into her eyes. "I want you more than I've ever wanted anything in my life, Nellie, but I've got to know."

She placed her hands on either side of Jack's face. "Know what? That I was foolish? That I wished a thousand times I had stayed that night? Fought for you, for what I felt for you?"

"No, that's all passed," he whispered, lowering his head to pepper soft kisses along her jaw. He lifted his head. His blue eyes glittered in the waning light of the day. "I got to know if it's real. If you want us, Nellie."

She slid one of his hands from her cheek and softly kissed the pad of each finger. It was a lover's caress, meant to be sweet, to impart all the swirling feelings inside her. "If I didn't, you wouldn't be here now, lying in my bed. The same bed I lay in and dreamed in for so many years. Dreamed about love, about the man I would call mine one day."

She felt moisture gather in her eyes. She was helpless to stop its path down her cheeks. "I love you, Jack. I've loved you since Vegas."

His mouth covered hers, so soft, so tender. His fingers wiped the tears away. For as long as she lived and breathed upon the earth, she would never forget that moment—the moment she gave her heart away to Jack Darby. So simple, and so profound. Emotion choked her, yet her heart soared at the wonder of it.

Jack lifted his mouth from hers and smoothed back the tendrils curling about her cheeks. His eyes spoke a million words. She smiled at him. "Is that what you needed?"

"It's a start," he whispered against her mouth before capturing it again in a soft kiss. She surrendered to him as tenderness ebbed, replaced by passion. She enjoyed the way his lips played against hers, the way his hands softly stroked her face. She twined her arms around his shoulders and caressed the hair brushing his neck.

Jack pulled away and rolled to his side, propping his head on one hand. He stared down at her, his eyes teasing. His hands trailed down her chin to her neck, dipped into the hollow above her collarbone before plunging between her breasts.

"This is the ugliest apron I've ever seen," he said, tracing the ruffled edge over her breasts. She felt molten desire flow through her. It pooled deep in her stomach, uncurling and snaking its way to the inner recesses of her body.

"It was my grandmother's," she said, gazing down at his finger as it traced the top of her breast. Her breath grew labored. She wanted to rip the apron off and let him put his hands all over her.

"Let's ditch it," he whispered, dropping a kiss on her shoulder. The room was nearly dark, but she could still see the desire raging in Jack's eyes when she slowly rolled over onto her stomach, leaving her backside completely bare.

"Sweet, sweet Nellie." His hands feathered down her back, resting on the dimple right above her bottom. "I don't think I'll need any dinner. I could eat you up, baby."

Nellie couldn't even affect a giggle. His words were lava hot and made her feel like her skin was on fire. "Hurry, Jack."

His hands leisurely plucked at the apron strings knotted at her waist. They came free, but Jack seemed content to stroke her skin, sliding his hands from the top of her shoulders to the curve just under her bottom. It was slow, sweet torment.

She wriggled. "Jack, please."

He chuckled, "Slow down, Nellie. This is our time, babe. The beginning for us. We've got all night. All night."

Nellie pushed herself up onto one elbow. She slid a hand up and pulled the pins from her hair then tossed them onto her nightstand. A mass of curls tumbled about her shoulders. Jack's eyes didn't even follow the progress of her hand or the way the light played on her hair. He was staring at her breasts, at the way they jiggled as she shook her hair free, at the way her rosy nipples brushed the homespun quilt covering her bed.

"Let's ditch your clothes, Jack."

She watched as he scrambled out of his clothes like a man possessed. She was certain he broke record times for undressing. She delivered a sultry laugh as she looped the apron over her head and pulled it free. She tossed it behind her and lay before him, absolutely naked except for the high-heeled sandals on her feet.

Nellie rolled over onto her side. One hand cushioned her head, the other cupped one of her breasts. She smiled.

"Damn," he muttered, yanking his boxers off and kicking them into a corner. Then he just stood and stared.

She felt naughty. She could see the raw need in his eyes. Not to mention the very hard and protruding evidence much lower.

She allowed her hand to slide away from her breast, over her flat stomach, toward the juncture of her thighs. Jack's eyes glittered. His nostrils flared.

So she lifted one knee and trailed her fingers over the smooth inside of her thigh. She could already feel the dampness there. She was more than ready for Jack. But first, a bit of fun.

Nellie rolled onto her back but left her leg bent. It opened her to his gaze. She used one hand to cup a breast, the other she allowed to slide down her stomach toward the place that ached for him. "Wanna help a girl out, Jack?"

She didn't have to ask twice. He grabbed one of her ankles and jerked her to him. She flew across the bed. There was nothing graceful or sexy about it. "Jack!"

"You're about to pay for that little peep show," he ground out, pulling her to the edge of the bed and settling between her legs. He leaned forward, allowing his erection to rub her most intimate place. She was slick and the friction of Jack against her made her groan. God, she wanted him inside her.

He caught one of her nipples with his mouth. She nearly launched off the bed.

"Make me pay," Nellie managed to beg, trying to catch her breath. She spun out of control. Beyond caring.

While Jack made love to her breasts, she twined her arms about his neck, stroking and encouraging him. His tongue laved her nipples, teeth grazing against the sensitive flesh, pulling her higher and higher all the while his hips ground into hers. His member probed the entrance to her body, dipping inside and back out, teasing her beyond reason.

Nellie wrapped her legs round his waist and pulled him to her. "Please, Jack. I can't wait."

He obliged, driving his hips forward and filling her. Nellie nearly came undone. She lifted her hips and met each thrust. It felt like heaven. Jack's mouth captured hers, his tongue thrusting into her, mimicking the pace below.

His hands grasped her hips and lifted her off the bed. "Put your arms around my neck," he murmured against her. Nellie, lost in the throes of passion, would've done anything he suggested as long as he continued the tender torment. Wrapping her arms about him was easy. So was twining her legs around him.

He stood, raising her so she rode his length. His hands clasped her hips, lifting her up and down, each stroke deep and fulfilling. She had never felt so exquisite, so perfectly in tune.

His heart thumped against her breasts as his mouth nuzzled the side of her neck. Nellie could feel the orgasm building inside of her.

Jack took several steps and she felt the wall at her back. Using it as leverage, he increased the tempo, thrusting deep within her. Nellie clasped him tightly with her legs and pulled his mouth to hers.

"I love you, Nellie," he whispered against her lips before he took possession of her mouth.

Nellie shattered against him, her body trembling uncontrollably as she rode a wave of sheer orgasmic pleasure. It seemed never ending, cresting and breaking over and over until she fell limp against the wall. She was so caught up in her mind-altering orgasm she didn't realize Jack had reached his peak too.

He peeled her from the wall, cradling her and stroking her hair. She was replete, exhausted, yet every nerve sang.

"That was incredible," he whispered against her temple, kissing her forehead then tilting her head so he could look into her eyes.

So sweet the moment, her eyes glistened. Her heart contracted with love. Sheer happiness flooded her. She belonged to this man. She was his.

Jack smiled and walked to the bed. Gently he lowered her, never once breaking their intimate connection. His body covered hers. He was warm, sheened with sweat. Nellie twined her arms and legs about him and let him rest.

"I love you, Jack Darby," she whispered against the faint stubble of his five-o'clock shadow.

"I love you too, darling," Jack whispered back, his breath soft against her hair.

The ceiling fan whirred above them. The room was silent, the moment sacred. They lay, two lovers sated with pleasure.

Jack finally rolled off her. "Bathroom?"

She didn't move, just pointed to the door across the hall. He pulled her from the bed. "Let's wash up for dinner. I'm starving."

Nellie nearly fell as she rose to her feet. She'd forgotten she still wore the sandals. She pulled them off and followed Jack to the bathroom.

Two shakes of a lamb's tail later, they sat at the previously abandoned dining room table in just their undies, munching on cold fried chicken. It still tasted fabulous. In fact, Jack thought the potatoes were pretty damned good.

He took a gulp of wine. "Ready to talk?"

"What do you mean?" she replied, buttering her corn bread and taking a bite. "We just had the most amazing experience ever."

"Yeah, but we still got some things to decide. For example, I didn't wear a condom."

Nellie stopped chewing. She set her goblet of wine down and stared at it as if it was poison. "Oh, dear Lord, we didn't."

He wanted to laugh but stopped himself. He shouldn't have made such a stupid mistake. Children should be planned. "No. I didn't really think. Usually I do. It's just that it—"

"—didn't seem necessary?" she finished. "Like we did it on purpose?"

"No. Not on purpose." He scooped up a spoonful of peas. "Would it matter? I mean, are you going to marry me?" He looked at Nellie, his heart in his eyes. "Will you marry me?"

She had just taken a sip of wine. Her eyes bulged and then her face grew purple. It took a full five seconds before he realized she was choking.

He sprang from his chair and thumped her on the back. Nellie sputtered. Wine came out of her nose. Then huge racking coughs made her bend over to the side.

"Nell? You okay?"

Nellie nodded her head but remained hunched over. He patted her on the back. "Nellie?"

After a minute, she sat up and grabbed the snowy napkin next to her plate to wipe her mouth. "Did you just ask me to marry you?"

He crept back to his place, worried. She was probably mad. He was supposed to propose romantically. Do something cute, like hide the ring in a glass of champagne or on top of a piece of cake. Or flash his proposal on a JumboTron. Hell, he didn't have a ring. He'd screwed up big-time.

Jack sank back into his chair. "Uh, I guess I shouldn't have done it this way."

Nellie's eyes glistened.

He paused. He needed to rewind. Go back in time. "Look, forget about that. It wasn't right. We've got to clear some things. Okay?"

"So you don't want to marry me?" Her eyes flashed again.

"No. I mean, yes. I want to marry you. I just think—"

"—too much," Nellie interrupted. She smiled. "Look, you're right. We have some things between us. We need to put them behind us before we take a step into the future."

He nodded. Good. She understood.

She picked up her fork and stabbed it into her chicken breast. "So…I'll go first."

She looked at him across the flickering candles she'd lit when they'd returned. Her eyes softened, her features luminous in the glow. "I went to Vegas because I thought I wanted to be someone different. I thought I could make myself…better. Better than just a small-town, frumpy girl stuck in a rut."

He nodded. "I figured that out."

"No, not really. Maybe you can guess what it's been like for me. I mean, you don't have to feel sorry for me or anything. I've had a pretty happy existence. It's just I was stuck, you know?"

He nodded again.

"Everybody knows me here. I'm a Tucker and that's hard. There are expectations—unspoken, but still there. I was raised a certain way by a woman who believed in unwritten rules. She loved me, but expected me to follow the path." Nellie's eyes grew misty and she took another sip of her wine.

"Well then, why did you stay in Oak Stand? You could've left, gone somewhere else."

"Well, I did. I had a job in Plano right out of college, an internship with a computer company that needed a computer architect to create databases. Honestly, it's something I'm pretty good at, but two days before I started, my grandmother had her first stroke." Nellie paused. He could hear the resignation in her voice as she relived the past. "There wasn't a choice after that. I had to come home and take care of her."

He understood. He'd gleaned from others around the town the extent of Nellie's loyalty to her family. He'd have done the same thing.

"I got a part-time job at the library and fell in love with it. I love to read and to work with children. It just clicked for me. But as far as my social life, well, that kind of fell apart. Wasn't really anybody here for me. Most of the guys who were decent were already married, and we don't get a lot of strangers here, as I am sure you found out. But, anyway, I couldn't leave Grandmother alone in the evening."

Nellie took the last bite of her chicken. Jack had finished his dinner long ago. His plate was nearly licked clean. She scooted her chair back and scooped up her plate. Reaching across the table, she picked up his plate and disappeared into the kitchen.

She returned with the chocolate cake. "I put some coffee on. Decaf."

He grinned. "Should have made regular. I plan on being up late tonight." He reached out and snapped the band of her lacy panties.

She slapped his hand. "Behave."

Nellie cut a huge piece of cake and set it on a delicate china dessert plate. She passed it to him and then cut an equally huge one for herself. She hopped up, disappeared into the kitchen again, and came back with a tray holding two cups of coffee.

"So, back to my story. When my grandmother passed away, it was weird. I couldn't seem to shake myself out of that mold I'd created for myself. I knew I was grieving. I loved her and she was all I had. But then I just stopped caring about how I looked, whether I'd get married, or anything. It was like treading water."

"I know how that feels," he said, taking a bite of the heavenly cake. Yellow cake, chocolate frosting. His favorite. And it was good.

Nellie looked puzzled.

He smiled. "Until you walked into Agave Blue, I'd been in some sort of funk. Really dissatisfied with my life."

"You're kidding," she said, dipping her finger into the icing and licking it off. "You seemed to have everything a guy could want."

"I did," Jack agreed. "But it wasn't enough. See, it wasn't about being successful or having women or being in demand. I figured it out. I was lonely."

"Really?" Nellie looked dumbfounded. "Me, too."

"Yeah, I know."

"Funny. Who would have thought we were both suffering from the same thing, just in different ways?" She scooped up another dollop of frosting and popped it into her mouth.

"Keep doing that and we won't make it through this talking thing," Jack growled, waggling his eyebrows.

She smiled. "If you're a good boy, later I'll let you rub it on me then lick it off."

He clutched his chest and groaned. "You're killing me, woman."

"Okay, so I went to Vegas looking for change, a good time, something to kick-start me. I didn't want to live alone in this big house, all the kids in the neighborhood afraid to come into my yard and step on my tulips. I wanted my own kids, a husband to love. But I knew I had to do something to help myself get that, so I called Kate."

"Well, she did an amazing job. I got a hard-on the moment I saw you."

"No, you didn't," Nellie said. "You mean the second time you saw me."

"Touché. The second time. But I have to admit, the first time I saw you, I noticed what kind of person you were."

She cocked her head.

He sipped the French roast coffee. "You didn't really spill that wine. The fat guy next to you did. You took the fall. I remember thinking how genuine you were. I distinctly remember telling myself I needed to find a woman like you."

"You're joking," she accused, her eyes dancing, "No way. You didn't even give me the time of day."

"Cardinals fan, remember?" he said.

Nellie rolled her eyes and he laughed. "But I did remember you. Plus, things hadn't gone well that day. I had been scouting for land and couldn't find what we'd been looking for, my dad had signed the purchase papers on the horse, and I'd had four calls from my attorney about the club sale. I felt like acid was eating through my stomach. Truth was, I was scared shitless. Nothing was coming together and everything felt wrong."

"It felt right when you saw me?" Nellie looked intense.

"Yeah. It was strange, but it felt like this piece of me that had been floating around somewhere just settled in and clicked. I don't know what you'd call it, but I just had to try you on."

She smiled. "That's a different way of putting it."

"You were a perfect fit," he said, his eyes wandering over her lacy bra and bare shoulders before returning to her flushed cheeks. She'd placed the glasses back on, but her green eyes sparkled beneath the thick lenses. There was nothing nerdy about Nellie.

"So it was fate?" she asked.

"Or something like that," he said, taking another sip of coffee. "I just think we were destined, designed for one another. That's why I came here. It didn't even surprise me to find a farm for sale right outside your town."

Nellie thought about that. "True. You know, old Mrs. Henderson held on to that place for years. I couldn't believe she'd finally agreed to sell it. Bubba told me her grandson got into some trouble in Dallas and they needed the money it would bring for an attorney. Go figure."

Jack covered her hand with his. It seemed so delicate in his larger one and he rubbed the pad of his thumb over the smooth back of her hand. "So you found yourself? Figured out who you are?"

Nellie's lips twitched. "I have many sides to myself, and

what I was in Vegas is who I am as much as…uh, it sounds confusing. What I mean is, I don't have to sacrifice my naughty side so I can cling to what I've always been—responsible, practical, able to tell an Eastern bluebird from a Western one."

He raised his brows. "You can tell bluebirds apart? Hell, I didn't know there was more than one kind."

"Yep. And I feed the Eastern ones nearly daily when they're nesting." Nellie took a sip of coffee, realizing she enjoyed the dark roast as much as she had the martinis in Vegas. Hey, she was a coffee-drinking, martini-swilling sexually liberated tight-ass. Was there anything wrong with that?

Jack leaned back into his chair and sighed. "So we've straightened out the really important stuff, right? We both know where we stand?"

Nellie nodded. Could anyone ever know where she stands? Ever be sure of anything? She wasn't certain, but she felt where they were heading had to be a good place to plant their feet. And she could wear some sexy-ass shoes to stand in. Just keep her comfy slippers nearby.

Jack smiled as he stood and stretched, arching his back, making it crack like a machine gun. "I think you did throw out my back. You're gonna have to walk up those stairs this time."

Nellie crossed her arms and shook her head. "No way. We put the past to bed, but I'm not going back up those stairs with you until we move on to our future."

"Future? You mean as in—"

"*M-a-r-r-i-a-g-e.*" She ticked each letter off on her fingers. "You may have knocked me up, Jack Darby. I'm a Tucker. We aren't supposed to have children born on the wrong side of the blanket. Well, except for Aunt Clarice, and we aren't allowed to talk about her and the fact she was born four months early, weighing a healthy nine pounds even."

Jack grinned. "Knocked up. Tuckers say that?"

"Well, technically I'm a Hughes. Plus, I, too, was conceived on the wrong side of the blanket, so I guess that's blown out of the water." She threw him a mischievous grin. "So are you taking that proposal back? Because there's lots of frosting on this piece of cake."

"You're holding out for a proposal by using frosting as a weapon? You want our kids to know I proposed in my underwear?"

"They're really cute undies. I love the little penguins on them. They make me feel naughty." Nellie swirled one finger in the chocolate frosting and then slowly licked it off her finger.

He dropped to one knee. "Okay, I'm easy to convince."

She pulled her finger out of her mouth. "Really?"

"Really." Jack reached for her left hand. The one without the chocolate residue. "Nellie Hughes, will you do me the honor of becoming my wife?"

Nellie's sassiness fled. She sounded like a frog when she croaked, "Truly?"

"Truly. Forever. Always." He lifted her hand to his mouth and bestowed a soft, sweet kiss atop it.

She slid down to her knees. Right next to the buffet her great-grandfather had purchased for his bride on their wedding day, on the floor her grandfather had salvaged from an old Confederate warship, right next to the seat cushions her grandmother had embroidered with dahlias. Clad only in her underwear, Nellie said, "Yes."

"Good." Jack kissed her. Her knees would have turned

to jelly but she knelt on them. The kiss was passionate. Sweet. Tender. Full of promise.

"All right, now about that frosting. I'm wanting a little dessert to seal the deal. To celebrate."

"Okay, but you'll have to be quick," she murmured, licking his neck.

"Why?" Jack asked, angling his head so she could reach the tender spot under his earlobe.

"Cardinals." Nellie nipped his earlobe.

He yelped then swatted her behind. "Do you feed them too?"

Nellie pulled back. "Feed them? I thought we'd watch them."

Jack fumbled with the dessert plate, pulling it to the edge of the table. He swiped one finger in the icing and lifted it to Nellie's lips, reaching for her. "I'm not watching birds."

Nellie halted him with a hard kiss before whispering, "Baseball, dummy. They play the Dodgers at nine."

Jack's laughter bubbled as he clamped one hand on her bottom and pulled her hard against him. "Think I'd choose the Cardinals over you?"

"No, 'cause you don't have to. I'm gonna watch them with you. I read my book." Her lips hovered over his.

Jack captured her mouth and gave her a deep, toe-curling sexy kiss. "As long as you're naked and sit in my lap."

Nellie smiled. "No problem. I'm not Elle, but I *am* the real Nellie."

* * * * *

0411/06

0211/24/MB328

ULTIMATE ALPHA MALES:

Strong, sexy…and intent on seduction!

Mediterranean Tycoons
4th February 2011

Hot-Shot Heroes
4th March 2011

Powerful Protectors
1st April 2011

Passionate Playboys
6th May 2011

MILLS & BOON

Collect all four!

www.millsandboon.co.uk

M202_TTH

One innocent child
A secret that could destroy his life

Imprisoned for a heinous crime when she was a just a teenager, Allison Glenn is now free. Desperate for a second chance, Allison discovers that the world has moved on without her…

Shunned by those who once loved her, Allison is determined to make contact with her sister. But Brynn is trapped in her own world of regret and torment.

Their legacy of secrets is focused on one little boy. And if the truth is revealed, the consequences will be unimaginable for the adoptive mother who loves him, the girl who tried to protect him and the two sisters who hold the key to all that is hidden…

"Deeply moving and lyrical…it will haunt you…"
—*Company* magazine on *The Weight of Silence*

www.mirabooks.co.uk

MIRA

0411_S1ZED

2 FREE BOOKS
AND A SURPRISE GIFT

We would like to take this opportunity to thank you for reading this Mills & Boon® book by offering you the chance to take TWO more specially selected books from the Cherish™ series absolutely FREE! We're also making this offer to introduce you to the benefits of the Mills & Boon® Book Club™—

- **FREE home delivery**
- **FREE gifts and competitions**
- **FREE monthly Newsletter**
- **Exclusive Mills & Boon Book Club offers**
- **Books available before they're in the shops**

Accepting these FREE books and gift places you under no obligation to buy, you may cancel at any time, even after receiving your free books. Simply complete your details below and return the entire page to the address below. You don't even need a stamp!

YES Please send me 2 free Cherish books and a surprise gift. I understand that unless you hear from me, I will receive 5 superb new stories every month, including two 2-in-1 books priced at £5.30 each, and a single book priced at £3.30, postage and packing free. I am under no obligation to purchase any books and may cancel my subscription at any time. The free books and gift will be mine to keep in any case.

Ms/Mrs/Miss/Mr ______________ Initials ______________

____

Surname ______________________________

Address ______________________________

____

______________________ Postcode __________

E-mail ________________________________

Send this whole page to: Mills & Boon Book Club, Free Book Offer, FREEPOST NAT 10298, Richmond, TW9 1BR

Offer valid in UK only and is not available to current Mills & Boon Book Club subscribers to this series. Overseas and Eire please write for details. We reserve the right to refuse an application and applicants must be aged 18 years or over. Only one application per household. Terms and prices subject to change without notice. Offer expires 30th June 2011. As a result of this application, you may receive offers from Harlequin (UK) and other carefully selected companies. If you would prefer not to share in this opportunity please write to The Data Manager, PO Box 676, Richmond, TW9 1WU.